Early Bright

Ami Silber

EARLY BRIGHT

The Toby Press

Early Bright

First Edition 2008

The Toby Press LLC
POB 8531, New Milford, CT 06776-8531, USA
& POB 2455, London W1A 5WY, England
www.tobypress.com

ISBN 978 1 59264 241 0, *hardcover*

A CIP catalogue record for this title is
available from the British Library

Typeset by Koren Typesetting Services

Printed and bound in the United States

To Zack, with all my love

Chapter one

Being alone with the piano, only a soft scraping rhythm behind me on drums, that was as close to praying as I ever got, and that included my bar mitzvah. The air in the club was thick and alive, smelling of bodies, booze, reckless joy. If there was a better place to play, I didn't know it. The crowd quieted, breathing on my command, and I held them for as long as I could stand it. But I knew when to let them go.

Sonny had had a legitimate gig earlier, recording for a movie over at Paramount, and he'd run out of steam after half a dozen numbers. Since there weren't any other sax players ready to go up, Victor was backing me with brushes. Don't get me wrong, I dug playing with Sonny and other musicians, but soloing was the difference between smacking lips with the tired chick in the carnival kissing booth and the honeyed press of an eager, fresh girl in the privacy of night.

There was a moment, a weighted moment, when I would first sit down at the piano, my hands over the keys, just brushing against them, the coolness of the ivory kissing my fingertips, and the room was silent, the audience suspended and waiting for me, waiting for sound, and not any sound, but *my* sound. I could've drawn it out, that anticipation, the need and communal hunger of the crowd that only I could satisfy, until they threw themselves at my feet, sobbing with desperation. Or I could have shoved myself straight through the membrane of tension, hard as steel or iron, brutal and direct as I played without pause or mercy. There might have been other musicians onstage with me, but when I was the soloist, the melody I was about to bestow was all that mattered. In that moment, I was the most powerful man in the world.

It was a power I didn't get to taste often enough. My usual audiences didn't hear music, not at the front of their minds. At my weekly paid gig, banging out standards on an out-of-tune piano for chalky poker players, I wasn't powerful, wasn't the controller of destinies, just background atmosphere, and hardly even that.

No one paid me here at Dee's, and it didn't matter. I played "Night and Day," bringing everything down low and gentle, into a collective longing. Music wasn't a con, but even here I could lead folks along, make them feel what I wanted them to feel, the way I could make people cry, have them grow greedy when I wanted. I was the shadowed, gleaming man underneath the window, whispering promises of touch and taste to the woman inside. Her hand rested on the sill, slim and alive in the cool evening, and, hearing me, hearing how I would run my own hands over her, silky and rough, how I would then bring them up to thread my fingers into her hair, tilting her head back for the first dark kiss, she wanted so badly to push up the casement and invite me inside. She wanted to fall back onto the bed with me covering her, settling between her legs, sliding into her the way it was always meant to be. Every note I played was my pledge, the one vow I would never break.

Glancing up quickly at the audience, I gauged my success. Lights dazzled my eyes, but I could see enough—people with their eyes closed, swaying and nodding—to know that I had wooed and won. And this was not a small prize, lightly given. Mine was the only white face in the club, and so I always had to work even harder, make each seduction doubly sweet, irresistible. But I never doubted myself.

* * *

Central Avenue was a long stretch of road that ran from downtown Los Angeles to Watts, a colored neighborhood. During the day folks did their shopping, walked their kids to school, got their hair cut, not much different from any other neighborhood anywhere, but at night it lit up. Theaters and jazz clubs and after-hours joints elbowed next to each other. I'd see some other white folks down there, slumming, taking in high-end shows at the Club Alabam or the Jungle Room, celebrities, too, gilding their path from Bel Air and Beverly Hills, but mostly it was a Negro crowd, listening to the best jazz L.A. had to offer. And I'd open my ears and play right along with them. It was the dark heart in my chest, beating to keep me alive.

I loved the Central scene, loved it since I first got to town four years ago. It made me think of when I was back in New York, taking the train from the Bronx into Manhattan to vibe on 52nd Street. That's where the best spots were, between Fifth and Seventh Avenues. A gawky, gangly kid, nothing but limbs, trying to squeeze my way into the Spotlite, or the Three Deuces. When the juice got hold of me, I'd head over to Minton's on West 118th Street to try and catch the most with-it jazz out there and watch Charlie Parker and Dizzy Gillespie do their Monday night jams. I never got to see Bird or Diz, but just hanging around the place was enough. Between Minton's, 52nd Street and Leo Israel, my old piano teacher, I had myself a fine education. But once I got to Los Angeles, I needed to know where the best action was, music-wise. That's when I caught the word about Central Avenue.

Things weren't going well for me when I'd shown up in L.A. That was '44. I had a little money stashed, but I was wrung out, cheap, a wino's empty paper sack gusting down the wide streets of an unknown city. But all that changed once I got to Central—I filled up, fleshed out, grew up.

When I first started hanging around, I got more than a few strange looks from the regulars. You know: "Who's that jive white square trying to make it like he's a colored hepcat," that kind of business. Most everyone thought I was slumming, too, trying to sham that I was black, trying to score a little dark meat. But I finally weaseled my way into one of the after-hours clubs' jam sessions, the cutting duels. I got myself on the piano, and I couldn't be cut. They tried, the other musicians, but I knew I was playing for more than just bragging rights. I knew that if I wanted to get the rubber stamp, learn from the masters, I'd have to show I had the goods. Here was one thing, the only thing I couldn't fake or con—it had to be the honest Injun, or I'd be given a private tour of the way out by the seat of my pants.

I lost about fifteen pounds that night, hammering that piano like it was my one chance at salvation. We jammed "Ko-Ko" until about six o'clock in the morning. Then the alto sax player, a guy by the name of Sonny Rockwell, came over, wiping his inky, shining face with a hankie.

"What's your name, brother?" he had asked me.

"Louis Greenberg," I said, using my real name for the first time in years. Somehow I knew that this was one of the only safe places.

"Lou," he said, "I'm beat and you're way upstairs."

"That's a good thing?" I asked him. I'd been exiled from the Bronx, had been weaving across the country for two years, but in some ways I was still a little wet behind the ears. He laughed and looped his arm around my shoulder. "That's a good thing. Lemme introduce you to the gang."

So I stopped getting looks whenever I popped up at the clubs, and nobody threw bottles at me when I joined in the jam sessions. And it was my groove, after finishing a paying gig, to ease my way into the after-hours clubs, listen to and play some righteous jazz. Because liquor couldn't be sold after two A.M., most of the joints had to serve some kind of food; chicken, biscuits, malts, whathaveyou, with bootleg hootch discreetly offered to those who asked. There were plenty of raids, trying to keep the fair city clean, mostly hassling the colored folks trying to dress up and cut loose for the night. I never get roped in one of those raids—I mapped out the back exits pretty well and with these long legs of mine, I can make a good break for it. Though I'd had a few close calls.

There were all kinds of after-hours places, Jack's Basket Room at Thirty-Third and Central, Lovejoy's, piles more that didn't really have names. You wouldn't be able to find them, not if you went look-ing. The one I hung out at was Dee's, not as august as some of the other clubs, but what we'd call modernistic. It was behind a bakery, so that around four or five in the morning, we could start to smell the first bread of the day, and the bakers, when we came out to go home, would give us fresh, hot rolls for our breakfasts. Yeast and jazz, the two living creatures that gave lift and rise to a day. There wasn't anything better than standing out on the sidewalk with a loaf of bread, tearing off chunks to share and talking about the jam session we'd just left. For a while, I'd been fooling with a piano composition of my own, "Fresh Bread," a sprightly piece that held a note of blue, my ode to these quick, perfect moments, but it'd never been good enough to play for anyone. Not yet.

Dee's Parlor on Central was over ten miles from my weekly pay-ing gig at a card club in Gardena and ways away from my apartment in Santa Monica. I needed a fix of good company and better music after watching the bleak, ashen faces playing poker, numb to every-thing but their fifty-two friends. Tonight had been no different.

I'd followed my usual routine when I arrived, just after two in the morning. "What's shaking, Paulie?" I had asked the doorman. Paulie was at least eighty, but his eyes still glittered like jet buttons beneath the brim of his natty little hat.

"Good to see you, Louis," he'd answered, pushing the door open for me. As I passed him, I saw the mean-looking .45 he kept stashed under his seat, which he broke out only when things got ugly. Pau-lie hailed from Kay Cee, known for its slippery characters, less-than-wholesome lifestyle and Cab Calloway, not exactly the hometown of the Boy Scout Jamboree. Nobody doubted that Paulie'd done some shady things when he was a kid, but it was a peaceful scene here at Dee's, and that gat usually stayed nice and comfy in its hidey hole.

A riot of heat and sound had met me as I stepped inside. The band was already cooking, the room was packed. It was something of a joke to call Dee's a parlor. If my bubbe's parlor looked like this joint, nobody would've come over for mahjong. Nothing had changed here for the past fifteen years, and that was the way everybody liked it. Myself, I wouldn't have said no to maybe a hydraulic pump hose coming along and giving the place a thorough washing, but I guess I was in the minority on that score.

I had crossed the bare wood floor, edging past walls painted so many times it was hard to know what color they were, something like clotted blood. With the lights burning low, you couldn't see the cracks in the plasterwork. I made sure to stay away from the small bar, people draped around it four deep, hustling for their drinks. Eight years ago, in '40, City Hall had decided that booze couldn't be served after two in the A.M., but the after-hours crowd still demanded overpriced rotgut. They were there for a good time, for hard drinks and jazz.

The stage at Dee's was no bigger than a food stamp, but they had managed to crowd a drum kit, two saxes, a trumpet, a bass and a piano on there. Everyone was sweating and hollering, and within a minute, I'd soaked through my undershirt and shirt.

I knew most of the people in there, and I don't doubt that my father, hard working as Ernest Greenberg was, would have been shook up some by the company I kept. My pop, a bigot he wasn't, but he preferred his colored people on the radio, making music and telling jokes. To him, they'd always be *schvartzes*, separate, unknown and unknowing—which I'd become to him now.

I had shaken hands and clapped shoulders with a bunch of folks, then heard my name shouted off in the corner.

"Clipper, over here, man," someone had yelled, waving his arm in the air. I was called Clipper on account of my accent, and being from the Bronx, short for Yankee Clipper, like DiMaggio. They didn't know I clipped another way. Far as anybody there knew, I taught piano to squirrelly brats. Scales and other baloney. Nobody here at Dee's ever caught wise, though. It wouldn't be far off to say I scammed them, too, down at Central Avenue.

"Hey, Sonny," I'd said, shaking his hand as he got up to meet me. "You playing?"

"Up next." He had tipped his head towards the sax case on the floor. "Gonna sit in?"

"You'd have to barricade the way with barbed wire and broads to keep me out."

Sonny had grabbed a chair from somewhere and wedged it near the table. I managed to fold myself into it.

Along with Sonny, there was Opal Dennis, his girl, who worked as a seamstress downtown. She couldn't have weighed more than a kitten, but her arms were tight with muscle from hefting bolts of fabric. I gave her a buss on the cheek for hello. Sitting next to Opal was her cousin Wendel, a bus driver who loved to buy everyone drinks. Wendel wasn't satisfied until everyone in the room was good and embalmed. He'd shaken my hand like he was pumping a well. Wendel's girl was Lilah, a school teacher, always laughing, and sitting next to Lilah was her cousin, Beatrice Langston. Beatrice was a cool customer, a telephone operator who never danced and didn't say very much. Not to me, anyway. She had given me a little nod when I'd sat down and then returned to watching the band, a cigarette smoldering between her long fingers.

"How's the band tonight?" I had shouted over the noise.

"Too much," grinned Wendel, and Lilah had bust out laughing.

I'd had to agree with Wendel on that. It was everything good to finally hear decent bebop, as wild and improvisational as it wanted to be, not caring whether or not you danced, living only for the notes jangling together. I had eyed the guy at the piano, wanting him to finish so I could get up there and jam.

Here, jazz wasn't something to fill the background. It worked to hold the world together, like mortar, and at the same time it smashed all the edifices so you were left on a bare plain.

We had yelled at each other for a bit, but no one was really in the mood to talk. We all came to escape the sounds of our voices, the truths of our lives—Wendel was college educated but could only get a job driving buses, Opal's boss regularly skimmed the profits but there was no one to beef to, Lilah took two trolleys and a bus to get to her job. Sonny was one of the best sax-men out there, recording soundtracks for movies, but he couldn't get on camera, being too well endowed, pigment-wise. And then there was me. So the music was our voices, as jarring or spare or angry as we wanted them to be out in the street, but couldn't.

And, let's face it, no matter how welcoming and warm everyone was to me at Dee's and on Central, how much I could tear it up at the piano, an outsider I'd always be. Most of the people at Dee's made more money than I did, some even went to college, which I didn't, they had steady jobs and families and a few had their own houses. But I was white, a Jew, and that never went away.

I'd looked around the table. Sonny's skin was a deep blue-black, Wendel's more like a Hershey Bar, and Beatrice looked like coffee with a shot of cream. Me, I had the black hair and brown eyes of my Polish grandfather, and what the ladies' beauty magazines called an olive complexion. Lilah was even lighter than me, her skin just touched with cocoa freckles and her hair pulled up in a reddish pompadour. Still, a gulf stretched between us, and even when the looks stopped coming my way, the gap was something that was never really forgotten. But this crowd was another of my cons—only instead of taking their cash, I took their belief in who they thought I was. Even they didn't know how I earned my bread, and that was my choice, my doing.

Did I want to be colored? No. But I won't lie to you. I did have an itch for someplace where I was on the inside, part of a group, completely and altogether myself. Though I wasn't sure who that was, what with my aliases multiplying like kids born on the wrong side of the blanket.

I hadn't even bothered watching the guys onstage at Dee's. I shut my eyes to soak up the sounds, lose myself in the perfect world of rhythm and tone. I gave up all my names, and became ears only, something for the music to fill and move. My fingers had moved across the sticky table, playing along, giving myself over.

Opening my eyes, when the music stopped and the crowd clapped, I saw Beatrice had seen me, as shuttered as a speakeasy on Sunday. But I hadn't flushed or lost my cool.

"You're up," she'd said, gesturing to the stage with her cigarette. Then I had stopped caring about everything else and felt my pulse begin to jet through my body. Sonny and I stood to take our place onstage. What did it feel like? Like the time when I was sixteen, sneaking out after midnight to Van Cortlandt Park to meet Francine

Kuflick, and losing my cherry in the boathouse. Francine's cherry had been long gone, but I wasn't sorry about it. All that had mattered was that first rush when I slid into her, her pussy still tight even though she knew her way to the boathouse. I thought for sure I'd found my true calling, something to do just after piano. About fifteen seconds later, it was over. Fifteen seconds after that, I was ready to go again.

Music wasn't like that. I didn't go off like a rocket and have to wait to get it back up again. That feeling lasted, stretching out, so I could die from it. And it wasn't a con. It was all on the level, the straight shit. The only thing in my life I could say that about.

My hands had still been warm from the gig at the Carmel Club, although sometimes on a cool night I'd hold them under a hot tap to loosen the joints up. I'd walked straight to the bench and sat down, flexed my fingers once, twice, then set my hands lightly on top of the keys.

"Isn't that Monty Clift?" someone had shouted from the peanut gallery, and the crowd laughed. I'd smiled briefly down at the keyboard. It was a joke that was starting to get old, the same one that got yelled whenever I took the stage after "Red River" came out almost two months earlier. I'd heard that Clift and I could fool our mothers, and it sure did help, this face of mine. Folks believed good-looking people, wanted to be near them, soak up their grace, but all that was worth doughnut to me now that I was ready to play.

I'd looked over at Sonny and gave him a nod. He had eyed the drummer, a cat named Victor White, and given him the go-ahead. With a few introductory beats on his snare, we had gotten going.

We'd launched right into "I Got Rhythm," Sonny starting up on the melody while I comped him. The crowd howled with him as he had moved from melody to improv, soaring and wheeling, wringing notes out of his horn and then gently coaxing them out with a soft touch. I'd let him be, supplying the notes in the back to give it all structure and spine. Nothing beat a tight combo, Sonny, Victor and I shifting and moving together, weaving music, and maybe it's corny to say, but nobody cared who was black or white, Jew or goy, con or straight, it was all the music. Even if I could scam these folks, they still knew good sounds.

9

Sonny and I had traded eights for a bit, jiving off each other, him high, me low, and then it was my turn to solo. I don't dig that ornamental dreck, I wanted a sound as pure and spare as an empty room, echoing with resonance. My right hand had taken a fast melody line, my left comping on the chords, as though I had the whole trio just inside of me. My chords had been tiny, just three notes, barely brushing the harmony. Every now and then the chords gave the melody a kick right in its pants, waking it up, moving it forward.

Just for kicks, I had galloped into a Chopin waltz, thinking of Leopold Israel, but it was only a rolling hint before I shifted back to my improvisation. It was a pure thing to let the notes out like that, to wheedle or stroke or demand or caress, a love affair between me and the keys. I had taken it up in the middle of the eight bar, went right past it, shoving it aside. And then, too soon, it was time to let Victor have his solo, Sonny and I backing him up and beating it out. Then we'd all come together to finish the melody and it was over.

A hot roar of joy from the crowd nearly knocked me off the piano bench. Sonny and I exchanged grins, grills as wide as Cadillacs. Yeah, we'd broken it up. Then we played some more, courting bliss.

After that, Sonny, tired from his day, had sat down and left me to solo.

And now I played, taking the familiar standard "Night and Day" and transforming it, becoming not just some Cole Porter tune, but birth, sorrow, joy, destruction and resurrection. They were mine to bestow or take away, and I did so, without pity. The audience took what I gave it, grateful.

It went on like that as I played, and I forgot everything that had happened during the day. Such a sweet pleasure to wipe my mind clean, even if that blankness didn't last.

The killer thing about Dee's was that I could go every which way and nobody told me to can it, to stick to swing or comfortable pop. I raged, I wept, I seduced, I mourned. I could stop, turn a corner, start a whole new line of improv, and that was fine. Bebop was like life—it didn't follow just a single melody straight through to the end, you couldn't dance or sing to it. It was complicated, unpredictable, confusing, real and terrifying, but also joyous, wild, true. And all mine.

My jacket was long lost, my tie loosened, my shirtsleeves rolled up and my hair hanging in my face by the time I got down off that piano bench. I felt like I was waking up from a long sleep—aware only of a drink being pressed into my hand and hard thumps on my back from men as I found my way back to my seat.

"Shit," Wendel said with a shake of his head, "you don't need to go to Muscle Beach, Louis. You worked those ivories like a strong-man!"

"Opal, be a doll and hold my drink up for me," I managed to say with a wink. "My hands are beat." She made a face but obliged. I took a swig of whiskey and felt myself coming back into the room.

A swing combo took over, and space was cleared for jitterbugging. Since Sonny was too bushed to do much besides nurse his drink, Wendel had to oblige the ladies at our table and shake his feet with each of them. All except Beatrice, who steadily smoked and looked around with a kind of high-cheek insolence that drove some of the brothers wild.

"Hey, sugar." We all looked up as Roland Webber sidled up to the table and flashed his pearlies at Beatrice. He owned three laundries around town and thought that gave him a diamond-like edge and gleam, but he was held together with sizing and starch.

Beatrice barely raised her eyes to him. Roland gave us all a quick, nervous look, knowing he was on stage, and covered it with a flop-sweat grin.

"What say you and me cut a rug?"

She took the cigarette from her mouth, lit a fresh one with its tip, and ground out her old light with all the precise ceremony of a Torah being unwound. All the while Roland stood nearby, hovering, getting smaller. She dragged on her new cigarette, blew out the smoke.

"I just lit this cigarette," she said finally, "and it'd be such a shame to let it burn for nothing."

We just about heard the sound of Roland's nuts shriveling up raisin-like and falling to the floor. I almost felt sorry for him as he melted into a puddle and dripped away. But he had to know the score by now—cool Beatrice didn't dance with anyone, and only a dope with a taste for humiliation would even try and ask. Still, at least once a night, some knight errant in a zoot suit would try his luck and get burnt, crispy and charred.

Finally, after making sure that no man would ever take his dick for granted, she crushed out her cigarette.

"I'm hitting the hay," she said, and Sonny and I lurched to our feet as she stood. "Say goodnight to Lilah for me." And she turned on her heel and left.

Three seconds later, Lilah sat down at the table, holding the top of her blouse open and fanning herself.

"It's red hot out there," she said with a happy sigh.

"Lilah, what's the skinny on that cousin of yours?" Sonny asked her.

"Why?" She cocked an eyebrow at him. "You interested?"

"You know Opal's my girl," Sonny chided. "Beatrice, she may be a looker, but she's one icy broad." He shot me a look and I just shrugged.

That, like most everything, made Lilah laugh. "That's Bea's way. She's always had ideas. Back in Ohio, her daddy used to beat her whenever she got too uppity."

"How often'd that happen?" I asked.

She grinned. "A lot. But she got good at running, so he couldn't catch her no more. Just give her time," she said, sitting back and pushing up her hair to catch a non-existent breeze. "She warms up, eventual-like."

"How long is that gonna take? She been out here since forty-four," Sonny complained. He eyed the bottom of his glass and I saw him trying to decide if it was worth it to get up and fight to the bar, or suffer his thirst. He stayed rooted.

Lilah just laughed once more and looked at me. I shrugged again. I knew better than to talk about a colored woman, so I kept my trap shut. While me being at Dee's was tolerated and sometimes accepted, nobody'd cotton to the idea of me squiring a sister around town. It was bad enough when a white chick would latch herself onto a colored guy, which did happen. People got to muttering about white dames with black bucks, and the service at joints like Dee's would get noticeably frostier. And forget about one of those couples trying to go out on a date somewhere that didn't serve coloreds. If they were lucky, they'd just not get waited on. But if they weren't, dirty words got smeared around, fights broke out.

It was worse around Watts if a white guy tried anything with a black dame. The poor sap would win his own guts as a door prize. Maybe it was too much like Simon Legree sneaking into the shacks in the field—I couldn't rightly say. So I played it cool whenever I was on Central Avenue and had eyes only for the music scene.

I threw back the rest of my drink and stood. "That's it for me, cats and kittens."

"Aw, Clip, you ain't cutting out now?" Sonny complained as I eased into my jacket, which was soggy and hung from my shoulders like an excuse.

"I gotta blow, Jackson," I answered, putting on my hat. "It's a long drive back to Santa Monica." Lilah made a face. The sleepy town of beach bungalows and fog may as well have been a resort on the sunny shores of the Baltic. "Sorry, honey, but it's where I hang my hat. Rent's cheap."

"Well, you come and see us again real soon in the colored part of town."

I bent and gave her cheek a quick, brotherly kiss. "Can't stop me, sister." I shook Sonny's hand and waved at Victor, Wendel and Opal before heading out the door.

It was coming on to three thirty in the morning, and the late October air was dry and cool. I stood in front of Dee's and breathed it in deep. Back in New York, we'd be getting out the woolens, preparing for a long, bitter winter, but not here in L.A., where late fall meant Santa Ana winds blowing gusty and juiceless from the desert. The sweat along my back dried, my skin prickled.

There was still plenty of traffic on Central, even in the small hours. Some of the early birds had already called it a night. Those left were the diehard gin mill cowboys and bandrats, still wringing the party out of the last scraps of the day. I watched the passing parade for a little bit, smiling at the fizziness of it all, the hard-working folks out enjoying the night, music on the breeze. I was still coming off of the high from playing. Everything seemed swell.

With a last adjustment to my hat, I started to round the corner that lead to the alley beside Dee's. As I moved into the dark, a pair of hands grabbed my shoulders and roughly pulled me forward.

I tensed, then loosened as I felt her lips against mine.

"Dammit," Beatrice muttered into my mouth, "why'd you keep me waiting out here like a two-bit floozy?" Off balance, we stumbled so her back was against the brick wall. I cupped the back of her head, cradling it to keep it from slamming against the bricks, and tilted her face up. She tasted of cigarettes and whiskey and oranges. The alley stunk, sour and raunchy.

"Can't just go waltzing out right after you leave," I breathed. I groaned a little as her hands pushed their way under my jacket and roamed across my back. "Believe me, I was dying to go."

We ate at each other like black market sugar. Ferocious. We hadn't seen each other in almost a week, then had to sit and pretend like we had nothing to say, nothing to do. A sweet misery. I took my hand and moved it down to the hem of her dress, then pushed the fabric up. I almost whimpered as I touched the warm smooth skin above her stocking, the tips of my fingers brushing her garter.

"You know how hard it is for me," she growled, clawing at me, "watching you play, those hands of yours on the keys, and I just gotta sit there, acting like it's no big thing, like I don't know what it feels like to have you touch me," she gasped as I moved my hand up further, touching her between her legs where she was already wet and hot, "*like that.*"

"I think I know how hard," I said, rocking myself against her. She grabbed my ass, pushing me closer, raising up on her toes. My cock was rooting towards her, trying to push into her through the gabardine of my slacks.

God knows how much further we would have gone, if some wiseacre on the street hadn't hooted, "Go, man, go!" At least in the dark of the alley, nobody could see that she and I weren't the same color.

Still, Beatrice immediately let go of me, retreating as far into the shadows of the alley as she could. I pulled my hat down low and snarled at the punk, "Go pick yourself an orchid, jackass," before heading after her.

I could barely see her in the blackness of the alley as she adjusted her dress and tried to repair her lipstick. Her hand was shaking, I could see that much as she held her compact, but there wasn't enough light. She gave up making herself look decent.

"Follow me to my place," she said after putting her paint back in her purse.

"We always go to your place."

"That's because there ain't no black women in your neck of the woods. I'd sure as shit get hassled by the cops if they saw me tooling around Santa Monica."

An old argument. It was better to keep the dead leaves off the lawn than cut down the tree. I was long gone for her. "Whatever the lady wants."

"See you at my pad," she said, trailing her hands down my stomach as she passed. The muscles there jumped and tightened. I waited a few seconds before following, trying to get my heart down to a thousand BPM. And as I slid into the driver's seat of my jalopy, watching Beatrice drive off, I couldn't help thinking that for a stoop-ball-playing kid from the Bronx, I led more lives than even I could keep straight.

Chapter two

The next week, I saw my father waiting for the trolley. He stood at the corner of Bundy Drive, a short man wearing a hat and heavy overcoat in the bright, blank sun. A trim little mustache sat just under his nose, the rest of his face clean shaven and pink. He was as dapper as a baby in a suit. He wore spectacles, glossy circles shielding his eyes, and he carried a battered briefcase in one hand, a newspaper in the other. You'd think I was driving too fast to see such details, but all I needed was the shadowy suggestion of him to know the layout of his person as well as I know a recurring dream.

It wasn't my father, of course, because Ernest Greenberg of Jerome Avenue, the Bronx, has never been further west than Pittsburgh, Pennsylvania, and only then because my cousin Milton had played upon him a very cruel trick that caused poor Milton to be excommunicated for several months. And all for a joke, poor schlub.

But Los Angeles is a place my father does not go, never thought about, never wanted to. He'd say, Hollywood, who needs it? He thought every place in California was filled with movie stars drinking pink cocktails by their pink swimming pools. The picture shows were fine, but you didn't live at the bakery just because you like their challah. If it isn't New York—the cultural capital of Earth, the Milky Way, the Universe—why bother? And do I know Ann Sheridan? I do not.

Maybe there is a storehouse of short men, hardworking men who can replace each for the other at their jobs, in their houses. So you could be sitting by the radio listening to your program and the man behind the newspaper isn't your father at all, some other man has wandered in off the street and taken his place. It might make no difference at all. But excuse me for being cavalier. The truth is that I hadn't seen my father, or spoken to him, in six years, and if it had been him waiting at Bundy, I would have pulled my car over in two seconds, crying, Get in, get in. He wouldn't have gotten in, though. With my father you know you are out of favor because suddenly you are invisible, and whatever you say may as well be a bunch of childish gibbering, he pays as much attention.

I used to take the trolley all the time, everybody did. You couldn't get so much as a drop of gasoline for years and if you did somehow wind up with a gallon or two, then how unpatriotic to be tooling up and down La Cienega when our boys are overseas fighting Der Führer and Tojo and Mussolini. So the ladies working at the defense factories and I would cram ourselves on to the cars and shimmy around town. The best time to take the Red Car was when the factories let out in the evenings and the girls in their overalls would stand around gabbing like they were at a raucous tea party. They wouldn't admit it—being dedicated to the cause and all the men away fighting—but they were having a ball. Shouting and laughing and living their lives as if they'd only just been let out of a cage. For me it was as good as being at the Cocoanut Grove, and I never got off the trolley without some chick's number in my pocket.

By the end of the war, I had enough money saved to buy myself an automobile. A '37 Buick Coupe. New, it wasn't, but in my line of work I need to be able to get anywhere at any time. Sure, I was lonely, sometimes, and would take the trolley just for old times' sake, but it wasn't the same. Lockheed and Douglas had given all the girls their pink slips, so it would be me and a couple of *alter cockers* staring at each other until I couldn't take it anymore and jumped off the line. The party, as they say, was over. But the way business has been going for me lately, I may have to go back to riding the Red Car again, seeing as how it is now a choice: food or gasoline.

I'll be honest. I miss the war. I don't mean the rationing, the shortages, the blackouts and the pitches to sell bonds. Good riddance, I say. I'll eat meat on Tuesdays if I want to, I say. But one morning I awoke and there were women everywhere, like a wave had washed all the men except me out into the Gulf of Mexico. And as their cries and shouts were drowned, as they eddied and swirled down towards Panama, past Colombia, down Argentina and out into the polar seas, all the women took their places. Get a haircut, and your barber would be a woman. If you wanted to go to the lady butcher to get some chops, you'd have a lady bus driver, too. They made airplanes and collected the garbage. They sold you your shoes and directed the traffic. Imagine a planet of women. Brother, it was paradise.

So maybe the question comes up, what was I doing at home when I should have been serving my country? Didn't I want to fight and do my duty, defeat fascism and liberate Paris? Wasn't that what every red-blooded young man should have been doing? If you must know, I didn't go because I was listed 4-F, a poor physical specimen that wouldn't even make it through boot camp. So for three swell years I lived the best life a man can live.

Thinking on it now I realize that my very first con was the one I pulled on Uncle Sam.

I was on my way out to Pasadena when I passed the shade of my father. Seeing him, but not seeing him, threw me, and that was something I didn't want, especially on my way to work. For my line of business, I need to keep a cool head, stay level, otherwise a guy's got no confidence and if there's no confidence, there's no money. So I switched on the radio to whatever was playing—some swing—and ran my fingers up and down the steering wheel as though I was giving accompaniment. I made myself concentrate on the rhythm, the cool melody, but to tell the truth, I'd lost my taste for swing even while the rest of the country still ate it up. Radio stations wouldn't play bop. Can't dance to it. Can't sing to it. So, they figure, why play it? But that's what gets played late at night at Dee's, and even back in New York at Minton's. My music. But if I started thinking about jazz on my way to work, it always brought me low. If I had better-paying, steady gigs, I wouldn't need this other job.

I shut off the radio, to keep from getting too down, and went over my pitch, telling myself it was like warming up, playing scales, but I knew differently. I kept driving, taking the new Arroyo Seco Parkway, until I got to Pasadena.

The houses there were neat as building blocks, stamped out of the same punch card. Green boxed lawns and eucalyptus trees were everywhere, and it was easy to believe in lies under the warm, featureless sky. As I turned onto a side street, I thought, Yeah, maybe this is what I wanted: the house, the driveway, the cypress between me and my neighbors, the wife. But I saw the rows of cypress trees, and they were prison bars.

I double-checked the address and found the place I was looking for. A suburban house, just like all the rest, with the tiny picket fence and a brick walkway and the remains of a victory garden off the side. As I parked the car I gave the place a thorough looking-over because a guy can learn a lot about who he's dealing with, how to shape the tale, by picking up clues. I didn't buy this old Buick because I'm a handsome fella, no, I bought it because I keep my eyes open and I read the world like the Rosetta Stone.

So: a single-story house, built about twenty years ago. They must have moved here from someplace else, relocated from one of the cow towns even deeper in the Valley. The lawn was trimmed but it looked as though it could use some weeding, a few stray dandelions had shoved their way through the mortar in the walkway. Two chairs on the porch, all the plants in cheerful pots and arranged carefully, but paint peeled up in places on the wooden railing and there were leaves in the storm drain. Gingham curtains, an empty bird feeder. No bicycles in the driveway but a basketball hoop put up over the garage, like a halo. Everything was quiet, suspended in the haze of afternoon.

I grabbed my clipboard and hat, then slipped on the wedding

band I kept in my inside jacket pocket. This was my best suit, and I knew that I looked sharp. It was something that could be relied upon. I listened to the sound of my shoes on the brick path as I walked to the door, heard the rasp of the soles and just began to feel my sock coming through the left one. I would have to remember to keep that foot on the ground. It's common knowledge that you don't trust a man with a hole in his shoe. Even at the beginning, I knew that.

I rang the bell and waited. Nobody answered. I tried again. Someone had to be home. I looked around again and saw that there was no *mezuzah* on the door frame. In all my years of work, I saw only one and decided to call it a day after that. You can't work your own people. After a minute of cooling my heels, the door opened and a woman stood wiping her hands on her apron. She was nearing sixty, maybe more, one of those women who came into mothering late and threw themselves into it with terrified abandon. Older mothers are more attached, in my opinion, because they didn't take it for granted, their children. They had been despairing about ever having a baby, the years creeping by, and their husbands and mothers looking at them narrowly, all wondering to themselves, *Failure?* Until, at last, came the one child and relief followed soon. Then the fear.

"I'm sorry," the woman said, "I was washing dishes. Can I help you?"

I consulted my clipboard, which wasn't necessary, but it looked official. I had a few friends working at the film studios, and they all said the same thing, that a guy with a prop is more believable than a guy with empty hands. "Are you Mrs. Phyllis Donaldson?"

Her face creased up a bit, the way everybody's does, to hear a stranger ask for them by name. I'd see the old fear come back, watch them relive a day much like today, when their lives were interrupted by a polite stranger who brought them the end of the world. "Yes, I'm Mrs. Donaldson. What is it?"

"May I come in?"

"Of course." She stepped back and I followed her into the cool of the house. I wish I could recall every foyer, every parlor, every sitting room that I had been in, but this is a job and things become routine after a while. I used to get a real kick out of being in other people's homes, as though I were learning a secret. Now I'm stuffed full of secrets and they're about as interesting as soda crackers. What can I tell you about this room that marked it as different from any of the hundreds I had already seen?

"You have a lovely home," I said.

"Thank you." She shut the door. "What is this about, Mister…"

"Silvio, Louis Silvio." When I worked, I usually picked Italian names, having been told on several occasions that I could pass for Italian. I took off my hat. "Well, Mrs. Donaldson, I've come here about your son."

"Paul?" she asked, her hand flying to her mouth. Her eyes began to brim and I looked away.

"Mrs. Donaldson, you wouldn't happen to have some lemonade in the icebox? It's quite warm out today."

"I have some iced tea."

"That would be swell."

She left for the kitchen, grateful. I usually gave the mothers or the wives or sisters a few minutes to collect themselves. All it took was a word to get them going, but their public grief embarrassed them. When women are ashamed, they don't listen.

I could hear Mrs. Donaldson in the kitchen, weeping into her apron. So I strolled softly through the house, stopping in the parlor. I ran my eye over her knickknacks: a porcelain shepherd and shepherdess, an old clock, a chipped vase holding daisies—which made me sad for some reason, those hopeful but plain flowers. A photograph from her wedding day hung on the wall, everyone dressed in the sacks of the twenties and staring glumly at the photographer. Mr. Donaldson looked particularly like a brisket in a suit, a beefy man with unsmiling eyebrows. And the younger Phyllis, pale and oval with her marcelled hair and smooth face.

Next to the wedding picture was a photo of Paul Donaldson in his naval uniform. It was a studio picture, the kind where people pay photographers to make them look like actors in publicity stills, looking away into the distance as though toward a future filled with glamour and romance. I've seen albums full of pictures like this one, though the uniform differs. Sometimes the kids look proud, borrowing the uniform's importance. Feeling consequential because of tailored wool and brass buttons, or a snappy hat. You can see in some boys' faces their understanding that signing on to fight will be the single most important or interesting thing in their lives. I pity those poor saps, whose only use is to kill or be killed. And if they made it back, just think how boring they would have become, telling the same damned stories about the same damned bunch of GIs and everyone having to take it. Who'd deny a veteran? I only see these pictures once the kid's dead, so the face of the boy in uniform becomes the face of a saint, a lost prince. In their shrines they are immortal and flat, preserved in the moments before going off to face death, eternally innocent but also courageous.

Often, the mother, wife, sister or even father will say something about the photo, about the boy, how proud they all were on the day the picture was taken, he was so handsome, so strong, so smart, et cetera. They never see what I do. I've been given a special gift. I see in their eyes, shining in the dark of their pupils like a doomed beacon, their fear. Whatever talk they talked before shipping out, whatever the families tell me about their boundless fortitude, I can see it plainly. The kids are terrified, I mean out of their minds wild with fear about what they're going to face, and beneath all that, they know there isn't a person they can speak to about it. So what do they do? They put on a few *schmattes* issued by the government and hope nobody can see their hands shaking, then take some pictures. At the portrait studio, on the front lawn or standing on the sidewalk. And they know these pictures will outlive them, so they keep smiling or looking off towards that promised future of adventure.

Paul Donaldson had a big face, meaty like his father's, also with heavy eyebrows and cumbersome lips. He looked like the kind of kid that played the tuba, who kept to himself at school and fantasized about girls in sweaters. In short, a loser, saved by the war.

I heard the chiming of ice cubes in a glass and I turned around. Mrs. Donaldson carried two glasses of iced tea that had already begun to sweat. She was clearly ashamed of herself, even as her eyes puddled with thoughts of her dear, lost son, and I smiled good-naturedly as I took one glass from her trembling hand. We studied each other over the rims of our glasses, but I had already seen enough to know who I was looking at. We pretended as though she had never shed a tear.

I turned back to the picture of Paul Donaldson. "A good-looking boy," I said.

Mrs. Donaldson walked forward and traced one fingertip along the frame. There was no dust, she cleaned his memorial regularly. "He was so like his father," she said, unaware that I had heard the same thing said about dozens of other kids. "Henry, my late husband, fought in the Great War and Paul always said that if he ever got a chance, he'd serve his country, too. That was all he ever wanted."

"You must be very proud of them both."

She didn't answer and I saw that she was still angry with her son for going to fight. Angry, but desperate for his impossible return. After a moment she said, "Why don't we sit down, Mr. Silvio, and you can tell me what this is about."

We sat down and I kept my left shoe on the ground. She sat at the edge of her seat, but I made sure to lean back, confident, relaxed. I had every business being in her house. The chairs were stiff and unused, the kind reserved for company. Somewhere in the house was her usual chair, where she would sit and listen to the radio while mending, and across from her would be another chair, once her husband's, once her son's, now unoccupied. How long would it be before she got rid of that other chair?

"I understand you're a busy woman, Mrs. Donaldson, so I'll get right to the point. Your son fought in the Pacific, is that right? He was a Petty Officer, Third Class on the *Gambier Bay*."

"That's right," she said slowly. Her hands were clasped together between her knees and she worked her thumb at the knuckle. "Aside from the name of the ship and his rank, his letters were rather vague, especially concerning his whereabouts. I never knew where he was. He said it was too risky to say exactly where he was."

Typical that this kid would think his letters held any interesting information for the Japs. "Of course," I said, nodding attentively. "I was stationed in England, myself." She didn't seem to care, so I continued. "Paul carried certain personal effects with him when he went overseas, isn't that correct?"

Her mouth folded up again with ill-concealed grief. "He had his father's pocketwatch with him. Paul would play with it when he was a little boy. I gave it to him the day he left, and I told him to wind it every day otherwise it would run down. Henry always kept it wound. Every morning he would get up and wind it, after he shaved and brushed his teeth. He'd get so angry when Paul would take the watch, but I knew he would want his boy to have it after he passed on. Paul was only twelve when his father died."

She was getting off the subject, but I let her have those rambling memories. The late Henry sounded like a dream of a man to live with, full of whimsical spontaneity, a wife's delight and a son's joy. I never could tell how much men like Henry were missed after they died. My opinion is that it isn't their loss that is felt, but their absence, something familiar now gone.

Sometimes I think of myself like a cowboy, steering, herding conversations and words to keep them from getting stuck in rivers of nostalgia. So I corralled Mrs. Donaldson back to where I wanted her. "He also had some photographs?" This was a guess which almost always turned out to be true.

"Yes." She reached into her apron pocket and pulled out a handkerchief, which she dabbed at her reddening nose. "I gave him a picture of me and his father, and he was also seeing Mary Kinkel from church, so she likely gave him a picture, too. And," she added, "I bought him a little Bible just before he left."

"Did you ever receive any of these items after…?" I let my voice trail away tactfully. Nobody liked to hear the words all over again.

She shook her head. "I just assumed that they were lost."

"Ma'am," I said after a dramatic pause, "I'm here to tell you that they are not lost."

"What do you mean?"

"I'm from the Citizens' Memorial Foundation—we track the return of departed soldiers' remains and personal effects to ensure that grieving families, such as yourself, have something to remember their lost sons. The CMF was founded by a woman just like you, whose husband had given his life for his country."

She was nodding, but I could see that she wasn't following me anymore. So I knew I had to play my hand now. After a deep, dramatic breath, I announced, "Your boy's belongings are being held in a storage facility in Washington, D.C. They can be returned to you at last."

She pressed her hand to her heart and sat back in the chair and did not speak for a minute. "That's wonderful," she whispered. "I've wanted something of his to be returned for so long now, but I had given up hope." The handkerchief was raised again and she shook it back and forth over her nose. "When can I get them back?"

"That's why I'm here, Mrs. Donaldson." I smiled ruefully. "It's a crisis we're suffering at the CMF. The government hasn't got the funds to send them to you."

"What?" she cried, sitting up. "That's ridiculous!"

I shook my head as though disgusted and ashamed. "Believe me, I know. The greatest, richest country on Earth can't even afford to look after its veterans. It's unbelievable, is what it is. But Congress has all its money tied up right now, paying back contractors, sending GIs to college, you name it. There just isn't enough money to go around."

"But they have Paul's things," she protested. "I just identified them and everything. How can I get them back?"

"You might, someday," I continued. "There are a lot of folks like you, who lost a son, a husband, a brother. And they're also waiting for those precious objects to be returned to them. The CMF tries to help out where it can, but we need that money—the funds, to enable that. So there's nothing to do but wait."

"But I don't want to wait anymore! It's been four years since he died!"

I leaned forward and clasped my hands together, a picture of concerned efficiency. "There is something that you can do. That I can do to help you."

"Anything," pleaded Mrs. Donaldson, and she took hold of my wrist. I could feel in the strength of her hand that she was used to living alone, having few people around to take care of her. A dead husband, a lost son, no one but herself and an empty house.

"I'd come here today in an official capacity, you understand," I said. "Just confirming details of Paul's personal belongings, his next of kin. But…"

"Yes?"

"I've got some very powerful connections back East. They might be able to…move things along for you, make sure that Paul's things get to you much sooner. More quickly than, say, the families who are supposed to get their boys' belongings before you. There is a schedule, after all. And we know how Washington loves its schedules."

I watched her thinking—thinking about the other women in their parlors, their shelves reserved for their dead heroes, and the bitter unfairness of sacrifice.

This is where it paid to wait. I couldn't say anything, couldn't rush Mrs. Donaldson. It had to be her idea, even though I was leading her carefully to where she needed to go. I used to get impatient during this part, try to hurry things along, but that never really worked. I almost had it go bust a few times. I've learned a lot since then, at this, my higher education.

"What if…," she began, then stopped herself. She fought hard, I'll give her that, but, in the end, everybody's got the same goal—to get what someone else couldn't have, to play wise, to have the best of things.

"What if," she began again, "I could offer those connections of yours something. To speed things up. As it were." She turned white and then flushed. "I could make it worth their while."

I pretended to think this over, while inside me a little icebox opened and cool relief blew through me, followed by a fizzy pop of triumph. It doesn't matter how long I've been doing this, I can still catch a high when the mark takes the bait.

"Hmm," I said, "that might work. And," I added, "you would finally have those lost mementos of your son. The child you and your husband raised is gone forever, killed serving his country. He will never come home again. Never sit at the kitchen table and eat his favorite meal. Never sit next to you in church."

She began to cry openly, covering her face with her hands.

"But you can have something of him back," I continued, returning hope to her, "the few precious items he carried with him as he went off to defend his home. Just think, he held that pocketwatch in his hand as the enemy's gunfire shrieked around him. He looked at your picture as the bombs fell, maybe even as he expired. And you can hold what he held, look at the faces that comforted him in his final hours."

"Yes, yes," she said through her tears, "I want that."

I looked concerned. "My connections are taking an awful risk, though, putting you ahead of the other families."

"I don't care about those families," she snapped, wiping her face. She must have been tired of crying, it was too familiar to her and losing its power. "I just want Paul. Tell me how much you think I should send. How about fifty? Or is that enough?"

"Fifty, I think, will be more than ample."

"Will you take a check?"

"Of course."

She excused herself to get her purse. I waited for her to come back before fiddling around with my pen, making official-type marks on my clipboard. The small gestures that confirmed the wisdom of placing her confidence in a gent like myself. Saying nothing, she took out her checkbook.

"Do I make it out to the CMF?" she asked.

"'Cash' is better," I said, "since we're subverting the normal channels."

She nodded sagely and wrote her check. Then she handed me the little slip of paper.

I was slow to take it from her, not from lack of interest but exactly the opposite. How beautiful and noble that check looked to me, the vessel of Mrs. Donaldson's faith, her hope to reclaim the dead. It doesn't matter how much a person reads the paper or listens to the radio. They can watch all the pictures they want. Everything bears witness to the fact that friendly, this world isn't. There's always someone like me waiting for their chance to take advantage. Yet still, here was a lonely old woman who wanted only to trust me. Everyone wants to trust, to believe, despite what their eyes and ears and minds tell them. It's a lovely thing, that trust.

I held the check as she replaced her checkbook, but when she met my eyes, she said, "What's wrong, Mr. Silvio?"

"I can't take this."

Her eyes widened. "Why not?"

"Fifty is simply too much. Especially with you living on your own—I know it's a lot of money."

"But I want to pay it!"

"Listen," I said, lowering my voice like an old friend, "let me see what kind of strings I can pull on my end. The CMF isn't without influence. I think I might be able to convince my guy in Washington to release Paul's things, have him do me a favor. I draw a lot of water out there."

"Really? That would be so kind, but I—"

With a dramatic flourish, I held up the check and tore it into neat squares and let them drift to the floor like a tiny parade. Mrs. Donaldson couldn't resist the spectacle, and her hand flew to her mouth.

"Just give me thirty in bills and I will take care of everything."

If she liked the idea of getting one up on those other families, she liked saving twenty dollars even more. She smiled, and I saw a bit of the girl in her then, even before she had been a bride, joyriding in dad's Model T and thinking that no tragedy could ever befall her.

In a few moments, I had a stack of soft green cash in my hand, carefully extracted from Mrs. Donaldson's pocketbook. I tucked them securely into the inside pocket of my jacket.

"I can't tell you how happy I am that I'll have Paul's things back," she said to me once I'd pocketed the money.

"It may take just a little while," I warned as I stood. "There's a lot of paperwork to be sorted out in Washington."

She followed me to the door. "It doesn't matter. All that matters is knowing they're on their way."

She opened the door for me and I stepped out back into the afternoon. It was after three, and a group of kids were walking home from school. They wore dungarees and T-shirts and shouted gently to one another, swinging their lunchpails. Mrs. Donaldson smiled as she watched them go by.

"This is my favorite time of day," she said, putting her hands in her apron pockets. "Some people complain about the noise the children make, but I don't mind. I like it. Do you have any children, Mr. Silvio?"

I put on my hat. "Not yet, Ma'am, but me and my wife are trying."

Her eyes stayed on the space where the kids had been. "That's good. Just keep trying."

"I'd better get back to the office and make some phone calls for you."

"Yes, certainly." She reached out and shook my hand. "I appreciate all the trouble you've gone through, Mr. Silvio. I'm so grateful."

"It's no trouble at all, Mrs. Donaldson. And it was a pleasure meeting you. Here's my card, in case you need to call." I handed her a business card, one I'd had printed up for cheap in an underground joint downtown. The guy down at the ink shop even came up with a little logo for the fake CMF. It was a beauty, very inspiring and official. If Phyllis Donaldson tried to ring the number, she'd get a barber shop near Olvera Street that spoke only Spanish. For now, the card was a little flourish, a coda on the end of my grift. It wasn't necessary, but it made everything a little prettier, a little neater.

I stepped off the porch and walked towards my car. The door shut behind me. She might linger at her curtains to watch me go, but I didn't want to turn around to look. Too furtive. So, confidently, I got in my car and drove off, the bills safe in my inside jacket pocket and radiating gentle comfort. Also in my jacket was her check for fifty dollars, whole and pretty as an Easter egg. The check I had torn up was nothing but a dummy. I kept a stash of blank checks in my jacket at all times, different colors and sizes to suit my needs. And right then my needs wanted Phyllis Donaldson's eighty dollars.

Maybe in a few weeks I'd send her one of the Bibles I picked up cheaply, but I was flat as a matzo and I had to scrounge every penny I could. I had to make a choice between her memories of her dead hero and my own living needs. Mine won out every time.

Chapter three

A few wilted potted plants pushed up against the walls of the Carmel Club. Eventually, those sad plants would take on so much smoke, their roots crowded with ash and butts, that they'd wither and be tossed out by the Carmel Club's top schnook, the manager. Burnt, dried up, the leaves would curl into themselves and finally drop off. Or the whole thing would collapse all of a sudden, like a boxer taking a dive. They'd be replaced with another series of unlucky plants, that would wind up in the same place, the gutter.

I'd seen it happen enough in the plants to recognize the signs of a goner. I could say the same about the suckers who crowded the room, happy to have someplace close to home where they could throw away money without worrying that the cops might break down the door. Draw poker was legal in Gardena thanks to a '38 loophole, so folks would truck on over from Hollywood and Studio City to stake and lose and stake some more, and I was there to provide musical accompaniment to cheer them on.

When I started playing, dreaming of the gigs I'd have, the fancy spots heaped with prestige and gorgeous dames, I didn't know about places like the Carmel Club. Now it was most all I knew, with the exception being Dee's. Grimy wooden paneling lined the walls, coming up at the edges, kisses of cigarette burns dotting the surface. Waist-high plaid curtains, yellowed and dingy, cordoned off each gaming table. My piano was shoved into a corner, far away from the floor girls selling chips but close enough to the bar that I might be able to scrounge a tip every now and then from a customer wetting his whistle. But I only got tips when they first came in, feeling big, or when they were flush, otherwise the glass pitcher I kept on top of the upright piano stayed empty.

It crossed my mind more than once that I might end up like one of the sick plants chucked into the wastebin in the back, clapped-out with the smoke from too many *schlimazels* believing they had a chance at the tables. Maybe I'd be given the heave, too, after crumpling at the piano, stuck full of cigarettes and wadded napkins, queasy with so much losing.

Looking up at my tip pitcher now, I saw that it held a few sad dimes, even a lousy penny, but not a single bill. Not enough to cover my funeral expenses, not even a burial at sea. Guess I'd have to stay breathing a bit longer. I peered over my shoulder at the room. It was crowded, a Friday night, and there were customers waiting for a seat to open up so they could toss down their week's wages and pretend that they were high rollers. Everyone bluffed that come Monday morning, they wouldn't be back to the same insurance offices, gas pumps, and freight shipping. Smoking and betting, they tried to put that Monday out of their heads, and made like they were Rockefeller.

I saw them, though: their one-room apartments that waited, with a Murphy bed and a free calendar tacked on the wall, a big red X marking each day spent. I've got what they call grift sense. Each sucker and chump I meet is laid open to me, so I see their tiny little hopes, their wants, the rooms they live in and the windows they stare out of, dreaming. Those dreams are the keys that unlock each con, everybody wanting something else. Everyone thinks it's got to get better, there's something more than just *this*. That's what I sell them: their own secret souls.

Or I play piano at clip joints.

Nobody here paid any interest in my music. I could've been

playing "I'm an Old Cowhand," "Mood Indigo," or Bach's Goldberg
Variations, it would have mattered just as much. For kicks, I once
tried a chorus of "Brother, Can You Spare a Dime?" Nothing.

But a gig's a gig, and they're too rare to turn down. Fielding
calls from Billy Berg, I wasn't, trying to fill a spot for his swanky club
on Vine. If the Carmel Club wanted to line my pockets to fill the
air with some piano tunes, then I wouldn't turn them down. But it
wasn't the Savoy Ballroom, and it wasn't Dee's, so I saved the good
stuff for later.

Letting my hands run over the keys, I launched, without thinking, into "Bewitched, Bothered, and Bewildered." Once, I'd tried some
bebop, but Len Holstadt, the manager, had come running over and
honked to ixnay on the opbay, since it made the customers nervous.
And jittery customers aren't as likely to bet big. No improvisation, no
two-note phrases, just straight melody, and easy on the ear. Len said
there was something comforting about a live piano player, instead
of, say, a jukebox, like they've got at all of the other Gardena joints,
something that gave the place an air of refined respectability. I had
cast my eye over the slumped plants, the cheerless curtains, and the
tired floor girls drifting back and forth like blown dandelions, Len
in his shiny, often-pressed suit that fit him like a grimace, and said,
"You bet."

Playing standards, regular as you please, no bebop, no improv,
felt like trying to eat Lindy's cheesecake while wearing a muzzle. Just
enough sweetness got by so that I was straining with impatience and
boredom. And that was how I earned my bread. You could call it my
legit money, since the other half of my take came from the grift, but
neither felt exactly pure, true. At the Carmel Club I faked the music,
and on the C—the con—I faked everything else.

Would it surprise anybody that I started out on the violin? My
pop wanted me to be the next Yehudi Menuhin. I used to lug my
case up the Grand Concourse to take lessons from ancient Leopold
Israel, who'd been, according to my father, "A great man, a remarkable
man," back in Poland, conductor of his own orchestra and what my
father also called a *feinshmeker*—a big deal. Definitely swankier than
the Greenbergs of Jerome Avenue, with me sleeping on the couch in

the parlor and my two sisters sharing a room with our mostly deaf grandmother, only a thin wall between their bedroom and my parents'. It was no wonder my parents stopped at three kids—where would they have put them, the icebox?

But old Israel had had to leave Warsaw because the Poles weren't too wild about a Jew living the high life and telling a bunch of goy musicians what to do. He'd come home one day to find all of his antique instruments smashed, his sheaves of music torn and burned, and a lot of dirty words scrawled on the expensive French wallpaper. And then the phone calls started. So he packed it in and came to the *Goldene Medina* and put up his shingle out of his apartment off the Concourse, the ritziest street in the Bronx, advertising in the local paper for all budding Stravinskys to come on by for a dollar a lesson. Which was a long drop from where he'd been. Leading orchestras in Krakow in front of women dripping with flashy rocks, well-greased gentlemen in cutaway tailcoats, champagne flowing like Coca-Cola, a tidal wave of approval and praise washing over him, warm and flattering. And then he went on to whining, pale kids snapping gum in the stuffy parlor, as cosmopolitan as a stale bialy. The first time I went to take a lesson, I pocketed the money for trolley fare and walked, hoping to buy some candy later. So even then, my other talent was already there, a grenade ready to be thrown.

I passed the awnings and the doormen, who'd sniffed at a bony kid, painfully mired in childhood clumsiness, while I gawked like a rube at the apartment buildings that held so few people. The elevator jockey had to quiz me three times for the floor I wanted. I hadn't gained the confidence that would do me so well later on, not knowing that confidence was as much of a scam as anything. It didn't have to be real, just convincing.

I expected an old man with pea soup in his beard, smelling of naphthalene, with fingers so bent from arthritis they seemed to slide right off his hands. But the door opened and proved me wrong. Leopold Israel dressed like the sharpest cat on 52nd Street, smarter than Adolphe Menjou, the perfect gentleman at home. He had a debonair mustache, no streaky beard, and when he shook my hand to welcome me in—which almost nobody in my neighborhood did to an eleven-year-old kid, I might add—he could have crushed me with the strength of those straight, strong fingers. And he talked like Charles Boyer. When I told my mother, later, she gave an uncharacteristic sigh and said she wished she could accompany me to my lessons. My pop wasn't wild about that idea. I didn't tell my dad that Leo Israel was a guy with the fight beaten out of him, given up on the promise of his past self to drag along in the afterlife of the Bronx. How could a lousy kid, who only went into Manhattan twice a year, who drank U-Bet and was just starting to develop a friendship with his *schlong*, see all this? Like I said already: grift sense. You can't pretend you've got it, you can't make it, either. It's something you just have, or forget it, brother.

But Leo couldn't throw in the towel, not completely, even if everything around him said that nothing mattered on the Grand Concourse, not him, not his snotty students, not the kreplach and squeaky-shoe hallways. Mr. Israel wanted things done right. And after a month of lessons, with me sawing away at the violin like a tough steak, he made me sit down at his piano and play scales.

"Louie," he said, being the first to call me Louie, which I understood later to be the French way of saying my name, "unless you want to cause an international incident every time you play, we have got to work on the basics."

Thing was, I really took to that baby grand of his. How to explain it? Up to that point, I'd been your average eleven-year-old kid playing stickball and comparing the merits of spaldeens and baseball cards. It'd been my father who'd pressed the lessons on me. He was the one, born in the *shtetl*, who dreamed of something beyond managing a cardboard box factory. The radio was always on at our place, tuned to one concert or another. Tone-deaf but full of wonderment, my father loved music, and wanted me, his only son, to love it, too. That's why he was willing to part with so much money right smack in the middle of the Depression. He wanted what Leo Israel had lost, knowing that, at best, he could only brush past the traces of smoke left by burning dreams.

There are stories of babies born clutching musical notes in their mushroom fists, who are calmed from red-faced fury only when music plays, and as soon as they can lift their heads or crawl, seek out means of making their own music on pots and pans or trilling their still-unformed mouths into song. Prodigies, I think they're called, which, I've also heard, is another word for monster.

A prodigy, I wasn't. I gave the whole music lessons scheme a raspberry. Like most kids, I knew the popular songs, and screamed my way through "Yes, We Have No Bananas" on the playground with scabs on my knees. And when it was announced that I was going to start learning the violin from scary, stern Leopold Israel twice a week after school, I did not leap into the air and caper about like a frisky colt.

And grim it felt, too, schlepping back and forth with that violin case, while kids roared their way through stoopball and jumped rope and played jacks, but there goes Louis Greenberg, like a sap. My mother even made me change my clothes before going over, to make a nice impression. To make the best of it, I tried to pretend that I was Jimmy Cagney in "Public Enemy," and that my violin case held a tommy gun. But Jean Harlow wasn't waiting for me. Instead, I got a hard, old, disappointed Pollack who made me torture catgut. I didn't like Leo Israel's apartment, silent and empty, and was especially put out that I didn't even get penny candy at the end of each lesson, the way they might give out at the barbershop if you didn't bite anybody's hand.

Leo saw in me no musical inclination, no talent, no love, but a dollar's a dollar, he was scrounging for them now, and he stuck with me until that day he plopped me down at his piano and the world flowered and came into being.

Eventually, the violin was sold and a second-hand upright was hauled up the four flights to our apartment, while our neighbors shook their heads and predicted certain doom. Why doom from a piano, I couldn't say, but these were not what you might call the most forward-thinking minds our country had to offer. So when the radio wasn't on, I played. I played with the radio, too, and soon after everyone in the building called our place the Cotton Club, not necessarily with love and fondness in their hearts, but because I never let up with the piano. I played along with Art Tatum, Duke Ellington, Count Basie, Oscar Peterson—name somebody and I followed them, anyone coming over the airwaves. My sisters, twins Doris and Delia, stuffed cotton in their ears because, they said, they couldn't take it anymore. My mother smiled and nodded, not understanding a damn thing I did at that piano bench. My father seemed to become a much bigger man. And Grandma Rifka couldn't hear anything, so it didn't matter to her.

I hadn't done a lot of listening to music before all this, not caring much for the piano, but it sure was different playing it. I could feel the hammer hitting the wires all the way up my arm, into my throat, down into the darkest, unknown part of myself, the part even I didn't know existed, that's where I was born. And though I played Haydn, Beethoven, and Liszt, it was the jazz coming in over the radio that went down into that dark, unknown part of me and brought me out into the world. How my father glowed, hearing me, how much he loved to talk about me to the doubting *farbisseners* at the barbershop or pretty much anyone he could get to stand still for half a minute.

To earn a father's pride, it's something else. It gives shape and meaning to a boy's life, a force propelling it forward, like a promise fulfilled. And then to lose that pride—but I was in the middle of a set at the Carmel Club, and couldn't think of that.

About two-thirds of the way into "Tenderly," I got the willies you get when someone stands behind you. I kept playing, but sat up straight. People coming up from the back made me jumpy. You never knew when a losing gambler might take it into his head to let out his frustrations on an innocent. Okay, so innocent I'm not, but the idea's the same. And it could always be a sore mark, come to beef. Now, if my life was like the movies, I'd have whipped out my gat and stuck it in the guy's belly while still playing "Paper Doll" with my solo hand. But, as if it wasn't obvious, I'm no Bogart. I'm not even George Raft. Few self-respecting C-men carry guns. We're not into the heavy rackets–e.g., something that might involve shooting somebody or getting blood on your clothes. So I debated whether or not to dive under my piano bench. Trouble was, it wasn't a very big piano bench, and I'm not a little guy.

"Greenberg," the Joe behind me said, and I relaxed.

"Mack. You almost stopped my ticker."

Wes Macklin came around me and leaned against the piano. Normally, I don't like folks leaning on my piano, it muddies up the sound, but the piano they had at the Carmel Club was older than Jumbo and twice as out of key, so it didn't matter. He was still in his work clothes, ink staining his fingers. His face was as rumpled as his suit, but not as elegant.

"Fancy meeting you here," he said.

"Fancy." I caught Len giving me the skunk eye from across the room, and said to Mack, "My break's in fifteen. Grab a flop at the bar 'til then."

Mack tipped his head toward the gaming tables. "Maybe I'll try my hand tonight."

I snorted. "This place is just a clip joint."

"Crooked, huh?"

"As your mother's back. You're better off just walking to the gutter and throwing your money down a storm drain."

With a whistle, Mack turned and headed toward the bar. The bar was a racket, too, serving watered-down well drinks and charging three times the price. Whiskey as potent as flat ginger ale, only less stimulating. But as they say, it's the only game in town.

I ran through the rest of my set, the old playlist of standards and popular ballads, and then, to no applause whatsoever, stood to take my bow. That must've been exactly how Leo Israel felt, roses and accolades tossed at his feet after a concert performance. Once I got up, I had to plug in the jukebox and fire up a few records. Len liked to keep the music going all night. It drowned out the sound of losing.

"So," Mack asked as I slid next to him at the bar, "you holding anything for me, brother?"

The bartender put a straight whiskey in front of me, my usual, and I threw it back as fast as I could so I wouldn't have to taste it. But I wasn't fast enough and cheap booze burned its way down my throat. To chase the taste away, I lit up a cigarette, and offered one to Mack. He waved it away, chummy, but what he wanted was to get his cut soon. We acted as though we were buddies, but there wasn't much I could get from Mack besides my leads. Maybe years ago Mack believed he was going to change the face of newspapers, make some kind of difference and set everybody straight with the skinny on how it really is, but there's no profit in truth-telling and by the time I'd gotten to know him, he'd rolled over and taken it right on the ass just to get through another lousy day. Guy like him had no confidence, ambition wrung out of him, and it was all I could do to keep our little get-togethers as brief as possible. I may grift guys like him, but I didn't like keeping company with dupes, like they had some virus or something I could catch from breathing too close.

From the inside pocket of my jacket, I took a slim envelope and pushed it to him across the sticky bar. He opened it and ran his fingers over the bills inside.

"Doncha trust me?" I said. "It's all there, forty bucks."

"I trust you, pal," Mack grinned, stuffing the envelope into his own pocket. "But it's hard to break an old habit. I've had other partners try to scam me out of my cut of the score."

I pressed a hand to my chest. "It shocks and saddens me that I'm not your first insideman. You're nothing but a floozy."

"But you're my *best* insideman," Mack countered. He swirled the watery contents of his glass around, grimaced in distaste and shoved it away.

"I bet you say that to all the girls." I took a few drags of my cigarette. Ghosts of my father still drifted through my head and I wanted to banish them with smoke and booze. "So, my ears are flapping, lay it on me. You're my main man down at the newspaper archives."

Mack shook his head sadly. "Things are bad, Lou. We're almost out of Gold Star mothers. And I've been combing the records, but there's aren't too many war widows and bereft moms left. War's been over three years now."

"Lousy peace," I muttered. "It's killing all my business."

"You and me both, brother." He watched the bartender squirrel back and forth between customers, who were bawling for liquid comfort after taking a bath at the poker tables. "Does it ever bother you," he asked after a while, not looking at me, "what we do?"

I shrugged. "If we didn't do it, someone else would. "

"You didn't fight, did you, Lou?"

"4-F."

"Me, too." He held out one leg for my inspection. I looked at it.

"That's a leg, all right. Betty Grable's got no competition."

"Flat feet," he said. "What about you?"

I took a deep drag and blew out some smoke. "Bad lungs."

His eyebrows curved, surprised. "I wouldn't have figured that about you."

"World's full of mystery."

"I sometimes feel bad about it, you know? Seeing all the guys in uniform. Staying behind like a chump."

Of course Mack felt that way—he was tiny. He wanted the borrowed wonder of the uniform and charm of killing, anything to lift him above the sameness and smallness of himself.

"The only thing I felt bad about was not being able to wear one of those snappy suits, myself," I said. "The ladies sure liked 'em. But that's it. I didn't lose any sleep over the fact that I wasn't getting the chance to be shot at." Which wasn't entirely true, but it was as much of the truth as I was going to give my roper.

Mack made a grab for his glass, but then came to his senses and left it where it was. "I felt like such a goddamned heel, Lou," he said, rubbing at his creased mug. "Sitting on my duff, instead of killing Krauts." He leaned towards me, taking his hand from his face, more earnest and close than I would've liked. "Some guy down at the office, he came back from the Pacific with a necklace made from Jap ears. Showed it to me. Looked like dried mushrooms. I was so damned jealous, I could've puked."

"I think I'm gonna puke," I said. "*Ears?* Jesus." I dragged on my cigarette to keep my gorge down and my cool up. I'll tell you, I don't take a shine to being surprised, and figured that I had people down pretty pat, but now and then something would come along, and it got me then that there were depths folks would sink to even I couldn't guess. The newsreels, for instance, of GIs liberating the camps. Hadn't counted on that, not at all.

"I didn't figure you for a necklace-wearing kinda guy, Mack," I said. "You've got it hard enough with that tie of yours. What chain gang did you pick that thing up from?"

Mack fingered the heap of cheap paisley dangling loose from his collar. He smirked, but was still thinking about the trophy he hankered for.

I wanted to change the subject. Sometimes Mack's Catholic morality and blood lust would raise their heads and blink sleepily in the glare, and I always made sure that they went back to napping. "What's the skinny on the new mark? Make it quick, my break's almost up."

"Yeah, sure," he answered. He took a scrap of paper from his pocket and nudged it towards me. "Mrs. Nora Edwards, widow of dearly departed Floyd Edwards."

I looked at the address and my gut wallowed around my shoes. "She's in Culver City, man. You know I like the marks at least eight miles from me."

"Times are rough, Lou. Can't be picky."

Goddamn it, he was right. "Where was this hero axed?"

"Italy. The Il Giogo Pass."

I knew enough about that campaign to get me through some small talk. And even though the Widow Edwards was too close to my own stomping grounds, I was starting to get as worn down and desperate as the schmucks at the Carmel Club.

"Aces. I'll give it a buzz."

I saw Len shooting daggers at me from across the room, and he pointed to his watch. That thing was like his mom's tit. Standing, I held out my hand to Mack. "Catch you on the flip side."

"Lou," he said, shaking my hand, "you're not colored."

I stubbed out my cigarette. "Square." He gave me a salute and then left.

Sitting back down at the piano, I eased my way into "S'Wonderful," and got to thinking about what Mack said. I had my own code, for whatever it got me. The touch from Phyllis Donaldson had been eighty bucks, and I'd split it with Mack. I didn't have to. I could have told him the score had only been sixty, or even forty, but I was level with him and gave him his cut. It was the straight thing to do. I was a *gonif*, but I was an honest *gonif*. Few out there could say the same.

If the world was a different place, a better place, I'd make plenty of money doing what I loved. Nothing but me and the ivory keys. But six years ago I learned that what we expect and what we get are as different as chalk from cheese. Here I was, twenty-eight, hammering on an off-pitch piano for a gambling dive. Most of my income came from grieving women. I snuck around with a colored woman. My apartment was a dump in Santa Monica and I hadn't spoken to my father since 1942. And I doubted that he'd appreciate my painfully constructed code of honor.

Chapter four

Beatrice lived just off Western Avenue, and, just like last week, and the week before that, and the week before that, I followed the taillights of her Olds all the way from Watts to Inglewood. Even though it was a Friday night, most of the city had already bunked down. Forget what you think you know about how groovy and swinging Los Angeles is supposed to be, the way they show it on the newsreels with the classy parties and nightspots, red carpets and flashing cameras. L.A. was still just a country cousin to New York. Central Avenue, Sunset Boulevard—it was no contest with the all-night flame of Times Square or Harlem. So down the dark streets I tailed her, as I'd been doing for the past two years, since we'd been keeping company on the sly.

Beatrice and I had circled each other for a while, trading looks across the tiny tables at Dee's. I dug the way she really grooved to the music, closing her eyes when something particularly fine was played, and nodding like she was hearing the Good Word being preached. And that reserve that Sonny had complained about, and sucker Roland had gotten straight in the nuts, let me know she put herself at a high price, she was worth something, bullshit wasn't something she'd abide. She was a honey, too, one of the finest looking women I'd ever seen, black or white.

One night, after about a year and a half of me being hot in the zipper for her and doing nothing about it, she and I were alone at our table, everyone else either off getting soused or boogying on the floor. She took a cigarette from her enameled case and I offered her a light.

I said, "What do you say you and I cut out of here and grab a cup of coffee, someplace nice and quiet?" Couldn't really tell you what got into me that night, why I was willing to take my manly pride in my hands and hold it out for her to spit on. It wasn't that I was hard up for action—for the love of Trigger, the smartest horse in the movies, I was a confidence man and if I couldn't talk my way into a dame's underdrawers, then I was in the wrong line of work. Just about any night of the week I could find some woman to bounce mattresses with, if that's what I wanted. That's no fish story, and not bragging, either, it's the truth. A lot of C men are good-looking guys, they have to be. Trust is gained more easily by the beautiful. Handsome guys and beautiful women also have that confidence in themselves that the usual plain-faced folks don't have. And if ever a con goes south, marks are reluctant to believe that somebody so touched by the artistry of God would ever lead them astray. They might even come back for a second or third helping of bunko. And the grift goes on.

But don't let anyone tell you a grifter can't be conned right back by a pretty face, because we're just as susceptible as the next mark when it comes to lovely women. And, let's face it, folks, you couldn't get better merchandise than Beatrice Langston, smooth and cool, a smart aleck, with a waist and curves just right for a man's hands, and a *punim* that belonged on a magazine cover, if they'd put colored women on the covers. Maybe because no one could get close to her, nobody had a shot, especially me, that's what first pushed me to get to know her better, one of the only women I couldn't, shouldn't, have.

So I held the match to the end of her cigarette and watched it glow red as she took a deep drag. She just looked at me through the smoke. The flame from the match crept closer to my fingers, until finally I had to shake it out.

That minute she stared at me was a long one. I didn't have any reason to think she'd take me up on my offer other than I wanted her to, badly. Every night I saw her, I watched the inevitable train wreck of guys trying to make their move on her, and, well, you've seen what she can do to a man. Here I was, some white cat playing it hep. My palms grew damp. This bothered me. My line in grifting needs me to be on top of the situation, always. It wasn't called the confidence racket for nothing. Usually, I could put it on and off like a damper pedal. But here was this woman throwing me for more loops than a ride at Coney Island. What the hell was I trying to get myself mixed up in?

Finally, when I was just about ready to pack up and put my head in the oven, she said, so cool I could barely believe it, "Come over to my place. It's private."

She stubbed out her cigarette and rose to leave. I was going to get up, too, happily leaping to my feet and slamming on my hat like a sophisticated gent, but she hissed at me, "Wait five minutes. I'll be in the back."

And those five minutes, like the lead time I always gave her, were sure rough. I just wanted to run after her, be alone with her for as long as I could, find out if she ran hot or cold when the lights were off. But we had to keep up the act. I won't tell you that I didn't get a kick when Beatrice shot down a schnook like Roland, me sitting right at the table, and all the other fools in the place tearing their tongues out to get a little of her action, knowing that later I'd touch and taste and smell her as much as I liked.

Every week, I anticipated those secret tastes until I could hardly take anything into my mouth except her. Sitting in my car now, I already felt the press of her skin against my lips, as if I could carve her from memory alone. But it wouldn't be a memory for much longer. At least, not tonight. Beatrice parked her car in the driveway of her little house and walked up the path to her porch as I was parking across the street. Breezy, she took her key out and unlocked the door, then stepped inside. In the quiet of the early morning, I could hear that she left her door unlocked as she shut it behind her. That meant something. The porch light went off. I looked at my watch. If I went inside before at least two minutes had gone by, she'd be hopping mad and make me leave. I may be able to finesse my way into a chick's panties, but no one, not even a chiseler, can talk a woman down when she's steamed. It's a point of pride for all con artists that they don't get anyone to do what they don't really secretly want to do. I won't force a woman, never had cause to, and when Bea laid down the law, I toed it. So I had to stew, while every part of me was tuned to her.

Through the gauze of the front curtains, I could see Beatrice switch on the light in her bedroom. Then she shut the bedroom door and everything was dark again. It wouldn't matter. I knew the inside of her house; the little sofa, the radio, the tiny kitchen with the Formica-topped table, even the pictures of Egypt she had on the walls. It was nearly the same as any house of my marks, but other than the fact that Beatrice thought I was a music teacher, I never conned or scammed her. She knew me, better than anyone else, or as well as any person can get inside another.

I'd waited long enough. I got out of my car and closed the door as quietly as I could. But there wasn't anyone awake to hear me, not even the dogs in the yards. Inglewood was a working-class town, rows of neat houses sitting close together, kids' bikes left on the trimmed lawns. Even though the spreads weren't exactly substantial, I still goggled at how wide and spacious the street was, how open compared to the crowded avenues of the Bronx. After all the years I left New York, that was still something I didn't quite get a bead on, how empty the streets of L.A. were in comparison. Or maybe I should say, the sidewalks, since it seemed like everybody and their dog drove in Los Angeles, nobody walked, and if you thought that maybe you'd take a constitutional in the middle of the day down Pico Boulevard—which I don't recommend, nothing to see except furniture shops and parking lots—folks would either gape at you like you were an escapee from a geek attraction or they'd stop and ask if you wanted a lift someplace while your car was in the shop. Sometimes I did get lonely for the jostle and company of a Bronx sidewalk, and went downtown near the Garment District for a fix, but those small skyscrapers felt like kids playing at being a tough guy, some schoolyard bullies instead of mob capos, and I'd usually shuffle home, sorry for even trying.

I hoofed it lightly across the street and walked on Beatrice's lawn to keep my footsteps muffled. Up the porch and to her door, where, no surprise but still a surprise, I found it unlocked. With a quick glance over my shoulder to make sure no buttinsky neighbor was peering through his curtains, I slipped inside and locked the door behind me.

As I said, I knew Beatrice's place well enough to not even need the glow of the streetlights to find my way around. I tossed my hat onto the palm-print sofa and went down the hall. For just a moment, I stood in front of her bedroom door, looking at the yellow light from under the door playing across the leather of my shoes. It's true, what you've heard, that there are times anticipation is better than the thing itself. I drew out that moment, listening to the faint music coming from inside on her record player—"I've Only Myself To Blame." I smiled at that and gently pushed the door open. There's drawing out the wait, and then there's just being a dope. A dope, I'm not. She didn't think so, either. She was waiting for me.

"Put on a new record, baby," Beatrice murmured. "Take the one from the top of the stack."

Though I was worn out and wrung dry, naked as a bumble-bee, I slid out of bed and padded over to the turntable on her dresser. She'd draped a scarf over the lamp on the bedside table, the way she always did when I came over, trying to make everything dim and rosy. It was one of those touches a guy would never think of, but women try all the time, even a woman with plenty of backbone, like Beatrice—trying to squeeze a little romance out of life when just about everything else screams that it isn't like it is in the pictures or tin pan alley ballads. But Beatrice's scarf over the lamp let me know that for all her hard-boiled talk, the way she cut would-be mashers and kept herself to herself, she still had a place set aside for the sugared dreams of girlhood.

I switched discs, easing one from its paper sleeve and putting the other back. I set the needle down and Bessie Smith's gravelly lament filled the room.

"No wonder you give everyone the brush-off," I said, turning back to Beatrice, who was stretched out, dark and slim, on the white sheets. "Listening to these blues would bring Andy Hardy down."

She held out her arms to me and I went straight to her, laying beside her and running my hand up and down the curve of her leg.

"I'll run out right now and buy me some Dinah Shore," she said, one corner of her mouth curling up. Just to drive me crazy, she started to hum, "Buttons and Bows," until I couldn't take it anymore and clamped my hand over her mouth. She gave my palm a lick with her tongue, and, not being a complete schmuck, I took my hand away and replaced it with my mouth.

While Bessie mourned yet another man treating her poorly, Beatrice and I got our second wind. She wrapped her legs around me and I trailed my lips down her throat, to take one of her breasts into my mouth. She gasped, holding my head tight against her as she arched back into the rumpled sheets. Her skin was salty, just a bit funky. I fumbled for the box of rubbers we kept nearby and just managed to cover myself. A man has got to watch out for himself. I'd heard too many hard-luck stories about guys getting shackled when they got too careless with their juice, or else running off and dodging private dicks hired to track them down. No sir, I may have a pretty face, but I've got brains enough to know that the last thing I needed was some crumb-snatchers hanging around my neck. Bea didn't want that, either, so she didn't much mind the little intermission in the show while I took care of things.

With a twist, she had me on my back and straddled me. I gripped her hips and brought her down hard. I almost thanked the rubber—if I could feel her wrap around me skin to skin, sure I'd finish in half a second, like a kid.

"They all think I'm frosty," she panted as I entered her, "down at Dee's."

"N-not me," I gulped. I wanted to watch her ride me, moving up and down with her black hair swaying and her head tipped back, but I knew that if I kept on watching her, I'd go right off. So I shut my eyes and felt her all around me, that sweet tightness of hers, hands raking down the front of my chest, hearing her breath come in shallower and shallower. With my eyes closed, it was like hearing the music back at Dee's, shutting everything out but primal sound—jazz, the rasp of Beatrice's breath in staccato bursts—that kept me alive.

"Am I cold 'cause I want things done *my* way?" she asked, slowing her pace.

Have you ever had somebody try and talk to you while you're in bed together? As though you're going to have a real heart-to-heart, but naked and grinding? Man, I don't know what the holy bejesus that is, but I don't need schmoozing while I'm deep inside a woman. Two words I couldn't string together, let alone answer her properly. I'd lose my mind in a minute. "No, sugar."

"So I'm a glacier bitch 'cause this here's *my* house, not my daddy's, not my husband's or my steady's?" She lifted herself up so that I was barely in her, just the tip of my cock grazing her. "'Cause I don't answer to anyone and come and go as I please?"

Somehow I got a strong hold of her and brought her back down, and I didn't know if it was her or me moaning. "Come and go as you like," I managed to gasp. "I'm not...holding you back." And that was true enough. Between my cons and juke joint gigging, I couldn't tell anyone else how to run their life, least of all a colored woman. I didn't want to, either. One of the best things about Beatrice was her demand for absolute freedom. And she gave me the same. She was complete as a dark pearl. But, sweet fancy Moses, why'd she have to go talking at a moment like now?

She brought her lips down to mine. "I know," she breathed, "and that's why I like you, Louis." Then she leaned back a bit, grinning. "Now can it, bub, we're in the middle of something."

Like I said, schmuck I was not, and didn't need to be told twice.

I grabbed her tight and we bucked, nearly knocking the lamp off the nightstand. She drew herself out in an arc, crying out, and I finally let myself go. I came hard, near turning myself inside out. Beatrice collapsed on top of me, arms and legs everywhere, panting, sated, our hearts zinging against each other, and still Bessie Smith grieved.

We sat in her kitchen, eating Hydrox cookies and drinking milk straight from the bottle, Beatrice wearing a yellow chenille robe, and me in my undershirt and trousers, suspenders hanging down my back. The Frigidaire hummed in the back, and everything was neat and warm under the single bulb hanging overhead. I can't tell you the last time I'd felt so content as I was then, looking at her, Beatrice comfortable in her own kitchen, swinging her legs and smiling at me. That coolness she kept close around her was gone—I was the only guy, the only person, who got to see her like this, making it extra sweet. I loved sharing her bed, but this came a close second.

So here we were, in her kitchen, in the afterglow. From the bedroom, Ma Rainey wailed about her black bottom, and Beatrice shut her eyes, swaying in her chair.

"Ma's something else, that sister," she said. "I could listen to her all day."

I twisted the top off a cookie and scraped at the white crème filling with my teeth. What's that filling made of, can you tell me? Likely nothing kosher. What did I care? I was noshing on cookies with my woman, the smell of our sex still on me. Her juices had dried on my fingers and I could taste her as I ate my cookie. It was so good, I was almost ready to buy a plot at the Beth Israel Memorial Park and end it all right then.

I said, "That'd get tiresome, don't you think? Always hearing someone moaning and wailing about everything that's gone wrong?"

"I love 'em."

"What for, kitten?"

Tracing her finger through the condensation on the milk bottle, she said, slowly and thoughtfully, "It don't matter how much those women are hurting, how down they are, how bad they've been played, they're always gonna pick themselves back up and start all over again." Her smile was wistful, far away.

For a while I studied her, trying to put myself into those far back thoughts, wondering where she'd go when her sight turned inward. Beatrice could turn corners I hadn't seen, and it amazed me that she kept shifting. "Lilah said your pop used to beat you," I said.

Her look came back into the room, to me. Now her smile was rueful. "She said that, huh?" When I nodded, she gave a little shrug. "He took his belt to all of us, my brothers and sisters, and my momma, too. It was just his way."

"She said he went after you particularly."

I knew things were different from family to family. Some might get spanked, or sent to their room without supper, and that's just how it was. Every family was like its own country, with its own language, money, law and punishment. I learned that from going into so many houses, crossing the borders, and though there might be some small lag while I picked up the lingo, eventually I found my way and took it all in without so much as a howdee do. Still, the idea of anyone hurting Beatrice boiled my potatoes.

Again, she shrugged. "I didn't wait on him, the way my momma did, and I had ideas about leaving Akron. Yeah, I was a schemer. Didn't want no house full of screaming kids. No husband bossing me. But daddy, he didn't cotton to that." She pushed a cookie around the tabletop then stopped and slammed the side of her fist down onto it. The milk bottle jumped, and I did, too. "That's what I say to him." Chocolate crumbs formed a circle on the table, some stuck to her hand.

She studied the crumbs for a minute before brushing them off with a napkin. "I squirreled my pennies away," she said, so quiet and calm, a body wouldn't have known she'd demolished an innocent cookie with her fist. "Pushed everything away and got a job in the defense plants. Worked at Northrop until '45. 'Course the colored folks got let go first." Something in my face must've told her that I didn't much dig this father of hers, because she said, sounding surprised, "Don't tell me your daddy never beat you when you was bad."

"Ernest Greenberg never hit me or my sisters or my mother. Raising his voice was something he wouldn't do, either."

She leaned back, her eyebrows raised. "Didn't he get mad at all?"

"Yeah, he got mad." I thought of the way he looked at me when I came home from the army physical, holding the 4-F papers, the fury and disappointment side by side in him.

"What'd he do?"

"Treat me like a pariah. Wouldn't talk to me, wouldn't look at me, not even, 'Delia, tell your brother to pass the peas.' That would mean I was still there. Still alive. And the rest of my family followed suit. They didn't have much choice, since I was cut off so completely."

She reached across the table and took my hand in hers. "That's rotten, baby. Happen a lot?"

I stared down at our interlinked hands, her fingers laced with mine. "Just once."

"What did you do, to have him act that way?"

Not for the first time, I thought about telling her everything that had happened. But I didn't know if even she would understand the choice I made that day, when I went down with all the other putzes in the neighborhood, to the local high school gymnasium where the army had set up its medical review for draftees. I acted, not giving much thought to the consequences, not knowing where that decision would take me, or who I had to keep silent around.

To answer her question, I just shrugged. She wanted to press me, but she held herself back, which I was grateful for.

Instead, I picked up Beatrice's hand and kissed it, crumbs and everything. "All that," I said, "it means nothing. Not your daddy, not my pop. They're back in Ohio and New York, but both of us, we're here now. That's plenty."

"It is," she agreed.

I couldn't help asking, "Would your old man whip you for running around with a white boy? A Jew white boy?"

She grinned. "Oh, he'd whip me good." Leaning forward, she kissed me, tasting of chocolate cookies and milk. I loved how her tastes shifted from one moment to the next, like she was a constantly changing banquet for me to sample. With other women, it was a single tune, an unadorned melody that had the simple cadence of a nursery chant. Not Beatrice. She had sharp turns, complex rhythms. You couldn't dance to the music she made—it was too hard to keep up without looking like a fool—but if you were after something more, something that held meaning and intricacy, then her sound was that and more.

With a dramatic sigh, I said, "Keeping company with me just to get back at your Daddy. Gee, I feel so used."

"Aw, but you love it."

"And how. Plant yourself over here and use me some more." I tugged on her hand, but she pulled back with a sleepy laugh.

"I'm too beat, baby. Had to work today and it's," she glanced at the starburst clock on the wall, "quarter to five." She stifled a yawn.

"I worked, too," I protested, "but I've always got something to spare for you, dollface *bubele*."

"I don't suppose you ever have recitals for those kids you teach," she said.

"Maybe a few. Why? You thinking of coming and watching?"

"I might. I just might like hearing Chopin and Mozart shredded to bits by little Dick and Jane."

"The only folks who deserve that kind of punishment are the parents."

Quietly, she added, "I wouldn't mind seeing you, too. Someplace outside of Dee's and my house." She shrugged. "Foolish. That's not gonna happen."

"I'm sorry, honey." Of course, these recitals didn't exist, and even if they did, she could only show up as an interested observer and not the sweetheart of the teacher.

Then she yawned hugely, covering her mouth.

"Sorry, baby, but I got me an appointment with my bed," she said. "And you know what that means."

I stood, grumbling. "Just once, I'd like to spend the whole night with you. Go to sleep together, wake up together." I walked over to her and put my arms around her low, cupping her juicy ass. "I've never seen you in the early bright."

"Early bright?"

"Morning."

She chuckled sleepily. "That jive you talk, sometimes. Between that and your Yiddish, sometimes I can't hardly understand you."

"Sugar, I can hardly understand myself."

She rested her forehead on my chest and I kissed the back of her hair, which I knew she spent hours straightening, using hot rollers and chemicals that burned. All colored women did, she told me, even though the idea, I thought, was ridiculous.

"Don't make me leave. I want to look at you lying beside me, first thing in the morning. I bet you're beautiful."

"It *is* first thing in the morning."

"So there's no problem, then."

"You can't stay," she murmured against me. "Believe me, I want you to. But this here's a colored neighborhood. Someone'd see you if you left when it was light out. And then there'd be plenty of trouble."

I sighed heavily. "Yeah. But that doesn't mean it's not lousy."

"That's the world we live in, sugar." She wrapped her arms around my waist and turned her face to press her cheek against my heart. "One lousy world full of stupidity and nonsense."

I ran my hands down her hair, her back, feeling her resting against me, her slim warmth that would never stay in my clothing long enough.

Like a back door man, I had to sneak out, first looking out the door to make sure no early birds were goggling from their front steps as they went to get the paper. Beatrice sat on the couch and watched me from the window, with the lights turned off. The sky was paling with morning, a high blue haze, and everything was hushed and damp. I shivered a little as I crossed the street, the sharp morning air working its way between the gaps of my hastily thrown on clothes. I stood by my car and quietly pulled out the keys from my pocket.

When I thought about where I could be, warm and loose in Beatrice's bed, just drifting off to sleep with her arm draped over my back and me breathing her in as I began to fall asleep, anger came and kicked me in the chest. But it wasn't her I was mad at. Mixed couples were given mad dog stares at Dee's until the couple got the hint and took off. And the looks outside of Central Avenue were no better, sometimes hidden, mostly out and rotting in the sun like garbage, nasty words trailing after you with their stink.

I got into my car and gave Beatrice a tiny wave before revving up and pulling out. I didn't know if she waved back, since there weren't any lights on in her place. Driving back to my side of town always hurt, like it hurt now. Something both sharp and dull, filling me up. That's when the crazy thoughts would start kicking around in my head, thoughts I wouldn't give much truck to unless I was crapped-out and stretched thin. Those thoughts went something like this: Maybe Bea and me could shack up. Hell, I might even ask her to marry me. But could we get away with it, a Jew and a colored? Mixed marriages were just made legal in California, but weren't in too many other places. And what the hey would that look like, us together under the same chimney? Her cooking and cleaning, me on the couch reading the paper, wearing a cardigan with elbow patches and a pipe between my teeth—nah. Damn, I stink something awful, somebody must've spilled some cheap hootch on me last night or this morning or who knows when. She wouldn't be Beatrice if she turned into an ordinary woman. What would happen to that sound of hers, the complex melody I needed? I couldn't stand it if she became another stale ballad. Things between us couldn't be better. And I'd have to go legit or let her in on the tale. I wouldn't mind giving up running cons if I had decent gigs, but when would that happen? When did they build that supermarket? I could go for some pancakes right about now but they don't sell pancakes at the supermarket, unless maybe I get some Bisquick and make a stack at home, but I don't even have a pan to cook them in, so there's no use going down that road. Even a guy on the grift can find all this tale-telling getting wearisome, especially with dawn coming on and me far from finding a bed. What's the difference between a flapjack and a pancake? Mom couldn't make either for shit. Manhole covers, but not as light. Dad threw them out the window when she wasn't looking. That was the funniest thing I ever saw, especially when one hit that pigeon and just about killed it. But even if Bea and I could get someone to marry us, what then? We couldn't go out to eat together, or see a picture, or shop, or any of the square, normal schtick I see couples doing. And if we had kids—forget it. Part black, part Jew. Not a combination that would get a standing ovation on the streets of Los Angeles. Or the Bronx. Or anywhere. Shit, I really want some pancakes.

. I drove north, heading towards Santa Monica and through the sleeping farmland that hadn't been taken over by new factories. The morning cool was thin, I could feel the heat just under it, waiting to burn through. To shut up my churning mind, I made myself think of playing at Dee's, being back at the piano. If I tried hard enough, I could feel the keys under my hands right then, comping chords, improvising. That was my perfect world, the pure space of music, where I didn't have to think about my next swindle, or disapproving eyes trailing me and Beatrice, or about how a single, quick decision sent me from the good graces of my family.

Chapter five

The sun was just up when I reached my own apartment building on Pacific Street. Because of the Santa Anas, the usual white fog that sat soft and dull over Santa Monica had been blown far out to sea. So when I pulled in to the curb, I blinked like a hick at my own apartment courtyard, yellow against a hot blue sky.

It was the kind of place you'd only see in L.A., and if you want to say that's good or bad, that's your call, brother. Built about twenty years ago for the beach bums coming into town, its sunny openness had gone to seed. If I'd been casing it for a con, I would have found plenty of ready marks inside, folks with faded aspirations, hoping for their own score, ready to screw everybody else. That's the best kind of mark—the type who thinks he's smarter, better than the rest, wanting something for nothing and ready to step onto the shady side of the street to get ahead. You'll seldom find someone who won't break the rules a little bit to get on, to pull one over and make everyone they know, and some they don't, bitter and envious. I could find all of that here, just the right type of character I could grift, but I don't con close to home, and this place was my own charming rattrap of a pad.

I walked into the central courtyard, surrounded by little

one-story bungalows, and threw the remains of my cigarette into the dry fountain that stood in the middle. Weeds knifed up through the cracked cement walkway. The spaces between each apartment had been used for victory gardens but were now bleeding with bougainvillea. The deco curves of the buildings didn't look so aerodynamic anymore, crumbling with beachbound rot. And the mitigating fog that normally hid these sad little details was gone for now, so I saw everything that early bright, even if I didn't want to.

What would this place tell me, if I was on the grift? That no one who lived there thought they'd amount to much. They were all clocking in time until the smell of their bodies slumped over in their chairs would bring a coroner's van out and the rest of the neighbors standing in their pajamas would shake their heads triumphantly with the sad waste of it all and wondering who was next.

Where I lived had a fancy name, Pacific Court, but you wouldn't find anybody living there that could live up to the expectations. When I first moved in, I thought for sure there'd be Goldwyn Girls living in the other apartments, and that every morning I'd rub the sleep out of my eyes to see them frolicking on the tiny lawns bordering each bungalow, wearing bathing costumes and begging me to polish their smooth brown shoulders with tanning oil. Instead, I got a few hard-bitten, snarling women who worked as taxi dancers and bathrobe-wearing creeps who'd sit on their front step waiting to catch an eyeful of the girls' gams as they stomped off to work.

One of those creeps in a velveteen bathrobe sat out now on a folding lawn chair, a weather-beaten guy by the name of Pomeroy who used to run hootch long ago, before repeal. I never saw him dressed and walking on the street, who knew what he did for money now? He cackled as I scuffled my way up the path. I couldn't dodge him, as my place was next to his, and I gave him a watery smile as I went by.

"Long night, huh, Greenberg?" he smirked, looking at my day-old suit and loosened tie.

I fumbled for my keys. "You said it."

Leaning so his chair creaked, his hairy belly peeping out of his robe like a leer, Pomeroy said with a conspiratorial wheeze, "Was she a real hotcha number? Didja get inta her stockings?" He took a deep sniff, trying to get a whiff of whatever action I'd had.

"G'night, Mister Pomeroy," I muttered, finally getting the door open.

"Dontcha mean g'mornin'?" he hooted.

I grabbed the paper and shut the door behind me, glad to rid myself of that sick old man and his smutty laugh. I threw my hat and the paper on the little table by the door and dragged a hand through my hair, looking around with a sinking feeling in my chest. I'd tell myself that I was just killing time here until the express line for better days left, but there were mornings, like this one, I couldn't quite sell myself that yarn. Beatrice's pad was small and tidy. Mine was small and sloppy. I tried to walk through the place, but issues of *Down Beat* magazine were everywhere, stacked up and sliding onto the floor. I thought about tossing myself onto the cracked red leather sofa, but records tottered on it in piles like drunk guests.

My shoulders brushed against the sheet music pinned to the walls, a kind of decoration that made the place rustle with every breeze that snuck through. I draped my jacket over the upright piano, which was shoved into the area that would've been a dining room, if I ever did anything remotely resembling "dining." As I undid the sickly knot of my tie and set it down on top of the jacket, my eyes moved restlessly, trying to find something to settle on that wouldn't make me want to jump off the pier. I didn't find much. A radio, one card table in front of the couch holding three full ashtrays, one chair. When I went into the kitchenette, I found an assembly of dead soldiers rattling on the counter, drained a long time ago but never taken back to the liquor store for the deposit.

The icebox, when I checked it, held an empty mustard jar and a single bottle of beer. It would have to do for breakfast. No one was going to make me Eggs Benedict. I popped open the beer and took a few swigs, swaying on my feet. Taking the beer out into the living room, I slumped down at the piano bench and began noodling out a little tune on the keys, nothing special, just notes strung together like bits of laundry on the line. It took me a lot of short cons and grift work to save up for the piano. It once sat in the lobby of a

Hollywood hotel that had since been torn down to make way for a giant drugstore. So I'd gotten it cheap, but it'd been hell to schlep it all the way from Highland Avenue to here. I loved it, though, the best thing in my apartment. The months without a piano, just after I'd gotten to L.A., had been the toughest, and I'd stepped up my cons to make sure I got one quickly.

After a few notes, I gave up trying to play. The dry wind rattling the windows had done something to the strings, and I sighed, thinking that I'd have to blow some hard-earned cash on a tuner. At least the guy I used wouldn't trim me.

I got up and closed the blinds, then shucked my clothes and left them on the floor on my way to the bathroom. Thinking better of it, I grabbed my suit, put it on a hanger, and hung it up on the ledge of the bathroom window. I stood under the shower, water spurting hot then cold, and nursed my beer. Beatrice was asleep by now, while the rest of the city was just waking up. Saturday morning, and I felt like a damp sponge that had been dragged up and down the bar a few times. At least I wasn't like the rest of the desk drones and suit-fillers, happy to have just a day or two to scrape out their lives before selling themselves to their bosses every Monday. Even Beatrice did the same, sticking quietly to her routine five days a week, saving the real meat of her life for the weekend. Monday through Friday, she connected people's telephone calls and dreamed of the blues.

Switching off the tap, I dripped in the shower for a few minutes, debating whether or not to shave. On the con, a guy has to look sharp and respectable, but I was so tired could hardly lift the beer bottle to my mouth, let alone carefully guide a razor across my face. I'd probably shave my nose right off into the sink. At any rate, the wrinkles in my suit had steamed out, so no visit to the cleaners needed.

I got out and toweled off. Would it kill anyone if I went a day without scraping off my whiskers? So I left them alone, and, naked, tapped, dragged myself down the hall and collapsed into my unmade bed. I could just hear the surf surging in at the beach as I spun into sleep.

* * *

Hard rattling slammed me awake. I lay in bed for a while, hearing the wind shaking the windows and ruffling the palm trees. Everything shook from the wind.

Reaching over to my nightstand, I pulled a cigarette from a pack and lit up, puffing steadily and staring at the ceiling fan as I stretched out. The room was hot and dry. The sheets bunched at my waist, but I didn't feel like getting up just to open a window and let a scorching wind come and blow sheet music around like leaves.

I watched the smoke clotting over the bed, hungry but too lazy to do anything about it for now. The clock read just after three— maybe I'd be able to haul myself out and get a burger at one of the drag-and-eat places down by the water. If I could get out of bed. Which was a prospect that seemed dim. I felt heavy, gooey, still waking up, so I smoked and listened to the Santa Anas trying to tear down Los Angeles and throw the city out to sea. I could just picture all the billboards, the twenty-four-hour cocktail lounges, studio flop houses, oil rigs, and every sad sucker edging by on lowered expectations, all of it being blown away and scattered over the water like dandelions.

The sound of it reminded me of when I was in St. Louis. This was back when I'd left New York, and was thumbing my way from one end of the U.S. to the other. I didn't know where I was going, didn't have much of a plan other than to get the hell out of the Bronx and the clouds of my father. The highways were already empty, what with the gas rationing, and I was lucky to find anybody to take me anywhere. I didn't have the funds to buy a train ticket, so I stood by the side of the road with a valise full of sheet music, issues of *Down Beat*, and my 4-F papers, waiting for a lift to someplace. There wasn't room in the little suitcase for my records. It had broken my heart to leave them behind.

St. Louis seemed as good a spot as any to hole up for a bit while I sorted things out. There was plenty of jazz, and I figured there had to be good horn players who needed a righteous piano sideman. I'd grown up listening to W.C. Handy's "St. Louis Blues," and saw myself as some busted-out bluesman walking the dirt track roads, making deals with shadowy figures for talent and damnation.

Except I didn't count on the fact that bluesmen don't walk dirt roads dragging pianos behind them.

I still had this picture in my mind when I headed to Missouri, but lost it quickly. The rooming house I found was right next to the railroad tracks, and the whole clapboard place shook when the trains came by. I'd lay in bed, just as I was doing now, hearing the place shudder around me, and it seemed like everything was ending. I was just a pip-squeak—never lived anywhere but my folks' place, knew nobody, trying to convince myself that getting the 4-F papers was the best thing to do, and feeling tiny. Damn if I didn't almost cry myself to sleep each night.

I tried to console myself with the idea of all the juicy gigs I would get. It took me a while to learn that a white cat from New York wasn't exactly welcome to sit in on gigs, and paying gigs, excuse me, but no. Meanwhile, the moths were having themselves a swell old time in my empty pocketbook.

That's when I met Arnie Marshall. He found me at a lunch counter, trying to make a stale danish and even staler coffee last. It was the biggest meal I'd had in three days.

I was trying like crazy to put the moves on the waitress, a frowzy blonde with sad black eyes and a mouth that looked like it could say a few choice words, and make good on them, too. She wasn't my usual type—if an unpicky guy like me could have something like a type—but I hadn't had a woman for a while and was willing to put just about anything on the bill of fare.

"So, whadaya say, dollface?" I said to her as she wobbled behind the counter. "I've got a regular gig on the east side of town—you should come and listen to me play. Then, maybe…" I let my voice trail off, pretending suggestive sophistication, even though I was twenty-two and had a cardboard suitcase.

She twisted that mouth of hers and swayed off without saying anything. Only a housecat could've been less interested. Sighing, I tried to take a sip of bitter coffee, but without a knife and fork, I wasn't going to make much progress with it. I didn't notice Arnie getting up from one end of the counter and moving closer.

Guys like Arnie don't come off the assembly line, and as he sat down next to me, sharper than a pickax, but me as green as a kosher dill, he said in that country gravy drawl of his, "Son, if you're going to try and chat up the local damsels, you won't make much of an impression dining on desiccated pastry." He eyed the danish with disgust.

I looked at him—he was a slick man, all right, distinguished in his charcoal pinstripe double-breasted suit. He kept his silvery hair neatly combed, and the way he folded his pocket square would've made Ronald Colman crap himself. The hat he set down on the chair beside him was a homburg, so I thought he had to be some kind of uptown banker or hotel detective. I'd never heard anyone use the word 'desiccated,' either. With all his gloss the guy reminded me of Leo Israel with a southern accent, but I'd seen enough Edward G. Robinson pictures to try and play tough.

"Peddle your bootblacking someplace else, Gramps," I pretended to snarl, hunching over my miserable danish and trying not to cry. "I ain't interested."

He ignored me and held up a hand for the waitress. "Coffee, please, black," he said to her, so politely and elegantly she would have run to Java just to pick the beans. Hell, I would've, if he'd asked me. A steaming cup of coffee appeared in front of him seconds later, and by the smell of it, freshly brewed, unlike the motor oil I'd been pouring down my gullet. He took a sip and shuddered tastefully.

"I simply cannot wait for the sugar rationing to end," he sighed. "I doubt I'll ever get used to drinking coffee without it."

Even though Arnie was old enough to be her father, the waitress hovered over him, black eyes glittering with long-dormant hope. A bell chimed behind her. An order was up, and she dragged her heels to grab it, reluctant to leave Arnie. Seeing this, I felt a quick, hard anger.

"Listen, bo," I growled at Arnie, "keep your nickel out of it. She's—"

"Not going to waste her time with a four-flusher like you," he said genially. "Anyway, ladies like her are firmly commercial. Strictly a pay-to-play operation." Then he leaned close to me and said, low and pointed, "Listen, my young punk, when you are offered a gift from above, you do not toss it aside like a comic book."

I started to get up, but he clamped a hand hard on my shoulder and shoved me back down, his grip like a longshoreman's even though he looked unruffled and genteel. If it wasn't for the ache he left behind in my shoulder, I would've thought sitting down had been my own idea.

"What's the grift?" I said, trying to sneer.

"Don't be a jackass, son," he drawled. "Just listen to what I have to tell you." So I sat, nothing better to do and no place to go, and he nodded, approving. He motioned for the waitress again. "Please give my friend here a fresh cup of coffee, please. And he looks hungry. How about a steak, too? Yes, a steak sounds just the ticket. With a baked potato and a green vegetable, on the side." He eyed the waitress. "You *do* know what a green vegetable looks like, don't you?"

She stared at him, her eyes watery and dark—a natural blonde, she wasn't—until he took out a bankroll that could have been used to finance a set of gold teeth for everyone in St. Louis. He sure saw mine as my jaw hung open.

"Green vegetable," the blonde repeated, staring hungrily at the wad of neat bills. "Comin' up." And she shimmied off. I was so dazed by this gent's gelt I didn't even look at her ass jiggling underneath her uniform. When she was gone, Arnie looked around the nearly empty lunchroom and then quickly unfolded the bankroll. He made sure I watched. The top bills were big ones, a hundred, a bunch of tens, fives, a lot of ones, and then, with a flash so quick I almost didn't believe it, a mess of worthless green paper. Then he folded up the bankroll, with its monogrammed genuine gold money clip, as impressive as the New York Public Library.

"This is called a Michigan bankroll. Also known as a Mish. The hundred on the outside, a few other bills, mostly clams, and trash underneath. You see," he said quietly, slipping the money back into his pocket, "it's all about making the right kind of impression with your mark. Whether you're the roper or insideman, the pigeon must never know you are behind the six—that's what we call being broke.

Always project wealth and prosperity, even if you only have enough to eat cans of beans for your supper. Ah, thank you, my dear." The waitress had returned and put a plate of food in front of me—a red, sizzling steak, plump potato, steaming away, and creamed spinach. She set a cup of coffee next to it, taking away the old cup. It all smelled so good I almost said a *shema*. But I was still pig-headed and proud, and so I didn't pick up my silverware. I just looked at the waitress.

"What's your name, sweetheart?" Arnie asked her.

"Hattie," she simpered.

Out came the wad of cash from Arnie's pocket and he peeled off a fiver. "Hattie, sugar, you are an angel come to earth. Now kindly scram." The bill disappeared inside the top of her uniform before he had even finished speaking, and she went soon after.

"Now eat, junior," Arnie commanded. "I have a feeling that just about everything on that plate will be rationed before too long. Besides, I have a lot to teach you and a hungry student seldom pays attention."

I wasn't quite stupid enough to turn down a free meal, and I figured I could bilk this gent out of a steak and then get the hell out of there. So, with all the elegance of a circus carnie, I began to shovel the food into my maw. Arnie laughed and shook his head.

He introduced himself as Arnold Marshall of Munford, Tennessee, aka Memphis Arnie, "Since Munford Arnie doesn't have the same zesty flavor."

"What's the pitch?" I asked, my mouth stuffed. "You some kinda Ethel or something? I don't go for none of that faggotry."

Arnie grimaced. "That will be one of your first lessons," he said. "Developing better table manners. No mark will ever break bread with a slob, and eating with your mark is one of the best ways to play the C. Sharing a meal builds trust, encourages friendship and intimacy, all of which are critical elements of the game."

"Mister, I don't know what the hell you're jabbing about."

"And we'll have to work on the way you speak. Too much slang. That accent of yours, also, does not inspire faith."

I was stung. Here I had been thinking that I was talking just as tough as the guys in the gangster pictures, but it seemed I just sounded like another boy on the playground pretending to be a Dead End Kid. That, and my pop always scolded me whenever I talked slang, and now Arnie made me recall that my father was gone from me forever. I stabbed a piece of steak and stuck it in my mouth, then pointed my fork at him. "Look, pal, I ain't—"

"'I am not,'" he corrected primly.

"I don't want no lessons, or whatever it is you're shilling. And I sure as hell don't want no fairy action. It's all dames for me."

He sighed. "Son, whether or not I prefer my amorous company betrousered isn't a matter of debate right now. What we are discussing is you, your future."

I couldn't think of a future at that moment, just the next five minutes. Ten if I was being rosy and optimistic. I swallowed some coffee, and it felt like a friendly slap across the face. "I'm swell."

He eyed me up and down, taking in my threadbare gabardine suit, worn-out shoes, bony shoulders and desperate eyes. "That is dubious, to say the least."

"Lessons in what, anyway?"

"Why, don't you know, son?" he asked me, and his smile was so warm and comfortable, right then I felt as if I knew him half my life, and the other half without him was empty.

I shook my head, already falling under his spell.

"Confidence."

I threw on a tee shirt and a pair of dungarees, dragged a comb through my mop, and, after checking in the mirror to make sure my exhausted face wouldn't send anybody to the hospital, set off to scrounge something to eat. I couldn't waste the whole day lying in bed, thinking about Arnie, St. Louis, and all the other phantoms crowding my head.

Pomeroy had crawled back into his bottle collection somewhere, and aside from a big orange cat splayed out on the walkway, the courtyard was deserted. Everything was yellow in the afternoon sun, dry and rustling, and I slipped on a pair of shades to shield my baked eyes. Heading west, I crossed Main and then Neilson, passing little shingle-roofed houses with scruffy gardens. Collections of seashells and bottle caps were strung up from the porticos, clattering against each other in the hot breeze. Even if I worked the turf close to home, I'd skip these places, having little to offer but the crap that washed up on the nearby beach.

Ocean Avenue fronted that beach, and I crossed it to Ocean Front Walk, a long, thin stretch of grass and palms that looked out at the sand and the water. I stood at the cement fence and smoked, watching the people crowding the beach. You'd never know it was almost November, what with the people running up and down in their swimming suits, throwing balls to one another and screaming. Striped parasols were grouped like thrown candy wrappers, little white legs sticking out into the sun from underneath them. A fat man slept on a blanket with a newspaper over his face, his belly huge and red, getting redder by the minute, while his chubby kid squatted nearby and tried to fill a bucket with sand, one grain at a time.

Couples were out, too, lying together on their towels. Whenever they thought no one was looking, they'd grope and nuzzle. The worst they could expect were a few sour looks pointed in their direction, maybe a loud tsk-tsk from some big-bosomed yenta trying to read about Tyrone Power and getting distracted by the heavy petting. No one would come and shove them apart, make them leave. No police or lifeguards taking the man aside and giving him a working over. They could lie side by side all day, necking and cuddling under the afternoon sun, building up a case of blue balls until they couldn't take it anymore and they'd rush home to peel off their swimsuits and get sand in the sheets. Beatrice and I could never have that privilege.

If I headed straight north, to where Pico Boulevard hit the beach, I'd find the Ink Well—where the colored people went if they wanted some time on the sand. I never knew if they couldn't go to the other beaches, if someone would get arrested for spreading their blanket too close to the white sunbathers, but legal or not, nobody crossed the invisible lines. Maybe a white guy could put his towel down in the Ink Well, but no one did. I didn't, either. And I never suggested to Beatrice that we try it together. It's one thing to go to the dives of Central Avenue late at night, but I wasn't going to take any chances on a bright Santa Monica beach on a Saturday afternoon.

Families were out for the day, toting their coolers, blankets, badminton rackets, ice cream cones, shovels, film magazines, bottles of soda pop, babies, suntan oil, paper-wrapped sandwiches, cameras, sandals, and the feeling that everything was fine. I watched fathers playing in the surf with their sons as their daughters crouched at the edge of the wet sand, poking at seaweed and sand crabs, wives looking on over the edge of their women's magazines.

Back home, we'd sometimes truck out to the seedy Orchard Beach when the mercury climbed too high for fire-escape sunbathing. We didn't go to the ritzy Shorehaven club—couldn't spare the money to use the pool—so mostly we sat around the apartment *schvitzing* until my sisters' bitching wore my pop down and all six of us piled into the Studebaker for the long, sticky haul out to Rockaway in Queens. While my sisters worked on their tans and my mother fussed about ruining her hair and old bubbe played bridge with whatever *tantes* she could find, my father and I took long walks up and down the beach. He'd elbow me, grinning and winking, when a particularly winsome girl passed by. I'd roll my eyes, beet-faced, but that didn't mean I didn't look.

Then I started to get older, and wouldn't go with them to Rockaway anymore. I'd rather hang around the drugstore soda fountain with my mob, sucking down egg creams, cracking wise and making like I was the coolest cat in the Bronx. Pop didn't argue it with me, but I can tell now that he was disappointed we wouldn't be taking our "men only" walks anymore.

He was the only man in the apartment, now. Even if bubbe was gone on to St. Peter's holy mahjong game, he'd still be outnumbered, three women to one. Did it bother him, all the stockings drying in the bathroom, the constant yapping, no other man to share the heartburn of living in a henhouse? I wondered, when the twins were squeaking about some new dreamy guy at the department store where they worked and my mom was clucking in sympathy, if just for a moment, my father missed me.

Blinking now in the sun, I turned from the beach. Hunger and brightness were making my eyes water. I needed to take off, get away from the happy families, couples and falseness. Everything, from my belly to my heart, was empty.

Chapter six

Alonesome melody pushed me away from the sand and water. So, after grabbing a hot dog from a boardwalk shack, I left the beach. The whole of l.a. was in the mood to have a good time, and I was the sad sack listening in from the apartment next door. With a red hot in one hand, a bottle of pop in the other, I threaded through the traffic lined up on Ocean Avenue and over to Strand. The day was winding down, folks were piling into their cars for the long trek back home. As I walked, I heard car radios blasting swing and sports scores, kids howling with exhaustion and sunburn, and dads *this close* to losing their shit and decking everybody.

On Fourth Street and Strand, there was a two-acre park, a big grassy slope with benches and a few trees. I sat myself down on one of the benches and had my breakfast or lunch or whatever the hell it was. Most everybody was at the beach, or trying to get away from it, so I had the place pretty much to myself. There was one guy with a cockatoo on his shoulder, walking up and down the stairs and talking to the bird like one half of a news report. He was talking so seriously, glancing over at the big white bird with a crease between his eyebrows, I nearly expected it to answer right back and give its two cents on the merits of the current Brooklyn Dodgers lineup. Personally, I thought Jackie Robinson was aces, though Roy Campanella could swat a few dingers, too.

It was coming on evening, the sun starting to reach for the horizon, and I was feeling mighty mellow now that my stomach was full. I shook out my usual post-meal smoke, closing my eyes to feel the last rays on my face, listening to the jazz of everyday life all around me. The tree limbs tapping against each other, the raspy brushwork of leaves moving in the wind, a bright, brassy car horn flaring out, some woman's laugh floating out a window. Maybe I could play this, too, translate these sounds into a defined melody and chords, and call it "End of October."

Thinking of that, I started itching to play, so after tossing my hot dog wrapper and soda in the trash, I headed the few blocks back to my pad. "Your Hit Parade" was coming on, I could hear the opening number "Lucky Day" through the screen doors facing the courtyard. I wasn't particularly excited about it. All pop and ballads—they'd never air bebop on a show like that.

I scooted right down in front of my piano as soon as I got inside. For a while I went at it, trying to figure out a way to capture the Indian summer sounds through the keys, but no matter how much I laid on the pedals, making it soft, filtered, I just couldn't nail the right tone. On top of the piano were some pages of notes I'd made for "Fresh Bread," and I worked on that for a while, trying out different chords and progressions, until I hit a wall and it stopped coming.

There was another melody in me, something spare and dark that had been slowly growing over the past six years, and I could only find it just on the edge of my hearing. The harder I searched for it, though, the less it would come, so I had to sneak up on it—no, that's not right. I had to wait for it to steal up on me. The best way to find that sound, the hidden notes reverberating deep down, was to distract myself, take myself away from the search.

I played a bit longer, standards with a fast tempo, agitated, then slowing it down to keep pace with the falling dusk. Each note came out like a star in the purple sky, glittering, solitary at first, then coming together in a constellation. I didn't turn on any lights, and sat in the growing dark until the keys were soft white glows at my fingertips and I was finding the sound by touch alone. That one nameless melody hadn't shown, no matter how hard I pretended not to seek it.

The wind had died down, leaving everything hot and still. A fog would roll in soon after, it usually did. I was powerfully lonely.

Getting up, I stumbled for the phone and rang Beatrice's exchange. She answered on the third ring.

"It's me, sugar," I said, cradling the receiver.

"Oh, hello, it's good to hear from you," she said, and from her cool politeness, not saying my name, I knew she had company.

"Who's there with you?"

"Just Lilah and Wendel. They're taking me out to the pictures in a minute, get a little relief from this heat." Someone said something in the background, asking her who it was on the other end of the line, and she covered the mouthpiece so I couldn't hear her reply. "Then we're heading out for a bite."

"I guess that means I'm a lone wolf tonight." I tried, without doing much good, to keep the disappointment out of my voice. "Unless you leave your door unlocked for me later."

"That's awful sweet of you to offer," she said as though she was turning down a slice of pie, "but I don't think I'll be home until late. Maybe I'll see you at church tomorrow."

I couldn't help but laugh at her joke. "Yeah, I'll be the yid in the first pew, singing 'Go Down, Moses' and shaking my tambourine."

Beatrice laughed, too, then she added, softly, "I'm sorry."

"Me, too, baby," and I was, but not just because I wanted to be in her bed. I would've been fine with just sitting and talking until it was time for me to leave. "Ring you tomorrow?"

"Sounds swell." And she cut the connection.

The room felt very dark all of a sudden, the apartment empty. I sat with the phone until the operator came on the line and told me to either dial another exchange or hang up. I almost put the receiver back in the cradle, but then changed my mind. "Get me MIchigan 45723."

The line rang a few times and then I heard a scratchy voice that belonged in a health department film say, "Yeah?"

"It's swell to talk to you, too, George."

"Greenberg?"

"That's what it says on the marquee."

"You lousy rat bastard! What the hell you callin' me for?"

"I got some new Dizzy Gillespie platters—wanna come by and listen?"

"Put out the lacey doilies, 'cause I'm comin' over."

George Lohr showed up about thirty minutes later with some chop suey takeout and a box of beers. Even though I was sitting right next to the door on the sofa, and we could see each other through the window, he stood and hung on the buzzer for a good minute. That was George's idea of a gag.

He lumbered in, a linebacker in a houndstooth jacket, and threw everything onto the card table. Magazines scattered across the floor like showgirls running offstage.

"This gonna be some kinda slipped disc party, or what?" he growled as I grabbed a beer. "Make with the tunes, sonny."

There'd be no talking to George until I got the music going. So I fired up the turntable and set the platter down. I flashed him the record cover: Diz, in his beret.

"Dig Chano Pozo on the conga drums," I said. "That's some crazy Afro-Cuban shit. Wait 'til you get an earful of 'Manteca' on the flip side. If you haven't ruined your pants, you've got no soul."

George popped his beer open and sprawled on the couch, still wearing his hat. Sweat gleamed on his forehead and stained the front of his shirt. His shaggy, white-blond eyebrows hung low over his flat blue eyes as he nodded with the music, and the light from the lamp caught on the grizzle of his stale shave. George came from the kind of people who used to ride into the villages of my people and destroy or rape everything in their path. Now he sat in my dingy living room grooving on bebop while I dished up some slimy Chinese noodles for supper. Progress was a beautiful thing.

But as hep as George was to the jazz, and there were plenty of white guys and girls who really dug it, most, George included, could never get inside bebop. He could appreciate it, parse it out, break it down, even learn from it, but he had as much musical talent as I could play forward for the Knickerbockers. And there are people who love and listen to bebop, and people who play bebop, and between the two is a stretch of black ice on the road. You may not see it, but try to cross it and you wind up flat on your ass. It takes a kind of anger that only a musician has to really crawl inside bebop.

"This here's my best china," I said, handing him the least chipped plate, "so don't get butterfingers on me and drop it."

"You live like a pig," he said through a mouthful of noodles.

"Pig ain't kosher, pal." With George on the couch, real estate was at a premium. I sat down on the floor and balanced my own plate in my lap, then took a long, cold swig of beer.

"Like a Jew pig," he repeated, wiping his mouth on the back of his sleeve and then grinning.

"And you're straight from the Sing Sing Finishing School, so let's call it even."

That seemed fine with big George, and he set to eating the chop suey with as much finesse as a guy nearly six-six and three hundred pounds could, which is to say, like a hippo bellying up to a smorgasbord.

I didn't mind, though. As one of the few guys I knew who dug both jazz and the con, George pretty much had my number. I met him a few months after I arrived in L.A. There was a cocktail lounge out on Las Palmas, one of those padded-door affairs that were kept dark and musty so no one would be bothered with nuisances like sunlight and fresh air. It was about three o'clock, so I knew I was sure to get the boozehounds who were gearing up to leave the amateurs and turn pro. One was already asleep in one of the high-backed green booths that lined one wall, and another was slumped over his drink at the bar. Two other customers, a regular schmo taking a long lunch and a battleship I'd later come to know as George, were also sitting at the bar.

I eyed George and knew that I didn't stand a chance with him. Arnie had taught me that there were just some citizens who wouldn't take to the con. Usually it's because they're too stupid to follow how they could profit from the scheme. But George, big as he was, looked thickly smart, unmovable. So I left him to himself. The other guy, however, looked like a fine mark, so ordinary that he was exactly what I needed. Sitting two seats down from him, I ordered a scotch.

I made myself hunch down and put my head in my hand. When the scotch came, I threw it back.

"Another, please," I said, sounding as low as a guy licking his own shoelaces.

The bar had been quiet, just the radio broadcast, so I got a lot of attention. I could feel George watching me from the far end of the bar, but I didn't pay him any notice. I was on the stroll and didn't have the minutes to spare for a rough-looking player like him. The other guy, however, was already nibbling the hook.

"Say, pal," he said, turning his watery eyes to me, "what seems to be the problem?"

I started to talk, then stopped, acting about as blue as a man could get without turning indigo. "You don't want to hear about it." I picked up my second drink and pretended I was taking a hefty gulp when I was just letting the scotch wet my lips. I couldn't allow myself to get drunk when telling the tale. Only a sloppy grifter gets drunk with his mark. Arnie taught me that.

Following the script he didn't even know he was reading, my mark said, "Sure I do. We're all chums here, aren't we?"

"I suppose," I said after a pause. I made sure to soften the Bronx in my voice, trying for something more mid-Atlantic and less Fordham Road. He'd never buy my tale if I talked how I normally did, so I made like I was in some George Cukor movie, smoother and more up in the nose, completely without place of origin. Only Arnie could really pull off that accent of his, recalling big white porches, mint juleps, happy darkies singing in the fields. Everyone loved a southerner, everyone white, that is, so he didn't try to hide his accent. But if I didn't do something about how I spoke, the New York came through and I was a Bowery Boy.

I got real friendly-like, as though I was desperate for company. "Can I buy you a drink? Whatever you just had. Single-malt whiskey, am I right?"

He gave a quick look down at his empty glass, which had been full of cheap rye. "Yup. You sure called it."

Right then I knew I had my sucker. He wanted the best of it, and I was just the guy for the job.

When the bartender set the drink down in front of my guy, I threw down a handful of bills. Nothing like flashing a little green to get a mark's attention. And it worked, too. He grabbed his booze and slid a seat closer to me.

"Thanks, pal," he said, and lifted his glass in a toast. After he threw his drink into his gullet, he smacked his lips and asked, "So now that we're buddies, you gonna tell me what's got you so gloomy?"

"Women," I answered. "Women have me gloomy. One in particular."

"Ah, woman-trouble," he said with a nod.

"What would you know about it?" I demanded. "You look like you do just swell with the ladies."

He barked out a laugh and held up his left hand, the ring gleaming morosely in the bar's dimness. "No ladies, my friend. Got me a ball and chain, and she's trouble enough. That's why I come here for lunch, 'stead of going home like all the other guys at the office." He was a mouth-breather, this one, with his trap hanging open and a cheap suit. I wondered who the lucky woman was who called him her hubby, all her pink ruffled daydreams squandered on this schmuck who drank their savings away and lived in a tiny box. She probably wasn't much of a prize, either, a terrible cook who slammed cabinet doors.

At the mention of a wife, I groaned sadly and made like I was taking another drink.

"Don't tell me," the mark said, "your old lady's giving you the run around."

I blinked at him. "I'm sorry—what do you mean?"

"Your girl. She's stepping out on you." When I kept looking dopey, a real square who wouldn't know the street if he was kissing it, my mark tried again. He liked sounding savvy, some older, wiser gent dispensing wisdom to a young acolyte. At the office, he probably got kicked around by management, jeered at behind the water cooler, another dope uselessly shoving papers around his desk. And at home—he may as well take his cock off as soon as he stepped inside the door and hand it over to his wife, who'd lock it up in the pantry until the next morning. But here, in this bar, he was smart and sharp. Meaningful. "Giving her attention to someone who ain't you."

I heaved a mournful sigh. "We were engaged. But the whole time she's wearing my ring, she was unfaithful."

"You?" He blinked, disbelieving. "But…lookit you. Like some kinda matinee idol."

"The only part I played was fool. Do you know," I went on, lowering my voice, confidential, "I even walked in on her. In bed. With my best friend." That last bit was a little over the top, but I figured he seemed the type who'd enjoy an extra lurid dash.

He shook his head with a sympathetic whistle, and I saw a flash of terror and possibility cross his mug. There's something in every man that's afraid of women, afraid of what they might do, the power they have. In a lot of ways, women are ten times smarter than guys, capable of doing anything, and it doesn't take much to convince a chump that some dame played him false. They know it could happen to them. I bet you're no different.

"Whatja do then?" he asked.

"What could I do?" I answered with a shrug. "I'm no tough guy. I left. Packed a bag and came straight here."

I motioned for the bartender again and had another whiskey set in front of my mark. He took it and drank it down without thought as I watched his mind turning inward, rolling over the possibility that even his own pain in the ass wife could tear his guts out.

"Packed a bag?" he said, coming around. "Where you going?"

"Serve my country. Go enlist. Maybe I'll kill a few Nazis. Maybe I'll meet a beautiful French girl and marry her." I gave a dry laugh. "That'll show Connie. Come back and introduce her to Fifi, my new French bride."

"Atta boy," the pigeon cheered. "I'm too old to sign on, but you nail them foreign broads for me."

I made myself wince a bit, like he was being too crude for my delicate sensibilities, and then I turned that wince into a smile. "Say, mister," I said, as though it was just coming to me, "I have a bunch of things that I won't need anymore, once I enlist. Books, some jewelry I gave Connie. You've been so swell, maybe I can give you some. You'd be doing me a favor. Taking it off my hands."

The gleam was in his eye, it lit up straight off, but he tried to play it cool, pretend to himself and me that he really was on the level and motivated from pure good will. "I couldn't do that, friend. It wouldn't be right."

"Maybe so. Nothing is very valuable," I reluctantly agreed, and I nearly tore myself open trying not to laugh when naked disappointment flickered across his face.

"Wait a moment," I said, snapping my fingers. "I have just the thing. Stay here—I'm going to get something out of my car."

Before he could say anything, I jumped up and headed out, leaving my hat on the seat so he knew I was coming back. I stood outside in the afternoon haze for a few minutes, watching traffic and the slim legs of girls walking up and down the sidewalk. I didn't have a car then, riding trolleys and buses to save cash, so I was just killing time. After a short while, I went back inside, hand in my pocket.

Sure enough, old sucker was still waiting for me. I made sure not to look at George at the end of the bar as I took my seat. He was on to me, I was pretty sure, but on account of him staying quiet about it, I figured he wasn't going to crack out of turn.

Taking my hand out of my pocket, I slid something across the bar to my chump.

"I suppose once I'm in the army, I won't be needing this anymore," I said.

When he saw it, his eyes grew to the size of ashtrays.

"How the hell'd you get a 'C' card?" he breathed.

"I'm a doctor."

"You look too young to be a doctor."

I flipped him a business card that read "Louis Vincent, M.D." I'd had it printed the same place I got the "C" card made up. "Just finished my residency," I said as he ran his eyeballs over it, "but it's enough."

He turned his eyes back to the "C" card. "That's up to twelve gallons of gas, isn't it?"

"Twenty, actually. You have an 'A' card?"

"Uh-huh. Five gallons." He touched the edge of the red card with the tip of his finger. "This thing real?"

"Of course it is. How do you think I got here?" When he continued to stare at the sticker, picturing himself tooling down Sunset like a high roller, I said quietly, "You take it. I don't need it. Think of all the places you could go. All the lunches away from the office, and from your wife."

He wanted it bad, boy, but there was still enough Sunday school in him to make him hedge. "Oh, I couldn't..." he murmured, half-hearted. Then, real slow, he said, "Maybe...if you want...I could...pay?"

"Gee, I'd feel rather bad about that. When I just want to give it to you."

"Really," he said, already fumbling for his wallet. "How about—twenty bucks?" I didn't answer right away, and he leapt in. "Okay, I got fifty, right here. That's fair, right?"

Who knew where that money came from? Probably he'd been skimming from his job the whole time, something from petty cash, a little here, a little there. I let on like I was reluctant, but I moved fast enough to pocket the cash. Smiling, I said, "Thanks, friend, thanks a lot. You cheered me up."

"Always glad to help out," he said, brimming with larcenous glee. Ordinary folks couldn't get their hands on "C" cards unless they were doctors, ministers, mail carriers, whoever Washington thought essential to the war effort. Some got "B" cards, but most everyone else got "A" cards, which were pretty well useless in L.A.

"Say, it sure is late, and I gotta get back to the office," he said, zippy and loud. He wanted to blow before I changed my mind about the gas rationing card, so he leapt down from his seat, clapped his hat on his head, and pumped my hand like a jack. "I sure am sorry to hear about your girl, but you have a dandy time killing Krauts." Letting go, he began backing up towards the door. "Watch out for stray bullets, ha-ha. When you get back, look me up. I'm in the phone book. I'm under—" And then he bolted before I could catch his name.

With fifty in cash nestling close, I eased it up a bit and was finally able to take a real sip of my drink. The scotch was hitting on all eight, something you'd put in a patent bottle, so I didn't mind it much. Feeling George's eyes on me, and thinking that my rube might be back, I decided to cop a heel. I tossed down some bills and, without a look behind, beat it.

I hoofed it real fast, but not fast enough to seem suspicious, making sure I wasn't being tailed, and didn't slow down until I got to Cahuenga. Around the corner from a liquor store, I stopped and, leaning against a wall in the shade, pulled out a cigarette to enjoy my score.

A giant mitt holding a Zippo appeared to light me. Jumping, I nearly ate the cigarette. But I tried to play it cool, and as I dragged, I gave the walking *Lusitania* a good up-and-down. He was sucking on the stump of a cigar, and it smelled Cuban. His suit had to be custom-made, there was no way all that yardage could come from off the rack. Some kind of triggerman. But, like the *Lusitania*, I figured this guy could be sunk.

"That was cute," he said and we puffed together. "Didn't even have to blow him off. Winchell did it himself."

I didn't know whether this huge guy was some kind of fakaloo artist or a cop, so I played dumb and shook my head like I couldn't figure him.

"Used to play the wire," he went on pleasantly, like we were chatting about daffodil bulbs at the garden show. "But that's old news. Now we do a bit of the rag, sometimes the pay-off. Could use a few shills like you for my boost." Arnie had taught me all the names for the different cons, names that meant nothing unless you were a con artist, but I made myself look blank when George rattled some of them off.

"Mister," I said, "you must have me confused with the Vienna Boys Choir. Only I don't sing."

He smiled at that, contemplating the end of his cigar. I

wondered how long it would be before I felt the burning end of that stogie in my eye.

"Sure, you're cute, all right. Think you'd work out fine."

"What for? You some shamus?"

He braced an enormous elbow against the wall, blocking out the sun as he shook his head. "See, I frame the store. Make it look good. Kinda like a stage manager. So when the roper steers the mark in to meet the insideman, the pigeon's gonna think everything's square. Then we take off the touch, blow off the mark, and put in the fix. Everything's white."

If he was a detective, he sure talked the cant. And if I had to, I could probably outrun him. Though, maybe not. He did catch up with me awful fast. And his legs could be used to span the East River. I couldn't play dumb for too long. Seemed like it would try this guy's patience, and I wasn't about to see how long or short his fuse was. He'd blow up when he needed to. I said, "I thought all those big store cons went the way of the silent picture."

He gave a little melancholy sigh that sounded like the ocean in an underground cavern. "Yeah," he admitted, puffing sadly on his stogie, "them glory days were twenty, thirty years back, but we C-men adapt with the times. And places. Got a sweet con that runs like a film production office. You oughta check it out."

"And I'd do that, why?"

He pushed away from the wall and I thought maybe that it was curtains for me, expecting to feel his King Kong fist come smashing through the top of my skull. Instead, he just flicked the end of his cigar away and said, bored, "Son, don't be a bunny. If you change your mind, I'm at the numbers parlor at Figueroa and Slauson every Tuesday. I give a half percent consideration, which is easy money for you when the touch is big. And the touch is always big."

Then he was gone as fast as he appeared, and I was left taking nervous, long drags off my cigarette to calm myself and wonder what the hell he wanted me to do, exactly, and why I wasn't getting fitted for a casket. Arnie'd told me about the big store, a con that sometimes took a week or more to play. Big con men took their marks to these places, sometimes set up like poolrooms, or racing parlors,

Western Union offices, even brokerages. The mark was always fleeced at the big store, where the boost—everyone from the teller to the bookies to the guys emptying the dustbins—were all in on the con. And there was always some guy who had to serve as manager of the big store, keeping it running and looking good. The bookmaker also broke the place down as soon as the con had been played, so that if the mark ever came back, to beef or to try again, he'd just find an empty room with nothing to show that it had ever been a ritzy gambling club. Pretty as an apple.

I'd run solo up to that point, taking in short cons as I needed the money, but there was something about George that caught me. If he was on the take, he'd pick his mob wisely, since the biggest flaw in a con usually came from the inside. He wouldn't have given me the heads-up unless he thought I was good. Lucky for me I wised up and met him the next week. He was on the level, and if I was sometimes short on funds, he'd been able to find me a nice bit part as a shill whenever the C was being played in a big store.

Turned out that not only did George act as bookmaker, he dug the latest in jazz, so whenever I'd score some new platters, I'd ring him up and we'd have ourselves a little listening party. More flush than me, George got to hang out at Billy Berg's, the Trouville on Beverly and Fairfax, Ciro's, even scooting up to San Francisco to go to Facks and the Say When, then come back and roast me by telling me all about it.

"Did I ever tell you 'bout the time I saw Bird at the Club Finale?" he asked me now after polishing off two cartons' worth of chop suey. "I think he was out of his gourd on the junk. But still an absolute phenom."

"Yeah, I read the libretto," I muttered. Two things killed me about George's stories. One was that he got to see legends play while I was stuck at home tuning them in on the radio. The other was that it wasn't me he was going to watch—that I hadn't gotten big enough to rate a gig at Club Finale, or pretty much any other class joint. Competition in l.a., and everywhere, was ferocious, and the best I'd been able to land so far was filling in at some of the smaller clubs when a sideman couldn't make it. Some days, I thought I'd wind up as played-out and shady as old Pomeroy, doing nothing but sitting in my bathrobe and disgusting the neighbors. Nope—I'd tie myself to the W in the Hollywood sign and set a torch to the whole thing first.

I got up and put another record on. "This is the sound of the future, Georgie. Brand new. From Blue Note. Open them elephant ears of yours and take a listen."

He cocked his head to one side, some kind of prehistoric spaniel catching a sound. Jangling, sideways piano chords filled the room, like a skeleton dancing up and down a staircase. Each note was a shot of cold light straight through my chest.

"Who the hell is that?" George demanded.

"Thelonious Monk. Used to play at Minton's and with Coleman Hawkins."

Once George stopped grimacing, he started to nod, digging the sounds. "Yeah," he said, "this kid rates. No one's gonna buy his shit, but he rates."

Me, I loved the angles of it, the bits and pieces of it, wholetone scales that mixed the simple with the knotted. Here was a cat who valued silence as much as sound, the negative spaces where so much happened, the way it did in life. Even the ballads seemed creepy, haunted.

I stood next to the record player and watched it turn. "Even if nobody gets this Monk guy," I said, "it doesn't matter. In ten, twenty, fifty years, folks'll still be listening to him play, talking about him. Maybe they'll say, 'What the good goddamn was that cat all about?' Or maybe they'll say, 'That motherfucker was a genius.' But he'll be there. His music's going to be heard. On account of this." I held up the sleeve of the record.

"You sound envious, Lou," George said, after taking a swallow of beer.

I wanted to laugh that off, but couldn't. "Shit, I won't lie. I'd goddamn kill your mom to have what Monk's got." I looked at the albums stacked all over my pad, the hundreds of hours of music forever captured and preserved, thinking about the men who made them.

"They why don't you record yourself one of these sides?" George asked. "I've heard you play. You're pretty sharp."

Walking over to the piano, I sank down onto the bench and stared at the keys while Thelonious Monk jittered along. There wasn't much in this stinking trap of life that I really believed in. Everything had a way of falling apart, nobody was as good as I wanted them to be, including myself. But the piano was so pure and clean—its strings and hammers, wood and brass—I felt it held something right, something that could wash all the other garbage away. Maybe I'd get washed away, too, but that'd also be okay.

My own record. Why the fuck not? Wasn't that what I'd been dreaming about all this time, even if I didn't know it for sure? I wouldn't have to sit around kvetching about some other hipster cutting wax—it'd be me, instead, on the turntable. My notes, my music. All those other rat bastards giving *me* a listen, for a change.

In my head, I pictured my own album, saw it being bought at record shops or sold by the shoeshine guys on Central Avenue, maybe played over the radio. It was a righteous feeling. Huge, expanding.

Then I thought of my father, holding my album as he stood in the middle of the cramped apartment on Jerome, seeing me on the jacket, putting the disc on the turntable and hearing those notes, my notes, playing again after years of silence. His lost and dirty son making good. Being, finally, legit.

Chapter seven

She was already there by the time I pulled into the parking lot in Vernon. Standing in the late morning sunshine, leaning against her car, Beatrice wore dungarees and a burgundy plaid shirt, a scarf tied over her hair and a big pair of sunglasses, dressed down but about as glamorous as a film star on the newsreels, cavorting luxuriously at their fairy-tale Bel Air estates and making like they were real folks, only better. There wasn't anything pretend about Beatrice, though.

"What's with the britches, Miss Hollywood?" I called to her through my open window. I parked and got out, squinting beneath the brim of my straw porkpie hat.

"I took a shine to 'em, working in the defense plant," she said, pushing away from the side of her car. "Stretch my legs as much as I please. Like a fella. And you said to dress comfortable, so here I am."

"Here you are," I said, smiling. She met me halfway and put her arms around me. There was nobody around, it being Sunday, and I'd been careful to pick a spot that was empty. I held her tight and kissed her. I wasn't like other guys who minded women in pants, grousing that they looked like boys—I figured I wouldn't want to wear a skirt all the time, either, so why cause a ruckus if a girl needed to cut loose every now and then? Besides, I dug seeing the motion of their legs, their energy and action, and the way their trousers hugged their asses. Beatrice looked mighty killer in her denim, the smallness of her waist and the bass curves of her hips, her sweet ripe ass, all of it there to see. Only a half-blind chump could mistake her for a boy.

"This feels good," I said against her mouth, "kissing you in the light."

"Got me pretty tickled about it, too," she murmured, and for a few minutes we just stood there, wrapped close to each other, with the sun on our shoulders and a wide, blue sky over our heads, nobody saying a damn thing about it or giving us rotten looks. It didn't matter to me that we were surrounded by the gray vacant hulks of silent machining plants, about as pretty as a welder's armpit, I could've stayed like that for years. I liked her ass, sure, and that she didn't hide what she wanted in bed, not some chick with a complex, but more than that, we had a good time together. I wouldn't have minded stretching it out longer than the few hours we could snatch here and there. Like we were doing now.

"So let's hear the story," she said after we leaned back. She looked so lovely in the daylight, her face familiar but strange. "You ring me on a Sunday morning, tell me to put on some clothes I don't mind getting dirty, and meet you in a parking lot next to McGruder's Aluminum in an hour. We aren't going to teach some kid how to play 'Chopsticks,' are we? I hope it's some cloak-and-dagger operation, fighting the Reds."

I let her go and walked back to my car. Opening the backseat, I pulled out a paper sack and showed it to Bea. Inside were some paper-wrapped sandwiches, bottles of pop, potato chips and a couple of oatmeal cookies. I'd bought it all from the market on Main, just around the corner from my place, after I'd called her earlier.

"Let's go for a spin," I said.

The fog never showed, and as we drove north up the coast, on the highway, the Pacific was a dark blue mirror under the paler sky. Instead of the hot gusts from the east, a soft warm breeze with its elbows in the cool came in off the water. We passed the Santa Monica Pier, the ballroom quiet, Ferris wheel turning slowly and the carousel grinding out its honky-tonk. If you want a grifter's paradise, then try a beach-side midway one of these days. You'll find every kind of con being played on the sunburned masses: carny cons, short cons, card cons, it's all there. Plus the usual pockets being picked while the crowd bumped against itself. So you'd think that'd be good hunting for me, but for one, I don't work the grift near my home, and for two, only the seediest and smallest of C-men prowl piers.

Funny thing was, all that brassy, cotton candy hooey was right next to the Gold Coast on Palisades Beach Road, where all the big name film people had their homes and beach clubs, big stucco Spanish-style piles and fancy white wooden heaps that seemed to prove the lie of the movies. We motored up the highway, hardly believing those houses were only a half a mile from where I strung my piano keys.

Just after Santa Monica, the crowds at the beach thinned, the beachside shacks selling pop and postcards straggling away, and Beatrice was able to sit up straight next to me and take in the whole scene. The hills that had been green in April and May were now edging brown and dried after another rainless summer. No August thunderstorms in Los Angeles, breaking the heat and making everything liquid. The shifts of seasons here were small, sometimes hardly noticeable, like a gambler's smile. Those dopes who complain about missing seasons, they can all live in an igloo somewhere wearing scratchy woolen underwear or roast on a shut-up subway car. Me, I'd keep the constant springtime, and no surprises, thanks all the same.

Further up the coast, we hit Malibu, and the Colony, where still more movie stars wrapped themselves up in a dream of California. They didn't know from clip joints in Gardena, or, "We've already got a piano player. Beat it."

"When I first got to L.A., I couldn't believe a place like this could be real," I said to Beatrice as we whizzed through the ritzy, sleepy little town. "I still don't." Folks came out to Los Angeles to make it in the pictures, to bask in the steady blank sun, live in the place between sleeping and waking. Me, I stayed because I was out of land, there wasn't any place further I could run without swimming to Hawaii and then on to our enemies in Japan. A whole country divided me from Ernest Greenberg. It'd have to be enough.

"I've never seen this before," she said. "Never been this far up the coast."

"And how does milady like it?"

She took a deep breath in, the light stink of seaweed and salt, and frowned. "Too different. Impossible."

"Like seeing a painting and wanting to live inside of it," I said.

"For a jazz man, you can sure be smart sometimes," she said, smiling.

I grinned back. "I ain't so bad, if you like the type."

"Fortunate for you, then, that I'm partial to the type."

"You mean fortunate for *you?*"

"Oh, buddy," she laughed, "you hit the jackpot with me, and that's for sure."

"No arguing there."

"Good, 'cause I'd win that argument."

"You're a smart-ass, you know?"

"Smartest there is. And it's a mighty cute ass, too."

"Amen, sister."

Off the smaller rocky beaches, there were guys riding huge long boards in the surf, paddling out and coasting back in. Their jalopies were parked by the side of the road, with shaggy mutts sleeping underneath in the shade. A few girls in bathing suits watched them from blankets spread on the sand.

"Dig those crazy cats out in the water," Beatrice said, with a shake of her head. "Sure nobody in Ohio ever thought of that. Hell, all we had was a swimming hole, but we had to be careful if we wanted to swim. Some white boys'd come along and flatten us for muddying their spot. Turning the water brown with our brown skin. And here these white guys have all this surf to play in."

I said, shrugging, "Seems pretty pointless to me. All that back and forth and never getting anywhere."

"Maybe that's the point." She adjusted her scarf, making sure the wind through the open windows didn't tug it off. "Isn't there anything you like to do just for fun?"

"Well…" I waggled my eyebrows at her.

"I should hook some kinda generator to your johnson," she laughed. "Power half the damn city."

"Just half?" I asked, taking her hand and kissing it.

"The Valley, too."

Both of us were feeling pretty high, giddy almost, as we wound our way along the shore. The heavy coat we wore back in the city fell from our shoulders, my whiteness, her blackness, the stories we carried inside us, all washed away in the Pacific surf. And at that moment, I could be Louis, a guy out with his best girl, Beatrice. That was it. Nothing else. When it was just us, I didn't have to think so much about the angle, the con, pulling one over. Beatrice didn't know everything about me, but I felt when I was around her, I could let go of the reins a little bit. If she had suspicions about the other life I lead away from Dee's, away from the warm enclave of her home, she didn't ask, didn't press for more. She could see that there were some things I needed to keep to myself, the way she held a part of herself separate from everyone, even me. She didn't ask for something I couldn't give her, and I didn't struggle to open the locked cabinet of her guarded self. If either of us wanted more, there'd been an unspoken understanding that there couldn't be more, and we left it alone.

I could write a piece about this, too, this day, this feeling. That was one of the things I dug so much about music—it could tap straight into a feeling like this without the bulk of words stumbling everything up.

It got damn near rustic as we motored up to the county line, losing most of the houses and cars, just me and Beatrice and the hills falling down into the sea. At Port Hueneme, we passed the Naval base then turned east, to Oxnard. I still didn't much care for guys in uniform—they were the ones that had got the most bothered seeing me in my civilian clothes and them in Uncle Sam's bull's-eye tailoring that shouted "Shoot here!" If it hadn't been for some smooth talking on my part, I would've wound up in more fistfights than a starlet on the casting couch. Folks think that calling someone a dodger is supposed to rile them, but bothered, I wasn't. People throw out names like they're supposed to have some power or meaning, some hurt, when all they do is make the idiot tossing them around look small. But I was in town back in '43 when the riots happened between the sailors and Mexicans, and it just proved what I already knew: boys in uniforms are just boys who can't piss without hitting their own shoes, and nothing, not even a funny little hat and a pair of bell-bottomed trousers, would change that.

"Now I know we gotta be on some spy job," Beatrice said. "We're out in the middle of nowhere."

"Exactly," I said. The sandy, busted-down sheds and sleepy towns flitted past until we were surrounded by orange groves, endless rows of trees that spoked and spiked away. I turned the car off the road onto a dusty track, and we rattled over the ruts, between the trees, until, sure that we were far from anyone, I stopped.

Beatrice got out before I did, taking off her scarf, and walking around for a few minutes while I got out the bag of food and an old blanket. The grove was a small mom-and-pop operation—nobody was out in the field picking, the only sound was the slight shifting of the branches, creaking a bit in the breeze. The trees weren't very big, only a kid could stand under the branches, but the leaves were dark green and glossy.

"You and me are gonna have ourselves a little picnic," I said to Beatrice as I spread out the blanket on the ground. "We don't need a lousy city park, when we can have all this to ourselves."

I could tell when she took off her sunglasses that the whole idea of a private picnic really pleased her. Her eyes were warm, rich. Coming over to me, she stood on her tiptoes and pressed a kiss to my mouth.

Seeing her happy like that, I felt like the biggest man in California, the whole USA, maybe even the world. At that moment, I didn't think there was anything I wouldn't do for her. No other woman got to me the way she did, but just then I didn't mind it a bit. I was glad.

The soda wasn't all that cold anymore, but it didn't matter as we sat down and popped the tops off the bottles. We unwrapped our sandwiches, ham and cheese for her, liverwurst for me—I sure missed the pastrami back home, but what can you do?—and ate, sharing the potato chips, having ourselves a fine old time. She talked a little about what was going on at the phone company, I told her about George coming by to listen to records, leaving out the bits about him being a con manager. Just gabbing, those rambling talks that circled and drifted like a leaf falling to the ground. Normally, I wasn't too keen on that kind of conversation. It wasn't real. It floated around and meant nothing. But there was some kind of kick out of making like we were some ordinary couple, playacting that part. That's what I did best. So for that hour or so, I made myself into Louis Greenberg, regular guy on a picnic with his regular girl. After we ate our oatmeal cookies, things started happening the way they ought when a healthy guy and a ripe girl were out in the warm October afternoon, on a blanket in the middle of a sweet-smelling orange grove, and I'll tell you, that didn't take any playacting. I was all there.

Beatrice stretched out and I lay down almost on top of her, running my hands up and down, over the cotton of her shirt, the rough denim of her dungarees, feeling the tough and soft yielding of her body underneath. We kissed for a while, and that's when I wasn't so wild about her wearing pants instead of a skirt. I tugged at the hem of her shirt, trying to pull it from the waistband of her jeans, half crazy wanting to touch her skin. She shifted underneath me, putting me between her legs, and my cock slid happily into place—exactly where it wanted to be, if we weren't so damned swaddled in clothes. We both sighed as I rocked against her, our eyes open, finally seeing each other in the light of day.

I was just starting on the buttons of her dungarees, when I heard the rustle and snap of fallen branches nearby. I sat up fast, and spotted some farmer standing by my car, frowning at it like he'd never seen a horseless carriage before. Right off I knew that the hick hadn't spotted Beatrice and me, and I also knew I had to make sure he left before he saw her.

I jumped to my feet and stuffed my hands in my pockets, on account of me still being ready as a rocket, and trucked it over to

Farmer Brown. Behind me, I could hear Beatrice putting her clothes straight, tying her scarf over her hair. I hoped she kept her back to the hayseed. If we rolled the dice right, he wouldn't see her, at least, not the color of her skin, and he'd take off without catching wise. I wasn't too worried, not yet.

"Hi, there," I said, cheerful as a Bible salesman. "How you doing today?"

The farmer had on a pair of worn overalls and a work shirt, a wide-brimmed hat shading his eyes. His face was deeply lined, made from cowhide, and as I got closer I made out the loose folds of skin hanging from his neck. He was an oldster. Sometimes conning a guy like this one could be the toughest kind. When you're trying to tell the tale, it's slow going if the mark's too thick to see the advantage you're showing him. It's like taking a sleepy baby by the hand and trying to get them to walk across a ledge. They'd never get there on their own. That can wear you out, especially if you have to make that trip a few times. But I wasn't trying to play the game with Farmer Brown, here, I just wanted him to take a powder. He and his chin came around the car.

"This here's private property," he said.

I gave him my two-dollar smile. "You're absolutely right, and I apologize for trespassing. It's just that your orange grove was so beautiful, I just couldn't keep myself from getting a better look."

"You from the city?" He spat out the word like a sour plum.

I kept on flashing my teeth. "The city's so ugly, but your orange grove is so beautiful. It's hard to resist." He still wasn't buying it, even though most people sop up compliments like Saltines on soup. "Who's that with you?" he demanded, trying to look around me. I sidestepped quickly, aiming to block his view, and held up my hands. That's when I made myself look sheepish, a kid caught in the outhouse with a dirty magazine and his pecker in his hand.

"Listen," I said, lowering my voice like he and I were buddies, men of the world, though by the looks of him, he probably thought a hot chick was something served up for Sunday supper, "I was just getting a little bit of private time with my girl. We don't see each other much and I thought I'd treat her to something real nice. Know what I mean?"

He tried even harder to look over my shoulder, the start of a knowing leer curling his mouth, but I sidestepped again. It made me want to puke, that sick, smutty grin foaming across his face, particularly since he was throwing moose eyes towards Beatrice. He wasn't pure-hearted country folk, he was one of those wheezy, groping backwoods creeps who couldn't wait for his daughters to grow up so he'd have someone new to fondle.

"Yeah," he said, licking his lips.

I had to get rid of this chump, fast. Before he got even uglier than he already was. I'm not wild about the idea of paying someone off—it's cheating if you're a grifter. Sure, you can flash a little green here and there, it gives the right impression, but a flat-out payoff is a pair of training wheels. I wasn't going to stand on principle here, though. I pulled out my wallet and handed the rustic a fiver. "You're swell, mack. We'll pack up right now and go. That okay?"

"You betcha." He stuffed the bill into his pocket. "Take your time. As much as you need." He gave me a wink, and I tried to wink back, though I was ready to throw my cookies. Then he turned and started off, whistling loudly. I let out a breath—he hadn't gotten a good look at Beatrice. But I didn't want to press our luck.

As soon as he was far enough away, I ran over to Beatrice and started grabbing our stuff. She was already on her feet, not bothering to pick the leaves off her clothes, folding up the blanket. Her face had gone tight.

"Don't bother with that," I panted, grabbing the blanket from her. Once we'd wadded everything up, we started running back to the car, trying to scram as fast as we could. So much for our romantic picnic. It was all a con one way or the other.

I tossed the blanket and remains of the lunch into the backseat. All the junk fell with a clatter to the floor of the car. Beatrice started over to her side, giving the knot of her scarf a hard tug. She stopped short and I turned to see what'd fazed her.

"Say, you and your lady friend could stop by the house for a glass of—" The hayseed was back, but because Beatrice and I had been busy trying to hightail it, we hadn't heard him coming. He also stopped short and stared at Beatrice, his eyes going round, then narrow. My gut hit the tops of my shoes. She shoved on her sunglasses. The hick started to turn purple. "What the hell?" he snarled. He fixed his eyes on me, sticky with hate. "You bring some colored whore to my place? What kinda sick son of a bitch are you?"

"Watch your lip, bo," I said, taking a step towards him.

His lip curled. "Or you're gonna what? I oughta call the damned cops. On you and your jigaboo floozy!"

The feel of my knuckles crashing into his face shot through me like a dark thrill. I hadn't decked anybody in a while and there was a little voice in the back of my head that wondered why I'd waited so long. I liked the crunch of bone, the jolt along my arm. The hick stumbled back, blood squirting from his nose and caking in the dust as he howled and fell onto his ass.

Beatrice shot around the car and jumped into her seat, slamming the door shut after her. "Louis," she shouted at me as I stepped towards the farmer, my fist curling again and ready, "we gotta go!"

I snapped back and got into the car. As we pulled away, tires grinding in the dirt, the hayseed yelled, "Goddamn nigger-loving wop!" Everything else he said was lost as we tore off back to the main road and the highway.

Neither of us said a thing the whole way back. For almost two hours, we were silent, not even turning on the radio. I'd glance over at Beatrice every now and then, but behind her sunglasses, she'd gone flat and still. It was all wrong. Me, the guy who could sell pants to a fish, had nothing to say, no way to spin it to make everything right. She sat next to me in the car, but she may as well have been back in Ohio. I couldn't reach her. I could taste disgust and liverwurst boiling up from my gut and it felt almost right to lean into it, have someone I could hate so purely. Most people were just sad, sorry little flecks, coming up to just about nothing, barely worth bothering with except on the con, but I saw in that shriveled, rotten farmer something I wanted to rip open, spit on, exterminate.

When we pulled into the parking lot in Vernon, the day winding down, Beatrice got out even before I'd stopped and walked over to her car, still silent. I pulled the parking brake and stood behind her as she went through her purse, looking for her keys.

"Sugar," I said, but she kept her back to me. "Baby. Beatrice."

Finally, she did turn around, but she didn't take off her sunglasses. She held her purse between us. "I keep hearing him, Louis. Seeing his face."

Me, too. But I tried to punch him away, bring up the feeling of my knuckles mashing into meat and bone. "Don't. It's a nasty face. Ugly. I'll go back and kick his teeth in."

"Maybe the words would stop, but not what they mean."

"They don't mean anything."

The sun was sinking away as she said, "I listen to people talk on the phone all day. Words. Holding everything. Happiness, rage, boredom. Someone's life being ruined, on account of what somebody else says." She drew her mouth into a line as she took off her sunglasses. "Words carry weight, baby. Lots of it."

The more she spoke, the angrier I got, until I was ready to get into my car and make good on what I said. I'd drive all the way back to Oxnard and rip out the hick's ribs, one by one, and set up a barbecue stand by the side of the road. "Some hayseed called us names. So what? Hottest date he ever had was with Elsie the Cow."

She didn't smile at that. It seemed like it'd take an act of Congress to get her to smile again. She went back to looking for her keys, found them, then opened the door to her car. I held it shut as she pulled on the handle, not letting her in.

"Come on, baby," I said. "Don't—"

"I can't right now," she said. "I just can't. I don't want to hear nobody, don't want to talk to nobody. I want silence. Nothing. Let me go."

I wanted to yell at her, take her by her shoulders and shake her hard until the doubt fell away. I wanted to ram my fist into the whole goddamned world.

I hated that rube for taking something from me. I was the taker, not him. And he ripped the day and my girl right away from me. I needed to grab it back, show him that I was the one on top, not him and his smutty words. But there didn't seem to be much of anything I could do just then to change Beatrice's mind. Maybe it'd be better to let her blow off steam for a while. She wasn't in the right place to be talked down. I let go of the car door and she slid behind the wheel. Gently, I shut the door after her, feeling like ten kinds of schmuck, not something I relished particularly.

"You'll call me tonight?" I asked, but I knew it wouldn't happen. She didn't nod, didn't shake her head, just looked at me and I saw hopelessness, anger, fear, everything I felt reflected right back at me. A face I couldn't con, couldn't charm and coax, not this time.

Without answering, she started the ignition, shifted the car into gear, and pulled out, leaving me standing alone in the empty parking lot, factories rising dark and looming just on the edges.

Chapter eight

Ten o'clock again at the Carmel Club. It was Sunday night and the place was full of die-hards, deadbeats and wasted nighthawks, nobody with a job, or willing to own that they had a job, eyes hollow and mouths twisted over their glasses. A different crowd from the good time Charlies on Friday. Sadder. Hungrier. Losers and loners.

And me. The guy at the piano, sitting on his bench twaddling out schmaltzy standards. Every last one about love. About a life that wasn't real. Gazing into each other's eyes in the moonlight. Dancing until dawn. Building gauzy, perfumed dreams in the sugared clouds. Flimflam, all of it. A classic bait-and-switch, and I was right in the middle, a sucker and a chump left with the gold brick.

I didn't lay it on Beatrice. My beef wasn't with her. When I got home earlier, I tried her exchange, but the operator came on after a while and said there was no answer. I rang her again, just before I left for the Carmel Club. Still no luck. Even so, I wasn't angry—at her. I hated this whole, stinking world, a pile of garbage just underneath the flower bed, and even the things that grew and smelled sweet were rotten beneath it all. White jerks listened to colored music, aped colored dancing, went to see pictures like "Cabin in the Sky," still it was nothing but niggers and coons to them. And kikes.

My right hand throbbed, still smarting after smashing that hick in the piehole. Probably it wasn't the brightest thing to do, walloping someone with my solo hand. I could've broken it, and then where would I be? I couldn't make myself give a rat's ass about it, though. If I had that hayseed in front of me now, I'd beat him until he was uglier than a schmear of chopped liver. I hoped the son of a bitch had to have his mouth permanently wired shut so he couldn't talk anymore. And what I hated more than anything was that some piece of crap I'd sooner wipe off my shoe than look at had gotten to me, thrown me so much and turned things sour. I hated giving him that. I don't give anything to anybody, especially two-bit shitkickers.

A finger tapped me hard on the shoulder. I didn't have to turn around to recognize Len Holstadt's cologne, so I went right on playing, facing forward.

"What the hell has gotten into you?" he snapped.

The cigarette bobbed in my mouth, ash dropped onto the keys. "Nothing."

Len came around so I had to look at him, crossing his arms over his narrow chest. "Whatever it is, snap out of it. The customers are complaining about the music."

Not that I cared, but I asked through the smoke curling up from the end of my light, "What's wrong with the music?"

"Can you hear what you're playing? It's like a car wreck on the way to a funeral. Got everybody edgy and uncomfortable. Nobody's betting."

I hadn't even been paying attention to the sounds I'd been making on the keys, it was just coming out of me, all reflex. Here I was thinking I'd been making nice and gentle with the sappy tunes. I looked over my shoulder and saw that, yeah, the chumps were acting ornery, eyes rolling like marbles, asses shifting in their seats. There was that melody I'd been chasing, again. It wouldn't come when I looked for it, but now, when I'd turned myself away from my search, it bubbled up underneath the glassy surface of pop standards, grimacing and wailing like a ghost under the ice. Most people would run away, or at least walk over it and pretend they didn't see it. I wanted to hack at the ice, smash it apart and let the ghost out, so it could finally possess me, and turn me into the instrument of its vengeance.

Tough shit, the customers didn't like the music. It scared them, and because I was playing it, *I* scared them. Maybe it was the first time in their lives they actually felt anything true, genuine, and nobody cared for it.

"Gee, that's too bad." I reached for the drink I had propped on the side of the piano and stopped playing just long enough to take the cig from my mouth and choke down some well whiskey. I wanted to feed the piano keys to some wiseacre, one by one, until they gagged.

"And you're not supposed to drink while you're on," he added, eyeing my empty glass sourly.

I shrugged and kept playing, but I noticed now how I was hitting the keys hard, beating them, heavy muscle. Sharp, barbed notes flung themselves from the piano and scattered like tacks on the floor. My right hand really throbbed, and I leaned into the pain. It was something real. Not like the hooey I was hired to play. I got an earful of the piano. It was supposed to be "Stardust." It sounded like a scream. Any minute now and the ice would shatter. I could've laughed. It was the best I'd played in a long time, and here was Len telling me to can it.

"I don't see why you're smirking," he groused. "There's nothing funny going on here."

"Just thinking of a dirty joke my rabbi told me."

Len didn't cotton to that at all. "Either start playing normal, or pack it in."

My hands stilled over the keys and I stared without seeing at the piano. I stood up, not bothering to push my seat back, so the bench went clattering to the ground. Everything went quiet. The cocktail waitresses stopped and goggled at me. The bartender held a glass, bottle suspended above it, ready to pour. Even the card players looked up from their hands, eyes red and stunned. Len gawked as I took the cigarette from my lips and ground it out on the piano keys.

"Get this piece of shit tuned one of these days," I said, then grabbed my hat from the nearby rack and headed out the door. As it started to swing shut behind me, I heard Len laughing nervously, telling the suckers that everything was fine, moving to plug in the jukebox. A sudden blare of swing filled the silence. The door shut.

I stood out in the parking lot and lit another cigarette. A watery lamp lit up the cars parked in rows, and every so often, another car groaned past. Gardena was a lot of flat, a lot of nothing, and I was alone, smoking, watching the faint stars wink on and off over my head. Far away, the mountains were dark teeth rising up to bite.

Possibly, I could go back inside and eat crow, make nice with Len and play whatever mush, corny crap he wanted me to play. Distract the losers and bottle-lifters. Keep my head down. Don't make trouble. The Carmel Club was the only steady gig I had. But the idea of crawling in on my belly to lick shoe leather made me sick. Already, I'd had one turkey get the up on me, crapping on what had been a good day, and I wasn't going to let a cheap weasel like Len Holstadt step on me, too.

I got in my car and drove off, not looking back. I almost went home—I'd tapped into something at the Carmel Club; that melody that shifted and hid when I wanted it, crept out and shivered in the air when I didn't. Now would have been the right time to get to my own piano and cage the animal with notes. But I couldn't go home. Even though Beatrice never went to my apartment, I'd spent too much time talking to her on the phone, staring at my walls, so that even those blank surfaces reflected her back to me.

In my car and driving, but I didn't stop to think about where I was or what I was doing until I woke up and found myself face-down on a Tijuana bar, pockets picked clean.

Whoever'd lifted my wallet hadn't taken the time to do the job right. My car keys still slept in my inside pocket, and when I stumbled out onto the street, early bright rays shooting right into the back of my head and exploding like artillery, there was my old Buick Coupe waiting with bitter reproach by the curb. I chased a couple of kids off the fender, bleating "*No dinero, no dinero,*" when they tugged on my jacket. What I really wanted was a big mug of steaming coffee, black and mean, but I didn't even have a dime for that.

So with a mouth like a trolley floor, my head broken wide open and stomping on my spine, I drove back north. The lines back across the border were short, it being Monday morning, and the cop at the gate didn't even bother to check my i.d. before waving me forward. Good thing, too, on account of me being without a license or passport. Some light-fingered Mexican was now the proud owner of a fake leather wallet that held $3.27, a library card, the driver's license of one Louis K. Greenberg (K for Karl, my father's favorite uncle, deceased, run over by a milk wagon on the streets of Warsaw), and a pawn ticket for an engraved watch given to me by my pop on the occasion of my bar mitzvah. I'd pawned it three years ago and never got enough scratch to get it out of hock. Maybe it was long gone into some clipster's pocket, but even so, I missed it now, knowing I'd never get it back. How could a body miss something they didn't even have in the first place? Maybe it was the idea of it, the final thing I had from my old life in the Bronx, and I'd gone and sold it. I guess I always figured someday I'd get it back, or I'd been fooling myself. Didn't matter much anymore.

I sped up the coast, feeling too septic to look at the passing scenery of San Diego, San Clemente, San Juan Capistrano, all the old Spanish towns with their red tile roofs and dull possibility. Going through Orange County, I went past endless rows of orange and grapefruit trees, and the reminder of yesterday made the tequila in my gut flip over and start to holler. A bunch of *braceros* in a strawberry field watched as I pulled over to the side of the road and chucked up everything I'd had to eat or drink, mostly drink, over the past day.

Bracing my hands on my knees, the sick, sweet stench of berries hovering in the late morning air, I felt like a conked-out sewer line, heaving up all the filth and misery stored up inside me onto the dust. I wished I could clean everything out the way I was puking now—the bristled face of the Okie that called Beatrice and me names, Len Holstadt's pinched mug, the hollow-cheeked kids demanding money from whatever *gringo* came their way, my dad, always there lurking. But no matter how much bitter bile I coughed up, everything stuck around.

Finally empty, I tried to straighten up, but the ground decided to practice its dance steps and I staggered back. I almost fell onto my ass, but just then I felt a strong supporting arm gently lower me to the ground to sit in the shade of my car. A tin dipper was pressed into my hand.

"*Agua, señor,*" a voice murmured next to me.

"*Gracias,*" I said, and took a long drink. The water was musty and stale, metal-tasting, but I gulped it down anyway. It beat a long, cold trail to my stomach. I started to feel only slightly dead, though I bet corpses smelled better and had a more cheerful attitude.

Looking up, I met the eyes of the *bracero* who'd bailed me out. He was wearing a broad-brimmed straw hat, the kind that'd seen about five hundred harvests. Guy must've been just over five feet tall, but he'd been able to hold me like a rag.

"*Gracias,*" I said again, and that was about the end of my Spanish.

He just smiled at me, a little smile that didn't get all the way up his face, then walked slowly back to his waiting buddies to fill crates with late-season strawberries. I heard someone murmur, "*Boracho,*" the word floating over the hot, still fields. There were women out there, too, some with babies on their backs, and kids, the sun hitting them hard and steady, it was still awful hot, but they kept going, picking, picking. Every now and then some white guy would swagger by, trying to look big-time, but mostly the pickers worked on their own, sometimes laughing, sometimes chatting softly, but mostly quiet.

I don't know how long I watched them, but after a while I felt like I could get back in my car and not drive off into the next ditch. I gave a wave to the guy who'd helped me out, and he nodded. I slid behind the wheel and drove off. There was still a ways to go.

There'd be no reaching Beatrice until later. She was at work, and I knew better than to try and see her down at the phone company.

Nothing to it but shower, scrape out the inside of my mouth with a straight razor and scrounge for coins in the back of my sofa so I could grab some coffee. Rent had eaten all the money I'd gotten off my last score. There wasn't anything at my pad that bore any resemblance to a bromo. I walked to Main, going past the Merle Norman building where tarted-up women and some sunk-chested men stood outside on their lunch breaks sucking on cigarettes, chewing stale sandwiches, and squawking to each other about that twat Betty in personnel, or that dreamy Dave up in accounting. Dragging as I was, I still felt one up on those folks, grabbing daylight for an hour before heading back upstairs to throw time away. Once I'd found the piano, I knew I'd never go that route, even if it meant pulling nickels out of my sofa to get coffee.

Pop tried to get me into Hunter College or City College, said there'd be music classes, but I didn't enroll. I kept going to Leo Israel after I graduated high school, taking jobs here and there, none of them lasting very long while I tried to audition for the big bands in the City. For a month or two, I'd be at the soda fountain, the messenger service, the printer shop. I lasted less than a day at the kosher butcher, hating the coppery smell of blood and the stacks of meat ready to carve. But either I'd be fired or I'd quit, and my pop would come home from work in the evening to see me at the piano, and he'd sigh and shake his head, but in secret I think he was glad that he didn't have an ordinary son, dribbling out life behind a desk or counter like another schmuck.

Yeah, but *kvell*, he wouldn't, to see me now. My reflection hopscotched from window to window, following me like a nasty idea. The beanery I found near Rose was crowded, it being around noon, but guys in suits edged away from me when I came in, and I was able to get a place at the counter with empty seats on either side. As I bent over my coffee, I felt the eyes of the pencil pushers skitter over to me, thinking I was some kind of seedy, dangerous character and not a heartsick, swindling piano player. I wasn't about to set them straight.

Through the window to the kitchen, I could see the cook

slinging hash, and the colored dishwasher piling plates and cups into a tub. The dishwasher had put on his mask of blankness and inwardness. I'd seen other colored folks put on the same mask whenever they were surrounded by mostly white people—turn inward, go unreadable and far off. If they looked sharper, some asshole snaps at them, tells them to be respectful and don't give no sass. Maybe that's why a lot of whites think Negroes are dumb—on account that they're always on guard, protecting themselves, smoothing over and clamming up.

In Houston, back when I was making my way west, I went to get my hair cut and wound up at some conking parlor where the colored guys went to straighten their moss. I got some queer eyeballs as I sat in the chair, narrowed gazes and hushed conversations, and, to tell the truth, I wasn't even sure what the hell I was doing there myself. There were plenty of white barbershops around, where the most notice I'd get was from my New Yawk accent. Trying to prove something, I guess, to me and my dad, about what it meant to be an outcast.

"There's Robert's, over on Spring Street, sir," the barber said to me as I threw myself into the chair. "They'd take nice care of you at Robert's."

He wanted to show me the door. Everyone there wanted me to just scram and leave them in peace, not caring about what I was proving. But that made me want to stay all the more. "No, thanks, this place is fine," I said. And with a shrug, just another daffy white guy throwing money around, he'd snapped out the cloth and tucked it around my neck.

As he was working the brush into a cup of foam for my shave, I asked him, "Doesn't it bother you?"

"What's that, sir?"

"That some creep like me can just walk in here and get a shave and haircut, but you couldn't go to Robert's without them working you over." He began to paint the shaving foam on my face, quiet and sealed off. "That'd steam me up, for sure, not being able to refuse a white guy but getting turned away left and right."

"You high yellow or something?" one of the other guys in the shop asked from his seat.

"No—Jew."

"Then it don't matter to you, do it?"

The razor blade was moving swift and steady down my face, rasping off the shadow. I watched myself in the chair, my face hovering over the white cloth, far from home, asking questions that might get my throat slashed, but I was reckless and full of piss.

"Just don't like the way the world works," I said, and the barber laughed.

He said, wiping my face, "Shit, mister, you don't know the half of it. Jew or not, you look white, so everything's swell for you. Can't complain when you don't gotta wear this skin out your door every morning."

"Got me a nephew who signed up to fight Hitler, they got 'im scrubbing latrines instead," the guy behind me threw in. "Said he'll be lucky if he gets anywhere near the front."

"He's lucky he doesn't have to fight," I answered.

The guy shook his head and rustled his newspaper. "And why wouldn't he want to do his duty, protect his country and his family, like any other American? That's what it's about, ain't it? He ain't no draft dodger." *Unlike you*, I saw him think. But he'd never say it, not to a white dude.

I didn't have an answer for him, but it was too bad that this cat's nephew wanted to get his head shot off so badly, and I was running from that bullet. Hell, I would've given the kid my spot, if I'd been able. But it didn't work that way, and he was cleaning toilets for Uncle Sam while I sat in a colored barbershop with a chip on my shoulder.

I kept my mouth shut while I got my hair cut, the air let out of me. Really, what did I know about it, being colored, taking hard knocks? When you're a Jew, unless you're walking around with *payes* curling over your ears and *tzitzit* hanging from under your shirt, the difference wasn't right out in the open. You carried it inside, invisible, and when I walked down the street, I was me first, not a color or race or anything other than just Lou. And, you'd be right if you said there wasn't a "just Lou," since I could make myself into anyone

I needed, and only I knew the constant of my self. Beatrice came the closest to finding the core of me.

Like some kind of *nochshlepper*, I parked in the alley behind her house. It was one thing to leave my car on the street late at night—a family neighborhood, everyone in bed or gathered around listening to Fibber McGee—but here it was Monday evening just after the sun went down, and there were still plenty of folks in front of their houses, getting their mail, walking the dogs, and I'd get too much attention if I rolled up like the Grand Marshal of the Whitey Parade and toddled up Beatrice's walkway.

She didn't seem surprised to see me at her back door. There was an awful, caved-in look on her face as she held the door open for me, not even yelling at me for coming around so early, just standing back and letting me in. Mamie Smith sung her blues from Beatrice's bedroom.

"You look like the winner of the Mister Long-Face Pageant," she said, but there was no heat or sass in her words. "When was the last time you ate something?"

I tried to think about it. It took a while. "Yesterday. Liverwurst sandwich." My gut was on fire, nothing but java rolling around in it, aching from being turned inside out on the side of an Orange County highway.

She drifted into the kitchen, me following after throwing down my hat onto a bench. She opened the icebox. "I got some cold chicken and potato salad. Fix you up a spread."

"I don't want anything to eat, Bea, I want to talk to you."

As if she didn't hear me, she starting pulling food from the icebox. And even though I talked big and noble, what she was dishing up did look mighty good. So I sat down at the kitchen table, mouth shut, while she made up the first real meal I'd had in over a day. It was out of tune, having Beatrice wait on me like she was a square chick fixing supper for her square old man. I didn't want to eat but my machinery yelled for it, and when she set the food down in front of me, I tucked it away.

She lit a cigarette and watched me while I ate, still far away.

I shoved a piece of bread in my mouth and chewed it down. "I've been calling since you got off of work hours ago. Why didn't you answer your phone?"

"Weren't around to get it."

"Where'd you go?"

She took a drag from her cigarette and breathed out smoke. "Blowing around."

"You rattled me, baby." I reached out to take hold of her hand. She sighed and slid away. It felt like hope itself edging back from me.

After a while, she said, "When I was a little kid, and my daddy'd whip me good, I found this place I'd go to, nothing special, a couple of scrub bushes in a vacant lot that formed some bit of shelter." The record was over and she got up to change it. Ida Cox held forth on any woman's blues. Beatrice drifted back into the kitchen and sat down, rubbing her thumb against the chrome siding of the table and taking hits off her cigarette.

"Nobody'd find me there, in my hiding place," she went on. "I could hear my brothers and sisters calling me, saying it was time for supper, I'd better get back before daddy tanned me some more, but I wouldn't move. Tried to stay there as long as I could even though I knew I'd get a walloping. He found out about it after a while, cut them bushes down, made me watch while he burned 'em." She almost smiled. "So I tore up his nudie pictures. Nearly wound up in the hospital after that."

I felt sick, sick because she'd been knocked around so much as a kid, and sick that her story could hurt me so much. "I won't burn you out, honey," I said. "But I don't want you holing up here, hiding."

"I couldn't hide if I wanted to. That ain't my way."

"That's why I like you so much, Bea. You got *chutzpah*. You stand up and fight." Which I never did, unless, like yesterday, I didn't have a choice and it had to happen.

"Just 'cause I'm standing don't mean I ain't hurting from the blows."

"I'll take them for you." As I said that, I realized I really did want to protect her.

"They're not yours to take." Restless, she stood up and walked to the sink, leaving her cigarette in an ashtray, smoldering. On the window ledge behind the sink, she had a little potted African violet, trim and dainty, and checked curtains over the window. It was all clean and regular.

I just couldn't seem to stop myself, and words leapt out of my mouth like the cliff divers jumping for pesetas in Baja. "Tell me who to hurt, Bea, and I'll make 'em beg."

She went over to a drawer and opened it, then pulled out a thick book. She slapped it down on the table in front of me. It was the phone directory for the whole of Los Angeles.

"That's for starters."

I looked up at her. "I have to make it right, but I don't know how."

She turned back, leaning against the counter, and looked at me, beat. She braced her elbows on the edge of the sink, the light from overhead casting long shadows on her face. "I'm burned out, Louis, sneaking around, making like you and me don't share a bed, lying to my family, my friends. I wear too many faces. It's all gone...stale."

She didn't know the life I lead, that putting on masks and bending the truth could wind a body up, not wear them down, but how could I explain that to her? "You want to send me packing?"

When she shook her head, my heart jumped like a high note even though I wanted to stay cool. "No, baby. Ending it—no. I need you around. But I need some time. Alone."

I got up and stood in front of her, taking hold of her hands and not letting her slide away from me. "You don't have to do this, sugar. You don't have to let all those assholes and schmucks win."

Beatrice stared up at me, and I wanted badly to believe that this wouldn't be it, that I'd see her alone again. She tipped her chin up, strong. "Time. That's what I want. And I'm not asking you, I'm telling."

That spine of hers, how I loved and hated it. It made Beatrice. And it tore us in two, took the control out of my hands. When she set her mind to something, not a damned thing could stand in her way. Even me, and my sappy, frustrated wishing. So I could wish and wish, and all that'd come of it was a big fat nothing. There we stood in her kitchen, hearing the blues in another room, and fainter, families in other houses, putting dinner together, yelling, laughing, breathing, the ordinary sounds of ordinary lives. I wish I could say I heard the sound of my heart break, or a catch of a sob in Beatrice's throat, but we faced each other, with nothing left to say, just silence.

Chapter nine

The exchange rang about ten times. I figured that because it was late there wasn't anyone in, but just before I cut the line someone picked up.

"Golden Platters Recording," a guy said, sounding like he'd been swapping chews with an ashtray. In the background I could hear a couple of voices laughing and yelling, and the *rat-a-tat* of the drums. Musicians. Most of them couldn't seem to leave their short pants behind, not in their minds, anyway, acting like a bunch of drunk baboons whenever they got the chance.

"Who'm I talking to?" I asked.

"Sam Knapp. Who the hell am *I* talking to?"

Since this was going to be on the up-and-up, I decided to give him my real name. "Lou Greenberg."

"Charmed, I'm sure. Now, what the fuck do you want?"

It was like chatting with Emily Post. I was ready to toss the phone over my shoulder and make friends with some scotch, but some of the musician cats I knew told me that Golden Platters was one of the best recording studios in L.A., and even better, cheap. "I'd like to know about booking studio time," I said. "How much it'll be, that kind of business."

Sam Knapp, or whoever the hell I was yakking at, shouted at someone, "You monkeys put that trombone down, or so help me I'll shove it up your ass." Someone blew a raspberry. Then he said, "What's your name again?"

"Who, me?" I asked.

"No, fucking Dorothy Lamour. Of course you."

This guy was proving to be one of the most charming conversationalists I'd met in a goodly while. I bet Memphis Arnie would've thrown a clot if he heard him. I couldn't wait to meet this Sam and bask in the glow of his bewitchery. "Lou Greenberg. I'm a friend of Sonny Rockwell's."

"Gee, that's sweet," he spat. "But I ain't got time for this now. Lousy bastards are tearing up my studio. Come in day after tomorrow—if you're serious—and I'll give you the rundown. But I'm busy, get me? If you ain't serious—"

"I am," I said.

"Dandy." And he cut the extension.

I squeezed out of the phone booth and stepped onto Venice Boulevard. A thick, damp fog pressed low onto the street, but there wasn't anyone out except me and a couple of hookers heading towards the Ocean Park Pier to see if they could score themselves a trick or two. I started to walk south, down Ocean and then over to Linnie, towards what remained of the old canals, now thick with weeds and green sludge. I'd seen postcards of what the place looked like twenty years ago—some guy's fantasy of the Adriatic—but now it wasn't much more than a bunch of crumbling cottages and rotten bridges, with a few dinghies in the soupy water bumping listlessly against their moorings. Whores and hopheads faded in and out of the fog as I walked. If I'd wanted a quick fuck or some horse, I would've been in heaven.

"Wanna date, handsome?" one of the hookers asked me slyly. She stopped and struck a pose, but it was so dim with fog, I couldn't see her that clearly.

"No, thanks," I said. "I'm on my way to a prayer meeting."

She shrugged and moved on, adjusting the hem of her skirt and softly clattering away. The Venice Pier had closed a little while ago, burning down just last year, so she'd have to find her johns a smidge north. You could find them late nights, the commercial dames, under the boardwalk, being screwed up against the pilings by sailors or drunk party boys, and whenever some light fell across their tired faces I could see that they'd taken themselves to the same place colored folks went when white folks were around.

Me, I never paid for pussy. For a few reasons. Some grifters hustle other working stiffs, but others give it a pass, since we save it for the pigeons and marks. Most of us hate to pay for anything if we can get it for free, which can usually mean a lot of fancy talk. But that also makes us good marks. That was something I got from old Memphis Arnie—he told me too many con men get suckered, turned into marks because they want the best of it, too. I never wanted to be anyone's chump, so when it came to paying for things—booze, clothes, music—I always played it square. That way, no one can get the jump on me.

But I won't pay for a chick. I won't con a whore into giving it away—she's got a job to do, too—and there isn't a bar or cocktail lounge I couldn't go into without finding myself a girl of the non-mercantile variety to press my pants. Listening to my own footsteps, walking without a place to go, I thought about Beatrice and almost ran to one of the bars on Main to get a little action, just to prove that I could. But I was beat and didn't feel like laying on the glitter talk with some chick for a few minutes in her trailer. I didn't want to talk to anyone, didn't want to have to make nice. There were bigger things kicking around in my head besides crawling between a woman's legs.

Taking my life into my hands, I stood on one of the creaking bridges and stared at the sulfurous reflections of the streetlamps. I thought about, then abandoned, the idea of tossing a penny in to make a wish. One, because I don't believe in wishes and the idea that some supernatural force would rise up out of the swamp to make my dreams come true. And two, I figured that recording time wasn't cheap, and I needed to save every bit of dough I had, even a lousy red cent.

Okay, so you just heard me say that I didn't believe in wishes, but I couldn't help dreaming. It rose up in me like a long-sleeping sickness and I didn't have a vaccine for it. I pictured my record hitting the stores, selling out, and the phone calls I'd get from Diz and Bird and Lady Day, begging me to back them up, though, no, thanks, I'm not a sideman any longer. And if I wanted to step out with a colored woman, then the hell with everyone else, I'd do what I like. I'd throw cash onto the floor and watch them all bend over to pick those bills up, but it'd be nothing to me, all that money. Already, they'd be clamoring for my next record, the money coming in, and then my father, Beatrice, everyone, they just couldn't turn me down.

Success was the passport to another world. When you were famous, you could say what you wanted, go where you pleased. There were a few Negro musicians who had white girlfriends or wives, maybe a handful, and it wasn't as though they were being given the keys to the city every day, but they didn't have to hide. And it'd always be better being a famous white guy with a colored woman. Beatrice and I could step into the hotel lobby, concierge and manager murmuring, If there was *anything* they could do to make our stay at the Waldorf-Astoria more comfortable, just *ask*, and I'd say, Send the manicurist up to our room in thirty minutes, Mrs. Greenberg wants to have her nails done. Thirty minutes later, up comes a woman in starched uniform, a bellhop pushing her wheeled manicurist station into the room. I'd sit in a leather club chair nearby, smoking and watching indulgently. Beatrice's hands are beautiful.

We'd never hear no. Sure, the strange looks wouldn't stop, not completely, but fame would shield us. Once we were out in public, protected by celebrity, there'd be no more private misery.

Day after tomorrow. It'd have to been soon enough. I didn't want to wait anymore. I was going to cut some sides, and soon. No more of this penny-ante baloney for me. Everything would change—the clothes I wore, where I slept, the earth on its axis and me with it—when I got to record.

The bridge gave off a low moan, wondering what it was still doing standing, something I wondered myself, so I went back to my car parked on Venice. I hadn't slept in two days and needed some shut-eye for tomorrow. It was finally time to pay a visit to Mrs. Nora Edwards, grieving widow. I'd put it off long enough, but now I was going to have to step it up. I had something to save for.

As much as I wanted some sleep, lying in bed my mind just wouldn't close down for the night. Whenever I did manage to fall into a doze, I kept going back to my first concert at the tender age of fourteen.

This wasn't my father's dream concert at Carnegie Hall or even the Windsor Theatre on Knightsbridge, but in the rec room in the basement of our synagogue, surely one of the more glamorous spots to be found anywhere in the five boroughs. As a little kid, I used to slide down the long, narrow room with my buddies during endless High Holy Days services, taking off our shoes and getting *schmutz* on our socks as we pretended we were ice skating. Meanwhile, our parents were upstairs atoning, a word and idea that I didn't get. Not at the time. After my bar mitzvah, I wasn't allowed to skate in the rec room on Yom Kippur, but had to sit between my pop and my bubbe while the rabbi droned on for what felt like days. I'd distract myself by trying to get a peek at Barbara Schliessman's legs—the ripest tomato at Temple Beth Shalom—and keep a hand pressed to my gut to keep it from growling too loud. I didn't think Jimmy Cagney let his stomach growl when putting the hurt on some punk.

The Beth Shalom rec room hosted more than just kids skidding around on their stockings. My bar mitzvah reception was held down there, so were plenty of wedding parties and the Purim carnival, and the walls smelled of stale matzo and Aqua Velva. A small stage stood at one end, with rust-colored velvet curtains, where kids dressed up for Hanukkah like Maccabees waved cardboard swords in front of their bored parents, who were grinning like maniacs to keep from running out into the streets, and nine of the littlest tykes came out with paper flames on their heads to stand for the menorah candles. The band for weddings and bar mitzvahs would also set up there—dinky three-piece combos, dumpy women in flowered dresses

trilling "Cheek to Cheek" between choruses of "My Yiddishe Mama."
And once in a while, some of the local music prodigies, such as yours
truly, put on our stiff miniature suits and starched pinafores, and had
ourselves a modest recital for the entertainment-starved masses.

My pop had been bugging me for a long time to perform in
one of these sight and sound spectaculars, but Leopold Israel didn't
want me clinking the keys like a trained monkey, the way most
kids did at those sorts of things, miserably pushing through Haydn
until the last note was shoved out of the piano and they jumped up,
folded themselves in a bow, and ran offstage to pick their noses. He
still had some pride, clinging to him like a lingering cold, and so he
flatly refused to have his students perform before he thought they
were ready. As you might suspect, many of the doting parents did
not turn cartwheels at this notion and applaud Leopold's dedica-
tion to his art. After all, they were blowing a whole buck per lesson,
and wanted to see a return on their investment. So get little Shirley
and Gordon and Florence and Myron up there and make with the
Beethoven, pronto. No sir, said Leo. He lost a lot of students that
way, but on account of my dad being grateful to Leo for introducing
me to the piano, I stayed on.

When I turned fourteen, Leo decided I was "good enough" to
play before a real audience. I might have told him his professional
pride was misplaced, that the rec room crowds surely didn't deserve
anything above the miserable Passover pageants and wedding combos
honking "Tiptoe Through the Tulips." The congregation listened to
Rudy Vallee croon through a megaphone on the *Fleischmann Yeast
Hour* and didn't know Grieg from gefilte fish. Old Leo didn't want to
admit to himself what he'd become, what he'd lost, so even the dingy
rec room with a row of high, narrow windows and clackety folding
chairs meant something to him the way an opera house might have
years before.

In the glorious year 1934, when "Anything Goes" debuted on
Broadway, I made my debut at Temple Beth Shalom. I'd argued with
Leo, wanting to play Ellington or Basie, not Chopin or Scarlatti,
something which pleased him about as much as an ice cold herring

in his cup of coffee. We stood in the echoing rec room, testing what Leo optimistically called "acoustics."

"So I am wasting my time with you, Louie," he said, tucking his hands into the pockets of his jacket, the way he did when he was angry. "We go over chord theory and progression, but meanwhile it is nothing but syncopation, all that stride piano *rupieć*."

I didn't know *rupieć* from Shinola, but the way Leo Israel's beard moved when he said it meant that it wasn't another word for genius.

"Those classical guys, Mr. Israel, they're swell and all," I said, "but that music, it's old."

"Of course it is old," he snapped. "Do you think we listen to it now because it is new and different? No. We play it, we listen to it, because it has withstood the passage of time. There were many, many composers and street musicians, all of them writing and performing, most of them terrible, but the filter of years gives us only the best. *Because* it is old, we know it is good."

Most kids would've shut their mouths at this point, letting their elders do the thinking for them, but I'd never been that kind of kid. So when Leo Israel thought he'd settled the argument, I said, "But I bet that folks just like us will look up to jazz composers, like the way we do for the classical composers."

"Absurd!" he snorted and I bet he was thinking of the Old Country, where kids were well-behaved and didn't mouth off, and sat at the table quietly, shoving fried liver and kraut into their faces without complaint. And not a one of those Old Country kids would've said something like what I was saying:

"I swear, Mr. Israel. Jazz will be the most popular kind of music, everybody's going to listen to it. They listen to it now on the radio." I got up on stage and tried my hand at a few bars of "The Pearls," sounding bright and kicking, even on that cornball piano, even in that musty rec room that had the looks and charm of a bowling alley.

"And that is what you want?" he asked me, and if he was grimacing because of the Jelly Roll Morton or the sour twang of the out-of-tune piano, I couldn't say. "To play for the dumb masses sitting like stones next to their radios who want to hear only what is pretty or, what is the word, 'swingy,' the same fools who bray with laughter at *The Cuckoo Hour*, who never pick up a book but paw through the *Digesting Readers*—"

"*Reader's Digest*," I corrected him, which, along with contradicting, was something I wasn't supposed to do. He shot me a cold look.

"Is that how you picture yourself?" he said. "A trained animal performing for imbeciles?" He shook his head and I felt myself growing tiny. Soon I'd slip underneath the piano bench and disappear under the foot pedals. "This disappoints me, Louie. I thought that perhaps out of all my students, you at the least had some genuine love for music, but I see now that all you want is to be adored, to be popular. Not a true artist."

He turned and walked slowly out of the rec room, and I sat, watching him go, shriveling into a blank. I tried to tell myself that for Leo Israel, this was nothing but a case of sour grapes, pining after something that was long gone and couldn't be gotten back. He was sorry for himself. Disappointed in what had become of him, not in me. Besides, the type of music he liked was strictly for Park Avenue longhairs, country-club types who didn't know *bubkes* from living in the Bronx, five to a tiny apartment, radios and voices and bumps on every side. Jazz was about living in the city, about running past trolleys and the bustle of folks crowded elbow-to-elbow, girls in summer dresses smoking on fire escapes, stealing handfuls of penny candy when the druggist's back was turned.

I sat at the piano for a while, plinking out notes, sullen and grouchy, trying to defend myself against him. I didn't like that word, "artist," it didn't mean anything to me. Music wasn't about art—I couldn't even figure what that was, art, how it had anything to do with anything. Music was life and life was music and what I knew, what got into me and rang out, was jazz. It was what I wanted, what I loved, and it didn't have anything to do with other people, whether or not they dug me and clapped when I played. The hell with them. And the hell with old, bitter Leopold Israel, too.

But when the recital rolled around, the long, stale room filling with all the locals dressed up in their shabby good clothes, and I saw Leo standing at the back of the rec room in his beautiful suit, straight and Continental in that sea of smallness, he and my father looking at me with their own forgotten hopes shining out of their eyes, I caved. I played Chopin's Nocturne in C Minor, doing pretty well, I might add, though each note splintered inside me. When I was done, my pop got to his feet, clapping wildly, and even Leo nodded and applauded, maybe not as crazily as my dad, but he did. I took my bow and then edged offstage to make room for Rose Bernhardt singing "Froggie Went a-Courtin'," and when it came time for all the kids to line themselves up and take a final bow, I wasn't there. I'd run all the way to the University Heights Bridge, and stood looking south at the lights of Manhattan, swearing that I wouldn't cave again. Not to Leo Israel, not to anyone. I had my own ideas—dreams, you might call them—and whenever I let someone else bend me, it was like I stood back and smiled while they stole my favorite handball. But never again. I rubbed my eyes on the sleeve of the suit my mom bought me from the discount store on 149th. The feel of that scratchy, cheap wool against my face was the seal of my promise.

I never really got what regret is, never quite wrapped my mind around what it means, why we feel something that can't help us at all. As much as it troubles us, there's no second take on the past. It sits and leers in the corners, won't leave even if you shout until you're ready to explode. You can't drink it away, can't screw it gone, even moving clear across the goddamn country changes nothing. So either you clean that dirty suit and get on with it, or throw everything away, curl into a ball, and live in your own crap. That's what regret is: a load of your own shit you rub in your own face.

Even after everything I've done, I can't quite scare up regret, won't let myself. Thinking on it now, it probably wasn't the smartest thing to go see Mrs. Nora Edwards, widow, at least not that soon after Beatrice and I hit the skids.

Beatrice kept kicking around my mind all night and all the next day, the way she looked in her kitchen, ground down, showing me the door. I was boiling—she'd sent me packing, at least for a while, and why? Because of an inbred hick cracking his jaw, some piece of shit who wasn't even worth conning. I just couldn't get my cool, hating that I'd been chumped by that hayseed, so when I drove down to Culver City, I was too riled up to prepare myself for the grift.

I tried to keep a lid on it by running my eyes over the scene. It was a sleepy burg, a bunch of marshes and low houses, the two biggest buildings being the Helms Bakery building on Venice and the MGM Studios on Washington—each the size of their own little cities. The smell of bread coming out of the bakery made me think of Dee's, and that just brought Beatrice back, so as soon as I thought I had my game face on, it slipped away again. I ought to have turned around. I should have known, followed Memphis Arnie's rule: "Never play the C when your confidence is at its ebb, son. Everything will go south unless you are in complete control of yourself. Best to call it off and try again another day." But I wasn't and I didn't—I kept thinking about how much it would cost to cut sides at the recording studio, how without my steady gig at the Carmel Club I was going to need some cash, how I'd show up at Beatrice's door in the middle of the day with the record in my hand—so I kept going.

Like a lot of places around L.A., Culver City was getting built up after the war. GIs who'd been stationed here decided they didn't want to leave the twenty-four-hour sunshine, and the hell with Mom and Pop back on the farm. Houses were going up fast, spreading like V.D., cheap bungalows with their little yards, little driveways, and little men and women cheerfully throwing themselves into the grinding gears of ordinary life after the glorious heroism of battle. No more shrapnel, no more watching your buddy's guts get blown out onto your combat boots and hating yourself for being glad that it wasn't you, no more stinking, stale barracks or cold C-rations, nosir, it was on to the dazzling future of management reports, mortgage payments, and washing machine repairs. And diaper service.

Wouldn't you know it, just after the war ended all these women started swelling up, toting their big bellies around town like they were proud of the fact that their husbands ran straight home from the front, hard-pressed for pussy, and knocked them up. And then came the inevitable flood of babies. Everywhere you looked, women were pushing carriages up and down the street, a parade of fat, squalling write-offs, the apple of their parents' eyes and the center of the universe, dumping and puking, the adorable angels. Fortunately, in my con, I didn't have to deal with those toddling crap factories, since the husbands or sweethearts were long dead and couldn't do any damage with their schlongs at least, not from beyond the grave.

Mrs. Nora Edwards' husband had taken the long dirt nap in Italy back in '44, so unless he'd had some leave and put a bun in his wife's oven, I wouldn't have to coo and tickle some chunky carpet crawler. I pulled up in front of her house and didn't see anything in the yard that'd show a kid was in residence, no toys, no sandbox, all clear. Getting out of my car, I gave my suit a quick once-over, making sure I was sharp. I looked at myself in the window of the Buick—a few rings under the eyes from a night spent revisiting Leopold Israel and my dad, but other than that, I still had a face that could make out like a foreign loan, so that was swell. Nothing to do but say howdeedo to my latest pigeon.

She lived in one of those new colonial-style homes, the kind with miniature white columns and green shutters, as straight as a first-time boxer's face just as he steps into the ring. Houses done up in that historical style made me laugh, in Los Angeles particularly. Everybody dreaming about a past that never was, an America that didn't exist, ye goode olde days of George Washington, Yankee Doodle, the fresh green yesterday now buried underneath highways and telephone lines. Sure as hell Los Angeles didn't have anything to do with those old, creaking Founding Fathers, their powdered wigs and buckled shoes—it was all Mexico way back then. At least the stucco Spanish apartments and houses around town tried just a little to recall what L.A. had been, and even they weren't more than a mirage of something unreal.

Nora Edwards' place was clean, neat. She didn't have weeds in the yard, no paint chipping up, nothing leaking or muddying up the stone walkway to her door. She must've been one of those Rosie the Riveter types, doing everything herself once her man had gone, the kind that was glad to kick men out of the picture, rolling up her sleeves, fixing the plumbing, rewiring the lamps, and switching to dungarees. Maybe she still wore them—like Beatrice.

I got rattled again, thinking about Bea, and it wasn't until after I'd rung the doorbell that I realized I had completely fucked up and left my clipboard in the car, the one I used to look official. I felt like a complete asshole. I'd never made that mistake before. If Memphis Arnie could've seen me, he would've choked on his boutonniere. I was just about to run back to the car and grab the clipboard when the front door opened and I was looking at Floyd Edwards' widow.

She looked around thirty, thirty-one, and not a tall drink of water—just a shot glass, the top of her head grazing the knot of my tie. She tilted her head back to get a good view of me, and I was sorry that she wasn't prettier, her being young and all, with hair the color of fine whiskey and round, blue-gray eyes. Her figure didn't know she was on the short side, something I appreciated, and I was able to get a decent view of her rack down the front of her blouse, me being so much taller. The pale freckles on her nose wrinkled when she gave me the up-and-down.

"Can I help you?" she asked, and I heard the Midwest in her voice, the long winters and boiled food, the boredom and heavy coats, and when the chance to move out west with some guy came along, the readiness to chuck it and skip another dreary Lutheran summer. I hoped her solid Iowan values hadn't burned away altogether in the hot California glare, and she'd be willing to wave farewell to some money in exchange for a memento of that guy who'd taken her away from pig wallows and stern, wide-hipped mothers.

I sure as hell wished I had my clipboard—I needed that prop. But I didn't, so I had to keep going. I told myself that I was in charge here, it was my con and I could make it go wherever I wanted.

"Are you Mrs. Nora Edwards?" I asked, cheerful but solemn, a special combination I'd tinkered with and perfected over the years.

"Yes?" She didn't sound all too sure about that, though, which would make the grift easier. She seemed sharp enough, but ready to be lead along.

"May I come in?"

And here's where I was right about her being a little sharp. Her round eyes narrowed and her small mouth creased in the corners. Maybe she wasn't as grain-fed as I'd thought. She held the door tight in one of her hands, as if she could actually keep me out of her house if she wanted to. I saw the ring still on her finger, which was good. "I'm sorry—what is this about?"

Telling my tale on the doorstep wasn't my favorite thing to do. Being in someone's house helped sell the story, I could use the things around me to my advantage, some photo or *tchotchke* to summon the dead, but I'd done my work before on the stoop and I could do it again, even without my goddamned clipboard.

Taking off my hat, as if I was being respectful, I said, "I hate to bring up painful memories, but your late husband—"

And just as regular as a boozehound getting the shakes, she said on cue, "Floyd? This is about him?"

I gave a somber nod but felt myself grinning inside. Sure, I'd bobbled it at the beginning, but I could pull off this con, with or without my props. "Captain Edwards was in the 350th Infantry, am I correct? And gave his life heroically breaking through the Gothic Line?"

She started to nod, the reliable grief coming on, but then she did something I'd never seen before when digging up the body of a lost husband: she smiled. A real smile, slow and cautious, but real, not one of those pasteboard types I've seen widows and mothers use to make themselves believe everything was going to be okay. I have to admit, I was stumped.

"Are you...you must be one of Floyd's army buddies," she said, naked hope parading before the curtains. This was new. Nobody had ever thought I was some old pal from the Front. But who knew what not having a clipboard would get you?

Before I could even nod or shake my head, she said, pressing a hand to her cheek, "Gosh, you must think me terribly rude, treating one of Floyd's pals so rotten and making you stand out here like some salesman." She held the door open wider, so I could see into her house, but it was so bright out, all I made out was a lot of darkness. "Come in."

I could have backed out then, could've muttered something about a mistake, or even gone ahead with the con, correcting her gaffe. But even as I was going over these odds, even as I thought about Beatrice and my pop and Memphis Arnie, the money I'd need for the recording time, even though no good could come of it, I heard myself say, "Thanks, Mrs. Edwards. Floyd said you were a good egg," and watched myself step across the threshold.

Chapter ten

Y ou're very lucky."

I'd stepped inside the hallway and my eyes were still getting used to the dark. Everything was sandy and blurred, I couldn't see much of anything. I turned to a small shape next to me, hoping it was her, but bumped into a potted palm.

"How so?" I asked, and I made a lunge for the plant, trying to stop it before I got dirt all over the floor.

I felt her cool, small hands fumble near mine as we straightened the palm. "I'm usually at work this time of day, but there was some kind of gas leak and they sent everybody in my department home."

Whether beloved Floyd would've said something about where his wife worked, I didn't know, so I just nodded and let myself enjoy the feeling of her hands touching me. I asked myself what the hell I was doing there at all, why I was even trucking down this path, was I some kind of grade-A Alvin for even going as far as I had with this scam which would probably net me nothing in the cash department. Maybe I was standing there, hat in hand, gripping a potted palm with some woman I didn't know from Stella Dallas because of what I saw in her eyes when she thought I was one of her dead husband's friends. Now, don't think that I'd gone soft or anything, that I'd blow a perfectly ripe chance to fleece a sucker, that I got all misty and schmaltzy, seeing a woman in need, and me being a regular Prince Valiant I rode in on my white charger to save the damsel. But I stewed over this a while, and the best I figured was that Nora Edwards was the first person in a dog's age who'd been honestly glad to see me. Beatrice, she always seemed almost mortified, a little bit sick with herself for bedding down on the sly with a white guy like me, and when she'd let me into her place, I felt her letdown. I don't think she'd ever admit it if I said anything, but it was there. And I sure couldn't say that any of my marks were ever giddy with joy when I stood on their front steps, resurrecting the dead. Who was left? I didn't have any gigs where the audience stood on their chairs and clapped like maniacs when I sat down at the piano. The folks at Dee's stomached me only because I played some righteous piano. And if I saw my pop again after all these years, he would not slay the fatted calf.

The last few days had left me feeling as flat and worn as a flophouse mattress, and Nora Edwards didn't really know who I was, so I was willing to be whoever she wanted if it would have her fix those blue-gray eyes of hers on me and be glad of it. For now, anyway.

She led me into a parlor, and I was finally able to see, getting used to the dark. There were the usual characters: framed prints of ladies in old-fashioned dresses, clattery wooden tables with turned legs holding dustcatchers, and, yep, the picture of Our Dead Hero, Captain Floyd Edwards. I gave him a glance. Not bad looking. As my bubbe would say, a real *goyishe punim*. Blond, square jaw, someone who'd eat a cheeseburger with bacon, that is to say, pure *trayf*. In the picture, he was standing in some park, wearing his uniform, his arm around his wife's waist, holding her against him like a kid trapping a ladybug in a jar. Both of them looked stunned, as if they'd just gotten off the bumper cars.

"It must be strange to see his face again after all this time," Nora Edwards said behind me.

She didn't need to know this was the first time I'd ever clapped eyes on the guy. I acted as though I was giving him a thorough look, like I was trying to recall the good times we'd had, the shrieking bombs we'd dodged. "Sure is."

She came and stood next to me, and I could smell a whiff of sweat and the babyish powder she dusted over her freckles. But then I caught another look at her chest, and that wasn't babyish at all. Maybe I could get something out of this crazy stunt of mine. She wasn't a beauty, but that shape of hers compensated nicely.

Touching her fingertips to the frame, she said quietly, "This was just before he shipped out, the last time I saw him. We both knew he'd be gone a long time. I guess we didn't know how long."

Even though I didn't know the script, I knew my lines. Sort of like comping somebody when they're on a tear. I had the basic melody, but the variations were wide open and all mine. "None of us did," I said.

She pried her eyes off the picture and looked at me, and I saw the quick flash of anger that I'd made it and her man hadn't. Why'd the war spare me, but not him? Who the hell was *I* anyway? I'd gotten that before, from the other widows and grieving mothers, but never so particular, so exact. After all, she thought I knew dear dead Floyd, maybe was with him when he cashed in his chips, a rare privilege that for some creepy reason many women seemed to wish for. Me, I'd rather be far away whenever someone's Christmas gets canceled. Why sit around and watch those moments of death? We're all going to buy it—some sooner than later—no point rubbing our noses in it.

So Nora Edwards held that against me, but she tucked it away fast, like a strand of hair behind her ear, and smiled at me again, a genuine smile. There was something about that smile, though, that seemed a bit too bright, but I was having a hard time figuring out why I'd feel that way. Mrs. Edwards seemed ordinary enough. All the same, it wouldn't hurt to stay on my toes.

"I was so happy to know you were one of Floyd's friends, I didn't even get your name," she said.

I held out my hand to shake, even though we'd already clasped hands in the hallway. "Louis Dante."

For a tiny girl, she had a strong grip. "It's a pleasure to meet you, Mr. Dante."

Why not? "Call me Lou."

"Can I get you something to drink, Lou? A cup of coffee maybe, or I think I have milk in the icebox." She screwed her mouth to one side, sheepish. "Sorry to have such poor hospitality for you. But I'm at the studio late most nights, and take a lot of my meals at the commissary."

"Don't worry yourself about it. I'm fine." The place was pretty small, so she didn't make much at whatever she did at the studio, wherever that was. The MGM lot was nearby, so my guess was that she earned her bread there, but what did she do? Most women in the movie business were either costume, makeup, or assistants to cigar-chomping moguls and hacks. I took a quick peek at Nora Edwards' hands again. They were small, the nails kept small and neat, with a tiny callus on the middle finger of her right hand. When she sat down in the parlor and motioned for me to do the same, she was compact in the way she moved her legs, the way a chick might if she had to run around answering phones and taking dictation from a pinhead jackass behind a desk, all the while dodging some guy's hands wanting to give those Model Ts on her chest a test drive. Somebody's secretary, and maybe she was good at her job, but more likely she was signed up because of her ripe figure and almost pretty face.

"They must rely on you quite a bit at the studio to keep you there so late," I said.

"When you work in accounts payable, everyone needs everything immediately," she said with a shrug. "And all the baloney they tell you about the movies is just that: baloney. The stars and directors, even stuntmen and set builders, all of that important stuff boils down to just one thing."

"What's that?"

"If there's ink in the mimeograph."

We were both pretty stunned to find ourselves in her parlor, laughing. But then she got quiet, less pretty. "I don't think Floyd would have been pleased about me getting a job. He didn't believe wives should work outside of the house."

Me, I've never formed much of an opinion on this subject, since, dreams of the Waldorf-Astoria and Beatrice aside, it wasn't in the cards for me to get hitched and raise a clutch of money-siphons. I suppose if a woman didn't want to spend all day wiping asses, noses and floors, only to have her husband come home at the end of the day hollering for his chow while smelling of his secretary's snatch, that was her business. I sure wouldn't want to do it.

"I bet he'd understand," I said, making myself solemn.

She folded her hands in her lap and came on all gloomy. "It was circumstance. I didn't want to get a job. I wanted to be a good wife and mother. But I just didn't get the chance."

We were separated by a little table with a doily and crystal candy dish on it, and I reached over to give her hand a consoling pat, friendly-like, letting my fingers brush a bit over her thigh. She didn't notice or didn't mind. I'd take either one.

"I think you're doing swell," I said.

She gave me a wobbly smile. "That's kind of you. I don't know how many other men would really approve of a woman supporting herself."

"I'm not like most guys," I said, winning the prize for biggest understatement of the year, which I guess was the world's smallest loving cup . But still, I kept asking myself, what the hell was I doing? What did I think I'd get out of this chick?

I knew quickly why she wanted me there, though. "Were you in Floyd's platoon?" she asked, looking hopefully at me.

Whatever pit I'd dug myself into, I didn't want it to be too deep that I couldn't leap out. "No, I met him when my battalion got to the Gothic Line." That left me a comfortable cushion of a few hundred GIs, so I didn't have to be too chummy with Edwards. "I'm sorry, I just didn't know him very well. There were a lot of men that'd come and go. You'd meet somebody, start to become friends, and then they were moving out. I almost never met the same guy twice who wasn't in my squad."

Nora didn't care for this idea, but that didn't surprise me. "Oh, I understand," she said, her voice small and disappointed. "So you couldn't tell me anything about when…"

See what I mean? Women all wanted the gruesome details of their man's last breaths, as though they could somehow put themselves there, maybe even keep it from happening, which makes no sense, since there just isn't a way to travel through time and stop a bullet or mortar shell.

I gave my head a glum shake as I started to wing it. "I only found out about it after we took Firenzuola. I saw a lot of good men cut down, but I was sure sorry to hear about Floyd. He was a real okay guy." While I'm not one of them sad schmucks spending long Saturday nights sitting around picturing my funeral, I sure hope that no one says about me after I'm dead, *That Lou, he was an okay guy.* What a bunch of applesauce. Better for somebody to say, *Man, that Lou was a heel. I'm sorry he's dead, on account that I'd have liked to pop him off myself.* At least then there'd be some feeling behind it, something more than a weak aftertaste, meaning nothing and rinsing away fast.

But Nora Edwards didn't seem to mind her dearly departed being just "okay," and she lapped it up. Then a little wrinkle appeared between her eyebrows and she asked, "If you didn't know Floyd very well, why are you here?"

It was time to play Truth or Consequences, and if I didn't answer right, I'd wind up at best out on my ass on the sidewalk. But then flimflam artists have to be able to improvise whole songs on the spot, and I didn't even have to pause and think before I said, smooth as Brylcreem, "One night, before we tried to take the Pass, a bunch of guys were sitting around talking about their sweethearts and wives, the girls they left behind. A lot of us were thinking we'd never see them again, and I guess," I cast a moist look at her, "they were right."

She was already reaching for her hanky, so I kept at it. "I was feeling pretty blue, because I didn't have me a girl waiting stateside. Well, I did, but she sent me a Dear John letter saying she was taking up with some flat-footed air raid warden."

"How awful," murmured the widow Edwards, and I'm not ashamed to admit that I'd work the pity angle on a chick.

So I made myself into the Heartbroken Hero, noble but a little dinged up, which no woman can resist. "Floyd tried to cheer me up, even though we'd just met, said that there were plenty of chicks—

ladies—who'd treat me right, nice girls who'd never sneak around and play me wrong. Then he started talking about you."

The poor little muffin. So easy to play. Like "Chopsticks." Pling pling pling. But there was the thrill of a good improv that kept it fresh. She sat up and smoothed her skirt. "He did?"

"Yep. He said what a great gal you were," I took a bit of a gamble here, "writing him all the time," she leaned in and nodded, so my gambit paid off, and it was like hitting just the right combo of chords, "that you two knew each other forever," okay, still going strong, "and it just about killed him to ship out." I sneaked a glance at a picture on the mantle, almost hidden by a vase, of Nora Edwards standing with some old broad in front of a church, and I thought that maybe it'd been Easter, seeing the lamentable hats covered with flowers and bows that perched on their heads like fruitcake vultures. "He said how much he loved that hat of yours, with the silk roses, that you looked like Spring, only more lovely."

Oh, brother, was I laying it on. She couldn't stop the water leaking from her eyes, and blew her nose twice. "I wore that hat our first Easter together as man and wife," she sniffed.

"That's what he said." I reached for a cigarette, then stopped myself. "Sorry, do you mind if I smoke?"

"Of course not." She pushed a small glass ashtray towards me that looked cleaner than a surgical theater, taking a match from a dainty china box painted with a shepherdess and lighting my cigarette. I liked the way she shook out the match, neat and sharp, then ground it into the ashtray.

I took a drag and blew out, noticing the careful and hungry way she watched me. "You sure this is all right?" I asked, waving my cigarette in the air.

She nodded so hard I thought she'd fall out of her chair. "I don't smoke, but Floyd did." Which explained why she kept everything waiting for him, just in case he came sauntering through the door and demanded a puff. So for now, I could be the stand-in, filling the house with tobacco and man. "Please, go on."

I drew on my light and went on. "Oh, yeah. Well, like I said, he couldn't say enough good things about you, but I could tell that everything he said was the truth. For some guys, being away from home, life looked a lot rosier than it was; girls were prettier, Mom's cooking was better, the whole megi—I mean, the whole nine yards. Not with you, though. I knew you were the real thing. He even showed me a few of your letters. I hope you don't mind."

"Not a bit," she answered, blowing her nose.

This story was getting good—I usually didn't have to tell this much of a tale, and it was kind of fun. I wondered if there were any openings for writers at the studio.

"Well, I read them," I said, "and I have to say, I was half nuts for you by the time I was done." I gave her a straight stare, right at her, and she went pink all over, even down her chest. She looked right back at me, even though she was redder than a Commie. It gave me a little zing right down to my goodies. "Then Floyd put your letters back in his diddy bag and he said to me, he said," and I pitched my voice, just a hair, making it deeper, the voice of a fallen champion, "'Dante, you seem like a straight arrow. I hope when all this is over you'll come and visit me and Nora. We'll have some beers together and talk about how we gave those Jerries a pounding. Then Nora and me will find you a girl.'"

I could hear the violins swelling and see the golden sun sinking into the horizon when I said, "When I heard about Floyd, that he didn't make it, I knew that if I ever got home, I'd be sure to see his widow and let her know that right before the end, he was thinking about her."

She was going to have to be mopped up, she was crying so hard. I almost thought she'd break a string, heaving and sobbing the way she did. I thought about just sitting there, letting her bawl. Some women don't want too much attention when they're crying, it's not ladylike or demure. Maybe it would've been the right time to just get up and leave, mission accomplished—though I still didn't know what that mission was. But in the end I was a bit of a chump and got up, and put my hand on her shaking shoulder.

Without stopping her wailing, she turned and threw her arms around me, but since I was standing and she was sitting, she wound up hugging my crotch. I felt her body shuddering all up and down my legs, and the quick seep of hot tears into the front of my pants.

"Thank you, thank you," she gasped, and she didn't seem to realize that her mouth was charmingly near my cock. I doubted she'd ever had her lips so close to a guy's schvantz. "I'm so glad you told me. I'm so grateful."

"Believe me," I said, resting my other hand on the top of her head and gently stroking her hair, "I'm happy to do this."

After she'd disentangled herself from my schlong, she went into the powder room to wash her face. I was glad she'd gone out of the room for a minute, because while the company of the girdled sex was something I was used to, you can't name me one guy who wouldn't raise the flagpole even just a little when a tomato's got her face near his goods. So I was glad for the breather.

I moseyed around her parlor some more, scanning the photos, the dustcatchers, everything showing a corn-fed girl who longed for a little movie romance in her life—all the pictures of women in old-timey dresses. She hadn't had a man in the house for a while. No guy would put up with so many china roses, couldn't pass gas or scratch his balls surrounded by that hooey. Nora wasn't around enough to keep the place completely clean. When I took out a book about fly-fishing, it left a line of dust on the shelf. Inside the cover was written: FLOYD MILTON EDWARDS and an inscription dated ten years ago, "Dear Floyd, Happy 21st Birthday, Maybe this will help you finally catch something, besides Nora, ha ha, Love, Your Father." A regular man of letters, this Pop Edwards. George S. Kaufman must be wetting himself from terror.

I slid the book back in its place and turned around when I heard her come back into the room. Her eyes were red and puffy, same with her nose, but she'd swept herself together. I smelled a fresh spritzing of perfume, and she'd put on a new coat of lipstick. Her grief had planted a little more life in her face.

"Feeling better?" I asked.

"Come with me into the kitchen. I'll put on some coffee."

I followed her through the narrow halls and was treated to a viewing of her caboose, which suited me fine. Maybe it was on account of Beatrice that I'd become what you might call an ass maven—though I liked women's legs and bodies, too—and I was glad to see that, WASP she may be, but the Widow Edwards was packing a picnic for two in her trunk. She had a good sway on her, too, when she walked.

I found myself in Nora Edwards' kitchen, more modern than the one at Bea's place, with new wood-grain Formica countertops and flat green cabinets that didn't look banged up or used. She had me sit while she put the coffee together, and by the way she was bouncing on her feet, almost humming to herself, I knew she liked waiting on a man, that she'd been ripe to do it for a while. For a minute, it felt a little queer, Nora Edwards brewing me up a cup of coffee, all square and regular, when a few nights ago, I'd been in Beatrice's kitchen eating cookies and smelling of her sex. And just last night, Bea had fixed me some food. She'd been my steady for almost two years and, sure, I'd screwed some other girls every now and then when Bea wasn't around, but I never meant anything by it. Maybe I could have me a little fun with this widow while I sorted out my problems with Beatrice.

"I can't tell you how long it's been since I made coffee for someone other than me," Nora Edwards said as she poured me a cup. "Oh, sometimes my girlfriends come over for a game of bridge, but it's not the same." She sat down across from me and held her cup in both hands, smiling. "For a while, after Floyd left, I kept making enough for two, and had to keep pouring it down the drain—this was before the rationing, of course. I didn't want to get out of the habit, for when Floyd came home." This made her sad again, and she studied the dark surface of her coffee.

You'd think that being a flimflam man means keeping the chatter up the whole time, sousing the mark with a nonstop gush of smooth words, but Memphis Arnie made sure back when I was a tyro that I knew the profit of keeping quiet. Marks do a lot of the work themselves, giving you what you need, opening every door. "Don't forget to listen," Arnie said, over and over. "Your mark is giving you the treasure map, and if you do not pay attention and hear them, even the smallest detail about their first beloved goldfish, you will walk ten paces instead of twenty, and get nothing but sand for your troubles."

So I kept it buttoned and let the little widow do her schtick. I'd figure all this out, eventually.

"I'm sure Floyd didn't tell you this," Nora Edwards said, "but before he left to fight, we were having some problems."

I made myself look blank, smooth. I was going to play rabbi, okay, chaplain, for Mrs. Edwards, but, hell, I'd heard so many damned secret stories that it didn't much matter anymore. Secrets were locked boxes of salt everyone kept stashed away, thinking they were valuable and prized, but the truth was that you could get the same stuff all over town, and for free at your nearest diner. But maybe she'd give me something I could use. "No, he didn't say anything about that."

She didn't seem too broken up about the trouble at home, like she'd gotten used to a wart—not too pretty, but what can you do? "In fact, we'd quarreled just before he shipped out," she said, "and the last thing he ever heard me say was...rather unkind." She gave me an apologetic shrug, but more that she was sorry what I'd think of her than what she'd done to ol' Floyd. I wondered what "rather unkind" really meant; if she'd screamed and thrown things, or pouted and slammed doors. Different women had different snits, and I didn't want anything to do with any of them. My own mom would bang around in the kitchen, opening and closing cabinets like she was blowing a safe, a pain to practice over, and her already rotten cooking would get even worse. Pop would sneak out with me after she'd gone to bed and get us some hot dogs, since none of us could choke down another cardboard chicken. I kind of liked it when he and Mom were digging up the tomahawk, since he and I could make believe we were undercover men, creeping around, buying Nathan's Famous under cover of night. But this woman, Mrs. Edwards, was from the Corn Belt, not a Jew from the Bronx, so her idea of being "rather unkind," was probably a cool peck on the cheek.

"I tried to make it up," she said, "writing him lots of letters,

V-mail. The few that I got from him were all blacked up from the censors. Then the letters just stopped. I never really knew if he'd forgiven me. And when he was killed—it just tore me up, not knowing."

So that explained it, why she fell so hard for my tale about Floyd showing me her letters, yammering on and on about what a swell girl she was, all that bull. She wanted to be sure that everything had been hunky-dory between them before he got his fatal case of lead poisoning.

I edged my cup away and put just the tips of my fingers against the back of her hand. This works better sometimes than outright grabbing a woman's hand. They like it because they think it's classy, Continental, straight out of the pictures. And it worked on tiny Nora Edwards, too. She clapped her eyes on my hand, liked what she saw, then turned her hand over to hold mine. Whoever said that women were hard to make out was one dumb schnook. Anybody can play them, you just have to know the right chords.

I fixed her with my best Paul Henreid. "I'm glad that I could help set your mind at ease."

She thought she was Bette Davis, too. She made herself look noble and suffering, but with Claude Rains' help, she'd get over it. "And I'm glad that Floyd met you in Italy."

The thing about any jazz piece is that you have to know the value of retreating, holding back, to make the rest sing, so I gently pulled my hand out from hers, got up, and went to grab my hat. She followed me to the parlor, trotting like a dog at my heels.

"Thanks for the coffee, Mrs. Edwards—"

"Nora." She hovered near me as I stood in the front hallway.

I gave her my ten dollar smile. "Nora." Oh, brother, did she dig hearing me say her name. I thought she'd faint right on my shoes. "I should be going."

She looked like she'd start bawling again. "Oh, but...must you leave so soon?"

"Time to get back to the office," I said, although I hadn't quite figured out what line of work Louis Dante was in.

I headed for the door, but slowly, waiting. It was a fight, let me tell you, for her to get the words out. I'm sure her stern momma and Bible-toting poppa wouldn't have cared for it, and she wanted to be one of those old-fashioned girls who sit around mooning and waiting to be asked to the ice cream social. But I wanted her to bend, hurt herself a bit to get to me. I felt like hurting somebody, what with the kicks I'd been taking lately.

"Mr. Dante—"

I turned. "Lou."

Now she smiled, but it cost her something. "Would you…perhaps be interested…." Then she stopped herself, and her eyes went round as poker chips. "Are you married?" she asked, and turned red for asking me so directly.

Not only had I left my clipboard in the car, I'd forgotten to put on my wedding ring, too. So I gave her my Wistful Lover, a look that brought women to heel without fail. And, as regular as four-four time, she sighed.

"I'm sorry to say that I never found any woman to take the place of Carla," I vamped.

"She's the girl who wrote you in Italy? The, um, Dear John letter?"

Then I tossed her my Revisiting Old Pain look, grimacing, acting as though bringing up the two-timing Carla hurt me. Nora Edwards put one hand to her cheek and the other on my arm.

"I'm so sorry, I didn't mean to be—"

"That's all right," I said, a man who was Suffering But Still In Command. "I need to put her behind me."

She went a bit sly on me, sliding her eyes off to the side as she said, as if it had only just come to her, "Perhaps, you and I…could have dinner together sometime, help each other move forward."

This was another of those times that I could have walked out the door, made some cop-out excuse and chalked everything up to a little fun, a shot glass of payback for all the crap I'd been taking. I'd made my point, hadn't I? If I wanted another woman besides Bea, I could get one, and not lose any starch in my shirt. I had done it, so why not just go? But a little man in my head ran over to the record player and put on a platter, and I heard myself say, "That's a wonderful idea."

And just as soon as the words popped out of my mouth, I thought that maybe it wasn't such a cockeyed scheme after all. I couldn't get money from her, but I could get something. What that something might be, I didn't know, but it'd show itself to me at some point. And I'd be ready.

I tried to tell myself it was a swell plan, seeing tiny Nora give her too-bright smile, but there was that bass note I couldn't lose, deep and low, that knew only trouble would come of it.

Chapter eleven

I'd get something from Mrs. Floyd Edwards, but I was going to have to wait and see what it might be. What I needed right now, though, was money. I was just as broke leaving her house as when I first walked up her front path, and boy, didn't I feel like ten kinds of idjit later, sitting on my cracked sofa and nursing a beer. The one woman I wanted, I couldn't reach. Now I had another dame on my hands, and not even a sugar momma. I required cash, moolah, gelt. There was nothing for it but to try and land a few more touches. After I'd gotten enough dough together, I could head downtown to Golden Platters. But, fuck, I sure didn't want to slick myself up and schlep to Union Station to run a few short cons on the chumps getting off the trains, to lift a few billfolds or sneak my hand into a chick's handbag to relieve her of her pin money.

I didn't go for that racket, not unless I was eating my own shoelaces. When I needed money fast, I did my usual routine. At ten the next morning, I rang George Lohr.

"Tell me you've got something for me, Georgie," I said.

"Greenberg, you gotta be some kinda mentalist or something," he bawled. "Not two minutes from now I was gonna call you."

I had no time to chew over the subtle mysteries of the universe. "Lay it on me, brother."

"Polish yourself up good, kid, 'cause I need you in Burbank in an hour." Behind him I could hear the frantic hammering of the con mob throwing together the big store. "I want you swank, you got me? Put a friggin' flower in your buttonhole, grease yourself up. But classy, you cocksucker."

"I dig. Classy. Like you."

"Go fuck yourself," he said cheerfully.

"What's the line?"

"Got some widget manufacturer's kid being strung along on the movie production game. We need you to come in and shill, wave some greenbacks around, the usual gag."

"And what's my take?"

He made himself sound hurt. "Lou, you wound me. Have I ever given you anything less than half a percent?"

"Make it one, Georgie. I'm flat busted."

I covered my ear as he chomped out a laugh. "When ain't you?"

"This is important, buddy."

"Awright," he muttered. "One, but only because you're the shill and not the boost." He sighed. "I hate getting the hard sell from one of my own mob."

"Thanks, Georgie. You're…what are the kids saying now? Oh, yeah. You're drooly."

"Me and Peter Lawford. Here's the address."

I took down the details, scribbling them on the back of a past-due water bill, then threw myself into the shower. I hoped my pinstripe suit wasn't stinking too much—I couldn't remember when I had it cleaned last. Still, if I smeared on enough cologne, the mark in question would just think I was some crass kike producer and buy the tale even more. After a quick hose-down, I shaved and grabbed my clothes. I saw myself in the foggy bathroom mirror. The good thing about my face was that it took well to living badly. Made the bones of my cheeks stand out and my eyes go dark, like a Hollywood dreamboat. I sure as hell felt dreamy, shoving on my least-frayed suspenders and giving my tie a solid shake to work the wrinkles out.

The whole time I was soldering myself together, I was saying a *brucha* for big goy Georgie, bailing me out of a tight spot. I didn't slap mustard and relish all over the idea of lifting wallets. It'd been years since I'd gotten that strapped, and I didn't want to fall. There's a pecking order when it comes to grifters. The big-con men like George Lohr sit at the top, what you might call the nabobs of the racket. Most of them don't rub elbows with us riffraff down below—George being one of the few exceptions. Those guys are cons for life. They've got no ambition past a big touch, the next fat score. Sure, they may live like J.P. Morgan, but grifters they are and all they'll ever be.

Short-con men like me are second on the ladder, not what you'd call high on the social registry, but we weren't billfold lifters or circus grifters working the midway. That's the bottom rung. Gamblers are down there, too, though Arnie showed me that just about all grifters gamble when they're not on the con. Most con men start out picking pockets, kids in crowds with light fingers. A lot get their training wheels with the short con and hope to move up to the big store, but I wasn't going to be in this racket forever. Now, a real pickpocket is his own kind of artist, and you'd flat out crap yourself if you ever saw the best at work. I'm talking about squirreling out wallets right out from under a cop's nose, and not getting collared. Real Houdini-type business. I don't pick pockets anymore if I can help it, but when it comes down to it, these piano-playing fingers of mine can smoothly hoist a purse or pocket.

As I stepped out into the weedy courtyard of my building, it struck me as funny—I was scraping myself together to pretend to be some moneybags out in Burbank when there wasn't anything to eat in my icebox but half a carton of rotten chow mein paid for by none other than George Lohr. The Health Department would piss all over themselves if they knew what lived in that icebox. Irony's a waste of time, though. I had other things to do with myself besides cry in my flat beer.

I didn't doubt, wouldn't let myself, that after I had that chance to cut some sides, things would change, and change large.

I got into my car and pulled out, thinking of the bright future.

The San Fernando Valley had just one thing going for it that the city of Los Angeles didn't—land. Acres of it, stretching out towards the San Gabriel mountains, flat and open. Well at least it used to be, but after a few studios and plants moved out there, some of the orchards and ranches went under the plow. All very country and charming, if you didn't mind the billion degree heat and thick gray cloud of smog that pushed down, stuck in the Valley's basin.

Me, I only hauled myself out to said environs when I was running a con. Things were a little more small town out there, more trusting, so a stranger on the doorstep didn't mean the G-men were after you. For marks, I couldn't beat the Valley. It was good and far away from Santa Monica, so I didn't have to sweat bumping into any suckers I'd played if I wanted to go grab myself a phosphate from the corner drugstore.

George's con mob usually ran their big store out of Hollywood, always someplace different, in case a mark beefed and tried to sniff out the place with some cops. Taking the store out to Burbank was new for Georgie, but I figured he and his gang had their reasons. They ran a tight setup, no crap shoot. For a big store like his, the nearby Warner Bros. lot and Disney studios made the slickest backdrop—and what was the movie business if not painted backdrops and false fronts? Maybe that's why L.A. or nearabouts was such a good spot for cons, everything already unreal and phony with the promise of glamour. And in this low-budget picture, I had my walk-on.

"Same as usual, George?" I asked after giving the peephole man the high sign. I stood in the middle of what looked like a really swank office—oriental carpets on the floor, big potted plants in Chinese vases, heavy wooden file cabinets, real leather chairs, some desks with new typewriters, telephones, and intercom boxes, and sitting behind the desks, sweater girls painting their lips like Michelangelo dabbing at the Sistine Chapel. Everything a rube might need to think he was in a legit producer's office.

George lumbered out of another room where three guys were

busy hanging a giant old oil painting of a racehorse over what looked like a warship-sized mahogany desk. He pulled the stogie out of the corner of his mouth to yell at some kid who'd dropped an armful of film canisters. He rolled his eyes at me. "Goddamn rookies. Kid's somebody's cousin or nephew or some such bullshit tryin' to learn the ropes. Anyway, you know the cross-fire, 'cept this time it's a sword-and-sandal picture."

"What? We gave up on the dancing girls?"

George smirked. "Sorry pal. No more starlets 'auditioning.'"

"The best part of the job," I complained. But then one of the sweater girls finished illuminating her face, caught my eye and gave me a wink while shoving her chest out. I ambled over and sat on the edge of her desk.

"Take a letter, sweetheart," I said. She looked at me like I was screwy. "'To the Angora Producers of the World: Thank you.'"

The girl turned the corners of her mouth up, the best smile she could make. "I don't take dictation," she said. Then she ran her eyes over me and liked what she saw. "Although in your case..."

George smacked me on the shoulder with a clipboard and dragged me away. "Son of a bitch, Greenberg," he laughed. "You and them goddamned dames. Like flies on shit."

"Man, I can't help it if I'm gifted."

"Keep that gift of yours wrapped until after Christmas, buddy. The mark's due in," he checked his watch, "half an hour. Roper called in from Musso & Frank to give us the heads up."

"Who's the roper?"

"Max Romero, one of the Indiana greats."

It's a little-known fact that the best of the C-men hail from Indiana. The word was that if you were at any country fair not but a few minutes, after watching a prized goat being led around a ring by a hayseed in overalls, you'd feel a tap on your shoulder and some farmer would be standing there, leading you to a tent to run a short con. Maybe it's because there's nothing to do in Indiana but think of ways to grift, scheming through the dull summers and dark winters. I never found out how many con men came from the Bronx, aside from yours truly.

I followed George into what was going to be the head honcho's office. His mob had put up nice wooden paneling, like what I thought an old library in some country house ought to look like, and a few of the guys, most of whom I recognized, were putting the last touches on the scene, even a few framed pictures of a wife and kiddies, though I don't think anybody knew just whose wife and whose kiddies.

"Swell job you apes did," I whistled.

"Used to shoot nudie pictures here," George said, ticking a few things off his clipboard, "'til a raid about three weeks ago. Cleared everything out, and I got it for cheap from the former owner."

"So that's what's in the film cans. No wonder the new guy dropped them."

His grin would've made kittens throw themselves into a furnace. "We'll give a private screening when we break the store down."

A heavyish gent in expensive clothes came waddling up to us, running a linen hanky over his mostly bald dome. George introduced him to me as the Philadelphia Kid, although I'd win the bet that his days as a kid were about thirty years stale. Some guys in the racket held on to their names long after they didn't matter anymore, but it was some sort of professional pride to stick with them. I wondered, though, why hold on to something if it doesn't mean anything?

"Philly here's our insideman," George said, draping one king-sized arm over the guy's shoulders. "Came to us from a pay-off store in San Diego. Kid, this is Lou Greenberg. He's gonna be our shill today."

"Didn't you run with Memphis Arnie?" Philly asked me. He drew himself back and worked his fleshy jaw.

"A while ago."

The guy shook his round, gleaming head like a bell tolling. "Shame what happened to him."

I didn't feel like kicking that can around the street, so I just nodded. Sometimes when Arnie's name came up, folks started looking at me cockeyed, so I tried to keep my trap shut whenever it happened. Maybe I was to blame for what happened to Arnie, maybe not. He was a big boy, he could take care of himself. Wasn't he the one who taught me the trade? And if he got himself into a tight spot with a beefing mark, then who wouldn't think he could handle the situation? I sure did, and left him to it, but next thing I knew, I was playing hobo and hopping trains to get the fuck out of Independence, Missouri, before the mark came gunning for me. There wasn't anything I could have done. I didn't pack heat, almost no grifters did, and I couldn't have clubbed the guy with a metronome.

I cried like a girl as the train carried me away—but none of that changed anything. Arnie was dead, facedown on the floor of a betting parlor with the marked-up tickets, his beautiful suit stained with blood and dirt, and I was still alive.

"Lou's okay," George said when I stayed mum. "Done this with me, what, a dozen times?"

"At least," I said, and didn't let my eyes stay too long on Philly. I didn't want to see the way he looked at me. I moved away from them both. "I'm going to have myself a smoke and get set for the show."

Before anyone could speak, I found a side door and slipped out, then made myself busy getting a cigarette. Outside, it was heavy and hot, the way it always was in Burbank, but I felt chilly all the way down. The alley was white and empty, stinging my eyes. I made myself blink over and over.

"Goddamned gorilla," I muttered to myself, trying to get my lighter to work. I clicked and clicked, but the flame wouldn't come up. I wanted to deck the big fat Philadelphia Kid. What the hell was the use of bringing up old sauerkraut? There wasn't anything I could do about it now, and didn't he think that if I could snap my fingers and go back, things might have been different? There were too many things I could waste time wishing I did or didn't do, and if I went down that alley, I'd get jumped for sure. Now here I was, knocked sideways by some fat schlub in a hundred dollar suit, and just before the show. You don't rattle someone in the mob right before the con goes down. Everybody knows that. Who was this joker, anyway? He couldn't have been a big deal if I hadn't heard of him. I'd learned all the old-time players, what their cons had been, what towns they operated out of, from Arnie. I kept working my Zippo, trying to get it to light. Still nothing.

"Can I help with that?"

I threw a glance over my shoulder and saw that one of the sweater girls—a brunette in something fuzzy and blue, the tweed of her skirt holding tight around her hips like a last chance—had come out the back and was shaking a box of matches at me with her long, painted fingers. In her other hand, she held a cigarette. Her story wouldn't be any different from any other pretty chick in this town: trying to be the next Linda Darnell, finding about thirty thousand other girls just like her all lined up outside Casting—most of them willing to get on their backs or suck a cock or two to get where they want to go—then stumbling onto the other side of the street, that is to say, where it's a bit more shady. And what could she do? She couldn't go back home, not after the way she left, and her name was different now. No, let them all think she went and made it big. She might even pen her best friend a postcard now and then, saying how gee-dandy everything was out in the Land of Dreams, she hoped her pal's job at the perfume counter wasn't dullsville, and then she would hustle out the door to play escort for good-time boys in the Hollywood Hills. Maybe she'd been one of the stars of the nudie picture ring and George got her a job pretending to be a secretary for the big store.

She was a distraction from butterball Philly and his fish eyes about Arnie, so I turned up the wattage with my smile. "Do you think you can handle the job?" I asked her.

She took out a match, lit her own smoke, then held the flame to mine. After it caught and I took a drag, she shook out the match and dropped it under the spike of her heel. "I do all right," she murmured and she wasn't bad at it, pretending to be Lauren Bacall in *To Have and Have Not*, which I could see was playing inside her head. If she couldn't land the part in the pictures, she figured, then she could play it on the streets. I almost whistled like Bogie, just to throw her a bone, poor kid.

We stood and leaned against the wall together, smoking under the gray heat of the Valley sun, not saying much because I knew what role she wanted me to play: the Silent, Handsome Tough Guy, with a little Troubled Soul thrown into the shaker. It didn't bother me to keep quiet. I wasn't much in the mood for schmoozing. Figured whatever she wanted, she'd get around to it, eventually.

"You do this kind of thing a lot?" she asked, tipping her head towards the door—it was propped open with a bust of Napoleon and we could see George's mob still arranging furniture.

I shrugged. "Once in a while." No sense giving her too much. That wasn't what she wanted, anyway.

She dragged on her cigarette and blew the smoke out, practiced and smooth. "This is my first."

I waited, then, "It's not so hard."

When she took her Lucky Strike out of her mouth, she left a ring of red paint around the end, which, for some reason, stuck me right through, something sharp and sad about it. "I keep telling myself that it's no different from acting," she said. "It's just a part like everything else."

"When it comes down to it, sweetheart, we're all acting." Kiss my ass, that wasn't bad: exactly the sort of thing one of her hard-boiled heroes might throw out when the lead starts flying. She ate it up, too. She turned and faced me, propping her hip against the wall, and with the late morning light coming down, I saw that she wasn't a newly-opened April bud, but hovering around twenty-eight, which for a woman, by Hollywood standards, was about as fresh as year-old eggs.

"What's your name?" she asked me.

"Louis."

"I'm Myrna." Or Violet, or Eloise, or Brenda, what did it matter?

"Pretty name," I said.

"You want to go get a drink when we finish up here?" She raised her eyes up to the sky then back down. She made a comic grimace, which didn't suit her. She did better with the hard-boiled stuff. "Or a cup of coffee. Maybe it's too early for a drink."

I couldn't figure it. When I get the come-on from a girl, a hot number like this one in particular, it wasn't much sweat to stir up some enthusiasm. At the least, this encounter would net me some kisses or gropes, and it was pretty likely I'd get a lay out of her. Never did Louis Greenberg refuse a blanket jam session with a nice-looking chick. But, standing in that alley with Minnie or Mabel, all I could find in my pockets was sadness. For her—a girl from the Carolinas who was told all her life she was beautiful and special, then came to Los Angeles and learned she was cheaper than newsprint, and all she wanted now was for somebody, anybody, to look at her again like she was beautiful and special, not last week's sausage—and me—pretending to be a big shot producer but scrounging for pennies to record some sides. And then Beatrice's face popped into my head, her dark stare full of sorrow and fire, and I couldn't even muster the energy for a pity fuck for the sweater girl standing next to me.

"It's never too early for a drink." Which wasn't an answer, exactly. Still hedging my bets.

I was saved from saying anything definite by George, sticking his enormous head out the door and snapping, "Come on, you two, the mark's gonna be here in five."

The girl fixed me with a *Well, here we go* look before dropping her cigarette to the ground and crushing it under the toe of her cheap shoe. She boom-chick-a-boomed past George, a walk perfected after years of trying it in front of a mirror. George stared at me.

"What?" I took a last drag then flicked the butt into the alley.

"I never met nobody who could land him so much pussy," he laughed.

"I didn't do anything," I bitched as I followed him in, but I won't kid you, it made me glad to hear the envy in that warship George's voice, and I sure didn't tell him that the most his hired floozy could get out of me was a case of the blues.

"One of these days, you and me are gonna sit down and you're gonna tell me how you do it."

"Grow another five inches, and then we'll talk."

"Five inches *where?*"

I fixed him with my Riddle of the Sphinx and walked away to take my place. I put away the gloomy pass made by Myrtle or Myrna, the Philadelphia Kid's exhuming of Arnie's body, Nora Edwards waiting for a man to walk through her door, Beatrice giving in to small and stupid minds. It was time to earn some cash and get myself out of this rotten little world.

The first few times I shilled, I got nervous, hands going cold, sweat down the back, the whole megillah. I didn't want to crack out of turn and ruin everything. Every now and then, I'd still get the hee-bie-jeebies when I waited before the big store con. I was a solo man, and didn't have to stew about somebody blowing their lines—I was writer, director, and star of the show. If I said the wrong thing at the wrong time, I could cover my tracks, no problem. Like when I played piano. It was just me at the keys. Even the backing band didn't count. When other guys came into the con picture, though, suddenly I had folks relying on me, banking that I'd give my patter to convince the mark. Sure, the guys of the mob were pros, dancing on the balls of their feet like prizefighters. They could smooth-talk anybody, even if some idiot threw a wrench into the machine. It took a lot to make a con curdle. But I didn't like folks counting on me.

Before Max, our roper, brought the mark in, everyone went over their lines, with George filling in for the outside man *and* the pigeon. A real jam-up guy, that George, wearing about fifty hats and never missing a cue. Once he was satisfied that we were airtight, he gave us the thumbs up to wait in our positions. That meant, I regret to say, being alone with the Philadelphia Kid in the private office.

We just stood there, two stopped grandfather clocks, cooling our heels until Max and the mark showed. There were times when I liked silence—when I was with a mark, sometimes with women, even by myself. I could lie around my apartment and not have the radio on or play record or sit at the piano—but in that phony producer's office as I stood at the bookcase, looking at but not reading the spines of the prop books, I felt Philly chewing slow and steady on a cigar, his eyes glued to me like I was going to filch his dear momma's cameo brooch. It sent crawlies up and down my hide.

"So, you guys already put the mark on the send?" I asked, trying to fill up that yawning gap in the room. I hated myself for even trying to play nice with the Philadelphia Kid, when I should have told him to go shove that stogie up his ass and let the smoke pour out of his ears.

Philly unplugged the stogie from his mouth and said, as flat as a beat cop's foot, "Yeah." That was it. He jammed the cigar back between his teeth and glared at me.

"Likewise, I'm sure," I said, then bowed. "Please give your majesty my regrets for trying to make conversation."

The cigar came out again. "Look kid," he started to bark.

"Aren't you the Kid?" I asked.

That matzo ball didn't like me getting fresh. He stomped over to me and stuck the glowing end of the stogie in my general direction. "I don't like you," he spat. "I heard what went down in Missouri with Memphis Arnie and don't think you aren't responsible, 'cause you are. You ratted him out. I can't believe you'd still show your mug after that. You're yellow."

It didn't bother me to be called yellow. I'd heard it all during the war, 4-F papers or no, and it got so that it meant about as much as a baby crying. Irritating, but I could shut it out with a snap of my newspaper—usually.

"I didn't rat Arnie out. Neither of us saw the guy coming until it was too late."

"You ran, though," Philly said, jabbing that stogie so close I thought he'd burn my buttons. "When you coulda stayed and done something."

"Done what? Sing 'Mammy?'"

Before the Philadelphia Kid could say anything else, George's voice came over the intercom box on the desk. "Mark's here. Wait for my sign. It'll be less than two."

Philly went back to gnawing on his cigar and I had to put about ten feet between us to stop myself popping him right in the face, which would not have been ideal timing. I made myself think of Ellington's "A Lull At Dawn" to cool down. It wasn't bop, but I needed something old and comfortable surrounding me, the slow liquid of it washing down, suspending me, like a sustained note that never faded.

George gave the sign, a quick buzz on the intercom, and Philly and I stepped forward, throwing open the doors to the office and laughing like old pals. He slapped me on the back a few times, and only I noticed how hard those slaps were. Standing in the middle of the office was Max and our chosen mark. The place was buzzing as if it were the real deal; phones ringing, girls walking back and forth with files. Nobody would ever have guessed that the whole thing was fake. Max, naturally, sported his killer suit, he was anybody's rich, generous brother-in-law. The mark gawped at us, some gangly guy with too much cash and not enough brains—which is every guy I've met who was rolling in it. I bet he was some steel baron's kid, with his low C average at Yale, amounting to a big disappointment to his folks and stuffed full of money to keep him from embarrassing himself. And now the kid was pushing forty and still Daddy wouldn't let him into the office, so here was his chance to show the old man that he wasn't a complete washout. The mark didn't know the con mob was onto him and about to fleece Pater's loser of a son.

"Charlie," I said, doing my best Well-Heeled Investor, and throwing in a bit of Rich Jew just for extra sauce, a guy with nothing but money in the bank and the wisdom to know what to do with it, "this picture's going to make you and me wealthy men. But I want in on it fast, understand? I don't want to lose my share to somebody else. A controlling interest, understand?"

"Of course, Mr. Kaplan," the Philadelphia Kid boomed. "It's a sure thing. Just write a check and we can start rolling."

"Check?" I repeated as if the idea was absurd. "No, no, Charlie. It'd have to clear the bank and all sorts of nonsense. I want in on this *now*."

I pulled from the inside pocket of my suit the boodle, a giant wad of real and fake cash I flashed in front of the mark. George had slipped it to me earlier, one of the props no big store con did without. It was supposed to be almost a hundred grand, but even with the paper and low bills, it still made up to almost twenty thousand, which I would've happily run off with if George and his gang didn't know where I lived. It felt good in my hand. I waved it around and took a few more loose bills from my pocket and wallet, just to let the mark see that cash was in abundance here at this producer's office. The boodle's key when playing the big store. It gets the mark excited, seeing how fast it flows in those parts and wanting some for himself. Nobody's honest, even the people who think they could stand up against Abe Lincoln and make the guy bawl his eyes out.

Seeing the huge bundle of money, the mark's eyes just about jumped out of his head and danced a hornpipe. He gave me the elevator, looking me up and down, checking me out, and I had him.

"Here's a hundred thousand dollars," I said, laid-back and casual, it didn't mean anything to me, just a tiny tile in the mosaic of my wealth. "That's merely a down payment to make sure I don't get ousted from the picture."

Philly snorted and hemmed, he couldn't possibly, not really necessary, but in the end, just like we rehearsed, I jammed it into his hand. Then I whammed him on the back, getting even. "Can't wait, Charlie. This gladiator picture is going to be fantastic."

"Sure is, Mr. Kaplan," he coughed. We shook hands, a little contest to see who could squeeze the other's bones into paste, and then with a wave I threw on my hat and glided out the door. Myrna or Myrtle tried to give me a wink on my way past her, but I didn't even toss her a look. Seymour Kaplan or whoever I was didn't waste his time with office bunnies. The sound I heard as I shut the door behind me was the sound of the mark falling right into the con. It was the same schtick we'd run over and over: the mark was an out-of-state investor laying down capital to finance a picture, but if he wanted to make any money on the deal, he'd have to pay up front, in cash, and quick, because of some business with filing papers. An under-the-table scheme that'd net a lot of profit for our dear mark. No paper trail would exist to "protect" the mark against nosy studios wanting everything square. Which would suit the mob fine, too. There would be no record of anything ever going down.

Just in case the mark was watching, there was a car waiting for me, a glossy Packard driven by a colored guy in a uniform. I checked myself to keep from talking to him. I didn't even know the guy's name, and Seymour Kaplan didn't talk to coloreds. The chauffer opened the door for me and, after I got in and settled, a hawk in his nest, we drove off to a bar around the corner to wait for George's all clear.

The bar was a studio watering hole, a real working man's joint, where grips and gaffers would head after work and gulp down beers, beef a while about the bastard assistant director or the wardrobe girl being a terrific fuck. At this hour of the day, only a few stuntmen sat at the bar, bragging about concussions and compound fractures. I had to leave the driver outside—the Valley was most decidedly not integrated, but I went outside a minute and took him a Coke, which he wasn't expecting.

Two hours later, George rang the bar and gave the all clear. I threw down some cash for the Postum—I hadn't wanted to get drunk before the meet-and-greet and Golden Platters—and stepped out into the dazzling nothing of Burbank. The driver and I went back and were met by a cheerful mob, though the Philadelphia Kid still wasn't handing me any prize ribbons.

The touch had been taken and the mark blown off. If he tried the phone number he was given, he'd get the operator telling him it wasn't in service anymore. If he went down to the producer's office, he'd find only blank walls. And if he tried to go to the cops, they wouldn't help him because of Dave, George's fixer, who set everything up with the law ahead of time with a juicy kickback. But the mark wouldn't go to the cops—if he did he'd have to admit that he'd been played for a dupe, hadn't been quite kosher with his money—so he'd have to explain to his pop that two hundred grand of his allowance had gone poof, and could he have an advance until next quarter.

I forgot about Philly and his skunk eye as I drove downtown to Golden Platters. I had close to two thou in my pocket, thanks to that morning's work, and what did I care who thought I was yellow, so long as the money was mine.

Chapter twelve

There are different ways folks look at you. Some of them are swell, such as, say, a woman, female loveliness packed into a girdle and garters, staring at you like a T-bone on Tuesdays. Or some jazz guy giving a look when you're at the piano and reckoning you to be as fine a musician as anyone within the Northern Hemisphere. Or a mark's open and generous faith, buying everything you say, gazing at you as if you were handing him salvation on a plate. Or even your father, in his chair late at night, turning his eyes to you over the top of his newspaper and in them, in his face, you see the full depths of a love you might think would never be lost.

But then there's ways people can look at you that aren't so swell. Like when a woman rolls over in the morning and her paint's smeared and you can tell she'd been hoping for the picket fence but wound up taking the wrong streetcar, and all you want is to get out of there before she reaches for the bottle next to the bed. Or the shut-down, hostile faces that ice you out when you're trying to audition for a gig and you aren't one of their set, so no thanks, no nightly show at the Paradise for you, bub. Sneering, borscht-faced GIs on leave, trying to act big in front of their good time girls and you just know that in a minute they're going to let on with a lot of names like "dodger," "shirker," "gutless creep," or "kike fink," and if you ignore them then they're going to get vinegary, but if you try and say something to them, it won't be long until you're trying to duck a clock cleaning.

Or maybe the look on a woman's face when she's given up the fight and tells you she needs to think, she needs time on her own, it doesn't matter if you and her have been together for nearly two years, that you knew each other upwards and down, you and she together sound as high and good as a tight duet, who cares what color your skin is, nosir, it's over, and because she's caved to the opinions of a bunch of folks with brains no bigger than a demisemiquaver.

I don't care for those looks, not a bit. But just when I thought I had my list of all-time worst ways a body can look at me, along came Sam Knapp of Golden Platters Recording, who stared at me across his desk like I was the squarest, thickest and most slaphappy ignoramus he'd ever clamped his eyes on. If you have not experienced such a look, I cannot offer you my recommendations on it.

"So you're just gonna walk in here, no producer, no nothing—"

"I've got money—"

"And throw down a wad of cash, and then, boom, presto, we got you a recording session? Then what? We cut some wax, press you up a few 78s, and you give 'em to your girl for Christmas?" He wanted to laugh but couldn't, just gawked at me with his mouth moving, like someone had come up behind him and walloped him with a sap, but he was too big and dumb to notice.

"It's not like that," I said, and I didn't know whether to deck this *k'nacker*, bawl into his hand, or wait patiently for the Cunard Line to fall from the sky and smash me flat. I was also entertaining the idea of running into traffic.

"Pal," the delightful Sam Knapp said as he lit a cigarette, "I don't know from under what motherfucking piano bench you've crawled, but there's no way I'm gonna let some piano jockey right off the street come into *my* recording studio and waste *my* goddamned time on some, what, ego project?"

"But I don't come from the street. I've got education. Studied with Leopold Israel."

"Who?" Knapp demanded without much interest.

"Let me at least play something for you." Man, I hated hearing myself beg like this. Made me want to turn myself inside out. I'd been laying down smooth patter for years, and did I once have to wheedle and plead? This is what I got for taking the straight scheme instead of working an angle. Like a schnook, I'd walked into Golden Platters and been completely legit with Knapp. So this honesty of mine, what did it get me? A fine thank-you.

Knapp showed what you would call no concern about my moral dilemma. I thought he might slide under his desk and fall asleep. Instead, he said, almost snoring, "You could be the next Vladimir Horowitz, but if you come ambling in here without a producer, or hell, anybody except your own self with your own fucking scratch, then we got nothing to talk about. And let me tell you, you're gonna hear the same story all over town. No studio will even sneeze at you."

"I'm no dope," I insisted.

He shook his head and pushed back the flips of hair that had come unstuck from his head. "Maybe not, but there's a whole lotta other names that fit you." Outside his office, there were folk walking up and down the hallway, acting important, and I could hear a singer rehearsing some pop tune with a five-piece combo. It was all boy scout and glossy, and, the way Knapp was looking at me, getting farther away by the second. He gave me a little wave forward, and even though I didn't want to, I found myself leaning in.

"If you want to cut sides, you gotta get yourself a producer," he said, a grown-up talking to a baby. I almost burped myself. Then I'd have the satisfaction of spitting up all over his face and big, important desk.

"So I'll get one," I said, and he did laugh then. I didn't like his teeth. There were too many of them, and I wouldn't have minded fixing that problem.

"Sure, sure," he snorted, "why doncha run out onto the corner and pick one up. They stand around like hookers, waiting for some musical john." He wiped his bulgy eyes. "You want a producer, then get yourself noticed. Headline at one of Billy Berg's clubs—"

"I'm not there, yet."

"Then get a gig as a sideman, sit in on one of the jam sessions. That's the way to do it, chum."

"Don't you think I've tried that?"

He was bored with me already. When the phone rang he picked it up straight off, barked into it, "Yeah?", then cupped his hand over the receiver. "Maybe you ought to consider a new line of work," he jeered. "I hear they're hiring at Santa Anita. You'd feel right at home there—all that horseshit." He cracked himself up as I stomped out of the office. "And tell Sonny not to send any more of his stumblebum friends without producers," he hollered after me.

Me on the street. After the fourth try and still my cigarette didn't light, I threw in the towel. My hands wouldn't stop shaking and the damned Zippo wouldn't spark. I tossed the unlit smoke into the gutter, and thought about doing the same with my lighter, but some girl in Albuquerque gave it to me when I was making my way out west, and even though I couldn't remember her name or her face, I'd kept it in a rare bout of sentimentality. A memento of the kid I used to be.

But even as I was stashing the Zippo inside my jacket I couldn't figure what use I had for mementos or even for that long-ago kid. None of them could stomp back inside and stuff a bass guitar up good ol' Sam Knapp's ass. I saw a phone booth and kicked around the idea of calling Sonny, giving him the what for, but I knew it wasn't Sonny's fault, just me being green, as green as I was when I thumbed my way out of New York. It'd been a long time since I'd felt like that, and I won't say that it was something I enjoyed.

The traffic on Alvarado kicked up dust, choking me. I had to get out of there, but I didn't want to drive, not yet. I had enough sense rolling around in my head to know that if I got behind the wheel, I'd wind up zooming all the way to Hermosa and straight into the ocean, taking a bunch of folks with me. So I started to walk. I didn't much care which way I was headed, so long as it was away from Golden Platters and the scene of my flop.

The worst of it was that I felt as much of a chump as any of my marks, but the one who'd done the conning was me. I'd duped myself into thinking it would be as easy as getting some gelt together and handing it over to the fine proprietor of Golden Platters. Nothing ever came so simple. But just like any mark, I'd believed the lie I told myself, that something decent and real could be gotten without a lot of trouble. Sure, I could lose something valuable, easy as a chorus girl, but the getting it, that's where the trouble came.

I was heading up the hill, crossing Temple, towards Echo Park. The midday sun hit down hard, a hammer blow to the head. I missed the cool fog of Santa Monica, and so I staggered towards the lake, thinking that there had to be some relief found in its phony, glassy water. But just like everything in this piece of crap town, Echo Lake was a sham, knocked together to seem romantic and pastoral in the middle of blasted city blocks and scrub hills. I'd pick up a paper and see a picture of boats on the lake, dragging for another body.

You wouldn't see me come floating up from the silty bottom any time soon, bloated and soggy, but as I crossed the fringe of park and sat down on a bench to stare at its surface, I sure felt like heaving myself into the drink right then. Here I was, having suckered myself, and Sam Knapp had been there with a front row seat. That'd been one of the worst parts. I knew that even as I watched kids casting their lines into Echo Lake, Knapp was yukking it up in his office, telling everybody about the sap pianist Louis Greenberg and getting a good laugh out of them. The very idea made me want to crawl inside my hat. Or set fire to that recording studio. Both options sounded pretty good at that point.

"*Helado, nieves, paletas.*" A tiny Mexican guy pushing an insulated cart stopped next to me, the bell on the handle chiming as it swung back and forth. "Ice cream, *señor*? Popsicle?"

I couldn't remember the last time I had ice cream in the park. More than a handful of years. Fuck, if I wanted to be a grown man sitting on a park bench eating an ice cream, then that was my business. "What flavors do you have?"

He opened the top of the cart and a gust of cloudy cold air whiffed out. "*Cajeta*, mamey, sapodilla, mango, guava."

"Uh…any chocolate?"

His dark arms disappeared into the white cart as he moved boxes around. "*No mas, señor.* The boys got the last ones." He pointed to the spill of kids sitting on the edge of the lake, fishing poles propped between their knees, lapping away at chocolate ice cream cones, smug.

"How about *paleta fresa?*" the vendor asked. "Strawberry popsicle?"

It wasn't the top of my hit parade, but at least I knew what a strawberry was. "Sure. How much?"

"Five cents."

I dug a dime from my pocket and handed it to the guy. He started to give me change, but I waved him off. "Us working slobs need to stick together."

He didn't know what the hell I was talking about, but he handed over a beautiful pink popsicle, rosy as a girl's tush, then rolled away. I heard him crying "*Helado, nieves, paletas,*" and the bling! of the bell, all the way down Bellevue Avenue, hitting a minor key, blue and dying, until it faded away under the sounds of traffic. It shifted and moved, that sound, weaving itself into the melody that I carried inside me, the one I always sought but could never quite pin down. Later, later, I promised myself, I would write it down and make it part of something real.

For now, though, I would let the music play in my head and leave it there. For a long while, I sat on that bench, sucking at the strawberry popsicle—it was pretty tasty, too, milky and fresh, like frozen summer—not letting my mind settle on any one thing for too long. I had to squeeze something good out of the day, even if it was just sitting with my *paleta* in the park. Here it was, four days to Halloween, and I was sweating under the palm trees, instead of wrapping myself up in heavy overcoats and dreading another bitter winter of mudrooms and slush. Not so bad. Nothing to knock the polish off your brogans, but not bad.

But popsicles melt and get your hand sticky and eventually you have to get up, throw the damp stick away, and find something to clean up with. I gave my hands a quick rinse in a drinking fountain and walked north on Glendale Boulevard. All kinds of garbage was blowing through my mind and I needed to get myself moving so I could work it out. My brain did its best work with me on foot.

North of the park I passed the big dome of the Angelus Temple. They still held revivalist meetings there every Sunday, with all that hollering and Praise Jesusing, which I can tell you, as a Jew, gave me the willies. Our congregation at Beth Shalom sat, shifting and squeaking, muttering their prayers in a language only half knew, then in a groaning wave, they'd stand when the ark was opened and the Torah paraded up and down the temple. It was just as exciting as you'd picture it, about the farthest thing from leaping up and down and shouting Hallelujah! a body could find. Even now as I went past the Foursquare Church, I heard yowling and deathly organ music inside, something like a funeral on a coke bender. Did all that squealing bring those folks any closer to God? Closer than Cantor Moskowitz and his long, slow slide of Hebrew? Either way, it was all just ways of plugging up the silence. If there was something like a guy upstairs leading the band, he probably didn't care for rackety tambourine-banging or the boring rise and fall of endless Hebrew chants. So I'd leave my worship to what I did at the piano.

I hadn't even been given a chance to play for Sam Knapp. He didn't care to know what I was capable of, the worlds I channeled when I sat down at the bench and put my hands onto the keys. I didn't want to believe that the princely Mister Knapp had pronounced a death sentence on me cutting sides, that from behind his desk he'd spewed out the final say on whether or not I was going to go anywhere as a musician.

As I kept heading north up the hill, past the oldest houses I'd seen since I got to Los Angeles, the gingerbread homes with pointed roofs and towers that already looked haunted, I couldn't figure a way around what Knapp had said. I wasn't sure he was being straight. Would other recording studios in the city tell me the same thing, that without a producer I was as useless as a blind man at a cootch-dancing show? I didn't want to believe it, but I had a churning in my gut that told me he wasn't feeding me a line. If every two-bit musician could scrape together enough money to cut sides, no one would be able to drive or walk or scratch their nose, there'd be too many records crowding up the sidewalks and spilling into the street. Discs full of painful music, slammed together by folks with no talent and less skill.

There had to be a way I could cut a record without a producer, but the how of it kept dancing away.

I'd never gone to San Francisco, but I'd heard plenty from George on his jazz trips to know that the hills they got up there would give a sherpa something to think about. But as I huffed my way up the steep streets around Echo Park, I bet that those same sherpas would take one look at these and sit right down to have a good strong snoot of whiskey. And then turn around and head for the gentle knolls of Tibet. At least some city planner thought to put in some stairs. I'm pretty sure my heart up and exploded as I went up the long steps at Baxter and Avon, and there couldn't have been any sweat left in me—it was all in my shirt—but something in me knew I had to get to the top of those hills.

When I reached the summit, I threw my *tuchus* down onto a low wall. Panting, exhausted, a degree away from self-combustion, I took off my hat, pulled out a cigarette and lit up. As I puffed, I looked out on my broad, dusty kingdom, a hazy mash of buildings spreading like gossip over the hills and flats of the Los Angeles basin. Down there were thousands of women adjusting the seam on their stockings, hoping someone would pay to see where those seams ended, cops getting cash slipped into their hands and looking the other way, downtown detectives sitting in late model cars and cooling their heels as they waited for the cheating husband to come out of the motel, hopheads slipping greasily into alleys to land a score, motorcycle thugs and evangelists, faded chorus girls and police line-up regulars, drag queens and jockeys, hash-slingers, finks, stud dogs, blab sheet scribblers, tab-lifters, whoopee mamas, and jazz musicians.

From up here, it looked puny and sad, the mice running their mazes, not even aware that mice they were and all they'd ever be. Tiny cars tootling from one end of the city to the other, as if they had somewhere to go, as if it mattered. Apartments being built to house another crop of suckers. The wheels of commerce that existed just to keep itself going, making nothing, serving nobody. All the pigeons and marks and suckers and chumps whose only use was to be fleeced. Sam Knapp could be crushed right under my pinkie finger from on top of that hill, him and every guy like him.

What a load of crap it seemed, the useless striving, the penny-ante moves towards significance. Didn't those saps know that no matter how much they dreamed of the movies, they were just the audience, eyes in the seats, who could only watch and wish and rot?

They were pegs on the cribbage board to be moved around to suit me. Screw Sam Knapp. He was nothing to me. He was nothing to anyone. My only mistake with him was being square with him, as if he operated on my level, which he didn't. I wanted to go back and find some way to bilk him, but even as I thought about it, I heard Arnie's voice in my head: "Son, once the con gets personal, it's time to disembark the ship. We are professionals, not hard-racket hooligans or street-corner vigilantes. Base emotion has no place in the cool playing arena of the grift."

Much as I hated to agree, I knew Arnie was right. The melody goes sour when the chords jar too hard.

I missed Arnie just then, his calm presence and the comfort of his tailoring. The beautiful suits he wore provided more reassurance than a rabbi's hand on my head. When I was just starting out as a grifter, if a con hadn't gone particularly well, it was almost worth it to have Arnie sit beside me in the excellence of his jacket and say it would be all right, tomorrow we would try again, this time for certain it will work, and I believed him, believed him with all my heart. I could trust him with that much.

Once I asked him why, out of all the sniveling kids at lunch counters across this grand and beautiful nation of ours, he had picked me as his protégé. It didn't make sense, me knowing cons about as well as my mother could play polo. Surely there had to be other young guys out there who showed more promise. All I showed that day in St. Louis were the bones of my wrists poking out from the cuffs of my too-small suit.

"But I saw it, *here*," Arnie had said to me as he laid his hand over my eyes. For a moment, I was in darkness, engulfed in the rough velvet of Arnie's hand, and his smell of tobacco and certainty. Then he took his hand away. "Your clever hunger, your belief in yourself at the expense of everyone around you. No, don't pretend you're insulted. It's a rare and beautiful gift to be so selfish. One that a grifter must have to succeed. And you, my dear boy," he had added with a slap on my shoulder, "have an abundance of that gift."

I didn't feel so gifted sitting at the top of that hill. Arnie existed only in memory, his reassurance and comfort gone. So I sat, alone, and smoked, and watched the tiny city go about its tiny business, running the problem through my mind, picking it apart, studying it from all angles. A pile of butts collected at my feet and the sun turned Los Angeles yellow as it slipped under the skyline. I got hungry, then smoked my hunger away. The streets started to clot with rush hour traffic, all the people running home after a long day doing nothing. Some of those folks had wives and kids waiting for them, ready to pounce and tear them apart with their disappointed hopes. But there were others who came home to a silent room, a single chair at a counter, a loaf of bread and cold cuts in the icebox, just the voices on the radio to keep them company until it was time for bed and then it all started up again. Men slipping in and out of life. Brown and pale. Like pieces of toast that fall under the table and nobody notices until they crunch and crumble under your shoe.

And that's when I got my answer. The little man inside my head ran over and put the needle down on the turntable. It seemed so obvious and plain, I actually laughed out loud. Which caused a guy walking his dog nearby not a little unease. He and the dog trotted away from me quickly, both man and beast casting looks over their shoulders like I was missing a baseball card or two, but I didn't care. I stood and flicked my cigarette away, then started down the long stairs. I couldn't tell if my head was spinning because I'd eaten nothing over the last twenty-four hours but a popsicle, or if it was my scheme getting me hopped up. It didn't matter, either way. I would show Sam Knapp and Beatrice and everybody else that there were some things even *I* would fight for.

Chapter thirteen

Cairo Jacks was the kind of waterfront place where sailors and longshoremen came in to be rolled, get into fights, swill cheap, watered rotgut, purchase the company of honky-tonk angels, and generally make their doting parents proud. You wouldn't think dives like that needed some guy on the piano for a pleasant atmosphere, but if that's what they wanted, I was there to give it to them. It was the only gig I'd been able to line up, and gigs I needed.

The scheme I'd hatched was going to cost me plenty, more than I'd scored from the big store con I helped George play earlier. So when I got back to my place after leaving Echo Park, I called around trying to scare up whatever I could. And with all the night-clubs, watering holes, lounges and private parties in Los Angeles, you'd think there'd be something, anything, for a guy such as myself. But, no. Nobody needed me, and I mean nobody. I almost rang the Carmel Club, but remembered that I'd quit, and Len Holstadt wasn't the sort of guy who'd take a faceful of smoke and then give me a kiss on both cheeks to welcome me in. After about the someteenth call and still no luck, I gave it a wild stab and tried somebody I knew from an after-hours club I played almost a year ago. And got what I was itching for. This guy needed somebody to fill in for him at a gig, and by the way, the joint was down in San Pedro but the pay wasn't all that bad, who was I to turn my nose up? I couldn't go back to Gardena, and I had no other prospects lined up. Okay, I said to this guy, I'll be there, why not?

Cairo Jacks hunched at the corner of Fifth and Beacon, right opposite the water. And with a name like Cairo Jacks, it was as charming as you'd suppose. I didn't know what to expect when I got down there, but you can imagine the glee that burst inside my heart when I found it at the end of a row of tattoo parlors, cooch dancer shacks, pool halls, and clip joints. As I pulled up, two sailors on liberty were busy investigating the contents of each other's heads by slamming them against the pavement. Seemed like a waste of effort—they wouldn't find anything in there. A b-girl shrieked at them from a doorway. I almost spun on my heel and left. Even the shabby Carmel Club was better than this. But I needed that cash, so long as it was promised. I just hoped that my car would still be waiting for me in one piece when I left, not broken down for a chop shop on Figueroa.

It didn't get better inside. You think you know what these kinds of dives look like, with them being so picturesquely portrayed in the movies, but once you actually plant your feet in a place like that, it doesn't seem quite so romantic. Dark and grimy, who-knows-what slopped and shining on the sticky floor, the smell of beer and piss, men tossing back their drinks with a steady and professional air, somebody hollering at someone else, and you don't doubt that any minute you're going to find a shank sticking out of your ribs. Some guy in a stained peacoat coughing away until you think his lungs are going to shoot out onto the ground and skitter off under the barstools, shivering. Me, I'd been in joints like this before, but that didn't mean I liked cooling my heels in them.

A woman as wide as a whaling ship met me at the bar. On her arm was enough ink for a city-wide edition. Somebody's daughter all grown up and scaring the shit out of adult men. She eyed my suit, my hands, saw that I wasn't a seaman. "I'm Shanghai Mary," she sneered.

I figured the only thing Chinese about her was her mustache. "You the piano player?"

"I'm from the Nobel Peace Prize Committee."

Maybe she smiled, or maybe it was indigestion; both looked uncomfortable. "Don't want nobody cute. Just play the goddamned piano. You get a dime note."

Ten bucks wasn't anything to write an opera about, but that two grand I had stashed in the sleeve of a Coleman Hawkins record had to stay untouched, and there was still rent to pay and maybe even food to buy, though cigarettes and booze came first. I wanted to say nuts to Shanghai Mary and nuts to Cairo Jacks, but I didn't have a choice. I followed her meaty digit as she pointed to a miserable upright crouching in the corner, right next to the guy hacking up his first Communion wafer.

"I won't tell you how to run your business," I said, "but what do you want a piano player for? You've got a jukebox already."

"The girls like it," she barked, and by girls, she must've meant the crapped-out chippies wearily getting felt up by plastered gobs. Those chicks didn't quite strike me as real music lovers, but who was I to argue with the meanest butch prowling the waterfront? "Now if you're done giving me the what for," grunted Miss Shanghai Mary, the delicate flower, "sit your fancy, scrawny ass down and play some fucking music awreddy."

Sat I did, and play I did, less 'cause I needed the money than I was afeared that if I didn't, Shanghai Mary would yank out my spine and make me play Moonlight Serenade on it. As gigs went, it wouldn't go down as one of the finer venues. I went through a set of standards and pop—I thought that bebop wasn't going to be much appreciated in such a class establishment—ducking the now and then bottle hitting the wall above the piano which served as a request from the patrons to kindly play another tune. The guy coughing himself blue served as my sideman. Rough-faced working girls leaned against the upright while slow, sticky tears coursed down their cheeks because I was playing some sentimental favorite that recalled their long-gone youth. Sometimes Shanghai Mary would stomp over and slam a greasy glass of beer on top of the piano for me, which I think was supposed to be some sort of reward or perk, but seemed more like corporal punishment. Not trusting anything that came out of her taps, I'd slosh most of the beer onto the floor and, like I figured, nobody noticed the mess.

On my breaks, I'd stand at the bar and smoke, sticking close to Shanghai Mary. I tallied that if there was going to be any trouble, it wouldn't happen anywhere around her. That was true enough—two fights broke out between longshoremen, four between sailors, and two between the girls. Of all of them, the one that had me near ducking for cover was when a girl lit into another one for poaching her business. If you've never seen women fight, brother, you are missing one of the most terrifying spectacles that never graced a Roman coliseum. Chicks don't follow rules, the way most guys do. It's all open season, the hair pulling, the scratching, biting and kicking, and for the more seasoned ladies, the straight razor kept in the garter. Maybe they should've sent women overseas to actually fight in the war, instead of having them building airplanes and running pharmacies. The whole thing would've been over in about two weeks.

Most trouble was handled quickly by Shanghai Mary. She gave plenty of guys the bum's rush, even socking a few so good they forgot most of the years they'd spent since the third grade. I thought about writing a letter to the War Department and suggesting the wilting lily Mary as an alternative to the A-bomb. Even as I was banging out "Near You" and heard the meaty thud of somebody's fist hitting somebody's kidney, I was trying to laugh at it, think what a funny story it'd all make later when I told it to Beatrice. Then I caught myself—no Beatrice to call—and slid into a blue funk.

By the time two o'clock in the morning rolled around, I'd played three sets and had more than a handful of attempts made on my life. The guy hauling up lung butter eventually passed out at his table, but I couldn't say if it was because of his cough or the steady shots of whiskey he'd pounded all night. The dive had cleared out, mostly, with the girls taking their johns upstairs for the hour or two it'd take to drag through their pockets, and the young sailors asleep in each other's arms on the floor, cute as puppies. Puppies with V.D.

"Here you go," Shanghai Mary said as she stuffed a grimy wad of bills into my hand. "That's ten plus five for doin' such a swell job."

What was swell about it, how should I know? The best I could figure was that the cops hadn't busted the joint and nobody got killed inside the bar. "It's all high, wide and handsome," I said, and maybe she was cheating me, but I took the money without counting it. Getting my hat on, I made for the door and remembered that I forgot to eat anything since the *paleta* I ate at Echo Park. Maybe tomorrow I'd finally get some food, but after the hot, close steam of Cairo Jacks, I didn't feel too much like noshing.

"You played good, bub," Shanghai said and walloped me so hard across the back I almost cleaned the floor with my cheek. "Maybe you come back sometime, insteada that other guy."

Wearing T-bone underpants in the lion pen at the zoo. Having a second bris. Marching up the stairs at Jerome Avenue, throwing open the door and demanding a five-course welcome back dinner, as prepared by my mother. These were all things I'd sooner do before coming back to San Pedro, and Cairo Jacks. "Just give me a ring," I trilled to America's next secret weapon, and bounced out of that bar as fast as I could. I didn't think I could be any happier to see my car all safe and in one piece, though the Seabee laid out on the running board gave me a little hassle as I shoved him onto the street. With fifteen bucks in my pocket and one of the worst headaches this end of a timpani, I started for home. There had to be better ways than this to scare up funds.

With my father, I don't think he ever thought much about how I was going to make any money at the piano. When we'd sit around the radio, listening to the big band leaders, not a one of us got out pen and paper to do the figures: how much does it pay, what's the overhead, and the rest. Me, I was just a kid who didn't know beans from the cost of living. I thought maybe money would just pop out of the piano as I played it, some kind of printing machine spitting out cash into my waiting hands. So when he and me would build bandstands in the air, he never said, Slow down, tiger, and let's think this through.

Maybe that was a good thing, him not harping on the monetary mechanics of being a piano player. Most other kids up and down my block were getting hounded from the minute after they got squeezed out of their moms and into the glare and chill of the new world. From the get-go, kids like Paulie Weinstein or Alan Mandelbaum were being groomed by their parents to be doctors, lawyers, accountants, or, at the worst, take over the family candy store, hawking Necco Wafers and newspapers to the neighborhood. And who cared about Paulie's dream of playing infield for the Yankees, or Alan wanting to be the Jewish Tom Mix? Deep down, everybody knew that they'd hang up their glove or put away their Woolworth chaps and do exactly what the parents wanted, trading big ideas for the ordinary, respectable life. No surprise then when the call came down and all the boys were told to go to war, they lined up like chumps and signed on to die.

So I couldn't rightly blame my dad for not teaching me the ABCs of earning my bacon. I think he was just as green as I was on the music business, that he thought if I had talent enough it'd see me through and on to fame and glory. When I was a little kid, before I found the piano, there'd been some talk kicked around the apartment that I'd do something in banking. Why, you ask, when the Greenbergs knew nothing about said profession? The Zimmermans, the richest family at Beth Shalom, were in banking, and who else to measure up to if not the guy with a new coat every winter, his wife in furs, and their kids sent to camp in the Adirondacks during the summer to canoe and swim, not hanging from fire escapes or jumping in front of open hydrants. That banking notion was scratched soon after I got music, even though my mom still held out hope I would at least take over for my father at the cardboard box factory. Which he thought of as a death in life, just a way to X out days on the calendar until retirement and then, who knows?

I'd be both our tickets out of that. We didn't waste our cranium space on practicalities. When the broadcasts would come on from the Panther Room in Chicago or the Savoy just over in Harlem, we'd listen to the music and dream of the future. I'd have a luxury apartment somewhere on the Upper West Side, maybe the whole floor, view of Central Park, a chauffer to drive me to and from gigs, plenty of women in satin dresses to sparkle on my arm. And when the summers got too hot, off to some huge spread in the Hamptons, right on the water, a private beach, and for my pop, his own three-bedroom guest house, rigged with a music library, every record available and the snappiest phonograph Philco could throw together. We would sit out on the back deck, scotch and sodas in hand, and listen to my latest hit as we watched the sandpipers scurry up and back with the waves. We had it all schemed out, except for the how to make any of it happen for real.

That'd make both of us marks, the kind of pipe-dreaming suckers that I used every day like toilet paper. My excuse would've been that I wasn't more than a borough-bound punk, a sapling who only knew the rest of the world from the pictures and radio, and from what my father told me. But what I still couldn't figure out was Ernest Greenberg himself, twaddling on Fifth Avenue dreams when he ought to have known better. Didn't his folks run like hell from pogroms back in the old country? Didn't he have a wife, three brats, and a doddering bubbe to keep in bagels and bialys, and in a miniscule apartment no less? Didn't he look up from his desk at the factory, stacked high with piles of work orders, accounts payable statements, cups of stale coffee and crusts of sandwiches, and see that the dreams he'd padded and quilted from his own youth were going, going, gone? Didn't he know that those dreams he stuck hard to were weaknesses, flaws that somebody, somebody like me, could come along and take advantage of?

Maybe those dreams were gone now, gone like his son, run off someplace so that they may as well not exist, and weren't spoken of at the dinner table. And to think of them now was a finger on a bruise—unless that bruise had faded and there was nothing left of the old hurt. Part of me wanted that, for both him and me, to be forgotten. But there was that other part that didn't want to be scabbed over, flaked off, the shadow son from another lifetime. I wanted him to think of me the way I did him, like now, stretched out on the sofa, smoking, watching the wind gently shake the tree branches. Soft and low-down sax on the phonograph. A downbeat haze draped over the world. But he wouldn't. For one, because my mom would kill him if he lay down on the sofa, even with his shoes off, messing with the upholstery. But as to the other reasons why not, those I couldn't guess.

It was nearly afternoon and I hadn't been able to shake the headache I'd picked up at Cairo Jacks the night before. I'd even downed some good booze to put the pain in its place, but no luck. Why my cigarette hadn't taken care of that, who knew? Didn't the doctors say in the Chesterfield ads that smokes help your head? My stomach was complaining, too. Empty like a gutted radio. That popsicle was a long time ago. No wonder my head felt like it was about to burst wide open.

I sat up and stubbed out my cigarette, then cleared my throat. That little operation took a bit longer than I'd planned; once I got started, it wasn't an easy task to stop. Eventually, I picked up the phone and dialed an exchange. I had a good idea what, or who, I should say, might help me get over this melancholy. The widow Edwards could jolly me up.

"Hello?"

I slammed the receiver down and lit up again, taking long, shaking drags off my cigarette. Fuck me in four-four time. I'd called Beatrice accidentally. My finger just went to the rotary and did its business. I hadn't heard her, except in my mind, for almost a week, the longest we'd ever gone without talking, and shit, it threw me hard. She'd sounded good, too, and I could just picture her long, cool hands on my hot forehead, the honeyed rasp of her voice. And with my head pounding the way it was, I needed her badly. Hearing her was like a cold needle in my heart—icy medicine that stabbed. It was too soon. I wanted to show up at her door, my record in hand, the key to the future and me as the mayor presenting it to her.

Took me almost fifteen minutes before I picked up the phone again to make another call, and a few hours later, after I'd dressed myself up halfway decently, there I was, in Nora Edward's kitchen.

A more domestic scene you couldn't find anywhere, with me sitting at the kitchen table set for two, and her standing at the stove with an apron tied around her waist. The strings of her apron went around twice before being tied in a great big bow that dropped lovingly over the sweet curve of her ass. I tried to let the last reverbs of Beatrice's voice bounce out of my head, and I almost got there. Stay glued to the now, Greenberg, I told myself. I couldn't have Beatrice, not right now, but I had Nora right here. And man, oh man, with her cooking for me and that compact, killer body of hers standing so close, it was almost enough to make me start crying. I couldn't remember the last time I'd been in a scene so wholesome and legit.

"I absolutely know my mother would be horrified," Nora said over her shoulder. She was frying up something in a pan, something I couldn't see but smelled like heaven's lunch counter.

"Why's that?"

She threw a grin at me, coming close to being pretty but not making it all the way. Her wheaty hair was tied back, the last of her workday paint nearly gone. I wished she'd touched up a little before I got there, but she was stumbling through this get-together, awkward and eager like a duckling in Van Cortlandt Lake, tripping over itself to get to a breadcrumb. "Inviting you over for supper," she said. "It's awfully bold of me, not proper or ladylike at all. And we hardly know each other."

"Sure we do." I wouldn't point out that she didn't exactly invite me over. I had worked the conversation on the phone around so that she thought it was all her own idea.

Her shoulders went up and down in a shrug. "Not to her mind, I'd bet." She made her face comical, some impression of a Midwestern biddy, and I saw that if she hadn't gotten away from there, she would have wound up not an impression of a biddy but the real McCoy. Sometimes coming out to l.a. did people favors. "Why, we haven't even seen each other at church a dozen times, and you haven't walked me home from Bible study."

The last time I'd been to church was for the confirmation of Maureen Nolan, one of five Catholics in the neighborhood and to my thinking one of the choicest girls anywhere in the Bronx. My mom almost had a stroke when I got myself slick and headed out the door, a fourteen-year-old making like a sugar daddy for some *shiksa*, but pop knew that a boy's schvantz didn't give any mind to religion. And it paid off, too, going to that church. Later, in the coat closet of St. Columba's, Maureen let me put my hand up her pretty confirmation dress.

"I'd be happy to take you to church," I said.

That made her laugh. "I haven't gone to Mass in years. Not since I moved west. What about you?"

I knew synagogue didn't count, and even that'd been a long while. "Like you, years. I'm something of a lapsed Catholic, which causes my mother no end of grief."

Nora and I shook our collective heads over the crazy business of mothers, then she went back to poking whatever sizzled in the pan. Seemed like she was worrying that meat something good, but what did I know from fine cuisine? I didn't know a ladle from a lathe, which tells you how much I knew about carpentry, too. The smell of whatever she was fixing made my head feel like a helium balloon bobbing against the ceiling. With me still feeling poorly, what I really craved was a big bowl of matzo ball soup, with noodles, maybe some pieces of carrot and celery floating in it, but seeing as how I was supposed to be somebody with the last name of Dante, I figured I would know a bocce ball better, and that didn't make for good soup.

"It's bad enough for my mother that I would even have you over for supper, us being near strangers," she said, chuckling, "but to serve you in the *kitchen* instead of the dining room, well, that's downright disgraceful. She'd near to have died, seeing this." Nora turned and stuck out a hip, thoughtful. She was built better than the Chrysler Building. "You don't mind, do you? Eating in the kitchen?"

We'd gone past the dining room on our way in, when Nora had taken my hat and kept finding reasons to brush those spectacular tits of hers against me. I'd been so sidetracked by wanting to play her chest like a grand piano, I didn't give any mind to any room.

"It's much more cozy in here," I said.

She gave me another almost lovely smile. "That's what I think." Then she seemed saddened by something, and I felt myself get low with her. I didn't have the energy to pep her up, not with my head about to burst into flames like the next Hindenburg. I just wanted some food and a halfway decent-looking woman to stare at across the table. Why should that be so hard to get around here? "Floyd didn't like to eat in the kitchen, though. He said we may as well be back on the farm, and now that we were city people, we should act right."

I tried to give her enough, but not so much that I'd tire myself out. "There are all kinds of folks here in Los Angeles," I said. "Who can say what's right and what isn't?"

Everybody likes to hear their opinions seconded, and little Nora wasn't an exception. What a doll. I never saw anybody smile so much, except grifters.

That's when a little tickle in my throat went bananas and came galloping up out of me. Suave, I wasn't, bending over and whipping out my hanky as fast as I could, sputtering like a rusted jalopy. I thought my lungs were going to jump up my windpipe and out my mouth, then take the next train to Fresno. When I came back up for air, wiping my eyes, she was standing over me and patting my back, all womanly concern. I hadn't seen that on anyone's face, not for too long, and I was almost glad I'd nearly chucked my windbags onto the linoleum.

"Are you all right?" she asked. "That sounded terrible."

I didn't know where the hell that cough had come from, but I sure didn't want a repeat performance. "Just a little cold I'm fighting." I didn't sound like a radio star just then, unless I was playing some black hat-wearing villain with the sinister plan to take over the world. Maybe all those evildoers were so ticked off because they were sick and just wanted a cough drop.

Nora tried to come over stern, but she was about as intimidating as an angry kitten. "Why didn't you say you weren't feeling well? I could have made my mother's *surströmming*. It always helped us feel better."

"What's *surströmming*?"

"Fermented herring." I must not have been my usual self, because she said with a laugh, "I know. It's worse than it sounds, but it chases away whatever's making you feel sick. I don't think anything can stand the smell of *surströmming*."

I wasn't keen on her being able to see how I felt about that rotten herring dish. Usually, I can keep a smooth face, even when somebody tells me or shows me something that makes me want to claw at my eyes. One of Arnie's early lessons was that C-men can't show what they're feeling inside; they have to be blanks to be filled up with the mark's needs. That's how they get what they want every time. But either I was really under the weather, or I'd dropped the polish and professional distance. Neither of those options much appealed to me. You're probably saying, Lou, come on, pal, don't worry so much about something so minor. So she saw that you didn't cotton to fermented herring. Big deal. But, see, that's where it starts. As soon as little bits of me start peeping through, even about some shitty fish, that's when I may as well throw in all my cards and step back from the table.

"I'm sure whatever you made will be just swell," I said. "Like I said, it's a little cold. It'll be gone by tomorrow."

Her small shoulders went up and down in a cute shrug. She finally turned the heat off the pan and dished up the food. After untying her apron, she set the plate down in front of me and took her seat, grinning like a jackpot. I looked down at my plate and almost laughed.

"I hope you like pork chops," she chirped.

Didn't that just fit it all into a pocketbook? I didn't keep kosher, not with all the hot dogs I gnawed on down at the beach which I know weren't Hebrew National, but to sit in Nora's kitchen with a big plate of trayf in front of me seemed the final capper on me pretending to be someone I wasn't.

"Got any applesauce?" I asked.

Her eyes went round and the smile fell right off her face. I thought any minute she'd start with the waterworks. Her moods went up and down like a harp glissando. "I forgot," she wailed. Great. Now her party was spoiled, she thought she'd blown it all, and what the hell was I supposed to do with that? She started to get up. "I'll just run to the store—"

I shoved her down into her seat. I didn't care if I wasn't giving her kid-glove treatment. If she went to the store, she'd be at least fifteen minutes, and I was too hungry to wait that long. The headache I'd been sporting started to creep back in again, gentle as a slugger. "Don't be silly," I said. "This will be fine. Better than fine. Wonderful."

Her eyes were pleading, bare need plain in her face. She had a racetrack-sized hole right in the middle of her. "Really? You aren't saying that to make me feel better?"

"Of course not." She nearly collapsed into a puddle on my shoes. With her alpine highs and subterranean lows, she was easy to play. "I can't remember when I had a home-cooked meal. It looks fantastic."

She shook out her napkin and draped it across her lap, grateful—too grateful by half. "And it's such a pleasure to cook for a man again, I just cannot tell you. When you called me at work, I was so excited, I got off early to go marketing."

"You didn't have to go to so much trouble," was my next line, and I said it, just like the script told me.

Adoring Lady: "But I did." She reached out and took my hand, giving me a damp look, Irene Dunne in *Love Affair*. "This is so wonderful, Louis, having you here. I can't thank you enough for calling me and coming over."

Chivalrous Gent: "The pleasure is mine." I'd had enough talking, I was ready to eat. Two days without real food, and I didn't give a fuck whether I was eating kosher, trayf, or cannibal, I needed to stuff my piehole. So I smiled, slid my hand out from under hers, and started cutting into my chop. And cutting. And cutting. I could have sawed through the whole Sequoia National Park. Figures. Finally I find a woman willing to cook for me, and turns out she can't do it any better than my own mother.

But I was about to eat my own shoes, so what did it matter? I popped a piece of meat into my mouth and began grinding away at it. I would have been better off eating my Oxfords. She watched me closely, so I swallowed and choked out, "Delicious."

With a smile, she got to hewing at her own chop, and when she put a piece in her mouth, her eyes went wide again. She grabbed her napkin from her lap and with a ladylike *hack*, spat out the meat. I thought for sure she'd start up with the tears, but she laughed instead, tits bouncing happily. I could have joined them.

"That is undoubtedly the worst pork chop anyone has ever made," she giggled.

"It was pretty terrible," I said. "Almost as bad as the service."

"I guess we know why I don't cook very often." She wiped her eyes. "I'd poison myself."

I looked at the chop, tough as a gambler, and bid it a wistful good-bye. When I'd actually eat something was anybody's guess. I could feel my stomach digesting my liver.

Nora pushed her chair back, and walked quickly from the room. I couldn't move. The script had been thrown out, and with no lines, no stage direction, I couldn't figure what the hell I was supposed to do. Just as I was about to get up and follow her, which seemed like the right idea, she came back and threw my hat into my lap. The light behind her turned her gauzy.

"Are you throwing me out?" I asked, sure that this was the end of whatever crazy business I'd gotten into with her. I couldn't tell whether I was sorry or not that it was over. But she threw me again.

"*We* are going to get a decent meal," she said. "My treat."

Most men wouldn't stand for a woman picking up the tab, but I'm not what you'd call your usual gentleman about town. Maybe she expected me to resist, be gallant. Now it was my turn to knock her sideways.

"Sounds great," I said, getting up and slapping on my hat. "Where to?"

Chapter fourteen

From outside, Hi-Life Records looked no different from any of the other low stucco buildings shouldering La Brea—it could have been an insurance company, dental office, or bookie's. A big window faced the sidewalk, and inside I saw a middle-aged woman with glasses on the phone, plus the usual bits and pieces that make up every office everywhere: file cabinets, typewriter, free calendar with a picture of a sickly mountain lake courtesy of your local mortician. But maybe for all that typical junk crowding the front room, some guy inside was right then recording the next "Nature Boy." Nobody passing on the street would have caught wise to the music inside except for the small, block-letter sign just over the door that said it was a record studio.

Because of Hi-Life looking about as impressive as a fifty-cent tuxedo, you might think that I'd be feeling mighty low. Who'd want to lay down tracks in a joint that looked like an accountant's office? But I'd done my homework, and right after that shithouse Golden Platters, word on the boulevard was that Hi-Life could set a guy up swell, pack, shack and stack. You didn't want a fancy-schmantzy set-up on the outside of a recording studio. Better to save the fireworks for what goes on inside. I knew they did quality, anyhow. Didn't I have a stack of discs from Hi-Life next to my phonograph? It was a fair omen, too, that the place was open late on a Saturday afternoon, Shabbos. Music didn't take days off or sit in synagogue. I'd done my own praying that same morning, working on the music that had been drifting through my body for the past few days. The melody was getting stronger. I'd catch it before its legs grew too strong to run away from me.

I was parked outside, across the street, nursing a paper cup of coffee that I'd gotten from a hash house on the corner. It was some of the worst joe I'd ever had the pleasure to choke on. But it kept me lively, when I would have nodded off sitting out in the car. I was scoping Hi-Life, waiting, watching the front, but my mind kept circling back to the night before with Nora.

She'd taken me to a café near her place, and while it wasn't Bullock's Tea Room, it was sure better than the lunch counters and hot dog stands that made up most of my fine dining experience. We actually walked there, instead of driving. She said, "Maybe I'm still stuck on the gasoline rationing. I don't believe in getting in the car to go about six blocks. Maybe ten, but six is too few." Then she looked worried. "Will you be all right to walk? I don't want to aggravate your cold."

I remembered the character I was supposed to be playing, and figured there wasn't any harm in me stretching my story out, like a pair of socks. "When I was in the army, we'd march twenty miles every day."

"Really?" she asked, eyes going wide and awed.

I dredged up a story that some vet I'd conned had told me, and played it back to Nora. "You couldn't imagine the number of boots we went through. Soles worn as thin as newsprint. But they never sent us enough new ones. Some men would find a dead soldier, measure their feet, then take their shoes if it was a close-enough fit."

Maybe I'd gone too far. She turned a little green, so I backpedaled. "Not Floyd and me, of course, but other guys. Anyway," I said, going jolly, "a few blocks to a restaurant is nothing. The fresh air will do me good." It turned out to be true. The cough settled down, just coming around now and then to check up on me, and once I got used to the idea, I actually enjoyed strolling down the quiet, wide streets of Culver City, a gentle warm Friday night, all the families in, nobody wild or kicking up trouble. I wasn't used to walking with anyone, and it took me a while to remember to shorten my stride. Nora had fine legs, but it was like walking next to a daschund. Beatrice and me had never been out on a stroll together, so I didn't know if our strides would match. Bea had good, long legs, though, and she wasn't a dawdler, so between my New York pace and her briskness, I'd bet we could have done well together. I missed her bad, wanted her next to me and not this little Midwest WASP. A growling started inside me, and it wasn't my stomach, but another kind of hunger that wasn't going to be satisfied.

Through the open curtains, Nora and I could see into the houses we passed; folks gathered around the radio or, in a few houses, staring at the creepy blue-white glow of television sets.

"Do you have one of those?" Nora asked, pointing. The screens were tiny glass windows inside giant wooden cabinets, and from the way everyone kept getting up and fiddling with the knobs, it didn't look like the signal was all that great. Somebody was watching a cowboy chase another cowboy across a flickering desert, and in another house, they seemed to be watching some lady trying to win a new washer/dryer from a guy in a loud suit.

I almost laughed at the idea that I would have enough money to buy one of those T.V. sets. Even the cheapest one was a hundred bucks, and for a three-inch screen. I'd be better off standing outside a movie theater and trying to watch the picture from the street.

"Oh, no," I said. "There's something rather lonely about television."

She turned up an eyebrow at me, a movement I was getting to recognize. I knew it meant she wanted me to explain myself. That cheered me a bit, knowing that I could read her like any mark. If I could read her, I could con her. Maybe it wouldn't be my usual grift for money, but it *would* be a con.

I said, "I'm used to listening to the radio by myself, but when I go to the pictures, there's the crowd all around me. How could I see a movie all by myself? I reckon if I was watching something on a screen, I'd want lots of people nearby, not just one or two." Whew! That was a lot for me to spill, especially around a dicey prospect. But she seemed to eat it up, and turned to me with a sly smile.

"Perhaps you just need to watch television with the right person."

We traded looks at that crack. She fought to keep her chin up, pretending she could play at being fast, she was a woman of the world. So, corn-fed Nora from Iowa was trying to turn into some racy number, the kind of woman who'd give sass to a guy, that her last name was Charles instead of Edwards and she had a dog named Asta. But she wore that pose about as comfortable as a Jew with a 4-H ribbon, and it wasn't long before she turned away and let the streetlamps cast shadows across her face.

I wasn't in a hurry to make her feel comfortable. Arnie's voice was in my head sternly reminding me that if I was going to take the touch, I should've had something planned by now, some angle to work. Easy, Arnie, I thought to him. Let's let Nora twist for a while.

We didn't say much more until we got to the café on Culver Boulevard. The guy who met us at the door knew Nora, gave her a big, high-wattage grin, which stuttered but didn't go out when he saw me. She came here all by herself, it seemed, no gents squiring her about the fair metropolis. I kept it level and smooth when Nora introduced me to the guy—some oily little Greek whose name ended with "opodopolous" or something—but I liked knowing that Nick or Chris or Socrates wanted a piece of her action and hadn't gotten any, and here I was, a guy right off the street, with my hand on her shoulder. Yeah, pal, keep looking, but you're getting none of this. And lookee here, if it wasn't Xantippe herself coming up from behind the counter, giving her old man the evil eye for being too solicitous to the Widow Edwards.

"Everything's good here," Nora said when we sat down in our booth. "I think I've tried it all." I ran my eyes over the menu, and, like I said, it wasn't the 21 Club, but I hadn't paid that much for food for a while. I did have that two grand from George's big store con, but I had plans for that money, plans that didn't involve a seventy-five cent lamb chop dinner, even if it did come with soup and potatoes. She did say she'd treat, however, and I aimed to hold her to that. Still and all, I didn't want her to throw a clot when I ordered the dollar steak, which sounded swell and was what my complaining stomach demanded—but wasn't in the cards that night. There were sugar mommas in Bel Air and Brentwood, but not Culver City.

When Hercules waddled over to take our order, full of greaseball charm for her and hinky looks for me, Nora said, "Veal cutlets, please, with vegetable soup and fruit cocktail to start."

I said, "Same for me," even though I didn't much like veal or vegetable soup and I hated fruit cocktail.

After the Greek hustled away with the orders, bawling to his wife, the cook, Nora gave me that grin of hers across the table, the one that wasn't fake but seemed too bright. "This place is my own personal dining room," she said. "I'm here almost every night. Do you like it?"

"It's swell—very nice," I said.

"You've already tasted the proof that I don't cook much. Have you recovered from the experience?" She played with the salt and pepper shakers, moving them this way and that like she was arranging flowers. It was tough not to watch her and think what those tiny hands would feel like around my cock.

"It will take a while before I can look at another pork chop," I said, "but the docs say I'm on the mend."

She'd spilled some pepper onto the tabletop and was pushing it around with the tip of a finger. A small blot of ink dotted her knuckle, which she didn't notice. "Floyd would be horrified to see me eat out so much. He'd say it was a waste of money, and wasn't that what a woman was for, anyway, to cook her husband's meals?"

I'm not what you'd call the jealous type, and there sure wasn't anyone I wanted to feel jealous of, but hearing dear dead Floyd's name thrown around didn't do me any favors. The more he came up, the more I'd have to talk about him, and the slug of information I had on him was spent.

"You're a busy woman," I said. "You can't be expected to work as hard as you do and cook, too. Besides," I added, making my voice go soft and thoughtful, taking a chance with what I said next, "you don't have a husband anymore."

My gamble paid off. Instead of her sobbing noisily, reminded of her loss, she looked up at me and lobbed another of those smiles. "That's true," she said quietly, "I'm an unmarried woman now." She started worrying the ring on her finger with her thumb, moving it back and forth so that it started to loosen its hold, not even knowing that she was doing it. Later that night, she'd probably take the thing off for good, but not just then.

I stopped thinking about Nora's wedding ring when the guy I'd been waiting for outside Hi-Life finally came out of the building, and I couldn't stew over her anymore. I knew who he was because of some telephone calls I'd made earlier. This guy sure wasn't at the top of the distinguished characters parade, still, I'd gotten enough information to recognize him when he showed. Just spot the most average-looking man, which you might think would be easy, but there are some guys who work hard to make themselves fade away into the drapery. I bet you know the type: the kid who sat at the back of the classroom and listlessly played handball at recess with his two friends, the pudgy kid and the kid who wore woolen sweaters even when it was eighty degrees. He was the kid you had to invite to birthday parties because your mom made you, and it wasn't that you didn't like him, exactly, but there wasn't anything *there*. He didn't have a favorite baseball team, didn't care if he got Root Beer Barrels or Tootsie Rolls—and when you looked at class pictures years later, you couldn't remember his name.

Kids like that grow up, some go to college, most make sure that they keep creeping through life by working at laundries or in shipping departments, and a few even get married to women just as gray and hidden as they are. And even if they were chumps enough to go to war, they came back exactly the same as when they left and continued with just what they were doing before: move air around, in and out, each breath lost under the sounds of traffic and footsteps.

What makes some guys like that? Why do they wash themselves out from day one? Don't they have any plans, any wishes? They have to read comic books, go to the pictures, listen to the radio. Wouldn't some of that make them think that just maybe there was more than wearing a rut in the pavement on the way to and from the bookbindery? The only thing I can take a stab at is that they learned to be carpet samples at home, from their folks, who either beat them down or preached the gospel of dullness. Even when I felt loaded down with my pop's dreams—sometimes it was like carrying a grand piano on my back—I was glad that he never let me forget there was more for me than Jerome Avenue, I wasn't a hokey, nowhere boy, and to be anything less than extraordinary was a flat disappointment.

Clearly, this guy I was tailing didn't have a father like mine, and unless I'd been looking for him, I would have missed him stepping out the front door of Hi-Life and heading down the street. Mid-thirties, he had light brown hair, skinny arms but a soft belly, and he had the kind of walk that bounced a little too much, like he wasn't all that comfortable in his own body. He bounced around to the parking lot next to the building, then got in a grimy Pontiac and pulled out. I gave him a few seconds' lead even though this guy probably kept his head down so low he wouldn't notice if he was being shadowed. I kept it smooth and easy, laying back a couple of cars, and followed him as he turned from La Brea to Olympic and over to Fairfax.

I always got the heebie-jeebies whenever I was on Fairfax. Something was uncanny about it, all off. Hasidim in their long coats and beards, walking and kibitzing under palm trees, the women with their covered hair leading giant packs of kids down the sidewalk, boys with *payos*, and the streets so wide and empty—about as far from the Lower East Side as you could find a piece of challah, but here they were, the ghosts of home. It was Sabbath, so everyone was on foot and clustered around the synagogues for the once-a-week holiday. My spine went icy, then the sharp dart of longing hit between my ribs. Back in the Bronx, the family Greenberg weren't the most observant of Jews. Like nearly everyone else I knew, we'd show up at temple for bar mitzvahs, Rosh Hashanah, Yom Kippur, and the occasional Purim carnival when me and my sisters were small. Passover wasn't more than a long, long meal, thick purple kosher wine like a black eye, nibbling on matzo until finally the roast chicken.

We didn't have two sets of plates, and if old bubbe found it strange that me and the twins drank glasses of milk with our meatloaf, she didn't say anything about it.

You'll find Jews just about anywhere these days, except maybe Poland and Germany, so why should it be a shock to see them here, in the bright hot nothing of Los Angeles? These Hasidim wouldn't even think me a Jew, driving around on Shabbos, trayf all the way down to my sock garters. A *shtick goy*. The only thing fully Jewish about me was my circumcised schvantz, and it was known to associate with too much gentile company. But to hear the Yiddish and Hebrew as I drove past the kosher bakeries, see the long, sad, worldly faces only Jews seem to carry—okay maybe some Greeks and Italians, too, but no WASPS—brought me back to the crowded, noisy avenues of New York, sitting on the stoop, newsstands under the El, everybody's face looking like mine, and my father at the top of the stairs, paper in hand, suspenders slipped from his shoulders and hanging down, waiting for me to come home from the induction center.

So when my mark parked his car at Fairfax and 6th, got out, and walked into an Irish bar, I almost tailed him right in and ordered myself a shot of something kindly. I wanted that drink pretty bad, but it was too soon to actually go inside, risk the mark seeing me before I wanted him to. I cooled it, instead, across the street, and made a note in my head that this guy knew his way to this Mick joint. He was what I never wanted to be at any bar anywhere—a regular. I could spot it in the way he slumped towards the front door, no hesitation, just heading straight in for liquid comfort and the companionship of a barstool. Here it was, coming on four thirty in the afternoon; this guy was no stranger to sousing himself before the sun went down.

There wasn't anything for me to do but sit tight until he came out again, and when that might be, who knew? But wait I would, so I lit a cigarette and watched the lights come on as the sky went a hazy purple, moving towards evening. I kept taking drags to stay sharp, which made that goddamn cough sit up and stretch its legs, but at least I wasn't falling asleep. It had been a late night for me.

Nora and I stayed at that café for longer than I thought we

would be, talking away like regular folks. If I'd gotten any more square, you could shoot craps with me.

"It's funny," Nora said to me between slurps of her vegetable soup, "I feel like I know you so well, but I don't even know what you do for a living."

My spoon didn't even stop. "Banking," I said, and slurped, too. I would have preferred some matzo balls, even my mom's, what with my raspy throat, but the vegetable soup wasn't bad. I'd give Aristotle his due—his joint had a swell cup of broth.

"What kind of banking?" she asked. "Corporate? Personal? Investments?"

I could have kicked myself. A green bobble on my part, since she was in the accounting department of the studio. I'd thought of myself as a real wiseacre by picking the one line my mom planned on for me, and instead I found myself ankle-deep in brine. I knew enough about the money racket to improv—every C-man knows bits and pieces about nearly every job there is, in case they have to schmooze a mark—but that was with the average mark, when I had my touch all lined up and waiting. I knew enough to get that Nora wasn't going to be my average mark.

I needn't have worried, though. Her Midwest breeding kicked in and she went red. "Goodness, how rude," she said, trying to laugh at herself. "Interrogating you like that. And I'm sure after a long day at the office, the last thing you would want to do is talk about work."

"Thanks for understanding," I said and gave her hand a little pat, the Weary Businessman soothed by a feminine presence, an act she got fully. I've looked through some of them women's magazines— I've found one or two at Beatrice's and my sisters read them, too. Any man who wants to get the inside track on women has to pick up some issues of *Vogue* or *Redbook*, or for you domesticated types, *Ladies' Home Journal*, maybe *Good Housekeeping*. It's like there's no universe without men in it. Everything women do is for us guys, so these magazines say. What they wear, how they paint their faces, the food they cook, even what they talk about. All for men, and the children, but usually men first. Women are supposed to be the soft cushion between the house and the world outside. Don't give your man the business when he gets home from a long day, ladies, but build him a cocktail, spritz on some perfume and keep smiling.

Nora had done her homework and swallowed the hooey those glossy magazines had peddled. She wanted a man in her life, badly, and lucky for me that I'd come along to play the part she'd already written. I didn't mind. If some woman's going to lay out the melody, I won't fight the accompaniment. I might throw down a riff or two, to make things interesting, but I'll be there straight through verse, chorus, bridge and coda. And when it came time to take the final bows, I'd already be in my car and halfway to Ensenada.

But I had to get the conversation away from me and back on to her. No chick is going to resist a chance to talk about herself. "What do you do when you aren't at work?" I asked.

Her shoulders fell up and down, a shrug she wasn't committing to, but she was pleased that I was asking about her. "When am I not at work?"

"You've got to come home sometime."

"Well...I'm here a lot," she said and wrinkled her tiny gentile nose at the thrilling prospect of it all.

"So you sit in the back and play canasta with the owner and his wife?"

That got a giggle out of her. She gave my hand a playful swat. "Of course not."

"Then what?"

She cast her big blue eyes around the room, trying like crazy to come up with something, and I almost felt sorry for her, having such a hard time figuring out where she misplaced her life. I had so many goddamned irons in the fire, I could have been a blacksmith.

"This may seem funny, but I do love the pictures," she admitted. "I go twice a week."

"Why would that be funny?"

"Because I work at a studio. You'd think I'd be sick to death of anything remotely connected to the movies."

"There's a world of difference between cutting checks and

watching some gumshoe track down a killer. Nothing wrong with a little escape."

"I'm glad you feel that way," she said, smiling. "I never tell anybody at work that I go to the picture show. They'd just turn their noses up at me."

"Then they're all a bunch of fools," I said.

She liked that. "I think so, too, sometimes. I get so tired of hearing them pretend to be clever and worldly, as if they were indifferent to everything. Being bored doesn't make a person sophisticated."

"So what makes someone sophisticated?"

"If I knew that, I'm sure I wouldn't eat at the same coffee shop every night."

Good point. "But at least you don't pretend."

A dry smile etched the corners of her mouth. "Not about that, anyway."

Costas or Plato brought us our veal, which I got down well enough, and Nora and I spent the next hour talking about our favorite pictures. It turned out she was a sucker for Errol Flynn, even though she knew he was ten kinds of a louse when it came to women, and went for the sauce. We went on for a while about who was a better swashbuckler, Flynn or Fairbanks. She told me a funny story she'd heard from one of the girls in the steno pool about Flynn coming into the studio to meet with some producer, and Flynn runs into the guy's office, looking nervous, eyes rolling around in his head, sweating, the whole megillah. He hustles in there and tells this producer that he has to lend him some money, there's a goon from a numbers racket after him because some bets went south and if he doesn't pay up, there'd be some unauthorized chiropractic work on his knees. Everybody knew that Flynn was into playing the ponies, and just about anything anybody could lay a bet on, he was game. The producer shouts for Flynn to get the hell out of his office, he doesn't want any of his trouble, and this is a *professional* movie studio.

"Then the girls out in the pool hear a terrible commotion," Nora said, "and a giant bruiser of a man comes barreling in and storms into Mr. Meyerson's office, waving a gun, demanding money or somebody was going to get it. Nobody knows what to do, but suddenly they hear Mr. Meyerson scream like a girl and then the poor man starts to cry. He's throwing fistfuls of cash onto the carpet and begging for his life.

"And do you know," she said, looking prettier than she had all night, eyes bright, hands flying around, honestly lovely, even if for just that moment, "it turns out that the thug was straight from Central Casting! It was all a joke. Mr. Flynn just laughed and laughed, and told Mr. Meyerson to take a nice vacation, then he went out and bought the thug a drink at the commissary."

"So what happened to Meyerson?"

"He spent the rest of the day under his desk, nursing a flask his wife bought him for their twentieth wedding anniversary." She couldn't stop laughing, and I joined her. I thought to myself but didn't say that Flynn could have been a good grifter, conning like a bunco man born and bred.

"Meyerson," I murmured. "Interesting name."

"Seems that half the studio heads are...you know...." She poked at her veal.

"Jewish?" I asked loudly.

She jumped, then nodded, with her eyes stuck to the table, like she'd said something slanderous.

"And that's strange?"

"Maybe not for you," she said. "There just weren't any...you know...not in Iowa. I didn't meet any until I got to Los Angeles."

"So, you met some Jews." She winced again. That word wasn't polite. "That had to change your opinion. Or maybe not."

"They're different," she said after a while, which told me nothing, so I stared at her until she went on. "Kind of...noisy. And they talk fast."

I said, slowly, "Sounds like they scare you."

"Well, I mean, everyone saw those newsreels about the camps," she said in a rush, "and it was horrible, horrible. So, I feel bad for them. But they're strange. In some ways, they keep themselves so separate from normal people, but then, they're kind of mixing in, and some of them, you wouldn't know they were…not unless you found out their last names or they just came out and told you." She gave a queer little shiver. "I don't like that. I don't like not knowing how someone is different."

"Like, say, if they were colored."

Her eyes turned to mine, finding them comfortable and familiar and everything she thought they should be. "You understand, don't you?"

"Yes, I do," I said.

I'd heard worse, but that didn't make my veal sit any better. That filthy-mouthed rube flashed into my head, and Bea's shut-down face, and I was so goddamned tired of fighting things I couldn't fight that I just sat there in that booth.

I moved the talk to music, wanting to know what kind she liked.

"I just adore music," she beamed, and things were improving a shade, until she added, "I listen to American Album of Familiar Music almost every week. Margaret Down, Evelyn MacGregor, and Jean Dickenson. They're all just swell!"

"They sure are," I said, ready to shoot myself. "How do you like jazz?"

"Mm, I do enjoy Guy Lombardo, and I can't stop myself from dancing whenever I hear Louis Prima."

She hadn't named one colored musician or composer, and it didn't seem likely that she would anytime soon. She'd think Bird was something you served for Thanksgiving. Which brought me down not a little, worse, almost, than what she'd said about Jews. Jazz was my true faith and it pained me terrible to hear it slandered.

My missing Beatrice came back again so hard I almost doubled up. If she and I were sitting in this booth, talking about music, we'd be at it for hours, comparing the merits of Ellington versus Basie, Powell against Tatum. And that's when it hit me. Here we were, me and Nora, sitting out in public having a regular conversation like regular folks. I didn't have to worry about whether some gink was going to throw us out, or make remarks, or even—with the exception of the jealous Greek—look at us cross-eyed. I never got that with

Beatrice. It was always veiled and secret, sneaking around after dark and pulling the blinds. Even when we were alone, there was always that something, that edge that kept us stretched tight, volatile. To me, it didn't matter if Beatrice was colored or not, but it did matter to everybody else.

I had to admit, sitting with Nora in public felt good, free, not thinking about whose skin was going to offend who, even if the woman I was with had a tin ear and seemed to be stretching hard towards something out of her reach.

But the fact that it did feel good just made me all the madder. I looked across the table at smiling Nora and thought, Wrong. The words that came out of her mouth were wrong. The soft roiling of ideas in her brain was wrong. Beatrice, not Nora, should have been sitting with me in that diner, and I hated that I could get some kind of pleasure out of something that received the world's approval. But just like a regular guy, I walked Nora home, stood on her front step, and when she opened the door to her house, I didn't try and go in. She stopped in the doorway and looked up at me, fear and excitement and curiosity and dismay all there in her face, with the porch light shining down and the moths hitting the glass like billiards balls. I could hear their soft thump thumps, almost the only sound on the quiet street, as her eyes ran over my face, down the length of me. She wanted to ask me in, wondered where it would go if I did step inside and take off my hat. Would I feel different against her, in her, than her husband? She wanted and didn't want to know.

"It's been a swell evening," I said. "I hope we can do this again, sometime."

She knew I wasn't going to come in. Relief and disappointment flicked on and off, a coin tossed into the air, before landing on what she hoped was gracious hospitality. "Yes, I think that would be lovely."

Then I did what I couldn't remember ever doing before. I bent down, took hold of her elbow, kissed her lightly on the mouth, then stepped back and said "Good night." A real gentleman. I didn't even try and get a feel of her tits.

She waved at me as I got into my car and pulled away, and

in my rearview mirror I saw her stand on her porch for a long time. She was still standing there when I turned the corner.

I kept thinking about that kiss, sitting outside the Irish bar and waiting for my mark. I bet I could have taken her straight to the mattress—she was ready for it. Unless she'd played around while Floyd was in the service, Nora hadn't gotten laid in years. And I was a pretty good prospect, too.

But what I wanted wasn't sex, but something else. It was nice to leave her wanting more. A nice, cold feeling that iced its way through my lungs and pooled in my stomach and chilled me completely. A painful numbness that I kept jabbing.

By the time nine o'clock rolled around, my mark still hadn't come out of the bar. I didn't want to spend my Saturday night on my can like a complete maroon. I'd gotten what I needed on my mark for now, anyway. I knew the kind of guy he was from how he spent his free time, and that'd come into play later. For now, it was time to head back to Santa Monica.

Why does the phone always start to ring when you can't find your keys just outside your door? Fortunately for me whoever was trying to reach me was a tenacious son of a bitch, because after about five minutes of solid ringing and me patting down my pockets for the key, I finally stumbled into my dark apartment and grabbed the phone.

"What?"

"That any way to talk to your buddy?"

"Sonny! What's shaking?"

"Where the hell you been, man? Haven't seen you all week, and you weren't down at Dee's last night. What's the matter, you got your glasses on, don't want to be seen with your old friends?"

"Been busy, man."

"I'm going to be there tonight. Why don't you cut out and meet me there later?"

"Who'll be there?"

"The usual mob."

I didn't want to ask if that meant Beatrice, too. And I didn't want to tell Sonny that the big reason I hadn't shown my hands on Central Avenue was because of running into her. "I don't know, Sonny. I'm awfully beat."

"Cowboy up, brother. Besides, I want to talk to you about a gig."

"Can't you tell me over the phone?"

He clicked his teeth, which I knew wasn't good. "I'm seriously beginning to think your piano needs tuning. Don't you want to hear some hot jazz?"

Sonny wasn't the kind of guy who liked to hear "no." He'd keep leaning and leaning until there was nothing you could do but give in. Anyway, I wasn't going to hide in my cave. I wouldn't let Beatrice hold that over me. And the idea of a paying gig sure sounded better than good. So I said okay, hung up, and sat in the dark for a while, smoking, wondering what it would be like to see her again, hear her voice in person, the voice I always heard when I thought of music.

Chapter fifteen

I'd never gone to Dee's on a Saturday night. After-hours Friday was my usual routine. Maybe on Saturdays they cleared the whole place out and held three-legged races, or set up archery targets near the stage, or served English trifle from the bar. What did I know? But after I'd salaamed Paulie by the front door and stepped inside, from what I saw, things seemed about the same. Crowds elbow-to-elbow. Chicks and guys in their sharp clothes. A planned wildness, some kind of antidote to whatever lay outside, whatever folks were trying to forget. Onstage a bop combo smashed its way through eight to the bar and came out the other side.

The joint seemed hotter and more cramped than a coat closet grope. I could've blown glass in there. I thought I was going to turn to ash, leaving nothing but a chalky smudge and a brown felt fedora on the floor. I almost got lost in that idea, seeing the women's high-heeled shoes stepping over me, the soles of dancers' feet grinding me into powder, into the century-old *schmutz* that coated the floorboards. I would have stayed there, too, caught up in the far-flung twists of my overheated brain, if some clumsy goon's elbow hadn't rammed me between my shoulders and brought me back to the room.

I hustled my way to the bar fast, before I'd even cased the room. I needed something liquid and fortifying, and I positively didn't want Ovaltine. Standing with my stomach shoved into the counter, knocked around like the whores at Cairo Jacks and waiting for my whiskey, my mouth felt coated and dry and I wanted that drink something bad. Maybe there were more folks at Dee's, and that's why it was so hot. Or maybe that headache and cough I had were shifting into a cold. And then there was the possibility that knowing I was going to see Beatrice, that maybe she was already here, somewhere in the room, turned me into an inferno in gabardine.

I threw down three dimes for the drink, then tossed it down my throat. I waited, one, two, but it didn't make me feel better. There were live coals in my lungs, and the courage I was hoping the booze might float my way had floated past me and downstream. For a few minutes, I toyed with the idea of hightailing it out of there, just running home to lie under the sofa and watch the dust collect on the carpets. But Sonny said he had a gig lined up, and if my glorious night at Cairo Jacks had showed me anything, it was that I'd do nearly anything for a buck.

"Clipper," Sonny yelled behind me, and his hand, made strong from working the sax keys, clasped my shoulder and I almost honked. "What's the belch?"

I turned around. "Hiya, pops," I said, making myself crisp and new as counterfeit money.

Sonny gave my hand a steady shake, saying, "When you didn't show last night, I near thought you'd gone and died."

"I did kick it," I said. "Can't you tell from my suit?"

He gave a shake of his head, meaning: *Lou, you don't change.* If that was a good thing or not, I couldn't tell. "Come on and grab a seat with me and the troops." He started to pull me away from the bar, and I stopped myself from looking around him to see if she was there. "We got a table and a chair all ready for you."

There was only one chair I wanted to sit in even less, and it was electric. "Can't we talk over here at the bar? I'm kind of in a hurry."

He eyed me like I'd suggested Jackie Robinson as the president of the Jefferson Davis Appreciation Society. "Is your roof leaking, man? Since when don't you have the minutes to spend with your old chums?"

"Fine, fine," I said. It didn't seem worth it to risk a gig by not sitting down with him. "You crack the whip, I'll make the trip."

"Just follow me, brother." He and me pushed through the mob—I couldn't figure if it was the heat or the crowd bumping us, but the room seemed to shift and shimmy. I watched Sonny ahead of me—the gleam of his suit, his close-cropped conk—and the edges seemed to grow hazed and dark. My eyeballs were sweating. Beatrice was close, getting closer. I thought maybe I saw the upsweep of her hair, some kind of flowered pin holding it. My breath was coming in short and hot. I felt myself drift off, a piece of paper gliding along runoff and then dropping into the gutter's darkness.

"Hey, buddy, you okay?"

Looking up, all these faces were floating over me. Sonny, Wendel, Opal, Lilah, and somewhere back there, Beatrice. The room still wiggled and the music came up from the bottom of the ocean. It took me five beats to realize I was sitting down, five more to remember I was wearing my own shoes. I didn't want to see Beatrice seeing me like this, so I pushed my eyes over to Sonny.

"What—?" That about fixed me for talking. The cough I'd been fighting decided it was time to make its move, now that I was unarmed. I hacked it up, until Wendel pounded me so hard on the back that my breath was gone completely. Somehow, somebody'd found a glass of water, which seemed strange to me, since water was the one liquid nobody drank at Dee's. Who could trust the tap? I'd get dysentery for certain. I tried to shove the glass away, but Wendel just about held my head and forced the water down. After I'd taken a few gulps, finally he stopped torturing me and set the smudged glass down.

"Man, you rattled us," he said, shaking his head.

"You almost fainted, gate." Sonny pulled up a chair and sat next to me. "Here I was, thinking you was right behind me, then I look back, and hell if you're not swaying like the Moonlight Serenade. I thought for sure you were going to kiss the rug, so me and Wendel grabbed you."

"You okay, baby?" Opal asked and pressed one of her tiny hands onto my forehead. I didn't even know my hat was gone until I saw it on the table, next to the empty bottles and cigarette wrappers. "You're awful warm."

I hated knowing that across from me, Beatrice was watching, that she'd seen me swoon like a girl. My skin was chalky and damp. I made myself sit up straight and pull a cigarette from my inside pocket, which was as easy as building the pyramids. "Don't sweat it," I said, lighting up. "It just got a mite balmy in here. Everything's hunky-dory." And then I thought, screw this, I'm going to look right at her, like it wasn't a big thing, her so beautiful and satin in the dark light of the club. Let her see how far I was willing to go for her.

Was it a mistake? The way it was a mistake to bring that cute wooden horse into Troy. The half light gleamed on her cheeks and then there were those lips of hers, plum-like, ripe. I'd forgotten how much I needed to see her and that with just a look, she could silence all the reverb and bring everything down to a single, smooth melody. I wanted to throw myself down in front of her.

Never had I seen her so worked up about me in public. In her eyes I saw real fear, for me. Or was it because she thought that, with me being a little sick and not wholly myself, I'd somehow forget everything and crack out of turn, maybe blurt out the fact that she and I had been together? We're not through, yet, I wanted to say, but didn't. Sick, I may have been, but not stupid. I'd tell her about my plan for the record when everything was in place, and not before.

Arnie had said to me, "Don't boast about a touch or take before it's been accomplished. That's the surest way to ruin any plan—as though you'd left the safe door wide open so the world could admire your diamonds." Arnie, on the floor, blood ruining his beautiful suit. I wish I'd been able to clean him up a little bit.

I brought my feverish mind back into the room with a snap. This cold of mine made it too easy to get lost in the swamp of memories and not come out again. Deliberate as a pool shark, I looked at everyone, even her. "Cool it, kids," I drawled. "Let's not pull the fire alarm just yet."

Lots of grumbling, feminine clucking from Opal and Lilah,

but after chairs got moved around and everybody got settled down, you'd hardly know that a few minutes earlier I'd almost blacked out. Except that my head stung like it was full of tacks, my breath was still at the bottom rung of the ladder, and Beatrice kept staring at me across the table.

"So, talk already," I said when Sonny had grabbed his seat. "Why'd you schlep me down here?"

"Word on the pavement is you hightailed it from the Carmel Club. Aside from making peanuts teaching piano, wasn't that your only steady gig?"

Maybe later I'd take Sonny out back and tenderize his kidneys, since he'd just informed everyone, even Beatrice, about my current state of enforced idleness. I couldn't do that now, so instead I shrugged like it was no big thing. "That place was a racket that didn't pay half what I drank at the bar every night. I'm not sorry I quit. I'll find something else, something better, soon."

"Like gigging at Cairo Jacks?"

Motherfucking musicians' grapevine. Some days, like this one, a body couldn't take a crap without everybody in the city knowing about it. I thought maybe Sonny would hand me some toilet paper in a minute and tell me to wipe up. "I was filling in for Doug Polone." I forced out what I wanted to sound like a laugh but mostly came out a raspy hack. "Are you getting mother hen on me, pal?"

"No, man," Sonny said, but I didn't buy that. Everyone at the table was still looking at me like I was picking out a casket, and I didn't know what burned me more, the scorching in my throat or the idea that Beatrice might feel sorry for me. I never wanted pity from her.

He continued. "You can take care of your own business. Everybody knows that."

So when I said, "You better fucking believe it," I didn't know until I saw everyone at the table jump that I was shouting. I got myself smoothed out by going through Parker's "All the Things You Are" in my mind, just to take my kettle off the gas. Everything around me was a painful clamor: shrieking laughter, yelled boasts, the slam and clank of bottles, and driving music underneath, sharp and staccato.

Through that soup I waded to find my calm, and it wasn't easy, I'll tell you. But I made myself do it, since I only had two choices: either get caught and drown in the oceans of noise, or hold tight to a raft of melody and keep my head. Once I'd calmed down, I said, "Tell me about this gig."

"I'm playing a private party tomorrow night. A producer's spread up in Bel Air. Some Halloween costume jump."

I wanted to nettle Beatrice, make sure that she hadn't shelved me away in the library of past loves. So I said with a leer worthy of Groucho Marx, "Give my regards to the starlets." Good. Yes. I had my answer. She turned in on herself, going far-off and sulky, the way she would whenever something got under her skin.

Sonny didn't notice, though. He and Beatrice never had much truck with each other, and if they socialized together outside of Dee's, I never heard about it. So he just said with a laugh, "Well, Clipper, you can give it to 'em yourself, if you want." He leaned forward, bracing his elbows on his knees, and got deep. "I need a piano player tomorrow night. You game?"

From what I'd heard, those private Hollywood parties could lay out some serious cash for the entertainment. Plus plenty of food passed around on silver trays, champagne, and high-class women looking to slum with the help. A good time to be had by some. But, as a fringe-dweller in the musicians' scene, I'd never landed a gig like that. So I was almost ready to leap up onto the sticky table and shout my *brucha*, but something stuck in my gullet.

"You never asked me before, Son," I said. "What about Stu Lyman or Benjy Allen? They're your usual go-to guys."

"Benjy's got another gig in Los Feliz."

"And Stu?"

Sonny pushed out another laugh, glanced around the room before coming back to me. "Come on, Louis. Don't raise needless dust. It's a solid gig."

"Sounds as solid as Mount McKinley, but what are you asking me for? Seems like there's basketsful of other pianists you know, guys from the studio." I didn't want to play this tune, I felt like the scrapings off a hash-house grill, so I said, "Don't throw me any charity, Sonny. I don't need it. I got those teaching gigs, remember?"

"Who said you needed it?" When I kept quiet, he said, "When I get hired for these gigs, it's *my* ass that's on the line. I wouldn't put some idiot on the piano just because I felt sorry for him. They have to be good, or else *I'm* the one that's going to look like a heel, and I wouldn't get hired at any more swell Bel Air parties. Do you think I'm going to risk my rep and my cash by taking you on because I'm throwing you a bone?" He leaned back, chorus at its coda, and said with a shake of his head, "Man, I like you, but not that much."

To buy myself time, I took long drags off my cigarette and just looked at him. Maybe I'd gotten my back up for nothing, the same thin-skinned baloney that would sometimes rile my pop if you even looked at him cockeyed. Who knew what'd get him—some word thrown out that you wouldn't even pay a penny for, forgetting to save him the *Moon Mullins* comics, taking the last piece of babka even though he was saving it but never told anybody—then he'd get quiet and stiff and you never could get out of him what'd pulled the pin. It took me a long while to get a handle on what was behind that. I couldn't piece it together until after I'd left New York, and those spells of his were far off. I even talked about it with Beatrice, and between us the best we figured was that my father blew a gasket over anything that made him feel small, some kind of proof that he wasn't much in the eyes of the world, hadn't gotten far and was destined for a lifetime of the minor leagues. But he'd always turn that disappointment and anger on whoever made him feel that way, the hundreds of tiny offenses that piled up throughout the years, the sulking tantrums. But forget about telling him it was all an honest mistake, that you didn't mean anything by it. He'd have to cool down on his own, and then suddenly it's back to surprise bottles of Nehi and, Let's all tune in to the Dorsey Brothers playing at the Oneida Country Club.

There'd been a time when all I wanted was to have Ernest Greenberg's approval, but that time ended six years ago, him at the top of the stairs waiting for me to come back from the induction center and me coming up, both of us holding something in our hands—him his *New York Times* and me my 4-F papers. Was Beatrice thinking the same thing? The times she and I lay in bed, letting our minds drift from one thing to the next, maybe her mother's way of using potato starch in their church clothes, maybe whether Joe Louis was going to come out from retirement, which she doubted but I held out hope, and maybe the hot and cold tap of my father's favor, which could shut off and leave you shivering. My eyes strayed to where she sat across from me at the table, but she was making herself busy lighting a fresh cigarette. I couldn't much take how familiar her movements were, the way I'd seen her pick out a cigarette a hundred times, running her fingers over the pack until she found the one she wanted—which I always razzed her about, weren't they all the same?—how she'd work the cigarette from the neat rows and light it a full minute after she'd put it between her lips, a habit she'd picked up from her time in the defense plants to stretch out her breaks.

"What time does this brannigan start?" I asked Sonny.

He knew better than to make a big flap about me taking the gig, something I liked about Sonny. "Band needs to get there at eight, party starts at nine," he said, cool and smooth. "I'll pick you up and then we come around back. They don't want none of us darkies and kikes using the front door."

"How I envy life on the plantation," I sighed.

"Yassuh," Sonny said.

He gave me the rest of the details on the clambake, the address way up on Roscomare Road, above the country club, where the atmosphere was rarified and colored folks were called "the help." Sure, there were some Jew producers that shacked up in Bel Air, but nobody was going to let them in the club. I wrote what Sonny told me down on a scrap of paper and jammed it into my pocket. What I needed was to find me a bed somewhere and sleep until eight o'clock the next night.

"Time for me to blow," I said, getting up. The floor had stopped shaking like a burlesque dancer, and was now gently swaying like a ballroom hostess. I shook Sonny and Wendel's hands, gave a tip of my hat to the ladies, even Beatrice, and said over my shoulder, "Plant you now, dig you later." I didn't wait for anybody else to make their good-byes, but headed for the door. What I needed was some air, and pronto, away from the heat and weight of Dee's, the attic doors that got unlocked from just looking at Beatrice and her cigarette.

Parking on Central Avenue was as rare as a Klansman at *shul*, so I'd stowed my car in some narrow, dark alley a few blocks from Dee's. I was standing next to my car, patting myself down for my keys, when I heard her heels clack-clacking on the pavement behind me. From the sound, she was wearing her green satin shoes, the ones with the cut-out toe and straps that wrapped around her ankles. Something popped into my head—the sight of her walking around her house wearing just those shoes and a little green felt hat. I wanted to sigh and press my forehead against the cool metal of the car's roof.

"Louis, wait," she said, putting her hand on my sleeve. It would have been nice if I could have gone hard-boiled on her, not turned around, just said something snappy and sharp like a dime-novel shamus, then gotten into my car and pulled away, never looking at her once. Playing the iceberg act. But maybe because I was feeling poorly, I didn't have enough pepper to hold out against her, Arnie's advice drowned out by her melody.

"Cairo Jacks—that's the sailors' dive down in San Pedro," she said, but there was no heat in her voice. She looked downright bleak, and more beautiful than I could remember.

"It's more tea salon than dive," I said. "Strictly a pinkies-up kind of place."

She screwed up her face, the way she always did when I'd said something fresh but she wanted it straight. "You hurting for money that bad?" she asked.

I thought of the two grand quietly sleeping inside a record sleeve, and what I had planned for that cash. "I'm doing swell," I said.

"You don't look swell," she said. "You look lousy."

What started as a laugh ended with me hacking something up into the dirt. "Thanks, sugar," I wheezed. "I can always count on you to get a rosy take."

"When are you going to see a doctor?"

"I don't need one. I'm jim-dandy. Tomorrow I'm going to swim out to Catalina."

That did it. She'd had enough of me and my lip. Saying nothing, she turned on her heel and started to stomp away. But I was already down on the mat and listening to the knockout count, so what did it matter if I reached out and took hold of her arm? I could've bawled right then like a sniveling tyke. Her skin was a Chopin Nocturne, soft and melancholy, bringing back the long nights we'd spent in her bed and the short day in an orange grove.

"Bea," I said. "Dollface *bubele*. Don't go."

She didn't throw herself into my arms, but she didn't pull away, either, which was enough for me right then. "Louis," she sighed. "Here I am, outside. Something keeps bringing me out here, and I don't know what."

"Maybe on account of you missing me," I said. I rubbed my thumb along the inside curve of her arm, coaxing her the way I'd coax a phrase from the keys. "Poor kid."

The light from the streetlamp made a gold half-circle on her cheek as she smiled. "That cough of yours must've rattled something loose upstairs."

I started to draw her closer, slow and easy, hoping that I wouldn't tip my hand and let her know how bad off I was, how I didn't think I was going to be able to take another breath unless she was near me and I could smell the soap and tang of her skin.

"I didn't drag you out to this parking lot. You followed me."

She wasn't resisting as I was bringing her in, even as she kept a small tension in the bend of her arm, but I loved it, the contrast of it, brass and woodwinds or melody and improvisation. I could have gone on like that all night, except I felt sure I was running a fever of over a hundred and I didn't have enough kick in me to last much past a quarter chime.

"Could be I'm the one who's out of their mind," she said. "Things are a lot easier when you're not in the picture."

"There's no music in easy—no blues, no bop. Just the same note over and over."

"Maybe I like that," she said.

"No," I said, and she was right next to me now, so close I could count the links of the gold chain draped around her neck, gleaming dull in the weak light of the parking lot, see the faint shine of sweat above her lip, and feel the fabric of her dress rustling against my legs, and it seemed that everything slowed down to a thick, clotted moment, as hot and endless as a July beach, suspended, the whole world, the pull of cotton and gabardine across my shoulders and the turn of her ankle, her and me in a cooling alley blocks away from the club, the traffic of Central Avenue muffled beneath the distance between her and me, chance dropping from the branches of an orange tree to rot on the ground, the sustained note of the moon near the skyline, and words coming from my mouth I couldn't hear and didn't understand, but still they came out and I listened to them and watched her close the space that couldn't be closed, "no, you don't like it flat. You're C major seven. You go from a march tempo to jump and straight into a waltz. Unpredictable. Dangerous, even. The way it's supposed to be played."

Chapter sixteen

What with all the women I'd ever done the laying-down jitterbug with—there've been plenty, and that's not me blowing hot air, it's de facto, starting way back in the Van Cortlandt park boathouse all the way to now, and if you want a body count, I'd be the last guy who could give you one, but if you twisted my arm I'd number out something over a hundred but less than five centuries—with all that, you'd think that I'd find the whole thing pretty beat, the same from woman to woman, pussy to pussy, with maybe one or two things different each time, blonde, brunette, short, tall, skinny, zaftig, but hardly enough to keep it all fresh in my mind.

I'd feel sorry for you, brother, if the girls you'd screwed turned into one sustained note instead of the full symphony. Sure, a lot of them aren't going to be much to write up on the marquee, it's what you might call the law of averages—that is, it's a law that most chicks are going to be average in the sack. But then if you can't strum out the differences between them, the small things, the sharps and minors that are each woman's body and the way they move when they're lying under you, that's just sad, is what that is. The only excuse you could have for not remembering different women is if at the time you were wearing your bespoke suit custom-tailored by Mr. Jim Beam, which is a low state of affairs for you and the woman. It's an ill-fitting suit, chum, for finessing the ladies.

For example, sure I've told you about that first time with Francine Kuflick, who'd worn a path to the boathouse and was a pretty decent girl, she didn't want anybody to be her steady, just liked going to the boathouse, what's wrong with that? She and me went down there a couple of times, but then she said I was getting to be a drip, hanging around her locker, walking up and down the street in front of her apartment building, trying to think of words that rhymed with Francine—nothing, by the way, unless you know different and if so, maybe you could tell me—so she wouldn't go there with me anymore and next up for her was Henry Glasser. And maybe some guys would have gone off to some shack to lick their wounds, swear off girls, but I liked that Francine had taught me something valuable: to keep moving. No point staying around just one girl, when there was so much more out there to be sampled.

Now lots of guys could sit you down and spin some stale yarn about their first time, that's a square cinch, but what about the second, or the fourth or seventh? Unless a guy is one of those Mormon-types who gets their rocks off for the first time on their wedding day and that's the end of their history, you aren't going to get a wealth of detail about the women that followed Milady Number One. I can tell you about near every time I sat down at the piano keys, every piece I've played, the intervals, blue notes, and progressions, and I also have enough stories about women to make Scheherazade rethink her strategy and try card tricks instead.

Chick Number Two was Ellen Goldberg, a sweet girl who played the clarinet and wore straight plaid wool skirts. She had a Rudy Vallee record collection, and when we cleared the stuffed animals off of her narrow bed, it was "Heigh-Ho! Everybody, Heigh-Ho!" coming out of the phonograph, and when I pulled her sweater up, Vallee crooned "Honey," and when I got her skirt off he sang "I'll Be Reminded of You," and by the time me and Ellen were busy knocking her headboard into the wall, ol' Rudy was cheering me on with

"The Stein Song." Even now I can't hear Rudy Vallee without raising the baton a little.

Another girl that I remember is Estelle Perlman, whose father ran a cleaners next door to the automotive supply store. She was two years older than me, going to school to become a nurse. When her old man would step out to run an errand, Estelle and me would scamper off to the back and go at it on top of a pile of wrapped, clean laundry. I really started to love the smell of starch and sizing, and my mom would wonder when I came home how my clothes could be so mussed but I smelled so clean. But I didn't tell her that the scent of bleach wasn't actually bleach.

There were lots of other girls I catted around with back in the Bronx, but I made sure that they all were hip to the fact I wasn't going to offer them any diamond-studded shackles and a cozy apartment for two off Fordham Road. Hell, I knew guys who were already set to get hitched by the time they were eighteen, wife picked out and everything. As soon as they finished college, they and the lucky chick were going to start housekeeping and the brats soon to follow. Things were decent between my pop and mom, nothing that Carole Lombard and Clark Gable needed to sweat about, but I didn't see any of the advantages of lashing myself to one girl. You don't listen to the same piece of music over and over for the rest of your life.

But I'm not kidding when I say that each of those girls left something behind, some small memory or sense that even now, ten years later, I could give you a little detail about every one of them—Helen Liebow giggled whenever she came, Sylvia Gould wouldn't do it at home because she was afraid her mom might bust in at any minute, but she was fine with us going up to the roof of her building and screwing against a heating duct, Shirley David kept one hand clapped over my eyes the whole time so I couldn't look at her.

And there were the women I met after I left New York. There was the first chick I ever laid that wasn't Jewish, I didn't catch her name, but I found her at a bus station in Philly. I was feeling low, what with the way I'd had to leave the Bronx and me not knowing what each day was going to bring, and so I loped into the station trying to figure where to go, and there she was, sitting on the bench, a tender little bud in a plaid traveling coat, with a cardboard hatbox at her feet. How do I know she wasn't Jewish? I saw the tiny gold crucifix nestled in the hollow of her throat, and if I hadn't been planning to screw her before, that cross clinched it. We went across the street to a coffee shop and I still had a few bills in my pocket, so I paid for her ham and cheese sandwich, and when we wound up fucking in the ladies' room, I could taste the ham on her lips. Instead of bringing me up, though, with the newness of the taste and how girls like her were trayf to guys like me, I wound up feeling so blue I was almost indigo. It hit me then that I was gone, exiled, and I wasn't going to return home, maybe ever. I don't think I said anything to the chick before leaving, what with me feeling so rotten. She was pulling down her skirt, eyes glassy, so I wonder if she made the 3:15 to Detroit.

As I trucked my way from coast to coast, I found myself plenty of women in cocktail lounges, all-night soda parlors, movie houses, midways, laundromats, and lunch counters. A bunch were waiting for their fellas to come back from overseas, even a couple of married women which I usually stay clear of, since I didn't want to waltz with any jealous husbands who always have a way of showing up just when it's not so convenient, like when your pants are around your ankles. When the menfolk shipped out to be suckers for Uncle Sam, the ladies back home tried to be Mrs. Miniver, valiant, chin-up, spectacular hats. A few even tried out lousy English accents. But Greer Garson they weren't, even without the bombs dropping and blasted-out church sermons, so they'd turn to me when I was conveniently nearby.

I had plenty of unspectacular lays during the war years. Maybe the women thought that if they didn't move much or make like they were enjoying themselves, it didn't count. Or maybe they just weren't good in the hay. I found with those women, the stiff, eyes squeezed shut types, when it was over they'd get up, business-like, neatly button their dresses, smooth out their hair, spritz on perfume, and sail out of the room, thinking to themselves, "Well, *that's* taken care of. And now on to the Victory garden."

The ones who liked it, though, they were a different tune. One minute, they'd be clawing at my back, hollering in my ear, wriggling around so much it was like screwing a trout. And then when I was putting my britches back on, they'd start to cry, pianissimo, and wouldn't stop even after I left. Others would get really steamed afterwards, screaming at me, how *dare* I violate them like that, and I didn't think it was worth mentioning, as I ducked flying lamps and bottles of toilet water, that she had jumped *me* and it had been *her* tongue swabbing my uvula and her scratch-marks on my ass where she'd grabbed me and shoved me deeper inside of her. It didn't take much of a genius to figure that they were mad at themselves but that good old Louis could serve when blame needed to be handed out. I don't care for scapegoating, so I made sure to beat it whenever they got that look in their eye like they were Spud Chandler practicing their pitching skills with a nearby vase.

And as the war schlepped on, like I said, guys got more and more rare, rationed like sugar or coffee, especially young men such as yours truly. A paradise of women, the America I always wanted to live in. By the time '44 rolled around, there were enough women who'd lost boyfriends and husbands that they didn't work the violins when they wanted a little bedside action, and I had so much play I didn't even bother to try and learn all their names, just called them "Baby," which worked out nicely. Some of them got angry with me, you know, why was I home when all those brave young men were out putting their lives on the line in defense of freedom and their country, etc. That's why I kept my 4-F papers always in my pocket, getting so tattered that I held them all together with cellophane tape. Even so, they'd still be calling me a dodger and yellow, with their legs wrapped around my waist and their hips going up and down like drumbeats.

What did I care? I was getting as much pussy as I wanted and it didn't look like it was going to change soon. I was one of the only people not making with the whoop-whoop on V-E Day. Say *arrive-derci* to the parade of women. I saw all the young chicks lining up to make husbands out of the guys who'd been chasing foreign tail, and those chumps posing for wedding pictures in the cheap glamour of their uniforms. Nuts to that. It turned out to be hunky-dory for me, anyway. It wasn't the cornucopia that it had been during the war, don't mistake me, but I had this pretty face of mine and smooth patter, so maybe it wasn't a different girl every night of the week, maybe two or three times, instead. I figured anyway I was getting older, it was more seemly to take the tempo down.

With Beatrice and me, right from the starting line we ran a fine race together. In the hay she was tough and demanding, not too different from her out of the hay, and I liked how she didn't try and pin anything cornball on our action together. Even the most hard-boiled girl can take a perfectly good fuck and turn it to mush with just a look or touch. Those fillies, they'd come on as if all they wanted was what one of them called "base gratification," this from a chick who went to Vassar and considered herself a New Woman, but when the whole business was over and I was fixing to leave, they'd hop up and started making omelets or pancakes, and when I'd say I didn't want any, they'd practically knock my block off with a frying pan. Don't tell me I haven't faced enemy bombardment, I've got the scars on my forehead to show for it.

And for all that satisfying of base gratification, there was some part of all the tough chicks that needed more out of what the world dished up, the cored-out, lonesome baby wailing inside all of them, and they chased it by chasing me.

I didn't get any of that with Beatrice. She'd learned back in Ohio to take what she wanted and no beg-your-pardon about it. Our first time, we didn't make it to the bed, but went at it like kids in the rec room right there on the sofa. She'd kept it level enough to close the blinds and snap off the lights first. And then when we had finished, I thought she'd throw my hat and pants at me and tell me to take a powder, but instead she drew a bath and sudsed me up good, and the wood floors just outside the bathroom are still somewhat warped because of all the water that got splashed on them. It wasn't just the gusto she had for sex, but that I could always feel somehow that there wasn't any empty space inside of her, no searching part trying to hunt down an answer. She was total and complete—front line and rhythm section all present and accounted for. She didn't need me to make up the band, but maybe come in and jam for a while just to keep things interesting.

Over the next two years, she was my main concubine, and it got so that sometimes I'd find myself grinding some coatcheck girl's coffee in a storage room, or meeting a chick at a gin mill and going back to her apartment, and I'd lose my taste for them and finish up quickly just to keep from nodding off. Beatrice was my treat at the end of each week, the one woman I'd want to see again and again. Every now and then I'd kick around the idea that maybe I didn't want any other chicks, and could wait until Friday, but that never worked. I didn't think I could stick to one woman, even if she was somebody like Beatrice.

But I'd be pulling a Pinocchio on you if I said I wasn't reconsidering that idea after she'd followed me to my car. And I couldn't remember when we'd gone to bed together that could've been sweeter than that night. I can't remember how we got to her place, though I must've followed her, what with my car waiting for me outside and hers already in the driveway. With my fever, everything swam and turned liquid, a nonstop arpeggio swirling up and down the scale, and it was like she had a hundred hands, a hundred mouths, a honeyed, enveloping pussy that pulled me in so deep I thought I'd be smothered, though I wasn't complaining, no, that was one way to meet death that didn't seem so awful. And maybe with my fever, it was like I was running on extra steam power. We fucked and fucked and no matter how many times I came, my cock never went down, staying hard for so long it was like everything I was or would ever be was concentrated right there, between my legs, between hers, and the future stretched out before me as a lifetime buried inside Beatrice, and I didn't want to come back to the surface, with the blood a chord in my ears, sounding over and over, and her breath against my neck, her fingers threaded in my hair, the rest of the world flooded and drifting.

We must've stopped sometime, what with me coming to as an icy bottle of beer was pressed into my hand. And as I took a pull—one of the best sensations out there, I can tell you, a cold brew after who knows how many hours of uninterrupted sex, when it's a pretty sure bet that all your bodily fluids have taken the express train to the sheets—I finally got a good look at her. She'd wrapped herself up in the chenille bathrobe, and the complicated pompadour of her hair had come down in snags. In the lamplight, a soft shine traced along her skin, makeup long gone, either smeared off or maybe I'd eaten most of it. The murk of pleasure started to fade around me when I saw her. A sharp pitch and drop uncurled in my gut.

Then she said, "That was…good," but she didn't sound too tickled. She picked at the corner of the sheet and ran it under her fingernail—she'd said to me once that the feeling of the cloth rubbing up against the tender skin gave her a sweet pain, not entirely unlike watching her now, with the movement I'd seen her make a hundred times, almost always after we'd finished with the main action and were laying around talking about nothing in particular. Those times and this one seemed far apart.

"Pretty good," I said, and my voice came out sounding like a cross between a beat-up saxophone and a blender, not the silky, suave tones of a debonair man-about-town. Nope, I wasn't feeling so hot.

She'd been leaning against the bed, but now she pulled her legs up and curled them under, and I'd gotten enough juice back to see that she was drawing herself close, already pulling back even though not fifteen minutes before we'd come close to crossing the River Jordan together. I couldn't figure if that stab down in my stomach came from us tearing up the sheets, the flu I was battling, or seeing her curl up like a salted snail. She watched me as she drank from her own bottle of beer.

So that was it—that was how it was going to be, how it would end.

"Louis," she said, turning those dark eyes of hers on me.

Should I tell her about the plans I'd made, the record I would cut that would, amongst other things, bring us the means of being together? Until I had it in my hand, until the day I came to her door and showed her the disc, it would only sound like another far-stretching dream. I couldn't let myself turn into one of those guys, clinging, stooping, promising everything, anything, offering only words. A crawling spectacle of a man. She'd never take me back, then, hating weakness in others as much as she hated it in herself.

I was able to push myself up on my elbows. "Hey, babe," I said and offered up a cheap tin smile, "why are you looking so down in the mouth? Didn't we have fun, you and me?"

"This was—"

I reached out and tapped the underside of her chin with my finger. What good would it do me to storm and howl? I didn't have the steam for it. If I'd jumped to my feet and let fly, I bet that in half a second I'd be joining the rag rug spiraled on the floor.

"Fun," I said. Since when did that hard brass creep into my voice? It rang tight and edged. "Really brought back old times, didn't it?"

She sat back a little and something like disappointment moved across her face, which scuttled cold down my back.

"So you're going to be like that," she said.

"Like what? I wasn't being like anything except agreeable, right, sugar?" I looked at the bed and the clawed-up linens, and through the open door I saw picture frames knocked sideways, a little table lying on the floor, the trail of clothes that had fallen as we'd made our way into the bedroom. The silent record of how much she and I needed each other. It killed me that it hurt so much. "We had ourselves some kicks, but I've got to go." I couldn't take it anymore, I got up and dragged on my trousers, which I found wadded underneath the chair of her vanity. My head buzzed as I stood and for half a second I was afraid that right in the middle of my sophisticated patter, I'd wind up out cold.

I watched her watching me pull on my clothes. She could keep herself contained, and maybe some other guy might think she was hardly bothered by what was going on in her bedroom at four in the morning, but for me, I saw it differently. From deep under the smooth satin of her face came something like resignation and sadness—or I think it was sadness, and if it wasn't, I didn't want to know. "I should have known," she murmured, and her words weren't meant for me. "Same old Louis."

I was going to fire off my own salvo, but then the coughing got a hold of me and I spent the next few minutes staring at my bare feet on her carpet as I scoured out the inside of my lungs. When it was done, I had to sit down on the vanity chair to get my air back.

She walked slowly towards me and handed me the bottle I'd left by the side of the bed. I took a few pulls, but it didn't help my throat much, so instead I pressed the cool, slick glass against my forehead and closed my eyes. It took everything I had not to put that bottle down and wrap my arms around her waist, press the side of my hot face into the plush of her robe. In my mind, her name kept rolling over and over, a needle stuck in the groove.

"You sick for real?" she asked, and I opened my eyes.

"I thought I'd give you a guided tour of my lungs just for yuks," I rasped. "Don't forget to stop by the gift shop on your way out."

She took a step back from me and sat on the edge of the bed, shaking her head. "I never know with you, Louis."

"Know what?"

"What's real and what isn't."

A cold wind shook the eucalyptus trees outside. The street was quiet and ghostly. Four in the morning. Who knew what was going on across the city, what scraps of joy or misery were being blown against the base of the Hollywood Hills? The half-finished drinks with cigarette butts floating in them, the handfuls of cold cream rubbing out the last of the night's makeup, the unconscious, used and partly-dressed bodies of girls being loaded into the backs of cabs and the drivers told to drop them off anywhere, so long as it wasn't nearby. And me and Beatrice, in a small, yellow-lit room.

"I don't get you," I said.

"You do," she said. "You get everything."

I stood up again and padded down the hall, where I had a hazy picture of kicking off my shoes about three hours earlier. They were tumbled against each other by the bookcase in the front parlor, and I shoved my feet into them. Leather scraped my ankles—I was getting bonier, my flesh dropping away. The picture of me hunting down and putting on my socks didn't sit well, so I'd have to take a loss on them. Small price, I figured, for getting the hell out of her house before I did or said something that would chew me apart.

She followed me, her arms across her chest, and leaned against the wall. My jacket was out there, too, and my hat, and as I jerked my arms through the sleeves and jammed the hat on, she skimmed the room in the ashy light coming in from the street. She saw it too, the turned-over table, the heap of her dress left near the radio, and the picture hanging crazily on its peg, which she straightened. I was sick and glad. I wanted her to see what we'd done.

"Kitten, it's been swell," I said. "But I really do have to take a powder. Big night tomorrow, and I got to get my beauty sleep. Maybe I'll meet one of those bored producer's wives and she'll take me on for private music lessons."

Beatrice wouldn't go for it. Her sigh came out as cool and sorrowful as the wind outside, and my skin went hot and icy at the same time. "If you really are sick, you ought to get checked out."

I tugged the front door open, even though it felt like it weighed six hundred pounds, maybe because I was sick, or maybe I wasn't ready to leave yet, not quite. If I waited until I *was* ready to go, who knew how long I'd stay there, standing in her front parlor with the small and big space of the room stretched out between us. But open it I did and stood there halfway between the outside and the inside.

"I'm going to be fine, baby," I said.

"Take care of yourself, Louis," she said, and then I heard the low scuff of her laugh, which was more of a choked rasp. Just before the door shut behind me, before I was back out in the cold morning and wondering if it really could be over before it'd begun, I heard her say, "You always do."

Chapter seventeen

The mask I wore itched. I wanted to take it off, but Sonny'd said that the *feinshmeker* in charge—my word, not his—wanted all of the help to wear them, the girls passing canapés, the colored guy behind the bar, and, yep, the band. The starched Limey in the tux, whose accent, I might add, came straight from West London by way of Sherman Oaks, had passed the word on, along with three black masks. As long as the guests could see us, we had to wear them, "to preserve the illusion of the masquerade," the San Fernando Valley Brit said through his snoot. Masquerade, shmasquerade, just shell out my money at the end of the night, I said to Sonny. So while him, me, and Wallace Boyd on skins softly tootled out "Moonglow" in the corner of a huge room, we looked like Zorro's backup band.

At least the piano was good. I'll tell you the truth, it was one of the best set of ivories I'd ever had the pleasure of fondling, a Model III Bechstein Grand, all ebony casing that glowed like a woman in love under the soft lights strung overhead. And the tone—I bet a chimp could have sat down at that bench and pounded his paws on the keyboard, and what'd emerge would make Debussy weep with joy. Not even Leo Israel had a piano that fine, nothing but silk and resonance. And to find it in this phony Spanish hacienda sprawled at the top of the hills, shipped all the way from Berlin, just to look classy, tuned monthly but never played—I wished I was one of those strongmen down at Muscle Beach so I could've picked the thing up and carried it home with me. It was one of those princesses in fairy tales, stuck at the top of a tower and waiting to be rescued. So lovely and alone. If that piano had been a woman, I would've fucked it.

As we'd been setting up, Wally with his kit and Sonny fitting together his sax, Sonny asked me, "You feeling better tonight, Clip?"

I'd woken up earlier, I guess around three or so, and found that my cough had gone down enough so I could smoke without risking turning my esophagus inside out. I sat at my own piano, which was going to feel like wearing sandpaper underpants after this gorgeous Bechstein, a cigarette hanging from my lips and ash falling onto my hands as I warmed them up. Going through scales, it took me some time to tally up all the people who'd slipped away. Each time it happened, I thought I was getting better at it, the falling off, so that I could consider myself a kind of turnstile, spinning, spitting them out, but fixed in place. Some things you can practice. I unhitched my mind and let whatever came to my hands take over, and the scales shifted and reshaped until there came that melody, low and blue. I fumbled for a pencil and looked down a few minutes later: there, on the lined pages, I had scrawled a few bars, and when I played those bars back, they sounded like genuine music.

The phone was in my hand before I realized that I couldn't call Beatrice and have her listen to what I'd written, even though she was part of the melody.

So I didn't feel like I was burning up anymore, but instead there was this cold hollowness way inside that wouldn't budge.

"Fire up the stove, Jackson, 'cause I'm ready to cook," I said, and, to seal the deal, gave him a wink.

Sometimes when playing pop-style standards, my mind wandered off to find its fun elsewhere. Where it would go, that depends. Sometimes I'd think about the picture I'd seen the night before, or a radio broadcast, sometimes I'd lay out the next grift, or what I was going to have for dinner, when was the last time I'd had a decent crap, the usual potluck of nonsense that came to a mind at rest. It could even be kind of nice, cutting the rope that tied me to the dock so I could drift free on a sea of nothing.

Then there were times like tonight when, as soon as I undid that rope, I'd hit rocky waters and make myself sick. I raked myself over what had gone down the night before at Beatrice's place and every time I touched on it, felt I was ready to sink to the bottom. I'd think of her face, what she said—did she really know I was on the con, or was that what women say when everything's falling to pieces?—how much, when I touched her, I missed the feel of her skin, that she'd been the one woman, hell, the one person, who kept me from floating off into the soupy air of Los Angeles.

No—this was temporary. If I had to lash myself to my piano to get that piece right, I'd do it. And I'd finish the con I was setting up and cut that record and present to everyone my vindication on black vinyl. I just hoped that Beatrice wouldn't find herself another man while I was putting everything to rights.

I almost stumbled over "Time On My Hands," but caught Sonny staring at me, curious. The stumble was tiny, nobody but he would have caught it, but I sobered quickly. If I was going to brood on this anymore—which, I told myself I wasn't, close curtain—I couldn't do it here, now. A swell paying gig like this one didn't come around too often. Maybe I'd hamstrung myself in the past, but this night would be different. Instead, I tried to let myself sink into the velvet fullness of the Bechstein under my fingers.

Beatrice was too strong-minded to take another guy into her bed, or not for a long time, anyway. Look how long it took before she and me had finally made it to her couch and thence to her bed. Most of the guys at Dee's wanted her more than salvation, but she'd rather be alone than suffer some jackass' fumblings. Good. Fine. That left me some room.

From my bench, I got a good look at the room. Real cozy, like Versailles. And stuffed full of rich folks in costumes. Jesters, pirates, cowboys, angels, witches, and, my favorite, French maids, grabbing flutes of champagne from real maids in uniforms, who looked back with dull eyes and moved on. The costumes showed what everyone felt inside, what they wanted to be: the weasly yes-man duded up like Louis xiv, prim society mavens dolled up like harem girls, a guy in a superhero's cape and tights who probably never lifted anything heavier than a telephone receiver to fire somebody. Better they should've written signs and hung them around their necks, letting everyone see where their weak spots were.

Out there, too, were actors, some famous, some not. A guy I recognized from one of those fighter pilot pictures, not the hero, but the one who cracked wise and didn't make it but died bravely. The girl who played a detective's long-suffering secretary. But also John Lund, Van Heflin, Jane Greer, looking good enough to spread on a bialy. And wouldn't you know it, Montgomery Clift, too, but he didn't stay long.

Swank parties for swank folks are no different than the rent parties you know. Maybe the quality of the booze is higher, but drunk they still got. People laughed, raucous, got red in the face, said things they shouldn't have, made passes at somebody's wife, wives danced too close with men who weren't their husbands. Everyone spilled drinks, slumped in chairs, hoarded canapés like it was still the Depression, boasted, bawled, swore and hustled.

As the band, we were somewhere between the guests and the servants, in a sheltered bubble near the potted palms. The peons didn't say "yassuh" and "nosuh" to us, maybe because Wally and Sonny were colored and didn't deserve such fawning scorn. We didn't get the welcome mat, though, no long-lost cousins showing up at the family reunion. Nobody used our first names, gave us instead a cool civility. We were the tuxedoed ghosts.

Ghost or no, I toyed with the idea of getting one of the girls serving cocktails into the powder room during our next break, to prove to myself that I still could. Maybe just a little old-fashioned necking, the way I used to way back in the Bronx before Francine Kuflick surrendered the goods. A fine-looking dame with black hair and brown eyes had been giving me the vamp routine whenever she passed by with her tray of martinis. I didn't know how she could keep all those glasses on her tray when she was knocking her hips from side to side like a metronome.

On the band's first break, I'd watched where the girl with the Theda Bara eyes had ambled off to, then, hands in pockets, not rushing for the train, I went after her. When the fifteen minutes were up and it was time to get back to the serious business of party music, I'd learned that her name was Cynthia, she'd come out from Florida to see if there was more to life than orange groves and sunburns, she wanted to be a teacher or manicurist, and she'd noticed my long, slim hands.

I went back to the band in a slow mosey. "You make that chick yet, Clipper?" Sonny asked. He said to Wallace, "This here cat's the fastest gun in the West. Can't go no place with him without some doll tossing her panties in his face."

"That so?" Wallace asked, and hit the ride cymbal, ching-chick-a-ching. "Hot damn!"

I pulled the bench up and sat down. "So young," I said, playing a quick, improv *toccata*, "and so talented. Pity me, fellas, it's a heavy burden I bear."

"Maybe you can give me some pointers I can use with the hot looker I saw in the kitchen," Wallace said.

"That peola number?" Sonny asked. "Gate, you too dark for her. Light-skinned dames don't want no sooty man straight from the jungle. They like to set their sights high."

"Step aside, Wally, and I won't just *tell* you how it's done with that muffin, I'll *show* you," I said, and even though Sonny and Wallace laughed, Wallace looked a little funny at the idea that an ofay like me would try and squire a colored woman. Getting that, I kept talking to wash over everything and make him forget that I'd suggested making a pass across the color line. "With that stilt-walking chick, Wall, you've got to play the Eskimo. If you go pawing at her, she won't care and she'll send you packing to Loserburgh, but try and hold out a bit. If she thinks that you couldn't give a horse's rear about her, it'll drive her bats."

"I don't know 'bout that," Wally said, and I saw that I hadn't won him back yet.

So I kept at it. "Meek girls need to feel special," I said, "as if they're rare butterflies you chased to net. But those chicks puffed up with pride, they can't resist it when you treat 'em like yesterday's lottery numbers. They need the challenge, they need to know that they can conquer you, that they're just too mouth-watering for you to resist."

"Yeah," Wally said, fiddling with his drumsticks, "you may be on the level."

"Straight and level," Sonny said, nodding. He wasn't freezing me out, but he wasn't running up to slap me on the back and act jolly.

Wally said, "If Sonny says you know dames, well, I'll buy what you're selling."

Maybe détente had been reached with Wally, but that brief high I'd been feeling about Cynthia from Jacksonville got knocked out and landed on the damper pedals. Sure, I could play in his combo, comp his solos and be a good sideman, but white was white. Beatrice knew it. That's why she kept the blinds drawn and the lamps burning low.

With a faint chill along my neck, I studied the playlist. "Margie" was next, then "Stairway to the Stars." I wouldn't let myself stew over what just happened. It wasn't personal. That's how things were—for now. But I was feeling a little less well as we started the opening bars of the next number.

Four chords into it, I saw her. Walking in with Doctor Livingston and a ballerina. She was dressed as Little Red Riding Hood, but even under her cape I recognized that shape. Standing no taller than Livingston's shoulder. Then she pushed back her hood to get a view, and what with her not wearing a mask, it was plain. A good thing I knew the tune so well, or else I'd have blown it for sure. But behind my itchy mask I goggled. She was in accounting, and I couldn't figure how a low-rung studio girl like Nora Edwards got into a swank joint like this one. I was on *shpilkes*, wondering if she was wise to me sitting at the piano, when Louis Dante was a banker and not a professional piano player. I knew I couldn't leave right in the middle of a gig. So I sweated it through "Time on My Hands," and "Poor

Butterfly," wondering when she was going to come stomping over and clock me with the basket she carried.

The commotion never surfaced, though. I should have known that a woman who loved Jean Dickenson wouldn't give much attention to the jazz combo in the corner. She didn't even look my way. Instead, she let Livingston guide her through the guests, making introductions for her and the ballerina. When we played "Smiles," I let go of the breath I hadn't realized I'd been holding. She didn't see me, or, if she did, there was no recognition, no leap from the masked piano player Greenberg to her gallant suitor Dante.

I tried to let my gaze follow her around the room, and keep tabs on where she was. I couldn't do that and play, not without flubbing the tunes, so play I did, all the time wishing I could grow another set of eyes to tail her. If I knew where she was, then I wouldn't be caught off guard. I didn't want any surprises of the sneaking up kind. But I had to play and hope she didn't come up behind me. Our next break came. I didn't think about Cynthia waiting for me in the coat closet, I just wanted someplace quiet and dark. Trying to watch Nora while playing had worn me to a nub, and the breaks left me vulnerable to her finding me. I'd cased the house earlier and knew that there was a study not too far from the main room, a study with a balcony that looked out over the city. The noise of the party was a wave that pushed me away, carrying me towards a pocket of welcome solitude.

Los Angeles seasons aren't full of pomp and glory, no sharp winters when the air up your nose is a stab from an icicle, or thick summers that feel like breathing hot U-Bet syrup into your lungs. But every hundred years or so, rain falls from the Southern California sky, or the mercury might coyly slip beneath sixty-eight degrees. Fall is when you could notice it most—one day the Santa Anas dry everything out and all you can see is a yellow dust pooling in your eyes and the gutters, the air turning gold with the wildfires burning in the canyons, and the next a cold wind comes down from the San Gabriel Mountains drying the sweat on your back into a chill hand pressed too close.

So I stood on a private balcony outside the small study, gently shivering in my borrowed tuxedo. The party room inside had been too toasty, too many bodies, too much booze, and I wasn't yet back to the pink of health, so as soon as our set had ended, I'd made a break for it. I planned on sitting in the study for a while, but the outside seemed so welcoming and clear, I went straight out onto the balcony. Now I felt the last breath of October creep down my collar, but I wasn't ready to go back inside. The balcony looked out over the city. I could just picture the house's owner coming out each morning to stand on that balcony, and calling himself the King of Los Angeles. As kingdoms went, I wouldn't put much stock in that one—all the castles were made of foam rubber and the knights' armor a bunch of aluminum foil. Still, it was a fine view, one I wouldn't mind having myself some day, with the featureless expanse of the city turned into something strangely far away and beautiful, like coins on the floor of the ocean. My father would have loved that view, to him it would've been the dream made real—the house on the hill, the party inside, the hands of Hollywood spread wide in welcome.

I turned and went back inside, then shut off the lights. There were a few chairs in the study, both bathed in light from outside, but I didn't want to sit. I stretched out on the floor, on top of some plush Oriental rug, and sighed. I was in darkness and it was everything I needed it to be.

When the door to the study opened, then closed quickly as someone stepped inside, I wanted to yell at whoever it was to get lost. But doing that would have meant letting them know I was there, and I didn't think the gracious host would appreciate the help bawling out his guests or lying on his six-hundred-dollar rug. Still, I'd look a mite ridiculous when the trespasser turned on the lights and saw me there. I was trying to come up with an explanation, but it wasn't necessary. The guest walked through the dark study, not bothering with the desk lamps, and went to stand at the glass doors, staring at the view. I just about shoved my fist into my mouth to keep from blabbing out loud.

It was Nora.

I shouldn't have been surprised. The farm girl in her, much as it wanted out of Iowa, would start to feel a mite pinched at a party like this one. She ate almost every night at the same restaurant but ordered differently each time, a person who stuck close to the familiarly strange. A spread like this Bel Air place, stuffed to the expensive rafters with well-heeled heels—she was going to need a break from it all. She'd need someplace quiet, but not too far away from the action. She was a guest's guest, not welcome to wander far around the house. So to the study she came. In the darkness, she didn't see me. Instead, she put her hands to the glass doors and took in the city at night.

I thought about trying to edge out of the room before she noticed me, then checked that notion. It'd be almost impossible to leave without her noticing, and I wasn't your friendly gentleman cat burglar type who could creep through rooms unseen and unheard, then chuckle knowingly as I straightened my already immaculate bow tie in the hallway. So I lay on the floor, trying to keep my breathing to a quiet hurricane, hoping she wasn't going to clap eyes on me and blow everything to hell.

Then I realized I'd been given something. A gift. Gifts come from strange places. A diamond in snow. The song in the scream. And now, the chance to watch Nora.

Have you ever watched someone who thinks nobody can see them? Try it, sometime, and see what you learn. Sure, you might get someone scratching their ass or digging for gold in their nose, stuff we all do. But past that, you get an idea of what they're like offstage. Mostly all the corsets and camouflage comes off in the shelter of home, so to get someone absolutely pared down to their real selves out in the world, that happens not so much. It's only then that the bluster is peeled back and the fear emerges. Or the eyes kept trained on the sidewalk, meek and mousy, look up with hate. Or the bombshell doesn't have to fake it anymore and she looks at her body and what it can do with a sick despair. Or sometimes, when the wrapping comes off, all you find underneath is nothing.

And here was my chance to see Nora without being seen. Maybe she was going to be one of those hollow people rolling around like a spent cartridge.

She threw a fast look over her shoulder to make sure nobody was watching. I pressed my lips together to make sure not even a puff of air came out. Satisfied that she was alone, she scratched on the underside of her tits, where two crescents of sweat had formed. There wasn't anything sexy about it, more like an animal happily scooting on the grass, but it didn't bother me. Some guys, when they get proof that a woman isn't made of cotton candy and perfume, when they finally see that they have bodies just like theirs, bodies that sweat and smell and flake and need to shit and bleed and run down—when they see that, it makes them crazy or angry. Maybe they thought that their mommies were ice cream smooth, no holes to let crap in or out. But when they find out that women rot like the rest of us, sometimes they want nothing to do with them anymore. Sometimes, they knock girls around, as though they wanted to make them pay for being faulty, fragile skin.

Me, I didn't mind so much. I'd known so many women that there wasn't anything I hadn't seen—scars, sags, bruises, blotches, lumps, pocks, dents and bulges—and these were pretty girls, too, not the crusty broads outside burlesque houses. A little something like sweat and scratching didn't bother me. In a way, I find it comforting, that nobody's above their own bodies, even women.

With a soft groan, she rubbed her face gently—not hard enough to smear her makeup, just a little scrub. She looked over her shoulder, towards the door behind her, through which the sounds of the party came, dampened. Almost midnight and things were still going strong. Who knew how long we'd have to keep playing—maybe until the morning, which didn't make me want to dance up and down the stairs like a Ziegfeld girl—but green was the color of our host's cash, my favorite color, so if we had to play "Slap Happy" ten more times while the costumed schnooks lay on the floor sleeping off the last six bourbons, I'd do it, and thanks, mister.

Here I was, thinking over how long I was going to be stuck up on this hill, or laying on the floor, but then the light fell across Nora's face, and it was a hard punch in my gut. What was I expecting? Not that.

Sweet little Nora, all gee whiz and golly, at the Hollywood party. Alone now, or she thought she was, at any rate. And she wasn't beaming with pleasure at the fairy-tale sheen of the house, the guests, the glimmering city below. Those not pretty, almost cute features of hers had collapsed in on themselves as a wellspring of despair hit her. I couldn't remember seeing such a look of misery and loneliness, even with all the grieving women I'd conned. Underneath that, there was anger at her own sorrow. She turned back to the fairy-tale view and began to cry in big, gasping hiccups, taking her fists and grinding them into her eyes.

Say you were eating a big slice of cake: thick white frosting, sugar through and through, and then you bit down hard on something and spit it into your hand, and what lay there in your palm was a bullet. But I wasn't sorry to find that bullet. I was glad. The secret hidden heart of Nora Edwards. Uncovered and all mine.

Chapter eighteen

A few minutes of this, and she'd gotten herself together. Nora rubbed her palms over her cheeks, pulled a knuckle across each eye, and wiped her nose across the back of her hand. Satisfied that she wouldn't reveal her solitary misery to the merrie band inside, she turned and started for the door.

I sat up and leaned against the wall.

"Please don't turn on the light," I said, using Memphis Arnie's bourbon drawl.

She actually gasped and stumbled back, knocking into the desk.

"I beg your pardon," I said. "It's just that my head...and the lights make it worse."

Her voice came out half an octave too high. "I...can't see you."

"Yes, sorry. I need the darkness right now."

"How long have you been here?"

"Don't worry. I won't tell anyone."

"Oh," she said, breathless. "Thank you."

Make the mark feel indebted to you. Another of Arnie's lessons.

She wouldn't really know why she owed me something, only that she did, and that made everything so much easier.

"If your head hurts you so badly, I could go and find you an aspirin," she said, and that's when I noticed that it was gone. There was no sign of that hidden angry misery I'd seen not a few seconds earlier. Nope, she was back to cream and sugar, and if I hadn't heard her punishing sobs before, I would've never known what she was keeping locked away. I wondered what kind of woman could choke out furious tears, and not but a minute later seem as smooth as night.

"You are too gracious, but that won't be necessary," I said, the Courtly Southern Gentleman. "I just needed a little seclusion from the party."

Nora nodded with relief, finding a surprise comrade in the darkness. "Then I ought to leave you alone." Solid Midwestern modesty insisted she quit the room and let honey-voiced men seduce other maidens. She moved towards the door, but I wasn't ready to free her yet. Opportunity is made. Quarters are not pulled from young ears, except by nimble-fingered gents who've already palmed the coin.

Me as Ashley Wilkes said, "Now, my momma would surely give me a whipping if she thought I was being anything less than gallant where a lady was concerned. We can both stay here." I stayed in the shadow, and she took a step towards the study door, uncertain. This was something new for her. "I must insist," I said, pouring on the molasses. "Your company would be most welcome."

"But your headache?"

"Interesting, isn't it? The way a gentle female voice can be so soothing."

Women and accents. The Limey accent is tops for getting past the girdle, but I'm not into those European acts. Too far from home, too easy to bobble and say something you shouldn't. Then you're left with a phony accent hanging from your lips like bad herring. So I stick to Stateside. For sophistication, I throw on the Mid-Atlantic—boarding school, deck shoes, opera glasses and cigars with Father. Some women melt into schmaltz whenever the Bronx sneaks into my voice, maybe thinking that they've netted themselves some tough yegg with a heart of gold, a real Damon Runyon-type character. But when I don't want to take any chances, then I borrow a page from Arnie's sheet music and bring out Ole Dixie. Guess they all want to be on the porch of the plantation, slurping down juleps and listening to the happy darkies sing in the cotton fields.

And it worked on little Nora. She looked around, a touch nervous but quietly thrilled to be in the middle of the scene.

"Won't you sit?" I asked. "I'd pull a chair out for you, but my head just throbs like the devil when I stand."

She slurped up the half-finished courtliness. "Don't trouble yourself," she said, with what she hoped was a girlish trill, tossed me a shy smile and scooted into a stiff-backed chair parked next to the desk. Together we listened to the shards of laughter and talk barely muffled by the closed study door. Unlike the Carmel Club, when the band took a break here there wasn't a jukebox to plug in and soften the sounds of fevered merrymaking.

"Do you smoke?" she asked.

A nearly empty pack of cigarettes I'd begun this morning was stuffed into the inside pocket of my tuxedo jacket. "Once in a great while."

"Strange," she murmured. "I smell tobacco. It's very familiar."

"Is that so?"

"Yes. A…friend of mine smokes this one brand, and I could swear I smell it now."

"Might you be a dear and open the balcony doors? The fresh air is so welcome."

Silently, she got up and did just that, then went back to her chair, ankles crossed, hands folded in her lap. Waiting for the sermon, such a lady. I hoped the dry, cool breeze would scour away the traces of Louis Dante and leave only the Southern Gentleman in his place.

We both looked at the scenery that lay beyond the balcony. Los Angeles did its job and twinkled just outside. Aside from the clatter and commotion close at hand, the night itself was almost hushed. Far below, the headlights of a car rounded a corner, winding its way up the hills to some rich man's opium den. "Wonderful view, isn't it?" I asked. "Our host must be one lucky gent to have a panorama like this."

"I suppose," she said.

"Are you good friends with him—our host, I mean?"

She laughed like someone who didn't know what a laugh was supposed to sound like. "Hardly." Then she remembered that I might be chummy with Daddy Warbucks, and said more pleasantly, "And you?"

"A distant acquaintance." Then I added, in the soft, intimate voice that makes folks want to trust you, "If I may make a private confession, I'm rather uneasy in opulent settings such as this. I hope it doesn't show."

Everyone loves being let in on a secret, especially women, and especially from guys with Southern accents in posh shadowed studies. Playfully, in a whisper, she said, "Your secret's safe with me. If I can be honest—"

"Please, do."

"All this," she waved a hand around to take in the house, the view, the guests, the money, "makes me a bit uncomfortable, too."

I smiled, the kind of smile that would make sure she and me were the closest of bosom companions, the repository of each other's darkest self. Then I remembered that she couldn't see me, and I could make my smile have more facets than the Hope Diamond, but it wouldn't matter. Words, not flash, would win this prize.

"I'm glad we're of a like mind," I said. "But why come here, at all, if you don't enjoy the setting, and if you aren't acquainted with the host?"

"His accountant is a friend of mine."

"Ah," I said. I waited a few beats. "And when you say that this accountant is a friend…." I let my voice trail off.

She got me right away. "A *married* friend," she said with a laugh. "I came here with him and his wife."

"Of course, of course," I said, and laughed a bit, too, making sure I sounded jokey and a hair relieved at the same time. And then, because it's what the Georgia Gent might say, and also because I wanted to nose her out, I said, "So where is your beau this evening, if not with you?"

When she looked thoughtful, her head tilted to one side, and said, "I don't know where Louis is tonight," I could hear the tentative affection for me in the way she said my name, like she was getting sweet on me but wasn't so sure that she could let herself, if it was safe yet, and even the tiny sting of hurt that where the hell was I, anyway, with her not knowing. It didn't sneak past me, either, that when I'd asked after her beau, she'd named yours truly. Awful fast, with us not knowing each other more than a handful of days.

"This Louis is a lucky fellow," I said, coming on rueful but being a good egg about it, "but rather feebleminded, I'm afraid. Shouldn't he be here with you, on this festive occasion?"

"We never talked about it," she said, getting her back up a bit. "We just went out Friday, and it would be forward if he tried to see me so soon afterwards." She was making excuses for me, not something I generally take a shine to, but she was more protecting herself than me. "And I didn't want to seem too forward, either, by asking him."

"You're right, of course," I said, nice and apologetic, but no groveler, either, "and I shouldn't say anything unpleasant about something I don't really understand. In fact," I went on, "it seems to me that your Louis is a pretty good man, to be so courteous where a woman's concerned."

"He's a real gentleman," she said, and I knew she was thinking of Friday, when I gave her just a kiss goodnight instead of trying to angle my way inside. She'd decided to be pleased about it, see it as something good—and not give any thought to her wanting me to come in, what that might mean.

"Here's to the last of the real gentlemen," I said with a tip of my imaginary hat, throwing in a touch of Tyrone Power along with my deep-fried charm.

A cool wind blew up from the base of the hills and shifted the trees, making them sound like girls adjusting their petticoats.

"Do you miss him?" I asked.

"Louis?"

"Your late husband."

She looked surprised. "How did you know I'm a widow?"

"Well," I drawled, "you've the air about you of a woman, not a girl, the kind of knowing that comes only from marriage. And it stands to reason that if this Louis has been squiring you lately, it's likely your husband wasn't waiting at home."

"Maybe I'm divorced." She smiled.

"I'd wager you weren't raised to believe in divorce. That's for fast girls."

"You're right. I lost my husband in the war."

"I'm very sorry."

"Thank you. I've had a few years since then, however, time to say my good-byes to Floyd." And she sounded like that was the truth, too. There were pictures of him at her house, but they were already becoming images of herself and some stranger. Poor Floyd, stuck in a hole somewhere in Italy, rotted away in body and memory. Sad, that's what that was, and more proof that it doesn't matter how you die—a hero, a coward, alone, with someone—nothing kept you fixed to this earth past somebody remembering you, and even that thinned to disappear.

"Now there's Louis." It's a queer feeling to talk about yourself as if you weren't you, like giving your own eulogy.

"Now there's Louis."

There's something about night, something about time creeping on to the smaller numbers, that maybe the dark is going to last forever, the curtain won't be drawn back. And also everybody was wearing costumes and masks, so it was safe, whatever was said didn't count, it wasn't you. Here we were, near, but not on, a romantic balcony, a wild party steps away, and my voice coming out of the shadows, but friendly, and her in the light. Nora was ready to give me the key to the library. She probably didn't even know she was talking until the words had jumped out of her mouth.

"I wonder about him, though," she said. "I wonder what he wants."

"Why must he want anything?"

Her shoulders came up in a half-shrug. "Most people want something from you. Or it seems that way, anyhow."

"That's very cynical," I said, and I'll own that I hadn't expected her to talk like that. But then, having seen her secret despair just a few minutes ago, I was starting to believe that anything could be possible with Nora.

"Perhaps so," she sighed. "I ought to be more trusting. That's how I was raised."

"Something changed."

Her smile came out like a twist of lemon at the bottom of a dry martini. "I got married." In that one word, "married," I heard her whole disappointed history, the lines she'd been fed since she was in kneesocks, the vow of a better life reneged upon.

Pondering the matrimonial state wasn't something I wanted her to do. "I suppose the more important question to ask yourself is, what do *you* want from *him*?" Something I wanted to know but couldn't ask, not as myself.

Maybe that wasn't something she'd thought about. She turned as silent as Harold Lloyd. She actually opened and shut her mouth a few times, nothing coming out. "He's different from other men," she finally said. "He's not a wolf, and he knows how to make me smile."

"So he's ugly."

Nora laughed. "No, no. He's quite a handsome man."

"But you haven't answered my question. What do you want?"

"I want…" She opened and closed her hands, forming tiny fists that, if thrown, would maybe gently daze a butterfly. "I want what I was promised," she said.

I avoided promises. Opportunities for disaster and disappointment. I never made them to Beatrice, but felt the bitter edge of their wounding just the same and it fueled my anger's engine. I couldn't keep the grit from my voice when I said, "Maybe this Louis isn't the guy…the man who can give that to you."

She said, "I think he is," like she was meeting a challenge. What she really meant was, I'll *make* him into that man, whether he wants it or not.

What could she do to me, in her race to create the make-believe paradise of home, husband, children? "Then you're lucky you found him."

"He found me, actually," she said. "I'm glad he did. But he's so extraordinary, I wonder what he could possibly see in someone so plain like me. There's lots of beautiful women in this city."

"Ah, you're being modest."

"I'm not! I work at a film studio. I know there are girls who belong in front of the camera, and there are girls like me, with adding machines and typewriter ribbons. You know," she added wryly, "nice girls. Smart girls. Funny girls." She knew the code, what a woman might say about another woman to make her feel better, because of her buckteeth or bulgy eyeballs. But everyone knew those words meant nothing, paper prize ribbons handed out to keep the also-rans happy.

"I mean, who's to say," she went on, "that he isn't out tonight with another girl, someone younger or prettier?"

"Or," I added, "he could be sitting in a room right now, having a pleasant chat with a pleasant woman upon whom he has no designs."

She screwed up her face, skeptical, then sighed. "Maybe you're right. I hope you are."

"Perhaps, if you want things between you to become more… intimate, but he's too much of a gentleman to suggest something of that sort," I said, slowly and easily, "you might consider taking the initiative."

She started back a bit. "Are you suggesting—?" Sputtering. Knowing that the Iowa in her wouldn't even think the word 'cock' unless she was referring to the rooster in the yard, I could feel her turning red, and me three feet away and sitting on the floor. "I couldn't, I mean, I've never—"

"Maybe you should, maybe now you start. That would command his attention."

"But, but," she choked, "wouldn't he think less of me? That I was some sort of," her voice went raspy and low as she pushed out the suspect word, "strumpet?"

I'm not an expert in this area, since there hasn't been a single woman that I've screwed and thought to myself, Self, this girl's a tramp, and if I were you, which I am, I'd get my business finished and skip out, pronto, and forget about taking her to meet mom and pop after Shabbos services. I was never looking for one of those nice girls, marrying girls, so I didn't have an opinion to be lowered, no expectations dashed upon the cruel rocks of truth. For me, it was the opposite. If some woman decided she wants to hold out and dangle her pussy like a bingo prize, hoping to keep me around longer, that's when I shuffled off. Come to think of it, Nora was the only woman I'd taken out and *not* gotten into bed.

But most guys, I'm not, and I knew plenty of others who tried to get into a girl's girdle and once she surrendered, they didn't want anything to do with her anymore. Which doesn't make sense. But then most guys are chumps, buying the line that a girl who goes too willing to the sack isn't a good girl, a girl you'd bring home for mom's brisket and dad's sly winks.

"If this Louis is so special," I drawled, "then, on the contrary, he'll be delighted and charmed if you show him how you feel. No," I went on, "I don't believe he would be put off in the least. I know *I* wouldn't."

She mused, "I don't know. That's exactly what my mother told me not to do."

"Consider your mother's marriage," I said.

Toosh, as Memphis Arnie used to say. I had her there. But before I could say anything more, I heard the rat-a-tat of drums and the guttural moans of a sax, and knew that I'd gone way past my fifteen for a break. Sonny was sure to wring my neck.

"You know, I believe an aspirin might be just the thing," I said. "Would you...?"

She jumped to her feet, loving to be of use to a man. "Of course. Just wait here." Scurrying to the door, she opened it, then looked over her shoulder to get a good eyeful of my face. I turned away, futzing with my lapel, keeping myself in the darkness. She waited for me to turn so she could see me, but I didn't and, after a minute, she slipped from the room in search of aspirin.

As soon as I heard her footsteps disappear, I bolted from the study. The heat of the house pressed against me and my head twirled on account of rising in altitude so quickly. I was punched by sound after the relative quiet of the study. When I sat back down at the piano bench, Sonny giving me the what for with his eyes, the first notes of "How High the Moon?" came out stiff and blocky. Everybody at the party was too sauced to notice.

"Where the fuck were you?" Sonny snapped when the number was over. "Busy nailing that chick in the coat closet?"

"Who?"

"Her." Sonny tipped his horn towards a sourpuss girl in uniform standing by the entrance to the kitchen. Cynthia. She was steamed, and when I waved, she flounced out of the room. I shrugged. There were dozens of women like her, dozens of coat closets. And Nora. She had her usefulness. There wasn't any danger.

"We ain't got time for your shit, Louis," Sonny growled as Wally hit the opening to "Can't Help Lovin' That Man."

"Sorry, boss," I said, and Sonny scowled some more when he didn't see a fleck of remorse on me anywhere.

Chapter nineteen

How long does it take to make somebody trust you? If you could time it, how many minutes or hours would get used up before you became someone's new best friend? And when would you become the kind of friend that they'd tell anything to, believe whatever you say, split themselves open like rotten jack-o'-lanterns, and then hum cheerfully while you picked through the seeds and mushy flesh?

There's no one answer to that—some folks are just naturally suspect, and they'd throw even a bowlful of sugar right back at you. They're hard and rusted out. Maybe once they tried to ask for love but got batted down or slammed onto the ground with a boot on the neck, and they've been trying to hit back ever since at anybody they can. Those are the folks who slouch into the bar and sneer and snarl, then hours later pour themselves home and stare at the floor, cursing the whole stinking world that did them wrong. Fortunately for yours truly, and other grifters, they're not the only pebbles on the beach. Even in big cities, even in a place that guts you like Los Angeles, there are still plenty of folks who don't know they're empty until you offer to fill their glass. And lucky for me, that's just the kind

of guy Ronald Oates, sound engineer at Hi-Life Records, turned out
to be. So, to answer my own question, it took me all of two hours
and five Brandy Alexanders to hook this poor schlub.

I'd waited for him at the Irish pub off Fairfax I'd cased the other
day, and I played the C easy and smooth, so smooth I bet even Memphis Arnie would have forgiven me anything. Oates was used to being
hollered at by musicians and producers peppered with ulcers, blamed
for the singer blowing her lines, or the fact that nobody in the room
had any talent. He'd learned fast to keep his mouth shut up tight, to
become just part of the scenery, like the fake wooden panels and the
pea-colored carpeting—stuff you see, but don't see. Hardly anybody
talked to him in the bar, and nobody talked to him at home.

And here was I, no drip, a pretty swell-looking specimen and
full of manly companionship, not looking through or talking around
him, but sitting right by him at the watering hole and asking him to
settle a friendly tiff I was having with the bartender about who was the
better piano player, Oscar Peterson or Bud Powell. (Okay, I'll fess up:
there wasn't a tiff, not really, it was just some baloney I started spout-
ing ten minutes before I knew Ronald Oates was going to show, me
trying to get the bartender to talk and making sure I picked a subject
I knew Oates was hip to.) So when pal Oates hefted himself into his
usual seat at the bar, I could turn to him, natural as a blonde in Wis-
consin, and say, "Don't you think Bud Powell's got Oscar Peterson beat,
where comping's concerned?" which, you have to admit, isn't exactly
your typical "How 'bout them Knickerbockers?" and one I wouldn't
throw out with just anybody, but these were special circumstances.

It took a while yet to get chum Oates to break his habit of
silence, but when it came out that he was in the music line and so
was I, but I wasn't a big britches *artiste*, just someone who loved
music the way he did—which is why he got into recording in the
first place—we became bosom companions as fast as the highballs
were drained.

And I did feel a bit sorry for him. How could I not, with
him so full of words that had gone untapped for almost a decade,
nobody to talk to. Once I did crack him, he gushed palaver like a
broken fire hydrant.

On top of that, I was using my take from the big store con and throwing down cash to treat him, my new pal Ronnie. More booze, a one-dollar shrimp dinner from Doc Grimaldi's Sea Foods in Beverly Hills, and I shelled out the cover for him and me to catch some righteous jazz at a couple of clubs in Hollywood, pricey places I didn't usually frequent, but I was willing to take the hit to the pocketbook and ego for the greater good. I was laughing at Oates' jokes, but it was my fame, my future with Beatrice, that had me really laughing.

We wound up at a Mid-Wilshire cocktail lounge, a pretty dead place once the office squares finished guzzling their dinners and stumbled home. After three drinks, consulting the bottom of his glass, Oates said, "You're not so bad." I wasn't sure whether he was referring to me or the honorable Johnny Walker, Esq., but then he turned his eyes up to me. "I didn't think anybody in this town liked real music but me."

"You're not alone," I said.

He was one of those schmaltzy drunks, which is better than an ugly drunk, though instead of worrying if you were going to get smeared to a paste, you had to keep an umbrella handy for the inevitable gush of tears. And brim his eyes did, as he said, "Not anymore. Hardly anybody takes the time to really listen, you know? I mean, just because some music isn't pretty or simple, just because it's different from everything else, doesn't mean it's no good."

It didn't take the Manhattan Project to figure that he wasn't only talking about music. "I know, pal," I said. "Sometimes the best things are the most misunderstood."

"Exactly," he blubbered. "You appreciate what's valuable."

By the time the night wound down it was coming on three in the morning, and I was ready to vow undying love to my mattress. I dropped Oates off at his place off Kings Road and watched him fumble for his keys. It was all I could do to keep from slumping over the steering wheel to be found in the morning by an irate milkman. And tomorrow, I was going to have to do it all again.

I was busy trying to arm wrestle Ida Lupino with Richard Widmark officiating when the phone rang and woke me. Nora. Was I free for lunch? We could meet in the commissary—and Tuesdays were meatloaf.

It was quarter to twelve and my head was stuffed with old gym socks. The idea of choking down studio commissary meatloaf made me want to scour out my esophagus, and I doubted there'd be any beer, let alone whiskey.

"That'd be swell," I said, and cursed myself for being a lazy bum when the bottle I found in my nightstand was empty.

"Are you sure?" she asked. "I know it's awfully short notice. You probably have plans."

I was hanging off the side of my bed, the blood pooling gently in my head as I searched for maybe just a tiny drop of blue ruin sliding around the bottom of a bottle somewhere, anything to wash the taste of stained towel out of my mouth. "Nope, no plans."

"Wonderful," she chirped. So, she was in an up mood. "But you don't sound very good. Did your cold come back?"

"A little," I said after covering the receiver with one hand and giving my lungs a robust cleansing. "That's why I'm not at work."

"Gracious, I forgot about that. But we can get you some soup," Nora said. "They make a wonderful scotch broth."

I bet there wasn't any scotch in that broth. Tough luck. "Great. I'll see you in half an hour."

Forty-five minutes later, having soaked my head and put on my least stale suit, I met Nora at the studio gate. She was wearing a cute green jacket and skirt that didn't make any apologies, and even though I wanted to rest in a nice, quiet highball, I made myself smile back when she beamed at me from the other side of the guard's booth. Here she was, right out in public, smack in the middle of the day, in front of Stanley the studio guard and everybody else, smiling and waving like she couldn't have been happier to see me, and confident she could show that happiness without anyone giving her an ugly word or look. It was so different from what it was like with Beatrice that I just sat in my car for a few minutes, brimming with anger, until Stanley growled, "I ain't a carhop, bub," and I pulled forward, careful to wipe the resentment from my face.

Nora popped in to the passenger seat and didn't stop herself from giving me an enthusiastic buss on the cheek. She went pink a little, but I could see that the words of the mysterious Southern gent from Halloween had affected her.

She directed me through the maze of the studio. There was hardly anything to see. Some of the grifts I've run have brought me to different studios, waiting around between takes while the chorines got their tits powdered, and the little kick I first got to see where all the pictures came died quickly from boredom.

"This is pretty exciting," I said as I guided my car slowly past the prop department. A couple of union guys were putting the finishing touches on some phony Egyptian statues, but Israelites in bondage they weren't.

"I suppose it is," Nora laughed, "but I'm so used to all this. Every now and then, the farm girl in me sort of sits up and looks around and says, 'Golly,' but that doesn't happen very much anymore. Park here."

Soon as she jumped out of the car, I gave my cold, damp forehead a good swabbing with my hankie and made another promise to myself that as soon as I could, I'd get myself down to the Liq-R-King and shell out some money for some schnapps or muscatel or dago red—anything to punch this flu of mine right in the gut and leave it panting on the mat, KO. But that was going to have to wait through a whole lunch hour, and until then, there were about fifty coughs I was going to need to swallow.

She threaded her arm through mine as we started walking, and the feel of her chest in green wool pressed against my arm reminded me that she wasn't and wouldn't ever be Beatrice.

"Which would you like first," she asked, looking up at me with the sun washing down on her face so I could see the nervous excitement in the blue of her eyes. "Lunch, or a tour?"

I didn't want to eat. I didn't want to sit across from her in the commissary, and chat and be pleasant. I didn't know what I was doing there, with her, only that it wasn't right, not at all. But I couldn't make myself leave.

"If you don't mind waiting a bit to eat," I said, "I'd just love a tour." Then I remembered the fact that the studio was huge, and we were going to be stomping around for a goodly while.

"Swell!" She started to pull me along. "Anyway, it gets too crowded in the commissary at this hour. There's never enough chairs and it's just like being back in high school, wandering around with my tray in the cafeteria, hoping to find someplace decent to sit while everyone stares at me."

"There's always room at the debate team's table," I said.

"Or next to Elmer Hobart, who's repeated tenth grade three times."

"That was Marvin Bittleman at my school," I said. "He failed ninth grade so many times, they finally made him Principal."

She turned her head to one side and stared at me, just like a little bird in the park watching the guy on the bench throw crumbs.

"What?" I asked.

"I just can't understand it," Nora said, "how Carla could have preferred some other man to you."

Goddamn it, she really liked this guy, this Louis Dante, who was as real as an imaginary ghost. And I—he—found myself—himself—liking her, too. But whoever 'I' was, that didn't happen to me. I didn't go soft on the con. I couldn't figure who was being conned here, though.

I must've scowled, because Nora just about chewed her own lips off. "I'm so sorry," she jabbered. "Sometimes things just pop out of my mouth before I think, and I didn't mean to be rude, I just—"

"No, it's all right," I said, and lucky for me just then that my cold roughed up my voice a smidge, almost like I was holding back tears. "I understand what you meant."

"It was a compliment…really," she said, going pink again. This girl blushed like the nuns just kicked her out of the convent for giving them an inferiority complex.

"Then…thank you."

We stopped in her office first, and unless you looked outside the window and saw Linda Darnell and Cornel Wilde sharing a knish, you wouldn't know it was anything but a regular accounting office and not someplace attached to the movie business. The same water cooler in the corner, the same ceramic lights overhead turning everything pale, the same green glass-shaded lamps on heavy, scarred wooden desks, groaning under typewriters and adding machines, the same clanging file cabinets, and the same washed-out faces of women and men losing years as if they were minutes.

Nora had me meet some of her fellow bean counters: an old maid in a ruffled blouse who giggled when I took off my hat, some jowly schlub who wouldn't look up from unwrapping his bologna sandwich, a youngish girl who gave me the eyeball that said, What are you doing with *her?* Through all of it, I smiled and said not much, just enough, but don't think I didn't get what was happening. These sad specimens were giving me the okay, and Nora strutting me in front of them was making it more official, so that in the days and weeks to follow, the old maid or jowls or roving eyeball could ask about me and it was set and sure between us.

She showed me her desk. It was small and tidy, with a little potted violet and not much else. "Home sweet home," she laughed, and I made myself laugh, too, though I wasn't feeling much like it. When I was just a little runt, couldn't have been more than six or seven, my pop took me into his office, to show me off to the staff and give me a peek into where he spent his days. I guess I'd been picturing it like him disappearing into the clouds each morning, shaping the destinies of nations with a shrug of his shoulders or the neat comb of his moustache—even though, looking at our cracker box of an apartment, my folks, my sisters and me and my bubbe all heaped on top of each other, nobody who ever controlled the fate of millions would have stuffed himself in there. But what do kids know? Even when I'd ask him what he did all day and he explained it to me, I still never quite got what all those figures and balances and inventories meant. It wasn't like being a fireman or a doctor or even a plumber. Pop belonged to the vaporous world of adulthood, a place I wanted to see, but feared, too.

So to clear things up, one day during the summer I got to go to the cardboard box factory. My sisters were jealous, they kvetched why couldn't *they* go, too, and even though pop explained that it was too dangerous for three little children to be running around a factory, he would take them some other time, he and I both knew that there were some things only a father and his son could really appreciate—the manly business of work, the legacy handed down, seeing where men go to provide for their families. It was figured that even though I couldn't do my times tables very well, being a not-so-brilliant scholar who'd just finished second grade, eventually I'd do what all men had to and take a wife and start my own passel of tykes.

The factory itself was quite a spectacle—a brick building with FELDMAN & RUBINEK PAPERGOODS painted in white and yellow on one wall—and to my six-or-seven-year-old eyes, one of the biggest and most impressive structures I'd ever seen. (This, by the way, was a title soon wrested away by the New York Public Library when my class took a field trip into the city. But it's not possible to be too impressed with big buildings if you live in New York, and soon I would yawn at the Chrysler Building and roll my eyes at Grand Central Station.) Pop took me by the hand and showed me, from a safe distance, the factory floor where the giant, hissing machines pressed out the corrugated cardboard and cut it into shapes. The noise was terrific. I almost cried, but saw that my father just looked at them like they were faucets or bookends, nothing to be afraid of, so I made myself brave and didn't cover my ears. When we passed a row of workers in heavy denim clothes—some Italians, some Irish, and then the coloreds sweeping up—and they all tugged on their caps to say, "Morning, Mr. Greenberg, and little Mr. Greenberg," I felt like the prince touring his future kingdom.

Then he took me up a long flight of stairs to the actual offices. Back then, there weren't quite so many women out working, and those that did were either young chicks straight out of secretary school or else stern, unsmiling women who lived with their elderly mothers and thought children were an affront to decorum. I thought the young ones were too powdery and bosomy, squealing over little boy Louis and acting as though they hadn't seen any kids before and this one right here was a miracle straight from God's workshop. The old ones were scarier than the machines on the factory floor, and I clutched my pop's hand tight as we walked past.

When we came to the inevitable frosted glass door, I thought surely that someone so important as Ernest Greenberg, my father, would have his own office, but no, that's where the boss was, and pop's desk was just outside. Standing there, staring at that desk and holding his hand, I looked for something, some sign, that showed just how eminent and special he really was, him, the decision maker, the controller of destinies, but it was just a beat-up wooden desk with papers piled into wire baskets and an open ledger full of numbers.

I wondered, my belly getting heavier and heavier, if that was it. I kept hoping he'd bump my shoulder and say, just joshing, come on, and show me to a marble and chrome cavern with vaulted, painted ceilings and an ebony desk covered with ringing telephones, everyone demanding to speak with my father, the captain of industry. No such luck. This was him, this desk in a room of desks, not the important man behind the frosted glass door, just a guy who came in every day at eight and left at six, with a few breaks for cigarettes and sandwiches. And then, if that's what happened to him, what about me? Was I going to end up in a dusty office too, behind a desk, moving paper from one pile to the other?

When I started to cry, I told him it was because the machines downstairs had hurt my ears, but we both knew that wasn't true. I could tell, as he pulled out his pocket square to wipe at my cheeks, that he saw his desk, his office, his life, through my disappointed eyes, and that he would never be the untarnished hero for me again. We left soon after to have malteds at the candy counter, and I never again asked what my pop did and he didn't offer to bring me back to Feldman & Rubinek.

"Are you all right?" Nora asked me.

"Yeah, sure," I said, "why?"

"You looked...upset."

"I'm aces." I rubbed at my sticky eyes, forced out another laugh. "I always find adding machines moving. So many beautiful numbers."

She didn't look like she was buying it, so I asked her some question about interoffice memos, and that got her going for a little while. Curled up next to her telephone was a string of four paper clips hooked together. When she turned to point something out to me, I did a queer thing—I palmed that chain of paper clips and slipped it into my pocket. I didn't even know I'd done it until a lot later, when I went looking for my lighter and found the paper clips instead. And even then I didn't throw them away or even unhook and use them, but kept them in my pocket and I would find myself rubbing them between my fingers, the way I'd seen some Catholics with their rosaries, and a strange calm would come over me.

But I didn't know any of that until, like I said, later. We moved on. We stood outside on the little walkway in the colorless light of afternoon, the kind that washed everything pale, and she squinted up at me.

"I work with those people every day," Nora said, "but I never really talk to them. Nothing besides, 'Where are those files?' Or, 'So how was your weekend?' And even then I don't actually say much about what I do outside of the office."

"Because you go to the movies, and they think they're better than that."

"I just don't know what's wrong with believing in something."

I shrugged. "It's easier if you don't."

She thought about that for a minute. Not the movie business, but the girlish dream of marriage that died between trifling arguments and shriveling affection. "There's hope, isn't there? Hope for something better."

"Some people use that hope. Exploit it."

She looked away. "I know. That's what films do. But we keep coming back, keep hoping, because without it…there's nothing."

For a long time, she was quiet. Then she made herself bright. "So, what would you like to see next? Wardrobe, Makeup, Props?"

None of those options sounded as appealing as a vodka martini, so I said, "You are my guide. I'll leave the judgment in your hands."

A strange, sly look came over her, with a thread of doubt underneath it, so I knew that whatever was up next, she had something schemed. What that something was, I couldn't figure, so I guessed it best to just play along. "How about the back lot?" she asked.

"Sure. Sounds terrific."

We walked for a while and then turned a corner, and then, bang, there we were standing in the middle of a Lower East Side street, all brownstones and basement apartments. The idea that out here, where the eucalyptus trees swayed in the mild early November breeze and things like subways and walk-ups and 600% humidity on a 100° summer night couldn't be more unknown, they had to go and build a fake New York for the schmucks out in Indianapolis or anyplace else that wasn't Manhattan—the whole thing struck me as sad, really.

Even though I knew that this New York wasn't real, I couldn't help but feel like I'd been slammed to the mat. It'd been years since I was home, the closest thing I had was lying around, remembering. Standing in the middle of it, real but not real, was as if I walked the streets of my own memory. I could see it all in front of me, but there was no going inside of it. The streets were empty, the way they could be when we dream. It riled me, is what it did, dangling something in front of me that I couldn't have.

"Strange, isn't it?" Nora said. "They studied lots of photographs to get it right. Have you ever been to New York?"

I choked down my anger and said, lightly, "A couple of times."

"And?" She looked up at me, expectant. "How does this rate, compared to the real thing?"

I took in the gutters, the prop trash cans and plywood stoops. The ghost of my past taken shape in California. "Too clean."

She laughed. "I'll talk to the art department, maybe they can fabricate some nice, expensive garbage. Orange rinds at a dollar apiece, or crumpled newspaper for five dollars."

I walked over to a brick wall and rapped my fist against it. "It's hollow."

"Everything is," she said. I don't think she knew how true her words were. "Let me show you something."

I followed her up a stoop into one of the brownstones. But instead of it being a real apartment building, there were just bare plywood rooms with some scribbles here and there, support beams holding them together. I wanted to find it comforting, knowing that this New York wasn't my New York, but that comfort wouldn't come. "Rents must be cheap," I said.

She was starting to get jumpy, talking fast. "They shoot the interiors on soundstages. Some of the sets are small, like an apartment, and sometimes they're gigantic, like a whole hospital floor."

I wanted to know where this was leading, so all I said was, "Huh."

She gnawed on her lips for a minute, then seemed to make up her mind. "Let me show you the second floor." She went up a set of wooden stairs, me trailing behind. We stood at the window and looked out onto the phony street, where Public Enemy Number One and Little Caesar had leaned out of stunt cars and fired blanks at coppers, and it was home but not home, a phony substitute for something I couldn't get back. I was thinking about the years I'd spent on the real streets, the stickball and handball I'd played, safe in the knowledge that no matter what, I could always turn around and climb our own flight of stairs back up to my pop reading the paper, nothing could change that, except it did change, and here I was, marooned out in Los Angeles—and then I was pushed back away from the window and there was Nora sticking her tongue into my mouth and clawing at my jacket.

She tried to climb me like a cat on curtains, rubbing herself up and down me, her fingers going into my hair to pull my head down closer, what with me being a good foot taller than her. So I grabbed her ass and hauled her up close, and let me tell you, she must've practiced on bulls back on the farm, because this girl could kiss. Poor Floyd. He didn't have a chance.

Then her hand went to my crotch and I not gently pushed her hand away as I stepped back.

Nora looked like she was trying to decide between bursting into tears or eating my liver. "Don't you...want to?" she asked.

"Of course I do, sweetheart," I said, and started to put myself back together again, tucking in my shirt, giving the jacket a tug. She looked relieved. "But not here on the backlot, in front of Sam Goldwyn and God and everyone."

Nora went limp and crestfallen. "I thought...he said that men liked...I thought you would like it if I was more...aggressive."

After straightening my tie, I stuffed my hands in my pockets to hide the fact that my body surely did appreciate her efforts, even if other parts of me seemed not to. "Honey, don't give a guy the wrong idea," I said. Rage had come back, hard and blistering, even though I'd gotten exactly what I thought I had wanted. I'd felt something when Nora kissed me, something more than just the bloodhound of my cock sniffing out the air. What was it? Another kind of pleasure, almost...relief. Happiness. That wasn't part of the plan. I looked at Nora and hated her for making me feel anything at all.

I never took an open hand or closed fist to a woman, so instead I said, "Maybe I've been mistaken this whole time about you. Maybe Floyd was wrong."

"What do you mean?" Her face had turned red and spotted.

"If you're the kind of girl who does this," I nodded at the plywood surrounding us, the scene of Nora's attempt at seduction, "how do I know that you weren't stepping out on Floyd while he was overseas?"

"I would never," she sputtered. "I didn't!" Tears started in her eyes and I stared at her without moving. "You have to believe that."

"Why should I?" This felt good, right. I wanted to hurt her, and I wanted her to hurt me back.

Nora stepped towards me, twisting her hands. "I never do this. Never. But...a friend told me...that I should..."

"You *talked* to someone about this?"

"It was nobody, nobody."

I shook my head and looked sadly at the ground. "I don't know, Nora."

She came closer, hiccupping with sobs, and reached for me. "Please, Louis. I'm sorry. So sorry. Can't we forget this?"

"Forget?" I asked, slipping away from her hands. They hung there, suspended in the air, like unrequited love. "I can't forget about Floyd, and his letters. Maybe you did, though."

"Not ever," she cried. I stared at her sadly until something started to crumble inside her. It fell away, leaving her white and shivering. "Once," she said, so quiet that hardly anything moved in the bare plywood room.

"Nora," I said after a good, long pause that left bruises, and there was so much disappointment heavy in my voice, you could grab hold of it and sink to the bottom of the ocean, drowning.

She'd gone past tears, now, and was dry with misery. "It was only one time," she said, in the flat listless way someone recounts tragedy. Her eyes were glassy. "Jack Hodges, from hiring. There was a party at someone's house, and we all had drinks and then...it wasn't very nice. I never spoke to Jack again. I never told anyone about it before today."

"Poor Floyd," I said. "He always believed in you. Even at the end." What the hell was it going to take to make her lash out at me?

She found a small reserve of tears and they crawled down her cheeks. "I'm sorry."

"I *want* to believe in you, Nora," I said softly. "Should I?"

Her voice was smaller than her. Soon, she would disappear altogether. "It was just the one time. And I felt so awful about it. Can't you see? I still do." She stared at me across the plain, blank floorboards, floors that would never support the weight of genuine lives. There wasn't much left in Nora anymore. I'd cleared her out like the room, and she was ready to be leveled or filled as I liked. No, she wouldn't try to cut me as I'd cut her, but at least I got to enjoy wounding myself. But even that didn't help. I felt ill. She said, "Louis. Louis, please."

I took a deep breath and thought. Not about what she was asking, but about other things, mostly Beatrice. She had this dress I loved, a white cotton dress that she would wear in the summer, that made her skin a wonderful torture, a dark soft glow. She could wear that dress when she met my father. I could see everyone hanging out of their windows and draped over fire escapes as I pulled Beatrice from the car, walked her up the stoop with my hand on her elbow. Neither of us would notice the staring, but it might be a little strange, a little strained, at first, when she and my parents would sit in the living room that smelled of burnt bread. They didn't talk to colored, much, my parents. But when our conversation would move to music, to the brilliance of me at the piano, then the burnt smell would be forgotten, the faded sofa forgotten, the evasions and untruths forgotten. We'd all pile into the car and drive into Manhattan, to the Rainbow Room. Then the Greenbergs of Jerome Avenue and the Greenbergs of Bel Air would be shown to the best table and everyone would think, "It was all worth it."

Where was Nora in all this? I'd banished her from my vision, just as I'd been banished from New York. But she wouldn't disappear. I wanted her to, but she wouldn't.

Eventually, I opened my arms to Nora. As she stepped into them, shaking with relief, I said, "Okay, honey. I'll try and put this behind us. I'll try to forget."

Chapter twenty

I had this game when I was a kid: I would try and walk down the hallway of our apartment building with my eyes closed. The game was to see how far I could get before I'd open them. Sometimes, I'd let my fingers brush against the walls, but usually I'd just try and walk straight ahead, testing myself. Would I reach the door to our apartment? Would I make it to the Kleins', or even further to the Lobells'?

I liked the pleasantly queasy, unbalanced feeling I'd get, moving forward slowly, never knowing if I was going to bump into any walls, or even if somebody would jump out from the stairs and knock me down. And every time I did it, I'd think, this time, I won't get scared, I'm going to make it all the way to the end, all the way to Mrs. Schulman's door.

Thing was, I never did get that far. Usually, I'd make it midway between us and the Kleins before I couldn't take it and opened my eyes. I don't know what I was afraid of, what might have happened if I'd kept my eyes shut—nothing too terrible, not really. I fell down and scraped myself up plenty playing stickball or horsing around in the street. Likely I wasn't going to fall onto a sword someone accidentally left out in the hallway, what with there not being so many Barbary pirates with scimitars or cutlasses in the Bronx. But eventually, I needed to know where I was. I couldn't go stumbling forward blind.

For two years, Beatrice and I had been idling, motors running but nowhere to go. It'd been enough to see each other at the end of each week, tearing up the sheets, listening to the blues, and never thinking past the next dawn. We each got what we needed and nobody stepped on anyone's lines. I could've gone on like that for a while, maybe forever, but that day in Oxnard had changed everything, pushed me from the comfortable, ambling path onto a highway. Blinking, dazed, I stood there like a schmuck, and might've gotten run over if I hadn't thought of the scheme to finally cut a record.

I understood what I needed, wanted with Beatrice. But Nora had been a puzzle. At first, I didn't know what I was getting out of her. Part of me thought I could use her for some mild enjoyment in bed. And I'd given myself the perfect opportunity to get between her thighs on the studio backlot. But that's when I understood that whatever I wanted from her was worth a hell of a lot more than five to seven minutes of halfhearted fucking.

And when it came to Ronald Oates, well, mystery there wasn't. I was strolling merrily down a flood-lit hallway. That's where I was, in the bright, each doorway and bump in the floorboards completely familiar, as I took Oates out to the far and sundry jazz watering holes in Los Angeles, never once doubting what I wanted and how I was going to get it, and why. My first solo long con, the one that meant everything. Money, time, I'd give them all.

One of the first things I did was take us to a cocktail lounge that I knew had a piano. As Oates wandered off to the washroom, I took the piano player aside and gave him ten bucks to take an extra-long break.

When Oates came back from the washroom, I was already ensconced at the piano, a drink left waiting for him. I was playing a moody "Body and Soul," and giving it everything I had.

Oates perched on a nearby stool and sipped his drink, watching me play. Different folks have different ways of listening to music, so you can tell what they're getting out of it. There are the recreational types—the head-bobbers or toe-tappers, who want music to jump and leap for them like a trained dog, and as soon as the music stops entertaining them, they immediately lunge for the radio dial to find something else upbeat and amusing. Some do nothing. They sit in their chairs and stare, blank. For them, music just ends silence, and in silence they can look inward and find nothing. They don't feel music, don't hear it, and when it plays, the best it can do is keep their thoughts from turning towards the yawning cavity of themselves.

Another type makes a big show of how they're true music lovers: they hunch over and screw up their faces, as if they were balancing each note, and should their attention flag for even a second, the whole crystalline structure would collapse into a pile of glass. Those folks claim to be the real audience, but I've been to too many shows—I see that what they're actually doing is boring their girlfriends.

Now Oates, I had to give it to him, he was the genuine article. His face stayed smooth but attentive as he tilted his head just a little. His eyes moved back and forth slightly, like he was reading the melody as it rolled out into the air. Every once in a while, he gave a little nod, not one of those exaggerated, cranium-shaking movements that the music snobs threw out there, but a small, private nod. Or sometimes he'd give a quick, intimate smile when I reached some ornamentation, a smile that'd be over almost before it began. We were having ourselves a conversation, and it felt strange to me, because I'd never tried to reach out to my audience and speak to them before, it had always been about me and the melody. Now, here I was, taking Oates into my confidence, asking him to hear, when I played, that I'd give everything up for this and this alone.

After I finished playing, Oates set down his empty glass, got down from his bar stool, walked over and put his hand on my shoulder. I didn't want to look back at him, worried that by combining the con with music, I'd overplayed my hand and given too much of myself away. So I stared at the keys, white and black, and heard him say, "You're lucky, Lou. You're very goddamned lucky."

I didn't know what he meant until we'd moved on to our next bar. For hours, I sat with him at a tiny, candle-lit cocktail table and got an earful of his life story: raised by his pop in Altoona, PA after his mom took sick and turned in her bingo card, just the two of them in an apartment over a radio repair shop, and the young Ronnie Oates going down to that shop to listen to the music programs because his own home was a void with no heart or sound. Down in that radio shop, Ronnie heard the same bands I heard miles away in the Bronx—Basie, Armstrong, Ellington—except I'd had the good fortune to also get musical instruction and ability. The young Oates took a job downstairs at the repair shop to pay for a saxophone and lessons, only to discover, twenty bucks and a few months later, that he had no talent. The teacher told him it wouldn't be right to take his money anymore, since he'd "heard more lovely sounds come from my flatulent uncle."

Where do the talentless go? Into production, of course. Oates, already used to being ignored or denied by his father, took to being a sound engineer, the blank of recording music. He just worked the levers and switches, nobody giving him much mind unless they felt like shredding someone to pieces. And he took it, of course, because what else was he going to do? But now I'd gone and opened him, and the lifetime of silence crumbled underneath the need to reach someone. Me. The guy who'd grind him into even less as I carved out my future with Beatrice.

"Here I've been running my mouth off," Oates said, looking at the bottom of his third highball. I'd told the waitress to keep 'em coming. "You've got to be bored senseless."

"Not a-tall," I said. "Do you want another drink?"

"Maybe I'll slow it down a bit."

I nudged another full glass towards him and he reached for it. Onstage, a combo was trying to murder "China Doll," but it wouldn't quite lay down and die, like Rasputin. Oates grimaced—at least he had a good ear.

"Hurts sometimes, doesn't it?" I asked. "Loving music, when there's so much rotten stuff out there."

Oates rolled his eyes. "The kind of crap I have to hear at Hi-Life, the acts they sign." He shuddered. "Really awful stuff. Novelty songs about puppy dogs or *trooo-hooo-hooo* love. I could puke."

"Don't they bring in any good bop?"

He snorted. "Goddamned studio owner doesn't think there's any money in it. 'That's for weedheads and uppity niggers,' is what he said." What a true gentleman scholar, this owner sounded. How I would love to serenade him by moonlight with an M1 Carbine. "I wish I could just get one bop act in there, just once." And then, bless him, he looked at me. "Somebody like you."

"Believe me," I said, trying to keep myself from capering around the table, "I'm trying. In fact," I said, lowering my voice as much as I could above the combo's continuing assassination, "I have a studio all lined up. But they want more money than I've got."

"I have..." Watery-eyed, Oates started digging through his pockets. He came up with two fistfuls of laundry tickets, lint and three crumpled singles. A couple of coins hit the table and rolled onto the floor. "I guess not a lot."

"That's mighty swell of you to try and help, Ron, but I doubt you've got that kind of bread just laying in your trousers." I heaved out a big sigh, almost gutting out the candle on the table. "I already made a deposit, but trouble is, the cat I've been talking to says that if I don't come up with the rest of the cash pronto, the deal's off."

He came on all flustered and alarmed. "We gotta do something!" Oates was already talking 'we.' "Maybe we can go to the racetrack."

"The ponies are crooked," I said. "And card clubs don't let you walk out with more than a few hundred bucks," I said, thinking of the many golden hours I spent watching the suckers win just enough to lose big at the Carmel Club. "I need more than that."

Oates was looking more and more glum, almost as if my misfortune was his. "There's gotta be some way to get money quick," he said, "but short of robbing a bank, I don't know how."

"But you work at a bank," I said.

He blinked at me. "No, I don't. I work at a recording studio."

"Yeah. The bank."

It took him a few minutes, but once he got my meaning, he stopped being drunk and started being scared. It was like he had to walk through broken glass just to get to a pair of shoes so he could navigate a minefield. "You mean, record at Hi-Life?" he gasped in a horrible, strangled voice.

"Just a thought," I shrugged. "You know the place, know its schedule. We could slip in and cut something. Nobody'd know."

That made him almost melt into his chair with fear. "Oh, no, no, no," he moaned. "Trying to sneak in recording time? Without paying? If Mr. Walsh found out, I'd be *lucky* to get fired." He tried to grab his glass, but couldn't pick it up with stiff, numb fingers.

I wondered what could be worse for Oates than getting fired. Maybe this Walsh had hired muscle. But whatever Walsh would or wouldn't do, Oates was ready to chew off a limb to get away from it.

I patted Oates' hand, and smiled comfortingly. "Don't worry about it, pal. I was just razzing you. That's what friends do—kid each other."

"Friends," he repeated, taking courage from that shining word. Eventually, he calmed down enough to go back to drinking.

I waited a few minutes, took a drink, put my glass back down, giving the moment plenty of space. "There is this one other lead I got, but…nah." I shook my head.

He skipped right into the snare. "What?" he demanded.

I took it slow. I didn't want to seem a runaway trolley car full of information. "Some cats I know, musician-types, get together once a week and play a few rounds of poker in somebody's hotel room. From what a buddy told me, it can get pretty high stakes, you know, blowing the rent in a night. That kind of thing." I shrugged like I could forget the whole thing and not cry about it. "I don't know, I'd thought about giving it a stab, but it seems mighty chancy to me."

Oates, as I'd hoped, wasn't ready to drop the idea. "But if these guys bet big enough, they could come away with a heap of cash, right?"

I shrugged again. "I guess so." Then, as if it just came to me, I said, "I think I remember hearing that Howard Bruce came away with six grand one time."

"That would more than cover the fees at a recording studio," Oates said. He was getting worked up now, bouncing a bit in his seat like a kid spotting the toy store from the window of the bus. "You oughta do it," he insisted, and his voice got loud enough to have some guys in the audience look over at us, their faces turning sour, what with us spoiling the racket of the band with conversation. "Get in on one of them card games."

I patted Oates on his shoulder to get him to muffle it, and he settled a bit. "A cardsharp, I'm not," I said. "I couldn't play poker well enough to risk the dough I do have."

Suddenly the candleholder got mighty interesting to him. He nudged the melted wax around so it made shapes as it cooled. "Maybe," he said after a bit, "you could use some sorta strategy to even the odds a bit, put the hands more in your favor."

"What?" I said, sounding like he was speaking Chinese. "You mean, like *cheat*?"

As if some big goon in a pinstripe suit with a heater was standing right behind him, Oates cast his eyes around and grimaced. "Not cheat, exactly," he hissed, a drunk guy trying to whisper, the least subtle sound this side of a steam train pulling out, "but get a little extra help."

I knew when to stop sounding shocked by the idea. "Sounds swell, but how can I do that? I'm not some type of hustler. I play piano, not people. I wouldn't even know where to start."

"There's gotta be a way," Ron said, but he was getting blue trying to piece everything together. I let him sit in glum silence, with the band hacking away at "I Can't Get Started," and I pretended to think.

Eventually, I said, "There was one gig I played in San Diego, and the drummer told me this story, which I didn't buy at first, but now it doesn't seem half bad."

"What's that?" Oates asked, still down.

"This guy told me how he made a pile of cash at a card game, using, like you said, 'a little extra help.' The extra help came from a friend." I leaned forward and said, quietly, but not so quiet that I couldn't be heard, "The drummer went to the poker game with a buddy. It was just them two and one other guy, a real uptown-type who liked to play for big stakes. After a couple of hands, his buddy loses all his money and is out. But he doesn't leave just yet. Instead, he goes and sits behind the moneybags while the drummer keeps playing poker. And do you know what his friend does?"

Oates shook his head in a slow, underwater way.

"His friend can see the other guy's cards. So all he has to do is let his chum know what the guy's holding, so he knows how to play each hand."

"How does he let him know?"

"Little hand signals, something real subtle, like," I scratched my nose, "means he's got a pair, but," I scratched the other side of my schnozz, "means it's a pair of jacks or better. Like that. They worked out a whole system ahead of time, and wound up cleaning the bankroll right out. Split the winnings between them. The drummer bought himself a whole new kit and spent the rest on a month in Tijuana."

Oates didn't notice when the cocktail waitress came and switched out his empty glass with a full one. "And that really worked for him?"

I said, "Yup," right back and gave his drink a little nudge towards him. He threw it back like it was seltzer and U-Bet, not gin and tonic. My pocketbook was taking a hit from the cost of booze, but it was a worthwhile investment.

"Then you oughta do something like that, too," he said. "Find yourself a partner and then get in on the poker game."

I shifted in my seat, making as though I wasn't sure about the scheme. "I dunno, Ron," I said, "that could be dicey. I'd need to find somebody I could trust, who wouldn't turn on me. Somebody who I know would split the dough afterwards and not take off with it." I waved my hand at the room. "You know this town. There aren't many stand-up guys to be found just hanging around under lampposts."

Bashful as a moonshiner, Oates said, "You should use me."

I looked at him as though I hadn't thought of that, the idea brand new and shiny. "You? Really?"

"Why not?" He started to get keyed up again, the notion starting to look mighty swell. "I'd be like one of those, what'dye call it, dark horses. Nobody'd suspect anything."

"Gee, Ron," I said, musing, "I don't know. It's not without risks."

The romance of it was becoming awfully alluring to gray Oates, who wasted his life away, barely looking up from the mixing board except to take a solitary drink, and now here was his chance to take part in something perilous and full of dark glamour, as the partner of a handsome, suave gent such as myself.

"Risks don't bother me," he said, and I saw he enjoyed the way such gallantry sounded coming from his own mouth. "I'm willing to take 'em. As long as I can help out my good pal Louis. We'll put bop right in the middle of the map. Get good music out there. C'mon," he wheedled, sounding more like the kid being picked last for Annie-Annie Over than a grown man trying to get in on a con, "you can trust me. I promise."

"Well…," I said, good and stretched out. He gripped my sleeve and gave my arm a little shake, his eyes pleading with me. Munificent, I finally said, "Okay."

He collapsed all over me, gushing his thanks, sure that it had all been his own idea and anything I asked of him was a gift on a silver salver. Oates was so grateful I almost believed that it *was* me who was doing him a favor, but I focused on what Arnie had said to me early in my education. "A C-man should sound convincing without actually believing himself. The biggest danger to him comes when his own lies start to sound like the truth."

It was too late to play by the time I made it back to my place. When I first got the piano, I celebrated by hitting the ivories until the small hours, but then one of my esteemed and cultured neighbors came by and instead of expressing his appreciation for quality music, threatened to fix me a finger sandwich—using my own digits. And as this gentleman earned his money training brawlers down in Venice, I decided to skip a debate, seeing as how there was little chance of me surviving such an exchange of words with my spinal column intact.

So that night the best I could do was grab a handful of blank sheets and try out some music in my head, jotting down whatever came to me. I tried to unhitch myself again, tapping into that melody that ran underneath my every day. Beatrice had her own leitmotif, so did the open streets of Los Angeles before the sun came up, and now, even Nora came through, the notes of her longing. Working late helped me break past any reticence daylight might impose. In the morning—okay, when I woke up, probably in the early afternoon—I'd give what I'd written a test drive. Sometimes these late night sessions produced pure dreck, what you wouldn't wish on your tone-deaf enemies, but other times I'd managed to rouse the genius that lives inside of me, the guy who mostly reads the paper and only now and then picks his head up to look around and offer up shining bands of gold. So I sat at the piano in the rathole I called my apartment and touched my fingertips to the keys, calling up the sounds in my head, then scribbled tangled knots of notes onto the paper.

It wasn't the most productive session I'd ever had, but by the time I saw the first picked edges of dawn creeping into the courtyard, I'd filled two pages. Eyes wet and tacky, I ran them over what I'd done that night. There they were, the notes like birds perched on telephone lines, ready to fly at any moment. I'd let them alone until the sun was higher up. In the meanwhile, I needed to grab some grub and then find me a nice mattress or bathtub to curl up in. I stared at the phone for a few minutes, trying to talk myself out of calling Beatrice. Her voice, even far away, separated from me by electrical wires and asphalt, would have been more welcome than a rabbi's murmured blessing.

I managed to tear my hand off the phone and shove myself out the door. What day it was, I didn't figure, somewhere in the middle of the week. I went in search of either a twenty-four-hour joint or someplace that opened early. The air was sharp and thin, stabbing down my collar even as I turned it up, reminding me of being up in the mountains. Memphis Arnie and me had hit up a few places in Colorado and I'd even been up to Lake Tahoe once. It was beautiful way up there, removed and clean. Walking through the early bright streets of Santa Monica was almost like that, no people around, the fine, pure avenues cold and silent. The sky, too, high and unreachable. It almost made me think that it wasn't so bad here, that I'd made the right choice and I could let go of everything behind me.

On Pico Boulevard I found a diner, and even though it wasn't more than five thirty in the morning, it was already packed full of long-haul truckers, dock workers and bartenders, all shoveling pancakes and fried eggs into their maws at the end of their day. Soon, they'd either slide back behind the wheel or else crawl back to their own ratholes to sleep off the stretched-out night that takes the place of day. Two waitresses scuttled back and forth, hurling plates of hash like discuses and topping off cups of scalding coffee. It was bright in there, no high pink sky but instead hard light from overhead that turned everyone inside into ash-white vampires. Even standing on the corner, I could hear the jukebox hawing out the latest bouncy pop tune.

For how long I stood out there, I didn't know. I had my hands stuffed into my pockets and I stared, puffs of steam powdering out of my mouth. My gut told me that whatever I'd eaten last was now just a fond memory. I needed food. But still, I stood on the corner, watching the inside of the diner, feeling the last of the quiet morning start to slip away. The rest of the world was going to be awake soon, crushing out whatever good will and hope I'd stashed during my solo walk through the streets.

A cop pulled up in his black-and-white, coming to grab a coffee and eggs before going back on patrol. He pushed himself out of his car and trundled to the front door. As he opened it, noise and clatter tumbled out. He held it open and asked me, "You comin' in, mack?"

"No, thanks, Officer," I said. "I'm not as hungry as I thought."

Chapter twenty-one

That bleak, hollow feeling I got standing out in the morning cold and staring at the diner was soon brushed off, or, at least forgotten for a while, when I took Nora out Saturday afternoon for a stroll down Ocean Front Walk. Sure, I was taking a chance parading with her in my neck of the burg—I usually worked my marks far from home, that was something Arnie told me early on, don't hunt and sleep in the same place—but I'd already stopped thinking of her as just a pigeon. Not completely a mark, and not completely a regular girl I was squiring. I thought to keep her hanging there in space for a measure or two. Anyway, it wasn't as if there'd be any danger of some schmuck popping up out of the sand and hollering at me, "Hey, Louis Greenberg, how's that grift business been wearing you?"

So I'd picked her up earlier and, with no particular destination in mind, wound up right back in my ole neighborhood. We ambled along Main until we got to Strand, then hooked it west until we came out to the grass and then the sand beyond. She wore a pretty little blue flowered dress and cork-wedge sandals that turned her tiny painted toes into penny candy, the kind I used to filch from the local candy store but wasn't able to eat on account of feeling guilty.

I threw those candies away every time, but that didn't stop me from stealing them again next time.

I thought about bringing up what happened on the studio backlot, but decided against it. First, it wouldn't be very gentlemanly of me to blurt, "Say, remember that time the other day when you hurled yourself at me and I called you a tramp?" As far as Nora was concerned, Louis Dante was a gentleman. It was better to keep her hovering at the edge of afraid, when I might use her unnatural desires against her. But also, I didn't know what to make of it myself.

We stood at the railing and watched the sunbathers gently braising, tots staggering with sand pails, he-men and thin-chested milk-sops competing for the attentions of exhausted manicurists in jersey swimsuits, and a dad tossing a chewed-up football with his kid.

"I don't know about you," I said to Nora, "but where I'm from, folks sure don't go promenading along the beachfront in November—not without getting bundled up like Nanook of the North."

"We'd put on our flannels around October and take them off in June," she said. "Or it seemed that way. Sometimes it felt like there was but two or three weeks of awful, sweating hot before the biting cold came back again." She made a dramatic shiver. "I did hate that cold. It just got me through and through." She looked up at me, shading her eyes with her hand. "I never knew it could be so pleasant anywhere."

I put my arm around her shoulder, and she was a tiny, warm toy. "I find it awfully pleasant here, too," I said. I'll own to it, it *was* mighty pleasant with Nora on that soft, balmy Saturday afternoon. I needed this, a small break from the nights I spent watching Oates getting soused and the days consumed with setting up the store, missing Beatrice something fiendish the whole time. Even with Nora tucked into my side, I wanted Bea and her complications that were easier to understand than the discordant jangle of notes Nora brought out in me.

Nora and I watched the folks romp or splay on the beach, even saw a few sailboats out there on the briny, bobbing up and down. They looked pretty, but I was content just to admire them from the shore. I'd never been on a boat before, aside from the chugging, tame ferries around New York which were more city bus than boat, and saw no reason why I should set myself up on one now. My grandparents had already done their big ocean schlep from Poland to New York, and the only reason they'd shut themselves up on a leaky, swaying ship was on account of the Cossacks burning down the shtetl. So unless there were going to be some big, mustachioed Polacks with swords at my heels, on dry land I would stay.

"You know, Louis," Nora said softly, and it almost made me laugh to hear her say my name that way, as if she was someone who really understood me, though the truth of it was that she knew only one note of a whole symphony, "you've heard me go on and on about Iowa, but I hardly know a thing about where you're from."

Which was no accident. The best lies are the simplest ones. "Back east," I said.

But it didn't seem like a quick answer was going to satisfy. "Boston?" she asked. "Philadelphia? Baltimore?" She sighed and shook her head. "Don't make me play 'Dr. IQ.'"

There are times when you need to give up a little to keep the peace, and I've found that sticking close to the truth is a grifter's best bet. "New York," I said at last.

She wouldn't leave it at that. "Upstate?"

"City." As to the Bronx, Jerome Avenue, that wasn't on the menu, not for her, anyhow.

"But the other day…on the lot," she said, stumbling over that last bit, "you said you'd only been there a few times."

"That was just me being cute," I said, and wondered how I could've bobbled something so simple like that. I thought for absolute she'd fry me.

But Nora just smiled a bit, and nodded, looking a little satisfied, as if she got a particularly fussy necklace clasp to finally hook. "Cute. That's you, all right. Well, I'm glad you're here now," was what she said. With her arm tucked in mine, we started to walk north.

I pointed over to the platforms set up on the south side of the pier. Just then, there were a few guys in little trunks hefting themselves up and down on some monkey bars. We're talking big slabs of guys who would be well suited to a long braise with some carrots and celery, with horseradish on the side. What this brain trust did all day was no secret. Every muscle save for those inside their skulls was beautifully developed, a small poem to the capacity of the body when the mind is napping and unbothered. Around them, a modest crowd watched their contortions, mildly interested and largely bored.

I caught Nora watching the gents in their trunks, and was surprised to feel the first splinter of something I recognized faintly as jealousy, but I reminded myself that that wasn't my style, and if a woman wanted to look at a man, then who was I to say no? Hell, if ogling girls was a crime, then I would've been sent to Rikers at the tender age of nine.

Just to prove that her staring didn't bother me, I stopped nearby so we could watch the Herculeses and Samsons of Santa Monica go about their feats of strength. One Tarzan was swinging around a bar until his feet were in the air, his arms holding him straight up like a radio antenna. He held it like that for a goodly minute or so, before swinging around again and landing on the sand. He looked around to see if anybody cared, and was met with two or three flaccid rounds of applause. Buddy, I thought to myself, I've been there.

"You should see this place come summer," I said to Nora. "Can't even see the sand, it's packed so full of people watching the goons—the bodybuilders."

"And they just come out here and pose and such?" she asked.

"Sure," I said, the Expert. Wherever you would go, some ass always became the Expert, gassing about crap he didn't even know about, could be those new jet airplanes, could be topiary, it didn't matter. They'd get smug and say garbage like, "Well, what they really need to do here is…," or "It's all a matter of…" And the poor schnooks with them could only nod their heads and murmur, "Is that so? Really?" when what they honestly wanted to do was borrow a nearby anvil and make a hat out of it. So here I was, coming on like the Expert, and only because I'd come down to the beach a few times in July and August and accidentally caught a few of the he-men contests. I wanted to stuff my own fist into my mouth to shut myself up, but somehow I couldn't stop. "Sometimes there's up to twenty guys out here, girls, too, even, showing off their muscles, lifting things, lifting each other. Competitions and whathaveyou. The crowds love it."

Nora shook her head, and, to my unwilling relief, it didn't seem that watching Johnny Weissmuller was lighting her rockets. "What could ever prompt a person to take up a hobby like that?"

"I guess the knitting circle was full up."

"And potting geraniums gets dirt under his fingernails."

Sometimes, for a WASPY woman, Nora wasn't too bad. She wanted to be one half of a nice average couple, two regular folks in the midst of the courtship dance. She wanted it so badly she was willing to gloss over things that should have given her pause. Grifters know without trying how to fill needs. I could be what she needed, and I was, for that moment. But it bothered me fierce that she and I were pretending together, her playing house, me substituting Nora for—

Beatrice, I said. Only I was able to keep myself from saying it out loud, although it almost slipped out.

And there she was. With some girlfriend I'd never seen before. They were walking south along the beachfront, her friend carrying a basket and Beatrice with a blanket. The two of them were talking, and from the few words I caught, the other woman was some pal from work at the telephone company. Bea was looking toothsome in her peach dress and sunglasses, but with the sight of her out in Santa Monica, a place that she and I never went to together, my head just emptied itself and left a clean space where thought should have been.

They must've been heading towards the Ink Well, where Pico Boulevard met the ocean, where the coloreds would go to enjoy the beach. Bea and her friend were chatting with each other, I couldn't even tell you now what her friend looked like, if she had three noses or green hair, I only saw her, Beatrice, gliding by like the last warm breeze of summer.

She saw me from about twenty feet away, and only I saw the tiny stutter step before she resumed her elegant, long-stemmed stride. A brief contraction of shock flicked across her face before draining away. She looked over at Nora, who I'd almost forgotten, and I glanced over at her too, to see if she'd caught me gaping at some colored woman, but Nora was busy watching some kids trying to heft themselves onto the parallel bars. I wished, just then, that Nora would get caught on an ocean breeze and be blown away, gently lifting into the air like an ice cream wrapper, to wind up bobbing on the waves miles from the coast. My eyes strayed from Nora back to Beatrice, pulled along because they couldn't stop themselves, and that's when I saw something dark and bitter seem to fill her mouth, before her eyes came over all droll and ironic. I saw what she saw. Me, with a white woman, cozy-like, and the bedsheets just finished cooling over at her place.

It's not like that, I wanted to tell her. Nora is a plaything, a hollow substitution. Whatever there is between her and me is as real as the New York City set on the studio backlot. A lot of plywood and paint.

I said none of this, of course. Beatrice didn't stop walking. But in those few beats where she strolled by, in the silence underneath the sounds of the waves washing in, the kids screaming on the sand, folks laughing or complaining about warm lemonade, cars circling and looking for parking, and all the other noise that made no noise, she and me went through a whole conversation as we stared at each other, her in motion, me standing still. Finally, Beatrice turned her face away from me, as deliberate as a knife. I felt the wound.

She flowed past us and it took all I had not to turn around and watch her walk away. Instead, I forced myself to stare out at the ocean, to watch the horizon and wonder if there was any place further I could go. From thirty thousand feet away, I heard Nora.

"I'd love to get an ice cream," she said.

There was rusted metal in my neck as I looked down at her, and I was surprised that she didn't hear the shriek and groan of my muscles grinding against each other. She beamed brightly at me. I wanted to push her down.

"Or maybe a pretzel," she added. "Louis?"

But I wasn't talking, wasn't saying anything, just took hold of her small hand and started walking fast. She almost dragged behind me, her short legs struggling to keep up with the length of my stride, as I wove through the Saturday crowds, away from the beach, away from—

"Louis?" she asked again, and this time something like fear or worry threaded through her voice, but I wasn't going to play the smooth operator now, didn't have time to pet and cajole and cover everything with honey. I had to keep moving. "Where are we going?"

Still, I kept quiet until we were blocks away and already in front of my car. I just about shoved her in, slammed the door after her, and then threw myself around and into the driver's seat. I had enough savvy to keep from going back to my place. Some part of my mind worked properly, so I started driving although I didn't quite know where I was headed until we pulled up outside her house. Looking over at her, her small face creased and uncertain, I realized I hadn't said anything for the whole drive, and still nothing would come out of my mouth, finding that there wasn't anything to say. Instead, I got out of the car, marched around it, hauled open her door and pulled her out.

Instead of taking her hand, I grabbed her wrist and towed her behind me as I took her up the front walkway. I didn't care about the neighbor watering his lawn or the kid slowly going up and down the sidewalk on his tricycle, both staring at me and Nora. I waited as she rummaged through her pocketbook—it was just a little thing, couldn't hold more than a lipstick and bobby pins, but somehow it had grown huge and full so it took forever before she found her keys. There wasn't going to be any idling as she tried to get the key in the lock, so I snatched it from her and got the door open in just enough time before I was going to have to bust it down.

Nora danced nervously inside and I slammed the door behind us. I pushed her towards the back of the house, her not weighing more than a damp eyelash. The hallway was dark, I was more shadow than anything, but I wouldn't let her stop, just kept shoving her forward and by now she couldn't speak. When she saw that I'd corralled her to her bedroom, she stopped and stared up at me.

"But it's the middle of the day," she said.

"Take your dress off."

Her fingers fumbled at the buttons, then she looked up again. "At least draw the curtains."

I jerked them shut, turning her bedroom hazy, and stripped off my own clothes. My hat, jacket, shirt, tie, trousers, everything into a heap at the foot of the bed. In the time I got naked, she had only managed to pull off her dress and was standing in the middle of the room in her brassiere and girdle. Her eyes turned into wide circles as I walked over to her, and I wondered somewhere in the back of my mind, how many men she'd seen without any clothes on, besides Jack Hodges from Hiring, and the late and unlamented Floyd. Those two guys likely weren't circumcised. She probably kept her eyes closed the whole time, anyway, and wouldn't know the difference between their cocks and mine. But thinking about Floyd, dead and rotting in Italy, set the machine of fury back into motion and I spun her around to undo the hooks on her underwear. I would have been more gentle roping steer than I was peeling those *gatkes* off of her. When she was shucked bare, I spun her around again. I didn't care if the look on her face was fear, excitement or sadness. I kissed her, or something like a kiss, and felt the satisfying weight of her tit in my hand, and then the tentative weaving of her fingers into my hair as she tried to meet me in the kiss. Then I pushed her onto the bed.

You're probably expecting me to give you the whole play-by-play on what happened next. What with all the buildup that came before, you probably think you deserve to hear about each stick and swivel. Not this time. What went on between me and Nora—I won't say that I'm embarrassed about it, I've got nothing to hide and nothing to complain about, all my parts functioned and she seemed to like it a little—but I'll tell you, I've given better performances, less rushed, and as a lay, Nora was on the fair to middling side of the scale. I did what I had to and have no room for regret.

But afterwards, we lay together and stared up at the afternoon light glazing the ceiling. I rolled onto my stomach so I wouldn't have to speak. She brushed back my hair with her fingers, saying over and over, "Shh," and I felt the pillow wet beneath my cheek.

Chapter twenty-two

Plenty of times on the road, I woke up and couldn't figure where I was. That happened a lot when I'd just left New York, coming to and—even with my eyes shut, knowing I wasn't home—the smell of the sheets was different, too bleached and clean or else musty with someone else's funk, the clatter on the street jarring in its strangeness, or, even worse, sometimes a flat silence I couldn't recognize. Opening my eyes didn't usually help much. A lamp on an anonymous table, a cheap litho of a farmhouse cottage, the window looking out to a view of a vacant lot, full of only weeds and emptiness and waiting. All across this grand nation of ours are hundreds of thousands of unknown, unnamed rooms, rooms that, no matter who sleeps in them, stay blank and void.

It took a while to shuck myself of the panic that would set in upon waking. But I did, I made myself, otherwise I'd have drifted away for sure, washed out in a foreign sea. Then it got so that I was used to waking up in a different room every day, so that if I pried my lids open and recognized something—the stuffed-full ashtray, the chip on the dresser's laminate—I'd get nervous and leave fast. I'd tell myself that it didn't matter, it was in my blood. Weren't us Jews the original wanderers? What should it matter if I hadn't anyplace that was mine, if the familiar became strange and the strange familiar?

And when I got to Los Angeles and found myself an apartment, I could sometimes smother the edginess by leaping from one girl's bed to another. Eventually, I settled into my life out here, and I lost my taste for waking up in some chick's boudoir, trying to recall if I was in Los Feliz or Hollywood or Arlington Heights and how to get back to Santa Monica. I made sure that, if she and I hit the mattress for a few jam sessions, I'd get up quickly afterwards and blow before I fell asleep.

So I wasn't expecting it when I managed to jimmy my eyes open and found myself staring up at a ceiling I didn't recognize right away. The shadows of trees moving back and forth told me it was sometime late in the afternoon, maybe early evening, streetlamps casting pale light into the room. Far off, someone had on their radio, but I couldn't catch the tune. It was that odd, muffled time, twilight, not the hustle of daytime, not the open hush of night.

I pushed myself up onto my elbows and took in the scene in the haze of dusk. I wasn't in my apartment—the furniture, what I could see of it, actually matched, and instead of sheet music tacked to the walls, I could see framed photographs, although in the darkness the faces in the photos looked like ghostly smears with black caves for eyes. My feet, lumps under the covers, seemed miles away. I rubbed my face and heard a clock gently killing minutes on the nightstand. A crescendo of panic started up in me, and I told myself that if I could just figure the time, I'd anchor myself back down and everything would be fine.

I started to reach for the clock, but then I heard Nora's voice in the darkness: "It's five thirty." When I went to turn on the lamp, I felt her little hand on mine, stopping me. "Leave it off," she said, and I couldn't read her, didn't know what she was thinking or feeling. Maybe it was because of me just waking up and not having my sea legs yet, or maybe she'd managed to pull herself back enough so I was left to fumble along a smooth, featureless wall. My jacket was somewhere at the foot of the bed, so I reached for it and found my pack of smokes. Leaning against the padded headboard, I played with my lighter but couldn't get it to catch. There was a flare and hiss, and

Nora held a match to the end of my cigarette. In the brief glow that came from the lit match, I saw her, wrapped up in a robe, her hair a tumbled mess of wheaty curls, her eyes searching and cool. Then the fire went out and we were back in the dark.

I smoked for a while, taking in and breathing out soothing tobacco air. A little plate showed up and I knocked ash into it. I heard her shifting around; she'd pulled up a chair and was sitting next to the bed. We both waited.

"Sometimes I forget," I said into the dark. "I can go whole days, weeks, even, without remembering or thinking about it. Telling myself that everything's swell and it's all smooth and easy from now on. And then, something happens. It doesn't have to be anything big, it could be so small, nobody'd ever notice. Just a sound, or the end of a gesture. Or a place that one day means nothing and the next day changes completely. That's when it comes back."

I took a drag of my cigarette and she listened to the way I breathed in and out, but she said nothing.

I said, "You've heard of Anzio. I was there—I saw it all happen. If Omaha was anything like it, well, God help those poor idiots, washing up onto the beach just to get killed. And not killed quick and clean, but bodies and blood and parts of men everywhere. Arms, legs, and other things I couldn't identify but knew were human, chunks of skin and slippery insides."

She sucked in some air, a little indrawn gasp of horror and disgust. She didn't tell me to stop, though.

I let my voice go flat, which always played better than hair-pulling and teeth-gnashing. "I remember lying in the sand next to half a guy who'd been chopped in two by a machine gun nest, and turning over onto my back and looking up at the sky. I heard the surf coming in, crashing onto the sand. I was scared, really scared, but it seemed so strange to me that all around me was death, that I could be dead or maimed terribly any second, but still there was this beach. The sand, the water. Maybe people even came there for seaside outings—before all this. And what did the beach care if men were dying right on top of it? It didn't.

"So I listened to the waves and tried to get some kind of comfort from them, but it never came. It never came even though I needed it. And then my CO ran by and I had to follow and fight my way up that beach, and eventually, I put that beach behind me because there was always another battle, from one day to the next, and maybe I'd make it and maybe I wouldn't. I was alive and dead at the same time. It's hard to get past that, hard to put it behind me, but when the war was over, I did, because that's what they told us to do, forget that we were alive and dead and just be alive once more. Until something comes along and brings it all back."

"The beach," she said, the way I wanted. "In Santa Monica."

"Yeah," I said. "The beach." My voice rasped, partway from the cigarette and partway from the cough, but it worked, so I didn't clear my throat. "And I know that doesn't excuse what I did, what I…made you do, but I wanted you to know. If not the why, then maybe how it began."

What she was going to do with all that guff I'd just fed her, I hadn't any idea. It made me wonder, too, as we both sat in the dark for a long time. All I could do was finish my cigarette, and I started to think if maybe I ought to get up and put my clothes on, maybe leave. But I was tired and raw, so instead of leaving, which would have been the safe, smart thing to do, I kept lying in Nora's bed and waiting for her to make the next move. Her robe rustled nearby, like the sound of a brush on a drum, and the bed tipped a little as she sat down on it. I wouldn't let myself look at her, though. Then I felt her fingers on my jaw, turning my head towards her. I still couldn't quite see her, she was a small shadow in the room, but she was near, and I smelled myself on her skin.

She put her mouth close to mine. "I'll fix you, Louis," she said against my lips. I could feel her shaking, a series of tremors that moved through her body into mine, but it wasn't from sorrow or fear. It was excitement, joy. She'd been given the role of a lifetime, the one she'd always wanted to play. "I'll heal you."

She could try, but she didn't know that everything was broken.

* * *

She gave me the gate at around four in the morning, so the neighbors wouldn't see me leave in the daylight.

Back to Santa Monica in the cold dark of the A.M. An icy ride home, but at least a shorter trip than my many schleps back from Inglewood. I had a strange notion to swing past Beatrice's place, see if, in the time since she'd seen me on the beach with Nora, she'd landed herself a new back-door Romeo. Maybe there'd be a Chinese guy creeping over the trash cans on his way out. That idea turned my knuckles white—I didn't want her catting around with anyone else—so I made sure to head directly home. I couldn't help but wonder what she would have made of my Anzio story, if she would've bought it or laughed in my face.

I passed maybe one or two other cars, but not many. L.A., especially the western part of town, was like a minister's wife, blamelessly sleeping the late night away while the sinners carried on elsewhere. It seemed as though out of all the hours in a day, I knew the empty ones the best.

Even exhausted and wrung out, I still found myself awake in bed later. And though I didn't want it to, my mind kept coming back to Nora. She didn't strike me as the kind of woman who'd cotton to years of nighttime dalliances and no promises. Marriage may have proved to be a rotten deal, but she wasn't Bolshevist enough to let some gent claim her bed full time without a ring on her finger. A ring other than Floyd's. My story had bound her tighter to me with ropes I didn't quite know how, didn't quite want to untie. I told myself that maybe something would work itself out, even though I had enough experience to know that something needed all the help it could get and never did anything for itself, the lazy bum.

So it was back to walking down the hallway with my eyes closed—a game I thought I'd dropped long ago.

Sometime just as the sun started to come up, I managed to nod off. But I had strange dreams, dreams of people and places I thought I'd forgotten, or at least I'd tried to, and when I pried my eyes open five or six hours later, it was like I hadn't slept at all. I found my pack of smokes next to the bed, lit up and went straight to the piano. Seeing as how it was near noon, I didn't think anyone would hassle me for getting on the ivories too early. I figured that I could salvage, somehow, the smashed bits of my sleep and turn them into something worthwhile.

The piece I'd been working on was scrawled all over stacks of sheet music and inside my own brain. I took it, the piece that had no name, and added to it, playing out seeing Beatrice at the beach and the blade of her disappointment, the soft shapes of Nora and the jangling edges of doubt, the careful planning of the grift and the empty spaces of everything else in between. I went at it for hours. I was clammy and hot and tearing through cigarettes one after the other. I never wrote home after I left New York, but there were times, like this one, when I had this strange feeling that every note coming out of my piano was making its way across the thousands of miles—past the deserts and canyons, the boomtowns and busted storefronts—all the way straight to my pop's heart. He wouldn't hear it, exactly, but he'd know through the vibrations of his sounding board what was up with me, what I needed. And had I got up from the bench and opened my door to find him standing on my step, ready to help his only son, it wouldn't seem peculiar.

He never showed at my door. Even thinking that he might, that I could somehow summon him like a *dybbuk*, made me feel small and babyish. Here I was, all grown up, and still waiting for my father to come and rescue me. Just in case the notes I was composing did make it to Jerome Avenue, I played that I didn't need him and that no matter what kind of fix I landed in here in California, I could get by without him. Almost a month, I waited through his stern silences, his deliberate abandonment, before realizing he wouldn't let go of his anger. I planned so that he wasn't home when I left. Let him come back from his empty job to find his son gone. He didn't search for me then, and I didn't want him now. So stow that luggage back under the bed and go back to reading your paper.

I took the swirl of smoke that made up each of my days and pushed it softly through the piano keys. The pack of cigarettes, the bottles of beer, even the plaster walls of my apartment—they were all bought and paid for with the grift, and the grift was made up of words. I spent my time spinning words, conning, so that the space all around me was thick with talk. Words cut everything apart into hard pieces, and being so small and separate turned me sour. But the piano keys brought me back together. I didn't have to worry about what scam I was pulling, who or what I was deceiving, there wasn't any story to keep straight. Beatrice and Nora, Los Angeles and New York, the music and the grift, all of it was me and I found something to give me a center when it didn't seem I could get it anywhere.

I played Beatrice: the secret warmth under a handful of hard edges, the hopeless rightness of her. There was Nora: something sweet and desperately, dangerously hopeful, each step forward surrounded by hazard and my own rage. And there was all of l.a., crowded and bare, and the Bronx, gray and colorful, and all the words I couldn't or didn't want to use became sound and me with them. Having played most of the day away, I staggered into my shower, hosed myself down, and, went out to scrounge something to eat. Maybe the guys at Muscle Beach could give me a few pointers—I walked only a couple of blocks and couldn't get my wind. And here was I thinking that spending all hours in nightclubs, drinking my dinner, would leave me a regular Charles Atlas. As I sat on a bench in the sunlight, taking a few calming drags of my cigarette, I told myself that once everything with Ronald Oates had been taken care of, I'd start eating regularly and getting more fresh air.

I did make it to the hash house and had a nourishing meal of a fried egg sandwich with potatoes, bacon and coffee, though I found I didn't have much appetite and had to make myself shove the food into my mouth. Still, the java went down smooth, and it gave me enough pep to get back home and work some more. Things were coming along dandy when the phone rang.

"Greenberg, you kike pantywaist," came bellowing out of the receiver when I picked it up.

"Have you considered a career in greeting cards, George?"

"'Dear Momma,'" he recited, "'on this special day, I just wanted to wish you a hot poker in the eye, you hairsplitting castrator, from your loving son, the hophead.'"

"I'll take two dozen, and four more for Sundays."

"Today is Sunday, hootch hound."

"Then I'll put on my plus fours and dance the turkey trot until I'm called for supper."

George decided he'd had enough. Through the receiver, I heard him take a large swallow of something, and if I had to bet what that something was, then the safe answer would be a fine tisane of the single-malt variety. "So lay it on me, brother," he said after his revivifying libation.

"Grab your ear trumpet and hearken to me, friend."

I put the receiver down and went over to my piano, then started to play the piece I'd been toiling on. I let myself forget about George on the line, about everything, and swam my way back to the place I'd been earlier, the place where the chipped plates of talking disappeared, I disappeared, but I was everywhere and everything was me. It didn't have an ending, not yet, but by the time I made it back to the phone, and asked, "Well?" George was breathing in slow, deep measures, the way he did when we had our platter parties and some particularly righteous tune came on the phonograph.

He didn't answer me straight off, and I started to sweat that maybe I'd gone and put him to sleep, or the music was so rotten he was trying to figure out what to say—though if there was an insult to be given, George would gladly wrap it up in pretty paper and hand it over with a grin on his face.

"Why've you been wasting my time with the grift," he finally said, sounding almost angry, "when you could have been doing *that*."

As compliments go, I doubt that he had much better in his arsenal. I tried to keep my happiness down to a deafening roar. "A fella's gotta pay his bills, Georgie," I said, instead of whooping.

"The bills can get lost." He took another gulp of Scottish lemonade. "I feel like I just seen the Earth from the Moon. Who wrote that?"

"Myself in the flesh."

"Then I don't figure it, Lou."

"What's that?"

"I've heard you play before, and you're good, but I never pegged you as the next Ellington, for chrissakes."

"Gee, what a swell bucket of herring."

"Don't get sore," George said. "What I'm telling you is that when you play other cats' stuff, you do all right, but playing your own music—hell!"

I took a chance. "It's working for you?"

He gave an angry snort into the phone. "Am I going to have to come down there and turn your kisser inside out? Yeah, it's good. It's fucking *great*. I think I crapped myself."

"That's exactly what I wanted to happen."

"Awright, I'm wearying of talking about the sunshine pouring outta your ass. Are we going to figure out your store, or what?"

He and me laid out our plan for the next few days and then, with a belch, he cut the connection. And, while George could use a few lessons in hefting a guy's ego, I was still riding high from what he'd said. The way I framed it, old George Lohr knew his jazz, and if he liked what I'd played him a few minutes ago, then what else could I want, a laurel wreath? What I did want, even George couldn't get for me. So I turned back to my piano and let it give me what nobody else could.

Chapter twenty-three

Ronald Oates and I walked into the lobby of the Imperial Hotel on Hollywood Boulevard and took in the chipped murals of Spanish conquest, the overfilled ashtrays and the guy in a funeral suit hunched in a torn club chair, staring into nothing. A decayed relic from glossier days. "Swell digs," I muttered to Oates. "Next time I decide to host the Boy Scout Jamboree, this place is going right to the top of the list."

Oates said nothing as a working girl brushed past us with a john on her arm. The girl looked like she'd rather be licking stamps somewhere, but she marched towards the elevators with her john, dutiful. I watched Ronald and saw on his face the same look of appalled interest worn by folks slowing down to view highway accidents.

"So the guy really wants to play *here?*" he stage-whispered.

"Yeah," I said, and tried to sound like I'd never been to the Imperial before and that the place gave me the jimjams, me being a decent citizen who wouldn't know a flophouse and creep-joint from his Sainted Aunt Esther. "Maybe we ought to blow."

"No!" he yelled, then lowered his voice as he grabbed my arm. I could feel the slight tremble in his hand, and didn't need to see him take out a hankie and dab at his melon to know that he was nervous. "We've already gotten this far," he said. "I won't turn back, I won't let you down."

How long had he been rehearsing those lines? Probably all his life. Ronald Oates the Hero.

And then he said my favorite line ever: "Trust me."

I gave him a dubious look, and Oates, with a meaningful stare, patted his inside jacket pocket, where he'd stashed his billfold full of my money. He thought that keeping his cash in the inside pocket actually hid it, but any grifter or cannon worth their bail would be able to spot it in a dark room. At least I was around to guard it in case any wiseacre decided to pull a brush up.

Oates didn't know that that very afternoon, I'd gathered up my combo for a rehearsal session at Dee's. While the acoustics at Dee's were as good as a urinal, it was the only place we could get that already had a piano—nohow were the fellas willing to rehearse at my place, not with the suspicious snoops peering from their windows and wondering what a whole gang of darkies was doing lurking around the joint. And professional rehearsal rooms cost bread, which was tied up and going nowhere. So, Dee's it was. We warmed up a bit on a clutch of standards—"Cotton Tail," "Smoke Gets In Your Eyes," "After You're Gone"—and then onto the piece I'd written, which still didn't have a name. Me on ivories, Sonny on sax, Wallace working the skins, and Morton Liddel on upright bass. It'd been a good jam after everyone got their parts down, and by the end of it, even Sonny smiled and said, "Righteous."

Oates hadn't an idea that I was already figuring my next move. To him, the only thing that mattered was about to happen, and he tried to convince himself and me that he'd see to it all, that he was the guy who called the shots. He didn't know that everything was all schemed and figured, all the improv scripted, almost like bebop: tightly controlled bedlam.

"Let's go upstairs," he said.

With a nod that I made sure looked full of misgiving, we headed towards the elevator. The concierge didn't look up from his

Weird Mystery comic book as we went by. As Oates pushed the button to call the lift, I said, "Maybe we should go over the signals again."

"Sure, sure."

Talking fast, I said, "If I close my eyes like this, it means he has a pair of jacks or better. If I close my left eye, then my right, it means he's got two pair, but if I close my right then my left, he's got three of a kind. Got it?"

"Uh, eyes closed, jacks or better, left then right is two pair, right then left is...uh..."

The elevator doors squealed open to reveal the world's most shriveled lift operator, a dried corncob in a red flannel jacket. "Tenth floor," I told him, but he just blinked watery eyes at me. "Tenth floor," I hollered, and with a heavy sigh, he pulled the gate shut and pulled the lever. We started to chug our way up ten flights. A sloth with a head cold could have beaten us there.

Since the elevator operator was deaf as my grandmother, I didn't see any harm to keep throwing information at Oates, getting him good and riled. "Right eye then left is three of a kind."

"Yeah, yeah, three of a kind. But if you bite your lip it means—"

"Straight. That's if I bite my lower lip. If I bite my top lip," I demonstrated, "that's a straight flush."

I breezed quickly through the rest, what my signal would be for a flush, a royal flush, a full house. It looked like he was starting to get the hang of it, so I threw in a few more as fast as I could until he started to look a little gray. Even after we reached our floor, the operator missing it by almost a foot and us ducking our heads and hopping down, I continued to pepper him with signals until we reached the door to room 1015.

I rapped sharply on the door. "Got it?" I said to Oates. Which I never would have done if I was going to fix a game for real—what could be more fishy than a guy saying to another guy "Got it?" just before a poker game—but these were special circumstances and I didn't need to play it so quietly.

"Wait," he said, "what does it mean when you—?"

He didn't get a chance to finish that. The door hauled open and a guy stood there in his shirtsleeves with a smoke hanging out of his mouth. "Yeah?" he demanded.

"Lou Peretti," I said, pointing to myself, "and Ron Capshaw. Jackson sent us."

The guy jerked his head, meaning, come in, and he peered over our shoulders like he thought we were being tailed. A good touch. As we walked into the room, I gave a quick glance and saw that it was the same as any of the dozens of cheap hotels I'd known: the faded curtains, the bolted-down nightstand to keep folks from shanghaiing the furniture, a bed I wouldn't get into without proper clearance from the Health Department. The window had a panoramic view of a wall. The only difference between this joint and the others was the table set up off to the side of the room, a wrapped deck of cards in the middle.

"You fellas want a drink or something?" the guy asked. "I brung a bottle of whiskey."

"I'll take a snootful," I said. "Ron?"

All Oates could do was nod. So the guy, he introduced himself as Alvin Lyde, poured three glasses. His and mine were a lot shorter than Oates's. "You wanna toast?" I asked as I picked up my glass.

"What for?" Lyde asked. "We're here to play poker, ain't we, not read from the Social Registry."

"I'll drink to that," I said, and both Lyde and I made like we were knocking our drinks back while Oates actually choked his down.

"Let's throw some cards," Lyde said, pushing his glass aside. "That's what I come to do."

I lit up a smoke, coughed just a bit, and pulled out a chair. Oates and Lyde did the same. The lamp overhead made a yellow circle on the burned brown tabletop. Lyde sliced open the deck, holding it up first to prove that it was legit and new, and started shuffling. Oates watched Lyde's hands as if he knew what he was looking for, which he didn't. Even I couldn't see all of Lyde's movements. We anted. Oates was trying to make as though he sat down to high-stakes poker games in frowzy hotels every day of his pure life, when all he'd done was sit behind a sound board or read pulp novels. He was jittered, but getting a kick out of it, too.

I'd sat in on a fair number of poker games, but Oates wasn't supposed to know that. What I had to do was play it like I was just as green as he was, but also try to come across as a cool customer, or enough so that Oates thought I was trying to be cool. It's a knotty business, getting inside someone's head, working all their angles, seeing the world from their eyes but also keeping them under your thumb. Another reason I hated the long con.

So there I was with all my plates spinning as Lyde dealt the first hand. He made sure to win the hand with a nice pair of ladies, and then got it so that I won the next off of two pair. Oates shot me a nervous look but I let him know with a sign that it was hunky-dory and less suspect if I won a hand or two before going bust. We took turns shuffling and dealing, and let me recite the praises now of a class-A cardsharp who makes it all sing like Nelson Eddie. I couldn't tell you how Alvin Lyde managed to fix that deck so completely, but it didn't matter who was dealing, him, me or Oates, everything went just as it needed to. A beautiful thing, that was.

And then, just like Oates and I had planned, I started losing. I made like I was getting sore, being beaten by a lousy trio of deuces, even though I'd held a straight and thrown it away. To make sure Oates thought I was keeping up the front, I'd snarl and lob my cards onto the table, saying things like, "Of all the rotten luck!" or "Go screw your bishop!" Alvin Lyde would look at me and shake his head, broadcasting without saying out loud what a bush leaguer he thought I was—which was exactly what he was supposed to do. And Oates, getting into the spirit, would also sadly shake his head and say, "Tough luck, buddy." Everybody putting on a show for everyone else—not unlike your typical Passover seder.

This scampered along until I finally lost to Oates and I had to snarl, "I'm tapped out, fellas. I got no more green."

"That's a raw deal, Lou," Oates said.

"Yeah, too bad, Peretti," Lyde added, sounding just bored enough.

"Ain't it, though?" I said, pushing away from the table.

"Should we pack it in?" Oates asked.

Dutifully, I answered, "Naw. You're doing swell. Keep playing. Mind if I read that?" I asked Lyde, pointing to a newspaper he had folded on a chair behind him. Thoughtful, that Lyde.

"Have yourself a time," he said, already dealing the next hand.

I made a big hoo-hah about sitting down, unfolding the paper, muttering some business about Truman and Dewey, the Red Army, whathaveyou, then placidly began what some might call reading the news. I wasn't right behind Lyde, but off just enough so I could see the cards in his paw, which he politely held high instead of keeping hidden. Oates sent me a glance—something any shyster could have spotted in a blackout, Lyde made like he didn't notice—and I gave him a wee nod of my head to let him know everything was dandy. Oates was keyed up: the second part of our scheme was about to begin.

We'd plotted it all out before, and we followed the rules: I signaled to Oates with a blink that Lyde held two ladies, and whatever Oates had been dealt was thrown away so Lyde could win. Then I blinked to Oates that Lyde was bluffing on the next hand and Oates took it. After that, I made sure that Lyde could win the next two hands—as Oates and I had worked it earlier, this way Lyde could feel comfortable and start betting higher, which he did, as he was supposed to—and that's when Lyde groused: "Man, this kitty's too small. Let's make it something worth a newsreel," all part of the patter, though Oates didn't know, but he did agree straight up so the cash could move bigger and faster. Up to then, they'd been betting with fins and sawbucks, but Lyde threw down a century and that's when it all took off.

One thing I didn't have to fake, not for Oates at least, was the weight of this con—what was riding on it. A chance to cut a record. A life for me and Beatrice. The tollway I'd taken cost more than money and I didn't want it all to be for nothing.

What we had here, in this hotel room at the Imperial, was something new for me: a grift that meant something. Not that the ones that came before didn't have meaning, but I'd been subsistence level. Each grift fed me, kept the rain off my head, but none meant that much.

When Oates threw down his first C-note, *my* C-note coming from his pocket, but then had to fold when I signaled him that Lyde held a full house, I knew that what we were doing was all part of the angle. Still and all, I couldn't help but sweat it a little. I made myself placidly read the paper, even though I ran my eyes over the same paragraph about a drug bust-up in Silverlake about fifteen-odd times, while I shifted or winked or rubbed my nose as the cards in Lyde's hand dictated.

In all my grifts, I'd never spent so much time with the mark. It was all short cons for me—the most I'd get with them was about an hour, though if the touch was going to be big, I'd stay a bit longer. Some of the big stores, they call for the roper to be with his sucker for days, weeks, even. Me, I couldn't stand to be around a mark for so long. I remembered all their faces, all their stories, it not being too much different from memorizing a piece of music. I took from those marks only what I needed to get my money, never had to be inside them as long as I'd crept into Oates. And knowing him as well as I did, all the corners of sadness and hope, made me appreciate my line as a short con operator. Who needed to crawl so deep inside that kind of misery?

But I had to be there, snuggled up against the longing in his heart, so that I knew exactly what move he'd play and when. Here was a guy who lived the life invisible until I came along, and suddenly he had shape and made noise and folks didn't see right through him anymore. Every mark's got his want and the trick is finding it and making it work for you.

As the pot grew, so did Oates's take. He was knee-deep into my cash, already past a grand, and things were starting to look mighty nice. Oates dealt and came up with a flush, beating Lyde's straight, and just like that, we were almost about to double three thou. If everything had been on the level...well, I could see how C men kept coming back to cards on their own dime. My heart was knocking around inside my ribs like a fighter on the ropes. Wouldn't you know, my son of a bitch cough started to come back in the midst of all this excitement, and Oates had to play a hand on his own while I went into the bathroom and hacked up a pound or two of something from the bottom of Loch Lomond.

I threw water onto my face and stared at myself in the mirror after toweling off. The lights in that bathroom didn't do me any favors—it was already three in the morning and I looked about as good as a man could look if he had been living under a freeway overpass. I searched for the reassurance of family resemblance in my face. I never did much resemble my father, I was taller than him by my bar mitzvah, and where he was round, I was long. We joked sometimes that I had the milkman's jaw. By the time my pop was my age, he'd been married four years and had a two-year-old son. I tried, but couldn't find that, couldn't find him, in my face. I wanted to see him looking back at me from the other side of the mirror, but he wasn't there. I made myself smile at myself, readjusted my tie, and came back out into the room, snapping the bathroom light off behind me.

"Who's up for another drink?" I asked with my hands spread wide, a genial host. "I'm fair parched."

"You okay, Lou?" Oates asked.

"Yeah," Lyde threw in. "You don't look so hot."

"Aw, fellas," I said as I poured myself a fine libation from Lyde's bottle, "I already got me a mommy. If I need her, I'll just ring her up." But they kept staring me, so I said, "Guys, everything's square," and to prove it, I took a strong gulp of whiskey followed by a drag from a therapeutic cigarette. "See?"

Lyde shrugged and started to deal while Oates sent me a look across the table: *You really okay?* I didn't give him an answer as I threw myself back down into the chair and read a fascinating article about what casserole to serve alongside Thanksgiving dinner, only a couple of weeks away. We always ate our Thanksgiving at my father's cousin Ira's place, because Ira was a dentist and had the biggest apartment out of anybody in the family. His place even had a separate dining room, with big double shutter doors that closed it off from the living room. So on the day, the shutter doors would be opened and five card tables would be lined up, and you always got a bum deal if you were one of the unlucky ones stuck in the doorway. It paid to get to Ira's early. There was nothing worse than trying to stuff your face with the doorjamb right in your back.

Thanksgiving dinners were a mixed bag. On account of us finally getting some decent home-cooked food instead of my mom's gutbombs—Aunt Erma's green beans, Cousin Nancy's creamed onions, Ira made his own stuffing—me and my pop and sisters could have wept with joy to eat such manna. And after dinner us younger cousins would go off to play board games in one of the kid's bedrooms while the old fogies smoked and the women played mahjong in the living room. All that was swell. But as soon as we got into the car to go home, my mom would start to sigh and mope, and want to know why Ira had such nice things and a big apartment, and with two children, yet, each with their own bedrooms, but here we were, schlepping back to our tiny apartment, hardly making it on my dad's salary from the box company, and three kids plus bubbe, a son sleeping on the sofa, and didn't my father have enough gumption to make something of himself besides shuffling paper, if not for his own gratification, then why not think of everyone who depended on him—and didn't Ira's wife Connie always look so Fifth Avenue in her new frocks while what did my mom get to wear but some old *schmatte* she picked up ages ago at Loehmann's. By the time we made it back to our place, all the good buzz we'd picked up from eating top-of-the-line food and playing games with the family was gone, weighted down with my mom's disappointed hopes.

I signaled Oates that Lyde held a trio of jacks, and Oates took another hand, getting our winnings up to almost five grand. Oates tried mightily to keep himself from squirming with joy in his seat—Miss Manners of Poker might have something to say about that—but here he was, the Victorious Hero doing me a good turn with the brilliance of the scheme. I couldn't not get a little leap of excitement, too, that every hand Oates won brought me closer to the recording studio and further away from a long car ride full of letdown.

But fun as this little dog-and-pony was, we couldn't sit here all night beaming sunshine at each other. I folded then unfolded the newspaper twice. Lyde dealt the next hand. I tipped Oates that Lyde only held one pair. Oates bet a century and Lyde raised him two hundred. They kept going like that, Oates staying with him. And Lyde finally said, "Listen, we going to make this interesting, or what?"

"Whatcha got in mind?" Oates asked.

"I'll bet you double or nothing on the hand you're holding now." He reached into his pocketbook and tossed down the largest heap of green outside of a lettuce farm. "How 'bout it?"

Oates looked at me and I gave him the tiniest shrug. "Gee, fellas," I said, "that seems a mite high."

"Now you're a babysitter all of a sudden?" Lyde said, looking over his shoulder. "Go warm us some milk if you wanna be useful." He turned back to Oates. "Seems like your buddy here don't think you can handle the play, that you don't got the spine for it."

"Hey, chum," I said, making like I was getting steamed, "I don't care for your tone." Starting to get up, I said to Oates, "Maybe you and me oughta cop a heel."

So there was me and Lyde, battling for the state of Oates's manhood and poor Ronnie, he was so torn. Here he had himself a chance to emerge more gallant and daring than even he'd ever imagined in the dark little cubbies of his heart. He could land us ten thou easy with just a single hand of cards, or lose it all and wind up with bubkes. We were already ahead—and now Lyde was calling Oates's courage into question. Oates wanted my gratitude more than anything.

Besides, I'm certain he thought to himself, I'd already let him know that Lyde's hand was just a pair and he had two pair. There'd be no losing. He reached over and slid his winnings into the middle of the table. I gave Oates a little smile to let him know I was onboard with the operation.

"Okee," Lyde said, "let's see what you got."

With a flourish, Oates tipped his hand and spread the two pair—fives and queens—onto the table. Lyde made an appreciative whistle and shook his head. "That's some hand, pal."

"Ain't it, though?" Oates said, trying to keep from sounding smug. He was hard-boiled and loving life.

Then Lyde set down his hand. First, a pair of threes and then—

"Motherfucker," I said.

Three eights.

Oates turned white then red and then he turned a color that hadn't gotten a name yet but wouldn't be showing up in your Crayolas any time soon.

"Thanks, boys," Lyde said, getting up and collecting his take. "It's been a time, but I gotta get home and kiss my mattress."

I saw that, after the shock of it, Oates's brain was working hard. I knew he was thinking that he couldn't call Lyde out for cheating, since that would reveal that he'd been the one with the inside tip the whole time. And Oates understood that there wasn't any bread left in our pantry to try and win it all back, or even some of it. As Lyde shrugged into his coat and put his hat on, Oates and I both just watched him, good and goggled. The sound of the hotel room door closing behind Lyde was the staccato of finality.

"Maybe I'm going to throw up," Oates offered, then put his head in his hands.

I sat back in my chair and looked at the ceiling, which wasn't much, your usual ceiling, a bulb burning whitely behind a ceramic shade, but I stared at it like it was a dying star.

Into his hands, Oates said, "You said he only had a pair."

"I said he had a pair *and* three of a kind," I said, my voice far off. "A full house."

Oates groaned and tried to crawl further into his skeleton, which I've tried before and found little success in that endeavor. I got up from my chair and floated over to the window, stuffing my hands in my pockets. Outside was dark, there wasn't anything to see but the glare of the hotel room light. The dark made the world huge and tiny at the same time, and I listened to it, the bigness and littleness, rushing in and out, with Oates's moans of agony underneath it all.

"So," I said after a pace, "no studio time for me, then."

"Lou, Lou, Lou," Oates whimpered. "I…"

"Yeah." I pressed the side of my cheek against the glass, and my face came to meet me, a lot closer than I cared for, as if I was about to kiss myself. The glass was cool, though. When I spoke, my words came out muffled. I'd thought about what I was going to say here and decided that the best plan was to stay simple. "Maybe I should have

known," I said. "Can't get anywhere without being crooked. Turned
around and bit us on the ass. Guess it's my fault."

Following the script he didn't know he was reading, Oates
said, "It's *my* fault. I didn't read the signs right and maybe...maybe
I oughta have quit before, not gotten so grabby."

I wasn't going to say whether or not I agreed that the flop was
his to shoulder, so I sighed instead, and said, "It'll take a while to get
that kind of cash again. But even if I did, the guy at the recording studio told me booking the room was a one-time deal. He might know
somebody else, though." I shrugged, Weary and Defeated, as I turned
back to face the room. "I don't know. This might be it for me."

When he looked up from his hands, Oates's eyes were wet. I
threw him my hankie and studied the surface of the table. "You and
me," he said, swabbing at his eyes, "we were going to get bop out to
the masses. We'd cut your record and it'd play on every radio station
in L.A.—on every station everywhere."

"Yep," I agreed. "It would have been sweet."

In the room next to ours, a door slammed and two voices, a
man and a woman's, started yelling. "...and you can tell Marty to
go fuck himself..." was about the most I could hear.

Also hearing it, Oates turned his head to one side and said,
"Go ahead."

"Go ahead and what?"

"You know—yell, scream, throw furniture. This is the part
where you're supposed to blow your fuse and beat the crap out of
me."

Maybe that's what he wanted after all. I wasn't going to let
him off the hook that way, and it wouldn't follow my plan, so I said,
"That wouldn't do anyone any good. Money's gone. 'Sides, you didn't
mean no harm. If you could get that dough back, you would."

Oates nodded, eager to redeem himself. "Sure would. In a
minute, pal. But," here he spread open his hands, empty and white,
"I can't get it back." He left his hands hanging there while his mind
churned and steamed, and this is where I had to wait, until Oates
could put the pieces together. He was halfway there when he said,
"Although..."

I didn't want to pounce too quick, so I futzed with the near-empty bottle of booze before asking, like an afterthought, "Although?"

He stood up so fast he almost knocked his chair back. Oates looked like he was stepping in front of the firing squad, but he'd do it, a proud martyr to the cause. "There's always Hi-Life."

"Ron," I said, sitting on the bed, "tell me what the holy hell you are talking about. You said we couldn't record there, even if we did have the money."

"We don't need money," he rasped.

"I don't get it."

"Listen," he said, as he started to transform from the Martyr to My Savior. "Usually the boss at Hi-Life books cats all the way through, from six at night until six the next morning. He likes to keep the joint open as long as possible to rake in money. Usually he can only get one or two recording sessions at night, though. Daytime is busy. He'd never shut down during the day. But I could fix it so that for one night, he doesn't book anyone."

"And how are you going to do that?"

Starting to roll now, he made like he was waving away a cloud of gnats, the idea was too small and simple to sweat out. "I dunno—tell him we gotta fumigate or something. Yeah, fumigate," he said, latching on to the idea and digging it. "That guy hates bugs, so all I gotta tell him is that I found roaches in the studio and he'd shut the whole place down. But I'll say that I'll handle getting the exterminators. So once he and everybody clears out," he slapped his hands together, "we got the whole place to ourselves. Equipment and everything."

I looked up at him like he was Edison, Marconi and Ford all rolled into one moist, doughy package. "The whole recording studio, empty for the night?"

Oates clomped over to me and put his hands on my shoulders. "If you came with your combo, dressed in coveralls—they could keep their instruments in a truck or something until the place cleared out—and we finished by sunrise, buddy, you and me, we could cut your record right that night."

"And your boss wouldn't know anything about anything."

Oates beamed at me. "Whaddaya think?"

"Gee, Ron, that's an awful large risk you're taking for me. Huge, even."

"But I owe you, Louis. I owe you big, and," he added damply, "you're my friend."

I made as though I was shaking my head slowly in admiration, when inside I was capering about the room and whooping. It'd taken such a long, long setup to get Oates to just this point, precisely where I needed him to be. He did dandy, though, even coming up with the fumigation angle and saving me from thinking of something myself. I'd have to tell George about it all later, and make sure that he gave Lyde not only the five centuries I'd promised but a little something extra, for getting all the pieces together. George, of course, would get his cut, too, two benjies for finding me the genius Lyde, and I'd be generous and throw in fifty to let him know I appreciated his work.

"You'd do that for me?" I asked in an awed whisper.

Oates got bashful but puffed up at his own brashness and ingenuity. He really did love this, his newfound role of courageous hero, especially since *I* was the one he was saving. "A 'course, Lou. It's the least I could do, considering I lost all your money. Anyway," he added, blushing, "things for me got a whole lot more interesting since you became my friend."

"That's right," I said, taking his hand off my shoulder and giving it a hearty shake. He'd been a perfect mark, that Ronald Oates. Arnie would have loved him, and loved me, for fleecing him good and proper. "You and me, we're pals right until the end."

Chapter twenty-four

I didn't even knock, and the door was being pulled open by Nora, a small, dark shape lit from behind. I bent forward and pressed a kiss onto her mouth, my hand resting on the guitar curves of her waist and hips. Her smell of powder and body was something I was getting familiar with.

She smiled up at me and then frowned over my shoulder. First I thought that maybe this old suit of mine was getting a smidge tatty around the edges, even though I'd worn my best—all my cash being tied up for a while in one scheme or another, I'd cancelled my regular appointments at Brooks Brothers for the next decade or so. But it wasn't my clothes that bothered her.

"Damn," she said. "The front porch bulb has burned out."

Unless she grew two feet in the next five minutes, there was no way Nora could reach the light. So I moved past her and started down the hall. "Where do you keep the spare lightbulbs?"

"In the pantry, in the kitchen," she said, trotting behind me.

"Right. Because keeping food in the kitchen would be just plain silly."

It felt strange, loping through her place as if I belonged there, grabbing the lightbulb, then coming back and switching out the fresh one for the busted. She watched me reach up, easy-like, not even stretching out that far, and perform the deed. A bright glare beamed down at us, and she lit up, too, as though I had changed out one star in a constellation for another. Playing knight-errant meant wearing a heavy suit of armor.

And in the fresh light of the porch, I looked at her. "Don't you look a lovely sight," I said, "straight out of a woman's picture show." She smiled and went coy, posing for me. She'd swept her hair up, as women are wont to do when they're dolling themselves up for a night out, and had put on some kind of deep blue dress with a pinched-in waist and full skirt. There was something pleasant about the feel of the extra fabric brushing against my legs as I stepped closer to kiss her again. She didn't put up what you'd call a fight, not with her tongue giving my mouth a good survey, but then she remembered we were standing right in view of the whole street. So she tugged me inside and we wound up necking against the front door.

I wasn't timid about touching her. She wasn't holding onto her Bible study shyness, but why would she, especially after we'd done a few things together the other day that would have made a fine ride at the State Fair. The crinkly fabric of her dress rustled as I gathered up her skirt, trying to get to her legs, and finding handfuls of petticoat instead. I dove back under her skirt until I found the ripe cheeks of her ass and grabbed. She squealed but didn't push me away. My hat fell onto the floor.

I wanted her, and not the way I wanted one of my recreational fucks. I liked how she looked at me—as if I was a better man. But I wasn't that man and everything we were together reminded me of that. I'd show her, show myself, who I really was.

"Let's go into the bedroom," she breathed.

I shook my head as I tugged on my zipper.

"Can I turn out the lights, at least?"

Again, I shook my head, and reached into my trousers, past my shorts, to take my hard cock in my hand. I pulled it out and she stared, stepping back. The hallway was brightly lit.

"You want to…make love…*here?*" she piped as her face turned red.

"Get on your knees."

"Why?" She really had no idea.

"Do it."

Eyes round and fearful, dancing back and forth between my dick and my face, she knelt in front of me. "I think I know what you want," she whispered, and started to put her hands on the ground, lifting her ass in the air. She'd been on the farm long enough.

"Not that."

"What then?"

I stepped closer to her, placed my free hand on the back of her head. "You and Floyd didn't do this."

"No, no. He never even asked."

"I'm not asking, either."

She was quiet, after that.

I was present and accounted for when Nora and I finally walked through the door of the nightclub. Tie straight, shirt tucked, all signs of lipstick on my face swabbed away, eyes bright and alert. Nora kept her eyes on the ground, unable to look up at anybody, patting her hair every ten seconds even though she'd fixed it decently before we'd left. She was wondering if anyone knew what she'd just done, and, if they did, whether she'd be thrown out into the streets and chased away. I almost told her that nearly all the women at Cookie's Silver Spoon, and probably half the men, had sucked a guy off before, and with better skill. I didn't though, being a gentleman.

And in the spirit of gentlemanliness, I took Nora out. Cookie's was a swank joint on Santa Monica Boulevard in West Hollywood. It was one of those nightclubs that had cocktails, dancing and candles in little frosted glasses on each table, and all for the reasonable sum of five bucks a head, plus the extra cost of two drinks, minimum. Cash was still tight for me, but I needed to give back to Nora, somehow.

As a hostess in a satin dress showed me and Nora to our table, we wove through clusters of folks polished to a blinding brilliance.

A decent combo and singer were working their way through a set of standards. Waiters in smart red jackets scurried around with bottles of champagne, one or two holding platters of oysters. Booze flowed fast and easy. I knew grifters who solely worked scenes like Cookie's—there was a short con, called the tat, and all a fella needed for it was some crooked dice and drunk, happy marks. Lots of times, the nightclub was a clip joint, getting its share of the touch in exchange for letting the C-man work the room.

I wasn't here to work. After we got to our table—I, the gentleman, holding out Nora's seat for her—I told myself that I'd do my best to shut off my mental gearworks for at least a little while. But there was the decision and the doing, and they weren't the same.

Across the table, I watched Nora. She stared at the table as if it held forgiveness. What kind of number had Floyd worked on her to make her endure everything I was throwing at her? She believed she deserved it, and there wasn't a thing I could do to her, say to her, that would make her leave. Beatrice wouldn't have stood for it, would've planted a fist in my face and a heel in my crotch, but not before ripping me apart with her words. And the more Nora took, the more I wanted to destroy.

Bea and I would never have been able to go to a place like Cookie's. The only colored folks I saw were parking cars and bussing tables. But it was her face I wanted across from mine, staring boldly back, challenging the room. Soon, I promised silently.

I wasn't with Beatrice, though. To keep Nora from sliding off of her chair and under the table, I reached out and took hold of her hand. At first, it just kind of sat there, my fingers wrapped around hers like a serpent, but after a few moments, her fingers slowly wove through mine. I smiled at her, and she returned the smile, but not without a little difficulty.

When the waiter came to take our cocktail orders—scotch for me, sloe gin rickey for her—she couldn't meet the waiter's eyes.

"How about a dance for your cavalier?" I asked as the band went into "East of the Sun." I was still having some trouble getting my wind back. Nora thought about it. I could just read her, know she was thinking that to take the dance floor meant having lots of people stare at her, and if they saw her, they would *know*.

"Just a dance or two," I said, standing.

Before she had a chance to say yes or no, I'd already pulled her to her feet.

The floor wasn't half so crowded as it was at Dee's, which is to say you could slide more than a dime between the shoulders of the dancers who barely heard the music they lurched to. When my record came out, this crowd would probably have no idea.

So maybe the high rollers and lacquered women wouldn't know when my music made it out into the grand, ignorant world— the big prize was getting it out there, having underground FM stations play it, booking gigs at sweaty little belowstairs clubs where the real jazz lovers met for excellent sounds. Maybe I'd wind up in New York, touring. Then—well, I'd wait until that happened before I planned my then.

"Louis," Nora said. "You're holding me kind of tight."

"How's that?" I asked, looking down at her. I'd crawled so far into my head, thinking about cutting that record, I'd hardly noticed that we were swaying back and forth together on the dance floor. Then I saw that my grip on her was hard, hard enough that she might bruise. I loosened my hold. "Don't want you trying to slip away."

"I'm not going anywhere."

I pulled her closer for the dance. It wasn't the best fit, so I had to hunch over a bit so that her nose wasn't straight into my ribcage. It'd been some time since I'd danced. Every now and then, when Beatrice was feeling kind of sentimental, we'd put on one of her blues platters and slow dance in her bathroom, far away from judging eyes. And with Beatrice being about as sentimental as a razor, we didn't dance together often. We matched together nicely, though, she being on the taller side and us able to put our arms around each other without me doubling over or her getting up on her toes. Nora was small, so small she could easily be crushed.

The band swung into the next number, an up-tempo "Oh, Lady Be Good." I had plenty of experience dancing with my sisters in our living room and later at dances held in school gymnasiums. So instead of beating a retreat when the swingier number kicked in, like half the crowd did, I took Nora's hands in mine and started into a low-key Lindy Hop. Maybe it wasn't the wisest thing to do, what with my lungs feeling like rusty radiator pipes, but when I went into the rock step, she suddenly smiled, forgetting the judging eyes around her. It felt kind of nice—the good, almost painful feeling of letting the girl go, then the resistance when she came out to the end of her spin, that little tug at the end of your arm where you had to keep your balance, holding onto her, else you'd both go flying into the bandstand, and then you pull her back again.

I turned her, spun her out. We moved pretty decently together, and that's when I looked up and saw that, even though we were right in the middle of some fancier maneuvers, she had her eyes closed.

You'd think that if you were being moved around in space by some guy, your eyes would be wide open, keeping sure that your partner didn't hurl you into other dancers or a wall or right out into the Milky Way. It took some trust to believe that the lead was going to do his job properly, keep you safe and not get trampled. I couldn't even walk down the hallway in my old building with my eyes shut, let alone dance.

By now, Nora should have known better.

I almost fumbled the steps, watching her like that. It made me feel really small, being handed a gift that I couldn't afford. I managed to finish the number, but when the band started to play "Lonesome Miss Pretty," I led Nora off the floor and back to our table.

The cigarette that I lit when we sat down again didn't help my lungs, exactly, but at least it gave me a few minutes to set myself back on the level. Nora had let the coat of embarrassment slip from her shoulders, and didn't seem to notice how much she'd shaken me with her trust.

"This is a nice place," she said, sipping at her fresh gin rickey. "I don't think I'd ever heard of it."

"It's not that new," I said.

She shrugged. "Sometimes, during the war, I'd volunteer at the USO dances."

"Not making sandwiches, I hope."

Laughing, she said, "And send our boys off to fight with food poisoning? Nosir. I'd help decorate the dance halls with red, white and blue bunting, as if it was the Fourth of July even in February."

I remember being force-fed Old Glory so much during those years, I could have puked stars and stripes. Everyone got to thinking that staring at some flag would make the whole country band together and sing patriotic songs for four years, that it was all worthwhile, the rationing, the death, and just on account of a scrap of fabric. A flag doesn't mean anything, not a guy's life, and would it provide any comfort for the kids shipping off to parts unknown, who'd come back in a box or with important bits of themselves missing? Even when they came back whole, I could tell that they'd lost something in the Pacific or the swampy fields of France, and no star-spangled rag would make up for it.

"I bet those boys appreciated it," I said. "I know I would have." I never went to one of those dances, since guys like me weren't welcome.

Nora and I were quiet for a while. The band kept playing and the room was filled with sound. She gripped my hand tightly, trying to cling to my good favor. I sweated, clammy. I had to end this before I wound up erasing both of us.

Tomorrow might hand me anything, and I had plenty of ideas about cutting my record, taking it to Beatrice, her contrition, my forgiveness, and the golden glow of the days and years that would follow. There wasn't room for Nora.

It was time to leave. Oates was going to call any day now to come into the studio—all last-minute, on account of the whole fumigation angle—and I was wiped.

"Do we have to go?" Nora asked, disappointed, as I helped her into her doll-sized coat.

"Long day at work," I said. "And tomorrow will be long, too." But I was already planning what I'd say. First, though, I wouldn't answer the phone for a few days, letting her fret and doubt. And then, when I finally did pick up, her relief at getting me on the line would crumble.

"I can tell that you feel better," she said, soft. Seemed she was willing to put up with whatever humiliation I could dish out, so long as she could dream of making me whole again through her grace.

I started walking her towards the door, threading through the tables, when I heard some gent say, "Nora?"

Nora stopped walking and stared at a guy sitting down at a table. "Jimmy?"

"Holy cow! It's you, all right," Jimmy bawled, leaping up from his chair. He turned to a dame, who was still sitting and not getting up for anyone. "Roberta, it's Nora Edwards."

This revelation somehow failed to excite Roberta beyond a tired smile and a "How'dya do?"

I just wanted to leave but, given the way Nora's face lit up when she was hallooed by Jimmy, we weren't going anywhere for a while. I couldn't bolt for the door—the path out was too crowded.

"Jimmy," Nora beamed and put a hand on his elbow, "this is Louis Dante. Louis, Jimmy Lomax."

"Nice to meet you," he said, shaking my paw. He wasn't a little fella, probably played football or rugby or Kick the Kike back in college. We hovered around the same height, but this guy had around thirty pounds on me, twenty-five of which seemed to be in his arm as he shook my hand. His face was as much forehead as anything else, what with his hairline beating a retreat towards the back of his neck. A mustache relieved the boredom of his face.

"A pleasure, likewise," I said. He was a peppy chap, smiling and pumping my arm up and down until I thought for sure I'd spout water.

Lomax finally let my hand go and I had to stop myself from shaking out the crushing he'd given it. He was one of those big dogs that knock you onto your back and lick your face until you suffocate. He didn't seem to get that we were wearing coats, and I stared at the exit with longing. "Why don't you join us?" he asked, and pulled two nearby empty chairs towards the table. They looked like bear traps.

"We don't want to disturb you," I said. Sleep and forgetting was what I wanted, needed.

"Only for a little while," Lomax insisted. He said to Nora, "What terrific luck, running into you like this. You can spare a few minutes for your old pal Jimmy, can't you?"

This idea struck Nora as one of the all-time greats. "You bet," she said, and then asked as she was halfway into her chair before looking up at me, "Will that be all right?"

"I—"

Lomax pointed to the remaining empty chair. "Have a seat."

I recognized the threat of his tone, his eyes. A cheerful bully. I folded myself down and felt the jaws of the trap slam shut around me.

Nora and Lomax talked away. Roberta, a thick, sandy-haired woman, watched the band and the dance floor without interest, not listening to the palaver. Seems as though Jimmy the Wunderkind knew Nora pretty well, and they were busy cataloguing all the friends they had in common. Dottie and Ken had popped out another papoose, this one a girl. Did you hear about Danny getting canned from his job at the accountants, tough luck? Seems like Vince and Janet were through—she'd given him back his ring and wouldn't take his calls.

Lomax was a cheerful blowhard who was afraid he'd evaporate unless he kept hearing the sound of his own voice. Roberta sure had heard it enough. She watched the dance floor, dreaming her dreams of quiet solitude and stacks of *Romantic Nurse Stories*.

"Me and Nora are old friends," Lomax hollered to me. "I guess you could say old, huh, Nora? Been three years now, hasn't it?"

She cast her mind back into the past, calculating. "That's right. Since just after the war."

Lomax explained as if I cared, "After I got deactivated, I came back out west—seemed like there'd be tons of opportunities for a guy like me."

I wondered how many opportunities a guy like him could have working as a human wrecking ball. I wouldn't much have minded if he'd been slammed into a side of a brick factory right about then. "You bet," I said. "Lots of possibility in California."

"Got me a job as a contractor. You wouldn't believe how many homes needed to be built when our boys came back—they were filling up as fast as we could build 'em!"

Didn't I see the crust of development spread over Los Angeles, filling it up with scrawny dreams of tidy front yards and semi-detached garages and electric ovens burning the roast, instead of fields, orchards and openness? When I got to L.A., it was half cow town, half defense plant, with a smear of glitter from Hollywood. It was only after Uncle Sam gave soldiers the heave-ho that space started to come at a premium, space I missed as the march to tomorrow plowed onwards, flattening anybody who didn't think that all men deserved a television and gray flannel suit.

"Progress is a beautiful thing," I said. "It's what brought me out west, too."

Lomax decided that he and me were going to be bosom pals, so he grinned his idiot grin at me, then turned solemn. "Me and Roberta, when we moved to L.A., I said to her, 'I got to go see Floyd's Nora. She's out here and I'd just perish on the spot if I didn't pay her a visit.'"

"Floyd and Jimmy were army buddies," Nora added. "He looked me up just like you did, Louis."

"That so?" I asked, and knew that I'd better corral this talk quick and steer it someplace else. "You come to Cookie's a lot?"

But that line didn't do me any good. Lomax believed that guys who got shipped out and shot at were somehow a big group of friends, instant brothers. "Where'd you serve?" he asked me.

Before I could get out anything, Nora chirped, "He was in Italy, too, Jimmy." The room was hot, but fingers of sleet began to work down my back. "And, you know, I met Louis because he knew Floyd overseas, too."

Lomax looked like he'd just won the lottery, the Triple Crown, and the Miss Springtime Tulips Pageant all at the same time. Meanwhile, I was getting colder by the second. "You knew Floyd?" he yowled.

"Yeah," I said. "I caught up with him briefly in Italy." I was trying like hell to stick to the rules: never give a sucker too much information or you'll get yourself into hot soup. Most chumps are satisfied with a nugget here or there, but not good ol' Jimmy. I was ready to throttle him. All I wanted to do was get Nora back to her place so I could head home and get some sleep, obliterating everything from the past, including today, but he wouldn't budge out of my way.

"Where in Italy?"

I had to dredge up the story I'd told Nora weeks ago, and I usually have a decent memory, but what with this flu I'd been fighting and everything else, it took me a second longer than normal to remember. "When my battalion got to the Gothic Line."

Lomax laughed and slapped his giant paw on the table. "Kick my cat! Floyd and me were in the same unit. I bet I met you, too."

"Gosh," I said, "I met lots of fellas. I don't know…"

"I was in the 85th Infantry, how 'bout you? 339th? 338th?"

I picked one he hadn't said. "337th."

"How about that! You boys came along and took Mount Verruca with us."

News to me. "A tough one, that was."

"Can you beat that?" Nora mused. She looked surprised but mighty pleased by this turn. I couldn't say that I felt the same way.

"Now I'm sure I must have met you before. When did you say you bumped into Floyd?"

"It was a long time ago," I hedged.

Lomax shouted a laugh. "Not that long, Lou! Most fellas I know remember everything from the war like it was just the other week."

I tried to play it like I was one of the guys who'd seen the ugliest and most awful things you couldn't even imagine. That way, when jerks like Lomax started prodding with the questions, I had a safe position to fall back on.

"I don't really like to think about it," I said, a Battle-Scarred Veteran.

Nora patted my hand and gave me some dewy eyes. Lomax, at least, nodded his cranium sadly. That was fine. I didn't want to keep down this road, seeing as how it didn't end at an ivy-covered cottage by the sea.

"It's tough, it sure is, coming home," Lomax said. "Took me months before Roberta and I could sleep in the same room. Isn't that right, Ro?"

Roberta didn't even turn to look at him as she said, "Uh-huh." Some unseen object continued to hold her fascination, floating off in the distance. If a galoot like Lomax was my husband, I'd probably start looking for pink elephants and will-o'-the-wisps, too. Better that than staring into his giant face all day.

If Lomax noticed his wife giving him the brush-off, he didn't let on. "I didn't want to talk much about it when I first got back," he droned, "but I found that things got easier once I started to open up."

"Yeah, maybe," was as much as I'd give him.

Nora gave me a small, sad smile as she squeezed my arm for comfort. She'd already had a brush with my war memories—that day at the beach when we'd hightailed it back to her house—so she didn't need further convincing that I was haunted.

"It's all right, Louis," she said, and I hoped that was the end of this.

But Lomax wouldn't let it go. "Still, I can't get over the fact that you and me may've met up over there," he dogged. "I don't think that's ever happened with anybody else I've talked to about it—meeting them overseas, I mean."

Man, this rube wasn't giving up and I was getting nervous, which was the opening strains of a con's collapse. "Really, I only met Floyd once," I said. "He just left an impression on me—him and his letters from Nora."

"Letters?" Lomax blinked slowly, frowning. "I don't remember him keeping any letters."

"They were rather private," I said.

"Yeah, but—" He rubbed at his mustache. "Me and Floyd were pretty tight, and he used to beef that he never got his mail. He even went to the co and tried to find out what the problem was, since everybody else was getting letters from home."

"I guess the co fixed the problem," I said, as my insides grew slippery and aquatic.

"See, here's the thing," Lomax said, staring at me like I was growing gills right there at the table, "he didn't. I used to let Floyd read my letters, just so he had something when mail call came around. That's why I looked Nora up when I got to L.A., to see whether or not she'd forgotten Floyd." He looked at her.

"You never said anything about the letters," she said to him.

"Because I could tell that you had written him, and it'd all been a mix-up. But I figured that if you knew he didn't get anything from you, it'd just upset you."

"I wrote him," Nora said. Her hand started to slide away from mine. "Every month while he was gone."

"What about the ones he sent you—they must've said something," Lomax pushed.

"I only got a few, and then they stopped. I figured it was because he was busy, or doing something top secret."

Now both Nora and Lomax were staring at me. Everything in the room had changed. The music wasn't pleasant and unassuming, but jangly and hard. The voices and laughter in the club broke apart into splinters. Everything retreated into a wash of sound and blur. "Louis?" Nora asked me from far away at my elbow. The notes were coming down on all sides, nothing musical about them, and I was being crushed underneath.

Chapter twenty-five

Sometimes, a guy just doesn't want to be right, and this was one of those times. When I first saw Jimmy Lomax, I'd thought he could beat me into nothing but a schmear, and I'd be unable to stop him. And lookee, kids, I'd been dead-on.

As Lomax's fist came up to smash into my ribcage, I tried like hell to do something about it. I even made a few swipes at him myself but only wound up brushing my knuckles past the shoulder of his jacket. It didn't make any difference, it just got Lomax sore, and the next time he punched me in the chest the little air I had in my lungs fell out onto the pavement and I sunk down onto my knees and into a puddle. The rain had begun sometime while we'd been inside the club, so now everything had turned to dirty water.

Nora had just got up from the table and left. She didn't say anything right after Lomax had caught me in my lies, just stood and headed for the door.

Before Lomax could say anything, I got up and went outside, finding gaps in the crowd to slip through.

Nora was outside, about to walk off in the rain, not even paying any mind to where she'd go. I took hold of her arm and dragged her under an awning. I stared down at her, her eyes wide and fixed but not looking at me, something like horror on her face. I wanted to leave, but her glassy eyes held me. I'd seen that look before, in the faces of men who'd lost everything and the next step was nothingness.

What I was going to say, I couldn't figure, and me the guy who always had a line. It was like running off a rooftop with no hope of growing feathers. "Nora," was the only word I could find.

"You didn't know Floyd," she said finally.

I considered hedging it a little, saying that he and I had met up just once for a few minutes but never actually talked about her, and instead I heard come out of my mouth, "No, I didn't know him. I never met him."

"Then how did you know anything about him, about me?"

"I…got your name from the newspaper archives." Out in public, the truth and I pretended that we didn't know each other. Yet here I was with Nora in the cold, the rain loud and staccato on the awning, cars hissing by on the wet streets, her face a white ghost, and me opening my mouth to spew out everything. "Everything else I guessed."

Her eyes flicked up to my face. There wasn't anything in them but glazed misery. No warmth, no concern, no hate, no nothing. "Tell me why," she said.

The sharp cold air shook my already unsteady lungs and I took on coughing. Before, when that'd happen, she'd put a comforting hand on my arm or gently pat my back. This time—nothing. It was tough to keep standing while my whole body shook with each spasm. When I could get my voice back a little, I rasped, "I was going to sell you something. Then you assumed I was one of Floyd's army buddies, and I never got to correct you."

"You're a salesman?" she asked and that last word came out like a cuss.

"Something like that."

"So all your talk about business and finance was more lies."

I shrugged. "Well, you thought—" I didn't get any further, what with her hard bark that was supposed to be a laugh.

"I see," she said. "*I* thought. It was *me*, not you. All this," she waved her hand in the space between us and in that space that used to hold warmth and now was nothing but fiction, "is *my* fault." She stared at me, a thorough up and down, and I wasn't exactly looking like the picture of rosy health, wheezing and pasty. "Did you even serve in the army?" she asked.

"4-F," I said, which was nearly the truth. I had the papers around somewhere, though I hadn't carried them for a couple of years. I could have thrown them away when the war was over, but they'd made me lose so much, I didn't have it in me to toss them into the ash can.

She made that queer laugh again, the one that hit me like hailstones. "Oh, that's swell," she said, voice full of smashed glass that cut me. "And that terrific story you told me, about being on the beach in Italy, men dead and dying, all of that. All of that was, was nothing."

Even if I'd tried, no words would have come out of me, they'd dried up in the icy air. I concentrated on staying on my feet, and tried to breathe with no success.

Nora dug the heels of her hands into her eye sockets, making as if she'd push her eyes all the way back into her head so they wouldn't have to see everything falling to pieces. "Is there anything you said to me that was true?"

I thought about it. "My name is Louis."

She ripped her arm from my grasp and ran into the street. A car swerved around her, honking. I bolted after her and dragged her back under the awning.

"Jesus fucking Christ," I shouted. "What the fuck are you doing?"

Nora forgot about trying to smash into traffic, and collapsed at my feet. Instead of hauling off and slapping me, she hunched over, grabbing at her middle and looking like she was about to give up the gin rickeys she'd drank. Here I was, right in the middle of the hallway, and no matter how much I tried, I couldn't get my eyes open, and all around me I heard the sounds of disaster.

Face wet, Nora pulled and shoved at her own body—she was trying to push me out of her. She was thinking that it wasn't so long ago, when I'd put my cock into her mouth, when I'd fucked her, that

I'd been deep inside of her, me, a stranger and not the man she'd figured me to be. And it wasn't just her body, but all the stuff we'd said to each other, what she'd revealed to me. I'd gotten into her. It was turning her sick. *I* was turning her sick, like a slow-acting poison. I think she was ready to turn herself inside out to clean me out of her, even while I stood nearby and watched.

I'd strung myself on her, using her as my torture rack. The pain I'd wanted had finally come but it didn't feel bright and scouring. It was thick and dark and viscous.

My head spun. I hadn't the strength to run or walk, barely enough to speak. Words came out of my mouth and fell to the damp ground like earthworms washed up by the rain, pale and wriggling and blind.

"Nora," I said, and just me saying her name made her curl up even tighter because I'd turned even that word foul, "this is good. It's good for you to know. What you're looking for, it can't be found. It's not real. I'm not real. You're just leaving yourself open to be conned." I couldn't figure the words out right, the time that I needed them most, when I wanted them to signify something, words I really did mean. I wasn't used to talking to anyone like I meant it—except Bea. I always tried to work some angle. There were too many angles now, a room designed by a lunatic.

She looked up at me with her own fever in her eyes, the fever of dying illusions. Then something in her eyes changed, turned to relief and gratitude, but it was a look she fixed over my shoulder. I didn't have to turn to know that Lomax was standing behind me. Arnie, in my head, looked solemn and disappointed.

Lomax put a huge hand on my shoulder and pulled me back, away from Nora, out into the rain. "Go home," he snarled as I lurched backwards. "Nobody wants you."

Roberta appeared, picking up Nora and putting her arms around her. She held Nora against her chest like a child.

"Get the fuck out of here," Lomax said, shaking me. Everything inside me knocked against itself, a boxful of broken dishes. He kept telling me to leave, but he blocked the only way out. Toying with me.

He shoved me back so hard I stumbled. He helped me along by pushing me into the nearby alley. It was close and dark, stinking of wet paper, old oranges and something sad and human. I took a step then slipped on the slick pavement, landing on my knees. Between chasing Nora out into the street and stumbling from the awning to the alley, I was soaked in cold rain. I couldn't have been any wetter if you'd tied me in a sack and dropped me off the pier. But I wasn't much worried about ruining my suit when Lomax came running up and slammed his fist straight into my face. My head filled with percussion.

"You pretend you're a veteran," Lomax snarled, bringing his fist back and then ramming it into my ribs, "and you insult all the decent guys who went out," he pulled back again and hit me straight in the gut so whatever little bit I'd eaten and most of the drinks I'd had came up, but didn't make it onto his shoes, "and fought and died for *you*, you piece of shit."

"I was 4-F," I gagged on my hands and knees.

"Yeah, sure." He kneed me in the chest and I heard something break—it wasn't his knee.

In the movies, any guy off the street can throw a punch. One second, they're a barber or businessman, and then put them in the middle of a fight and kapow! They're Jack Dempsey all of a sudden, and each punch they throw is dead-on, and not only that, they already know how to hit without smashing their hand into wee little pieces. They can take a hit, too, without collapsing like a card table. Never mind if they—the barber, the businessman—never hit anyone in their whole blessed lives.

I wasn't that guy and this wasn't the pictures. I tried to get up and take a swipe at Lomax, but between me not being a heavyweight champ and the network of fractures spreading throughout my body, I wasn't able to do much besides swing my arm through the rain and lose my balance so that I went face-first into the mud. Cold sludge crept under my collar as rain poured down the back of my neck, icy all the way down so that whatever part of my back wasn't already wet and chilled got an extra dose. I couldn't even shiver.

Another thing the movies don't tell you is how much it hurts to get punched and kicked. Think about the most painful thing you ever felt, like stubbing a toe or maybe even breaking an arm when you were a kid and fell out of the treehouse, or passing a stone or just about anything. Got it? Okay, now take that pain and make it happen over and over, and it doesn't stop, it keeps coming and even when you think it's just about done, that'll be it, another tractor slams into you and you hear the smashed glass of your bones.

Lomax grabbed my jacket and hauled me up. I swayed in his grip, my breath nothing but a hollow clattering in my lungs—one of the ribs he'd broken seemed to have dug in, stuck a hole in something important—and he kept whaling on me, driving his fist into my face, my shoulder, a domino chain of body blows, each one leading to the next. There was no way for me to stop him, my face was a lost cause. If it ever healed, I'd never look the same. Something around my eyeball was busted, and my nose was trying its best to crawl across my face to hide in my hair. I dimly thought, who was going to trust a C-man with a face like a hobo camp? It'd been my breadmaker, my pretty punim, and now it was gone. When Lomax got tired of holding me up, I slid onto the ground and curled up, tucking my hands under my arms and waiting waiting waiting for it to be over. For me it was years but for Lomax it probably wasn't more than two minutes. I'd seen fistfights before—in a betting parlor, a few bars, outside some cathouse—and they were short and sloppy, with both guys winding up on the ground in a flopping wrestling match. Nobody stayed up on their feet unless they were prizefighters, and there weren't too many of those walking around.

Then I heard women's shoes on the pavement, and something deep inside me lit up, thinking at least Nora had come to stop him, at least I got that much. But then I heard some other woman, it took a minute through the smoke of pain to figure who the woman was, and Roberta, not Nora, said, "Jimmy, get in the car and dry off! You'll catch your death of pneumonia out here."

"Be right there, honey," he said over his shoulder. Then to me he said, "I will fucking kill you, you yellow asshole, if you even think about Nora again. Got that?"

I couldn't answer, what with my mouth full of coppery blood, so he gave me a parting gift of a punch to the liver then picked me up again and threw me deeper into the alley, where I slammed into a few crates. I heard Lomax lumber off, the soft murmur of voices that was almost lost in the sound of the rain, and then I was alone.

Nobody called the cops, no ambulance showed up. I lay there for I don't know how long, lost inside a knot of bruises and misery. If I'd ever been lower, I couldn't figure when. I felt everything in my body, all the smashed bits, the wet rattling, the lacing together of muscle and meat that seemed to be unraveling with each minute I spent lying there. A drain spout emptied rainwater onto my ankle, and it continued on, the water that headed towards the storm drains and then the sea to get lost in the bigness of the ocean, taking most of my heat with it. The pavement grit rubbed into my face on one side while the rain hit me on the other.

The only thing that got me up was the idea that if I didn't move, someone in the club might have me hauled away and arrested for vagrancy—and what a guy like me doesn't need is a night or two in jail. As a C-man and not one of those guys into the heavy rackets, I'd fare about as well as a pastrami sandwich in the tiger's cage, that is to say, I'd be chewed up and shat out in a matter of moments.

With my blood turning the rainwater pink, I managed to lift myself up by clinging to the wall. I staggered to my car, half a block away. Nobody was out on the sidewalks because of the rain. Don't ask me how I was able to get my keys out and unlock the car door, or even how I made it into the front seat and turned on the ignition. I did all this in a stupor, both stuck inside the ruined machine that was my body and also somehow outside of it, watching from the backseat and telling the driver where to go. It took a while for me to be able to pick my head up from the steering wheel and turn on the windshield wipers. The rain drummed hard on the roof and hood of my car, reminding me of those movies about the French Revolution where some royal schmuck or self-sacrificing moron is led up to the guillotine and the drums go rat-a-tat until the blade comes down, snick, and the crowd goes berserk with joy.

At least in my car I didn't get rained on. I squinted at the street through the red fog in my eyes and knew that the day I stepped onto Nora Edwards' porch was the day I left the mapped world behind, plunging into unknown seas.

Some folks say that the Great Pyramids are miraculous, or even Barbara Stanwyck's legs, but I'm telling you that the greatest wonder this world has ever seen was me driving home from Cookie's and not crashing into a telephone pole. The drive to Santa Monica was like swimming through a thick soup of sight, everything covered in water and me barely able to stay conscious. A nightmare that drive was, one I couldn't get myself to wake up from, but filled with passing lights and dark turns and so much sound, sound that had no shape or meaning but wouldn't end. There wasn't any music in it, only the will to bury me alive in noise.

Then I was back out in the rain again, trying to make it from my car to my apartment. The black blocks of the other units surrounding the courtyard hulked over me as I dragged myself along the walkway. Everything was empty and dead, I was the only man left alive in the world, which was now so large and echoing I wanted to hide myself in fear. My keys slipped and jangled in my hand but I got the front door open. It could be the coda for Nora's melody, the sounds of my foolishness, my wish for retribution, metal against metal. I didn't snap on the lights—what was there to see that I hadn't seen already? There wasn't anything in my place that could help me. Even my piano squatted like a monster in the dark.

I used up all my juice making it back to the apartment. Just getting to the bedroom seemed a task even Hercules would shudder at. I fell onto my couch, knocking records onto the floor and not caring when I heard a few splinter into pieces. The idea of peeling off my wet clothes made me want to cry, I had nothing left to do it, so I lay and shivered and shook from the cold. Lying on my sofa, the white sheet music tacked to the walls floated like ghosts over me, their black notes a million eyes, the eyes of Nora, of Beatrice, my father, Memphis Arnie, millions of Jews lost in Poland and Germany, dead soldiers killed far from home, all staring at me, silent and wounded, blaming, hating, those eyes that wouldn't shut.

I buried my head under my arms even though it sent knives

of pain up and down me to move. The room swayed, tipped. Nora clawed at herself as she tried to scrape me away. Beatrice glided by, bitter and knowing. And my father at the top of the stairs. He would stand at the top of those stairs forever and I would be at the bottom of the steps, looking up, each of us not moving, and me knowing that I could never, never reach him up there, that the stairs would grow a hundred stories each time I tried to climb them, and he'd be pushed further back and it wasn't him that was moving away, it was me. Every step closer would only make more distance between us, the distance I'd made and now couldn't bridge.

The gym echoed hard with unknown voices, telling us to strip down to our shorts, step here, line up there, and us now a bunch of pink, shivering guys meek and obeying. Maybe outside, wearing our clothes, we'd been real. But standing inside the high school gym—it wasn't my old school, but the draft board set up shop there and so every guy from nearby had to show up, no choice in the matter, so what if you didn't want to kill anyone or if you had too much to lose to wind up dead yourself at 22—we, all of us and me most of all, became shucked down and raw. Could anybody tell, as I carried my clothes draped over my arm, that for me there was only music, and everything else, even the Japs and Germany, meant nothing? Most of the fellas were looking scared, and maybe it was on account of no one but their mommas seeing them in their altogether, but mostly it was plain fear of what was surely to come. We'd go through basic training and then be hauled overseas to places we couldn't find on maps and then each day face the possibility that we'd be killed, if not that morning, then maybe in the afternoon or at night. But it'd surely come, death, because that's what soldiering gets you. Not freedom, not victory. Just death. The guys who wanted to fight, the ones who bleated patriotism and said we'd show everybody who's boss, they'd already gone and enlisted on their own. As if chucking the meat of their bodies in front of bullets could somehow change things. What did it matter if the country won or lost if you weren't there to see it? I wasn't able to think about that long before I was stepping up to a couple of guys in uniform, one with a clipboard and papers, and I was told to sit in a chair. The metal was cold against my back. I opened my mouth when they told me to, and they peered down into my throat with a flashlight. They turned my head this way and that, stared into my eyes like they were falling in love. They put me on a scale and then made me step behind a screen, where some guy in gloves peered into my ass then took my balls in his hand. He asked if I had a social disease, and I was sorry that I'd been so careful with girls if that would have meant I didn't have to go. Coming out from behind the screen I saw the long line of men, white skin glowing in the light that hazed in from the high windows, and we all looked so fragile I wanted to cry. Why were they doing this to us? Did they want their sons dead so badly? Some other guy in uniform—I couldn't see their faces, no matter how hard I looked, and I know they didn't see mine—came up and looked at my feet then made a note on the paper I had been given. Then he pushed me along to somebody else with a stethoscope hanging around his neck. I thought the metal of the stethoscope would be cold, too, but it wasn't, it was warm from the heat of the bodies of all the other men it'd been pressed against, and that made it worse. My heart ricocheted inside my ribs but the guy listening seemed to expect that so he didn't make a note of it. He had me breathe in and out several times as he moved the stethoscope over my chest and back. He thumped me, too, and listened to the reverberations, then asked questions: Did I have shortness of breath? Asthma? Any childhood ailments that may've affected my lungs? No, no, and no. I wished I'd been one of those sickly kids that could only watch from the window as everyone else played stoopball, but no, I'd been right out there with them, racing around like a jackass running straight to his death. He pulled out a balloon from his pocket and made me blow it up. The bright red of the balloon glared in the flat dinginess of the gym, as festive as a merry-go-round in an operating theater. Then he took the paper from my hand, scribbled 1-A on it, and told me to get dressed. While I was putting my clothes back on, feeling like I was dressing my own corpse, I watched as the kid behind me went through the same rigmarole with the stethoscope, but he was struggling. He wasn't more than 19, thin and pale with a flat chest. Blonde hairs covered his arms and caught the light, so he appeared covered in baby fuzz. As he breathed in and out, even I could hear the rattling in his lungs, and when he was thumped he started coughing, and the balloon didn't inflate at all when he blew into it, just hung limp in hand. I hated that kid. I hated him so much I thought I'd puke with it. And when the soldier inspecting him wrote 4-F on his card, there wasn't anybody I hated more than him. They shouldn't send healthy guys to the front, it didn't make sense. Why not ship out all the rejects and misfits, the ones we could afford to lose? I took my time putting on the rest of my clothes, slowly tucking in my shirt and slipping my arms into the sleeves of my jacket, knotting my tie, waiting, waiting, for the kid to get his order to get dressed, and when he did, I stumbled into him so we tangled for a minute, me fumbling around apologizing and trying not to feel how breakable he was, this, somebody's son, but I was somebody's son, too, and then, when we separated, I walked out of the gym, in my hand his card that read 4-F, my 1-A card already shredded in my pocket, the kid left holding a piece of sheet music, and while I'd never forged anything beyond a sick note before I knew it wouldn't be much harder to change the name on the card so it read Louis Greenberg instead of Howard McGahey but, as I stood on the sidewalk and squinted in the glare of the day, thinking about the walk home, about my father waiting for me, I saw that everything was different now, I'd made my choice and there was nothing left for me but to disappear.

Chapter twenty-six

Of all the places I'd thought to wind up the day after getting beaten until barely conscious, the back of a truck hadn't been at the top of that list, and me wearing some exterminator's jumpsuit no less. But after seeing me, Oates, Sonny and the other fellas knew that nobody would buy me as your typical on-the-job guy, what with my bruised face being more black than blue, barely what you might call the color of skin, my nose crusted with blood, my eyes almost swollen shut. I couldn't stand upright on my own. Since we were going to have to convince the owner of Hi-Life to shut down the recording studio for the night while we "fumigated," it'd been decided that I ought to wait in the truck until the joint had been cleared out. I didn't much cotton to having this part of the con be out of my hands—wasn't I the one who needed this most?—but I saw their point and so there I was in the dark, the back of the truck open just a bit to keep the air moving, waiting until given the okay.

I don't know if it was even worth the trouble of keeping the back of the truck open. I wasn't getting much air anyhow. In the close darkness of the truck, I heard my breath coming in and out in short, shallow wheezes, hardly making it past my tonsils. And I whistled. But not "Sweet Georgia Brown." The sound I made was tuneless and raspy, telling the story of lungs that were a few minutes away from throwing in the towel and taking a nice vacation on some sunny beach somewhere. I'd like to join them, but only after my night at Hi-Life was over.

It almost looked like it wasn't going to happen. Oates had called me that morning and I'd somehow managed to answer the phone. Fortunately it was right next to the couch. Before I'd even gotten out a croak for hello, Oates was already whispering with happy urgency, "We're all set. I brought a couple of cockroaches in and the boss bought it. Come down to the studio tonight at around five in your gear. Got it?"

I was lying on my sofa in a damp suit that was stained with my blood. I felt as if I'd been clubbed over and over again with an aircraft carrier, and my head was stuffed with kasha. Even reaching for the phone had almost made me scream on account of me hurting so bad. The yellow morning light in my apartment glowed sick and hot, even when I shut my eyes. Here it was, what I'd been waiting and conning for, and the best I could work up was a gasped, "Yeah, sure."

"Holy fuck," Oates said, not much bothering to whisper now. "You sound like shit. What happened?"

Everything is gone and used up. If anybody ever cared about me, they're all lost now, because of me trying to play it all, and what I wound up with is a chest full of cracked ribs and a pair of lungs that even the Salvation Army would turn away. I'm twenty-eight and broken. What I actually said to Oates was, "Got into a little dust-up last night. It's nothing."

"Well, Christ, maybe you ought to see a doctor instead of coming here." I didn't like the worry in Oates's voice. "I could come and get you, maybe drive you to the hospital."

"Didn't you say we were set for tonight?"

"Yeah, but—"

"And your boss can't fall for the fumigation bit twice, right?"

"Gee, I don't know," he hedged, but he knew I was right. You didn't press your luck by trying to run the same con on the same guy, unless you really knew he was a live one. That only works when your mark thinks he stands to profit from the scheme. With Oates's boss, each time he shut down the studio at night, he lost money. I couldn't figure how long it would take to find a new reason to shut the place down, and time was one thing I knew was being lost.

So against Oates's protests, I set everything into play. There wasn't a chance that I could drive, so Sonny picked me up and we got the truck—the rental paid by Oates since he felt guilty about losing my dough—plus our drummer, Wallace, who loaded his kit into the back of the truck, and Morton, who put his bass in the back, too. When Sonny first saw me, he also wanted to take me straight to the doctor, but I was having none of it. I wouldn't blow my one chance. On the ride to Hi-Life, I gave everyone their music and tried to turn away whenever they looked at me with that look of pity and fear, but moving around didn't treat me so well, so I mostly kept my eyes shut. I needed the rest, anyhow.

Sonny and the fellas quietly joked about the jumpsuits they had on over their clothes, joshing that they'd gone into music to get away from wearing such low-down threads. They all had brothers and fathers and uncles and cousins who worked as mechanics' assistants, broomsmen at barber shops, porters, janitors—nothing that'd send a guy straight to the penthouse suite, unless it was to clean it. I felt like a grade-A asshole in my jumpsuit, too, and noticed that even with all my clothes on under it, it still hung off of my shoulders like a potato sack draped over a stick. I thought it was maybe a size or two too big, but the cuffs came inches above my wrists and if a flood came, the bottom of the pants wouldn't be getting much of a soaking. I knew I wasn't what you might call a beefy guy, but I didn't realize how much I'd whittled down until then. After this recording session, I was going to eat fifty cheeseburgers and drink a hundred milkshakes and lie on my couch reading back issues of *Downbeat* until I'd put some weight back on. Although that idea didn't sit too well with my guts—just thinking about food made me want to toss my chips.

Inside the truck, sitting with no light, I felt myself moving in and out of awareness. I couldn't figure where the darkness of the truck's inside ended and where the darkness of my floating mind started. Ghost sounds washed over me, voices of the hundreds of marks I'd known, their misery and greed and hope and need and hate. They smothered me—each breath I took fought to make its way to the surface. I was drowning in myself. I felt liquid in my chest, and when I coughed, the sound echoed like a drumbeat in my ear. I'd been buried alive.

I was about to start yelling when the doors were pulled open. Even though it was already dark outside, the glare of the streetlights burned my eyes, and Sonny and the other guys were just clouds of shape as they stood there, staring at me.

"Why the hell didn't you take him to a doctor?" I heard Oates say. It sounded like Oates but the words came out of a blob ringed with light.

"He wouldn't go," Sonny answered.

"But, Jesus, look at him—"

"Are we going to stand here all night and jaw like dames," I growled, "or are we going to record some music?" There was part of me that was glad I could still talk, even though it cost me. I tried to stand up, but my body wasn't having any of it, so eventually Sonny and Wallace jumped inside and hauled me up. Coming closer, I could focus better on their faces, and didn't miss the look they shot each other when they had my arms draped around their necks and me dragging between them like a wet sack. "So I'm not going to qualify for the heavyweight division," I said. "So what? Let's get to it."

It was all I could do to keep from screaming like a woman as they held me up and schlepped me out of the truck and onto the sidewalk. If I thought Lomax's punches hurt when he first gave them to me, they were a gift that kept on giving. Sometime during the night, while I shuddered and shivered on my couch, all my internal organs had gotten up and had themselves a hoedown, and when the dancing was over, nobody knew their way home.

"You really want to do this?" Oates asked me.

"'Course I do," I said. "I'm not getting another shot. Anyway," I added, trying to laugh but everything inside me yelling to stop, "I look worse than I feel."

"Then you must feel like crap," Oates said.

I didn't want to talk about this anymore—it was all time being lost. "Get me inside and we can start setting up," I said to Sonny.

There was another exchange of looks, this time between Sonny and Oates. Whole conversations were taking place right over my head, and even though I knew what they were saying, that didn't mean I wanted to hear it. At least Sonny had enough sense to finally say to me, "Sure, Clip."

Oates had done a good job clearing out the joint. There wasn't a secretary or cleaning lady to be found in any corner. But I wasn't at my most observant, so what do I know? Everything swam in and out, my head would shrink to the size of a quarter note then swell bigger than a Macy's Thanksgiving Day Parade float. It seemed to me that the inside of Hi-Life was a warren of rooms—offices, hallways, storage closets and finally, the room I'd been wanting to get inside more than I wanted inside a girl, the recording studio itself. Funny how a place that could change everything looked so plain. It wasn't more than a box with a window that looked into the tiny mixing booth. I had an idea what recording studios looked like, but there'd been some crazy hope of mine that when I finally stepped inside, it would burst into color, banners would unfurl themselves from the ceiling, and gauzy dress-wearing maidens would step forward with baskets of grapes and rose petals to herald their arriving hero. Instead, there were about three battered wooden stools, a bunch of music stands jumbled together in the corner, and a baby grand with a full ashtray on top.

After we'd ditched the jumpsuits for our regular clothes, Oates had the guys lean me against the doorjamb of the recording booth. He pointed at a panel of switches and levers. "This is where I'm going to mix while you guys play," he said. He tipped his head towards something that looked like a record player, only with a smooth black disk instead of a grooved record on it. "We're cutting straight to acetate, so you can't make any mistakes once we go."

I realized that Oates was telling me all this because I'd never been in a recording studio before—but for everybody else, Sonny, Wallace, Morton, it was familiar. I said, "Yeah, yeah, I got it," not only to cut the humiliating lesson short but also because I couldn't stand up much longer. Oates's voice was buried under a thick fog, so while his mouth kept moving, I could only hear every couple of words and then he'd fade out into a whoosh. It was like that with all the guys when they talked. I just hoped I'd be able to hear the music when we got down to it.

They draped me on the piano bench and I sat plunking on the keys to make sure it was tuned while the instruments and mikes got set up. Each note of the ivories rang true inside my head—I don't know how it worked, but all that blood and glop floating around in me turned me into the perfect sounding board. I couldn't remember a time when it sounded better and if I had Lomax to thank for something, it was reworking my body into a mass of pulp that absorbed and threw back notes with perfect clarity. I got absorbed into the strings of the piano, felt them ring against me while they stretched off towards the horizon, the hammers coming down onto me to make a clean, pure sound. I'd press a key and then get lost in it, closing my eyes and rising and falling with the tone.

It wasn't until I felt Sonny's hand on my shoulder that I opened my eyes and saw everyone staring at me. I thought I'd been testing the piano for a minute or two or maybe a only a millennium, but I saw that everything had been set up, the drums, Sonny's sax waiting in its stand, Morton holding his bass, the music propped on stands, and Oates had put all the mikes in place, even one under the piano lid, but I hadn't been onto any of it.

"Man," Sonny said, "we been saying your name for fifteen minutes and you just sat there, hitting keys and looking at nothing."

"Ready to rehearse?" I said. "It's got to be solid before we record."

Another decade passed. "Go ahead," Oates finally said. "I'll listen from the booth."

I was glad when nobody argued anymore. I didn't have much to give except what I had for the piano, so when the fellas all took up their positions to play I was glad. I rasped out a count to get us started, "Five, six, seven, eight," and we were gone. Don't get me wrong, it wasn't a prize winner when we began. First Wallace was on the beat too slow, then Sonny's cue had to be fixed properly, and me and Morton worked out when he was supposed to back me and when I wanted him to fall quiet. I scribbled notes on my sheets, the guys did the same, but to me the pencil felt like a ten-foot lead pipe in my hand. It almost toppled me over.

We kept at it for a long time. How I was staying up, I hadn't an idea. Even sitting at the piano bench was an endurance. While we played, Leo Israel came into the room and sat next to me on the bench. He laid his hands down over mine, but he didn't push down hard, just followed me as I played each note, feeling my tendons as they moved around the keyboard. He was wearing one of those natty suits of his, and in his pockets were peppermint candies. He was wise enough to keep from talking while I rehearsed, but when he did speak, no sound came out of his mouth except sometimes the low, pleasant whine of a cello. And then he got up and left, not once asking me what it was I played. I was sorry when he'd gone.

Sonny said, "If this was union, man, we'd be out of here after three hours. You lucky we're pals." So I figured they were due for a break. I didn't want it to be for too long.

"I'll send you a fruit basket," I said to him. "With plenty of lemons. Come back in five."

While me and Morton copped a smoke, Sonny disappeared. He wasn't crazy about cigarettes, said they did something to the way he blew his horn, and I was starting to think that maybe he was right, since after just one puff, I hacked and coughed hard. You know how in the pictures, when Garbo or Norma Talmadge or some other porcelain girl gets something wrong with her lungs and she coughs daintily into a lace hanky, and then swoons onto a perfumed sofa, and she still looks pretty good, good enough for Robert Taylor to press his face against hers and whisper undying words of love? Let me tell you something, that's just another example of what they show you in the movies being pure applesauce. I was sweating and clammy, and each cough shot hot nails through my chest. I was being turned inside out with rusty forceps over and over. Every time a fresh wave would hit me, I'd double up—there was no draping myself across some sofa, it was all I could do to keep from curling up into a ball and rolling under the piano for good. And when I pulled my hands away from my mouth, there were streaks of blood between my fingers. I wiped my hands on my pants to keep blood off the piano keys, and also so that nobody would call an ambulance. I wasn't going to give up.

Morton and Wallace were watching me hard, Oates, too, through the window of the booth. But I made sure not to pay them any mind. I wasn't going to look into their faces and see something I wasn't ready to see. When Sonny came strolling back in, I choked, "Let's get back to it."

"You want to start recording soon?" He wanted to cut the track, figuring that the sooner it was done, the sooner we'd get out of the studio and maybe ship me off to the doctor.

I couldn't get my voice to work properly, so I shook my head and held up two fingers to mean that we'd rehearse the number two more times before we finally put the thing onto wax. Maybe for other guys' music, I'd settle for something less than perfect, but not with this.

He picked up his sax, and, at his nod, Wallace got his sticks and Morton went back to his bass. They were humoring me, and while it wasn't my favorite thing to be humored, now I let it slide. I tapped lightly on the lid of the piano to count out beats, and we were back into the piece. I was pulling notes out of me, from somewhere deep down, each bass note sounding across the dark spin of the past. Memphis Arnie slid from inside the piano to stand behind me. I liked his hat, but it was strange to see him wearing it indoors, on account of him being very strict about manners. He was probably going someplace or leaving. He put a rock on top of the piano. With each note I comped, roses bloomed until Arnie was covered with petals and then the petals dried up and blew away when Sonny laid out a strong couple of bars on the sax.

We finished the second run-through and I looked up from the keys and Beatrice was standing in the doorway to the studio. She didn't look like she normally did out in public—it looked like she'd thrown a coat on over some pajamas and slid her feet into whatever shoes were close by. She wasn't wearing any makeup, either, and her hair was kind of mussed, like she'd just rolled out of bed. She stepped forward and everyone turned to look at her. Her heels click-clocked across the floor and she knelt beside me. Her hand was so cool against my forehead I almost fell over backwards.

"He's burning up," she snapped over her shoulder to Sonny. "Get him to the hospital."

"No hospital," I said and leaned into her hand with my eyes closed. Then I opened them. "You're here."

"Yeah, baby." Her voice was soft now, her face close to mine. She had warm brown eyes that moved over me.

"I mean, *really* here."

She didn't understand, but said, "Sonny called."

With a thousand pounds resting on my neck, I turned my head to stare at Sonny, who was leaning against the wall with his arms folded over his chest. His gaze came from a long way back, too far for me to really see. I didn't have enough breath to laugh, but I wanted to. Here Beatrice and I had been playing everything on the sly, thinking that no one was wise to us, being fool wrong the whole time. Sonny saw. Sonny saw and he knew and whether he approved or not, he wasn't going to say, but he'd been on it enough to ring Beatrice. Don't get me wrong, I was ready to collapse into sobs, having her with me now, so close and lovely. Still, the last time I'd seen her, I'd been with Nora and I didn't know if Beatrice could forgive me enough to get within touching distance, hit record or no. What had Sonny told her on the phone to get her out so late at night and for me? I had something of an idea.

"Please, baby," she said, holding my head now with both her hands. "You've got to stop and get some help."

I put my hands over hers and leaned forward so our foreheads rested against each other. Man, she was so sweet and cool and growing far away. I wanted to hold her like that for a long while. Forever, even. Right then, she was the one person I'd lost that made it back to me, and I didn't want to let her go. But—"I can't stop, sugar," I said, or made some noise like talking. "I've got this one chance. You get me?"

Something wet rolled down my face and she pulled her hands away to wipe at her eyes. "I get you."

"That's my girl," I said and kissed the curve of her wrist. "You go into the booth with Oates and watch me work."

Slowly, she got up and walked to the booth, drawing smoke behind her so I couldn't see her properly. In the window of the booth, she and Oates floated in dusk. I almost called her back to me, but I wouldn't get anything done with her that close by—at least she was near. We were driving up the coast towards Ventura and the water came in and out with a cymbal crash. I drove and she sat in the passenger seat, as we held hands underneath the dashboard. The breeze pushed at our faces and we were turning to the sea and points west, where if you kept going, you'd cross the whole earth and come back to home.

With a click from the booth, Oates said, "I think you guys sound great. Ready to record?"

The boulder that was supposed to be my head moved a bit, my version of a nod. Through the clouds, I was just able to spot Oates fiddling with some switches, Beatrice watching, and Nora darting in between the keys of Sonny's sax. Then Oates gave us the signal and we began to play.

I came in first, a solo piano, the early, empty streets of the Bronx and Santa Monica, passing dark windows and sometimes you could hear the wishful, blue rush of a delivery truck or bus heading who knew where but someplace not here. Morton plucked on his bass, only a few notes under mine and the streets fell away open and deep, a swallowing mouth. I was in space, holding everything together. Where was he? Everyone else had come by but where was he? I asked the keys. And what they told me was sound.

The drums and sax came in, what you wanted to hear from the fire escape but never did. As the piano met with the reed, strings and percussion, it was a long journey from New York to California and all the hotel rooms, the faces, the eyes, men in suits, men lying on the ground ruining their good suits but I turned them over and it was me, each man in each suit, my face staring back at me and the dirt on my lapels. The high notes of the sax was the keening of Nora, too, clutching at herself and bursting with disappointment, and boxes full of cheap Bibles and pens sent from a PO Box. I touched the piano keys, and they rang out with clear cool sorrow as I kept waiting at the bottom of the stairs, waiting for it to be different, waiting for him to come down the stairs holding his paper, but nobody came to meet me there, I kept waiting, wanting to go up them, and I wished he'd get here already, it had been a long time.

The piano was my other voice, the one inside me that went through its own change, not cracking with the awkward leap into adulthood but shifting and tuning with hard-won lessons. It said what there weren't words for, carving out the whole of the country and beyond, over Pacific seas staining beaches with their pink foam, over cold gray Atlantic waters and into cold gray European cities smashed flat by bombs and tank treads. And the other instruments chorused and comped, the newsreel announcers, as people squinted into the camera with eyes brimming with numb hopelessness.

White and black bones were under my hands, and I couldn't stop myself, even while we were playing, I coughed and red drops spattered onto the keys and once I got started, I couldn't stop so that I kept playing and tearing myself open and the red was on my hands and down my shirt, but he still wasn't coming and I couldn't hear his voice asking for me and I let go of the keys and everything swam in, grew small, even Oates and Sonny and Beatrice crowding in, seemed like they were shouting but what did I know from shouting, since he was silent and always silent and I was a little kid again in the hall closet playing hide-and-seek, a very young kid, my sisters not even born, me curled up in a ball under the coats, though it was hot and I couldn't breathe, I would try and stick it out for as long as I could take it, my lungs were molten and bubbling, destroying everything around them with their heat, and I was waiting to hear his steps in the hallway as he lifted up the hat stand, poked behind framed photographs, pretending to look for me, searching though he knew I wasn't there and I couldn't breathe, but I'd wait and wait for as long as it took to be found.

The walk up the stairs gets harder every year, it takes him just a little longer to reach each floor. He stands on the stoop and stamps the snow off his shoes, thinking about the stairs, and how, maybe now that the girls are married and gone, the old lady died some two years past, he and his wife could move someplace else, someplace with an elevator. As he goes inside, as he starts up the stairs, he remembers how the children used to play on them, galloping up and down on cold winter days like this one, not even breathing hard, and even though there are new children in the building, the sons and daughters of GIs come home, mostly those kids are too small to play in the hallway and on the stairs and, anyway, they aren't his.

One of his daughters has already had her first baby, a girl, and even though she and that schnook she calls a husband stop by to show them this baby and let her play on a blanket in the middle of the apartment floor, he can't feel the joy he's supposed to at a first grandchild. He'd been hoping for a boy. And the husband, well, he's a mumbling lump, so it just isn't the same.

He's reached his own door now on the third floor and stands outside the apartment for a moment. Inside, he can hear the television, which his wife insists on leaving on even when nobody's watching it. It had cost him almost half a paycheck to get the thing, and he's never found anything on it worth watching—he prefers the radio— but she turns it on first thing in the morning and leaves it on until the networks go off the air at night, and even then she switches it off with reluctance. Maybe she keeps it on because it is such a luxury. Only four other families in the whole building have televisions. But mostly, he believes she leaves it on to block out the silence that has come over their apartment. There used to be music, music all day and all night and now there isn't. He wouldn't let his wife sell the piano, although nobody plays it and it is long out of tune. He almost never argues, but this was something he insisted on. The piano stays.

Instead of music, there is the television and its brass-voiced actors and cheerful, hollow commercials, other voices and sounds and light to fill up what has now become a very empty home. He doesn't know what he minds more: the constant barrage of sound and studio audiences laughing, or the thick mire of silence. He supposes that if he still had someone to talk to, someone to open himself to and share the world as he knows it, he would demand that the television be quiet so there could be real conversation. But there isn't and there won't be and he knows this. Still, he's tired, it's been a long day at the box factory, and he can't stand in the hallway all night.

He unlocks the door and goes inside and is almost pushed back against the door by the noise of the television and the smell of frying onions. He yells out a greeting as he takes off his coat and hat and puts his briefcase down on the floor, and she yells back from the kitchen that there's a package for him, although she didn't think they knew anybody in California. Propped up on the table by the door is a flat, square parcel wrapped in padding with his name and address on the front. He checks the return address and can't remember anybody by the name of Beatrice Langston in Los Angeles. With his penknife, he carefully opens the protective wrapping and folds it into a neat square on the table.

It is a record, a record in a plain sleeve that has no writing or pictures on it. He's never seen a record like this before, and he opens the sleeve so the disk itself slides into his hand. There is no label on the record, and it looks as though only one side has been cut, the other side is smooth and black, no grooves at all. He's seen this a few times, records with music on just one side, but still, it puzzles him, and he tries to understand why a Miss Langston of California would send him a record, and then he notices the little slip of paper that fluttered out of the sleeve and onto the floor. He picks it up and reads the woman's letter.

His face is frozen as he reads, and everything is frozen as he walks to the turntable and puts the record on. He shuts off the television and pulls his chair closer to the turntable. He listens, staring straight ahead with unseeing eyes, as a piano begins to play a song he's never heard. It doesn't have words, but it does have the piano, and in it, he hears the lament of his son. Other instruments come in, a saxophone, drums, a bass, but all he hears is the piano and its pure, lonely sorrow. Then, faintly at first, then growing so that it can't be contained, is the sound of coughing. Abruptly, the music ends. The song is unfinished.

He picks up the needle and places it at the beginning of the song. He listens four times through and when his wife comes in, wiping her hands on her apron and demanding to know why he shut off the television to listen to some lousy record, she sees his face and falls silent. She sees the crumpled letter on the floor and reads it. Then she sits on the sofa and covers her face with her apron as she rocks back and forth. Every time the song ends, he picks up the needle and places it back at the beginning. He hasn't spoken and his only movement is to replace the needle.

Eventually, his wife gets up from the sofa, goes into the kitchen, and throws their dinner into the garbage. Then she goes into the bedroom and shuts the door.

He sits in his chair and listens, always picking up the needle and taking it back to the beginning whenever the song ends. He will sit there, listening, until morning.

Acknowledgments

I would like to thank my family for their constant support. I would also like to thank the readers of this novel's initial draft, who, not-so-coincidentally, are members of my family: Janice Fiskin; Pauline DiPego; Gene Fiskin; and Jerry DiPego. Thank you to my agent, Kevan Lyon, for keeping the faith, as well as Elisabeth James, for checking the fine print. Thank you to my editor, Deborah Meghnagi, and Matthew Miller of the Toby Press. I also want to thank Ho Nguyen of the Santa Monica Historical Society and Ian Bernard, who provided helpful information about the process of recording music during the age of acetate. Thanks, as well, to George Christian Gabriel, who offered guidance and suggestions in the history of jazz. This book was influenced by my father, Jeffrey Silber, and his abiding love for the 1940s, as well as the histories of my family, who traveled over treacherous waters from Poland and Russia to the Bronx and thence onward to California. My grandfathers, Louis Silber and Louis Garfield, gave Louis Greenberg his name only and not his means of employment, but this novel is a respectful homage to these good, hardworking men.

I consulted many books over the course of my research for this novel. These include: *The Big Con, The Story of the Confidence Man,* by David W. Maurer; Ted Gioia's *The History of Jazz* and *West Coast Jazz; Central Avenue Sounds,* edited by Clora Bryant, et al; Kevin Starr's *Embattled Dreams, California in War and Peace, 1940–1950; History in Asphalt, The Origin of Bronx Street and Place Names* by John McNamara; Jim Heimann's *Sins of the City, The Real Los Angeles Noir;* Cab Calloway's *Hepster's Dictionary; Rip-Off, A Writer's Guide to Crimes of Deception* by Fay Faron; *The Writer's Guide to Everyday Life from Prohibition Through World War II* by Marc McCutcheon; and *Straight From the Fridge, Dad, A Dictionary of Hipster Slang* by Max Décharné. I also urge anyone who is interested in hearing the music of the period to listen to artists such as Oscar Peterson, Bud Powell, Charlie Parker, Dizzy Gillespie and, for the more avant-garde, Thelonious Monk.

Finally, my deepest and most sincere gratitude to my husband, Zachary DiPego. He has seen this novel through every stage of its development, from the first germ of an idea to its ultimate publication. It would be impossible to overstate how instrumental he has been in the conceptualization, execution and refinement of this novel. He tirelessly read and critiqued not only the initial draft of this book, but every single iteration over the course of its writing. His support was and continues to be boundless in scope, which awes and humbles me. I am profoundly thankful that my life has been graced with such a man.

About the Author

Ami Silber

Ami Silber is a graduate of the Iowa Writers' Workshop, where she received her MFA. She also received an MA in Literature from UC San Diego. She won the Short Story Award for New Writers from Glimmer Train Press and her work has appeared in *Glimmer Train Stories*. She and her husband live in Los Angeles.

The fonts used in this book are from the Garamond family